A cry of terror

tore through the quiet Roman night. A woman's cry. Quick, startled, strangled into silence.

Bill Lammiter peered over the balcony railing outside his room.

The street was empty. Then two figures broke from the shadows. Lammiter could see the woman —a girl, really—locked in desperate struggle with a man. A small, black car nosed to the curb. A door was flung open.

The man had the girl pressed against him, one hand clamped over her mouth. He was trying to pull her into the car.

For a few seconds Lammiter froze. Then suddenly he let out a warning yell and raced for the stairs.

It occurred to him for a moment it was none of his business. But it was too late now. . . .

"Topnotch"
Best Sellers

NORTH FROM ROME

by Helen MacInnes

FAWCETT CREST • NEW YORK

NORTH FROM ROME

THIS BOOK CONTAINS THE COMPLETE TEXT OF
THE ORIGINAL HARDCOVER EDITION.

All characters in this book are fictional and any resemblance
to persons living or dead is purely coincidental.

Published by Fawcett Crest Books, CBS Educational and
Professional Publishing, a division of CBS Inc., by arrange-
ment with Harcourt, Brace Jovanovich, Inc.

ISBN: 0-449-24009-6

Printed in the United States of America

36   35   34   33   32   31   30   29   28   27

To my traveling companion

One

AT LAST, the city was quiet.

Quiet enough for sleep, William Lammiter thought as he finished his cigarette on the small balcony outside of his hotel bedroom. It was three o'clock in the morning —no, almost half-past three by his watch—and Rome was at peace. Practically. Only an occasional car now passed through the old Roman wall by the broad Pincian Gate, only a solitary Vespa roared its way up the wide sweep of the Via Vittorio Veneto. The café-table sitters, the coffee-drinkers and Cinzano-sippers had gone back to their rooms, leaving the broad sidewalks free at last. And, on the other side of the Roman wall, over the vast stretch of the Borghese Gardens, with its tall pine trees, pleasant pavilions, careful flower beds, sweet-smelling shrubs, there was now a cloak of darkness, darkness and silence, for even the night club which lay incongruously just within this entrance to the Borghese Gardens had stopped blowing its trumpets and banging its drums in steady four beats to the bar.

Time for sleep, Lammiter told himself again, but he still stayed on the balcony, a little narrow ledge of balustraded stone jutting over a street of parked cars, with a clear view over the Roman wall into the Borghese Gardens. He still watched the tall pines, with their straight trunks and massive crowns silhouetted against the city's night sky. They seemed as grateful for this hour of rest as he was. They sighed gently, as if they felt the same cool breath of air that had touched his cheek.

He ignored the group of young men who were walking smartly home, the two white-uniformed policemen who were pacing slowly from the Via Veneto through the Pincian Gate, the woman clacking lightly along on high heels in the darkened street below his balcony. He wanted to concentrate on the pine trees, on the feeling that this had once been the limits of ancient Rome, that wild and unknown country had once stretched outside there, north-ward, away from the old city. Then, that red brick wall, built to keep the barbarians out, had been manned by troops; and at a gateway such as this one, there would be soldiers on guard duty. On a warm summer evening in late July, such as this, nearly seventeen hundred years ago, a sentry must have stared northward, into the darkness, and wondered what lurked out there.

What was it like, Bill Lammiter wondered, to have been a Roman sentry standing guard duty at the Pincian Gate? Would the soldier, looking northward from his post on top of the high wall—there was a path there, broad enough for two men to march abreast—have felt loneliness, fear? Would he have stared out at the vast night, and felt a premonition stir uneasily in his mind? Or was he just bored, waiting for his relief to come marching along with the squad leader, hoping no trouble would break out tonight or any other night before he got out of the service and began farming that strip of land up near Perugia? Perugia in the Umbrian hills . . . That's where I ought to be right now, Lammiter thought. There's nothing to keep me in Rome any longer. I've been here a month. I haven't done a stroke of work. And I've lost my girl.

He stubbed out his cigarette angrily, straightened his shoulders, and turned to go indoors. From the now quiet street, beneath his balcony, he heard a woman's cry.

It was quick, startled, strangled into silence. He leaned over the stone balustrade. Under the shadow of the Aurelian Wall were spaced trees and street lights, a line of parked cars and two huge empty tourist buses. For a moment, that was all he saw, patches of bright light, patches of deep shadows, the small neat cars sheltering under thick tents of green leaves. Then, by one car, already pointing its nose out from the curb, ready to leave, waiting with its door open, he saw a woman and a man. They were standing rigid, it seemed, and then he realized it was the rigidity of force and resistance equally matched. The woman—a girl it was—drew back with desperate strength. The man, one hand on her wrist, another clamped over her mouth, was trying to draw her into the car.

Lammiter let out a yell, a loud call for help partly blotted out by the unmuffled roar of a solitary motor scooter, its rider oblivious of everything except the fine angle he cut as he swept through the Pincian Gate from the Borghese Gardens to curve down the Via Vittorio Veneto. But the two police officers, now pacing together so quietly on the other side of the wall, had stopped their earnest conversation and were looking searchingly in his direction. In a quick moment, Lammiter waved, shouted, pointed beneath him. "Here!—On this side!" He wondered if his English were understood, tried to think of the word for "Help!" in Italian, looked down once more at the startled man (who had heard the yell, all right), and shouted again. The girl broke loose as the man stared up at the balcony. She began to run, toward the brighter lights of the Pincian Gate.

Lammiter turned from the balcony and raced through his room into the red-carpeted hall. Behind him he left half-querulous, half-asleep voices, matching the dusty shoes standing outside their doors. He didn't wait for the elevator, a stately and shaky descent in a gilded cage, but ran down the three flights of steps that encircled its open shaft. He sprinted across the dimly lit hall, half sliding on the marble floor, giving the night porter scarcely time to look up from his desk, and was out on the wide sidewalk. He was breathless but pleased with himself. Not bad, not bad at all for a man of almost thirty, he decided. (Since his twenty-ninth birthday, he had become conscious of age.) He couldn't have taken more than two minutes to reach the street. Then he was amused by himself for being so pleased. He slackened his pace abruptly, and felt a stitch in his side just to keep him in his proper place. Ahead of him, in front of the Pincian Gate, the running girl had been stopped by the two policemen. The car, and the man with it, had vanished.

The policemen looked at him speculatively. For a moment he had the impulse to walk on, to pretend he was out for an early-morning stroll. Now that the girl was safe, there was no need to get mixed up in any complication. But he had been running, he was still breathing faster than normal with that proud burst of speed, and he was dressed exactly in the clothes he had worn on the balcony—a white shirt, sleeves rolled up, tie off, neck open, thin gabardine trousers. He glanced over his shoulder, to see how clearly the balcony was visible from the street. It had been extremely visible. He wasn't surprised when the grave-faced policemen identified him.

They were puzzled. The girl, even after she had regained her breath, was too frightened to speak sensibly. So now they turned on the stranger from the balcony.

An American, obviously. One could always tell most Americans; they had a young look to their faces, a peculiar expression of trust, a confidence in their eyes, a strange mixture of diffidence and decision in their movements. This one was no exception. They had to look up at him as they asked him their polite but puzzled questions, for he was tall, and thinner than they considered appropriate. (Strange that an American with money—his clothes were well-cut, his wrist watch expensive, he stayed at a good conservative hotel—should spend so little on food. But no stranger than the fact that he wore no tie, no jacket, and stood nonchalantly on the street, in this fashionable quarter of the city, without even being aware of how he was dressed.) His face was lean, strong-boned, with a good forehead and well-shaped chin and nose. His mouth was pleasant when he smiled. His teeth were excellent. Gray eyes under well-marked eyebrows, with a tendency to frown in concentration. His hair was brown, and—another peculiar American custom—cut short. His voice was agreeable to listen to, but his words were difficult to follow. A polite man, the policemen decided, for he was now trying to answer them in Italian. His words were still difficult to follow: his Italian was too careful, there was no natural flow to it. And he kept looking at the girl.

Why not? She might be stupid, or shy, or both, but she was extremely pretty, with shining black hair cut short, large dark eyes, an excellent figure, slender ankles, small feet in pointed-toe shoes with high Italian heels. "Thank you," she said huskily in English to the American.

"Excuse me, signore," one of the policemen said brusquely but tactfully, as he turned to the American. "You are staying at the Hotel Pinciana?"

"Yes. My name is Lammiter, William Lammiter." He added that he was an American, but no one seemed surprised. And then, as he tried to explain what he had seen from the balcony of his room, first in Italian, then in French, and then—defeated—in English, the two policemen tried to help him.

"No, no!" he had to insist. "The car wasn't passing by. It had been parked under my balcony. Over there! See? It must have been waiting. When I noticed it, it had its engine running, its nose pointed out, ready to leave. So there must have been two men, one driving, one trying to snatch the girl. No, I don't think there could have been three men. Why?—Well, there would have been two men on the sidewalk, one keeping her from screaming, one pulling her into the car. But why don't you ask her, herself?"

He turned to the girl standing back so quietly in the shadow of the wall. It was time she did a little explaining.

But she wasn't there.

The two policemen had turned, too. They stared at him. Then, quickly, they all moved through the broad archway of the Pincian Gate to the other side of the Roman wall. There she was, running across the wide empty street toward the entrance of the Borghese Gardens. And stopping near her, braking suddenly beside one of the islands formed by the circular wall guarding the roots of a giant pine tree, was a gray Fiat.

Lammiter had just time to say, "No, that isn't the same car. The other was smaller." Its door opened, the girl jumped in, and it streaked down the tree-shaded road that led through the gardens to the outskirts of Rome. The policemen looked at each other, and then at the American. One of them said a couple of lines in Italian, quick, low, tense. The other laughed and shrugged his shoulders. He said, "The price must have suited her that time."

"But—" Lammiter said, and then he, too, shrugged his shoulders and raised an eyebrow in his best Italian accent. There was really nothing else to do.

Briskly, the two policemen saluted him. They were no longer annoyed by the girl, but amused by him. It had become merely a slightly comic interlude to break the monotony of their night patrol. Now, hands clasped behind their backs, they began walking in step and grave talk of more serious matters, along the Aurelian Wall.

Lammiter went back to the hotel. The night porter in

front of his honeycomb of keys looked at him without much curiosity—Americans were a nation of eccentrics, he had decided years ago, and nothing they did surprised any hotel desk. The elevator wasn't working, anyway, so Lammiter climbed the three flights to his corridor. The shoes formed a jeering honor guard, right to his room. The voices had subsided into measured breathing and choking snores.

He went out onto the balcony. Beyond the Roman wall, the pine trees in the Borghese Gardens waited quietly for the dawn. And there it was, the first pale streak of gray, washed along the east rim of distant hills. A house swallow sounded its unmusical notes. Soon, others would form a vague chorus: they would start skimming over the mushroom-shaped trees, filling the air with the sound of their twittering and the swoop of their wings. And soon, too, the automobiles and the motor bicycles and the scooters and the horns and the unmuffled exhausts and the screeching brakes . . .

He closed both shutters, the windows, the heavy velvet curtains. Perhaps that would give him a chance to sleep. But long after he had had a quick shower and lay stretched on top of the heavy linen bedspread, he kept thinking of the girl who had said "Thank you" as if she had meant it. Eventually, to save himself from suffocation, he rose and opened all the layers of protection that covered his windows. The pale gray edge on the horizon had spread and changed to a fringe of green and gold. Above the renewed traffic, the swallows, in hundreds, were diving and soaring with their loud screams of frenzied delight.

"Idiots!" he told them angrily. And yet he had to smile. Bad-tempered as he was with lack of sleep and a surfeit of noise, the swallows were a comic mixture of graceful flight and ugly sound. "See, see, see!" they screeched in their thin scratched notes as they skimmed the tall pine trees, the old Roman wall, the hotel roof. "I'll leave Rome today," he told himself wearily. "I'll go up to an Umbrian hill town, and catch myself some quiet and some coolness." He had been saying that for two weeks, but now he knew he meant it. And either the pleasantness of the idea or his rediscovered powers of decision lulled him into sleep. Daylight or swallows or traffic or not, he didn't awaken until nine.

Two

EARLY, while it was still cool, he began to pack. He was traveling light: one two-suiter case and one grip besides his typewriter and camera. Yet, foot-free as he was, it was odd how he had seemed to have taken root in this hotel room—every small drawer and corner turned up another belonging, or something he had bought since he arrived four weeks ago. He was trying to fit some typing paper into the typewriter's neat case when the room waiter arrived to clear away the breakfast. It was the one Lammiter liked least, the small thin man, middle-aged, morose, who was never interested in anything except the size of the tip lying on the tray. But this morning he suddenly turned almost vivacious as he looked at the luggage. "The signore is leaving today?" The dull eyes were extremely clever, Lammiter noticed with some surprise.

"Yes," Lammiter said, and went on packing.

"The signore is a writer?"

Lammiter nodded. If you could call a man a writer who had written exactly one play. True, it had been successful enough, and that was something both unexpected and pleasant. But if he didn't write a second one pretty soon, and have another success, too, he would have to go back to Madison Avenue and advertising. In the last ten days or so, he had begun to wonder if he had resigned too rapidly from the steady job, the steady money, the rent and the butcher's bill and the dry Martinis all definitely paid for.

"The signore likes Rome?"

Lammiter nodded.

"The signore stayed a long time here. He has many friends in Rome?"

"The signore," Lammiter said firmly, "has no friends in Rome, at all." That was accurate enough. Eleanor Halley was in Rome, but after their last disagreement two weeks ago— Disagreement? Let's face it, he told himself: Eleanor and you have had your ultimate quarrel.

13

What had she called him? A man too jealous to be able
to accept with any kind of grace the fact that she had decided to marry someone else. A man too narrow-minded
to approve of her marrying a foreigner. A man too much
of a snob-in-reverse (it had taken him a few seconds to
puzzle that phrase out) to like anyone who had a title.
"Look," he had told her, "I don't care whether this new
fellow of yours has a title or not. I don't hate him because
he calls himself a count. I just want to know more about
him." But this phrase (calculated, he had to admit now)
—"this new fellow of yours"—had had a most final effect. Afterward, he had phoned Eleanor twice at the
Embassy, twice at the apartment she shared with two
other women secretaries. Miss Halley was not at her
desk. Miss Halley was not at home. And three days ago
he had loitered around the Embassy entrance, hoping to
have a few minutes' talk with her. But either she had
left early or she had seen him and taken another exit.

Now he would never be given the chance to make the
apology he ought to have offered in the first place, instead of letting his hurt pride sharpen his tongue. He
ought to have said, "You were right. I was letting the
theater swallow me up, I was turning into the re-write
machine, the rehearsal haunter, the director's little help-
er, the willing autograph-signer, the luncheon speaker;
the man who wanted to prove success hadn't gone to
his head; the man who couldn't say 'No,' trying to oblige
everybody, failing the only person who really mattered."
For a moment he was startled by the picture he had
drawn of himself. Was it just his eloquence, or had he
been as neglectful of Eleanor as all that?

The waiter coughed discreetly and arranged the breakfast tray's dishes once more. Lammiter searched automatically for a tip, but he was still thinking about Eleanor. If only she had complained. . . . Why hadn't she
spoken out, given him some warning? Instead, just as he
was about to leave for six weeks in Hollywood last
spring, she had taken off quietly for Rome. He ought to
have followed her, right then; but the Hollywood assignment was important: it was his own play, wasn't it, that
was being turned into a film script? Then the job was
postponed. Then it was scheduled for May. Then it was
delayed again. Then arranged eventually for the end of

June. By that time, he was ready to say, "The hell with all this, anyway," and join Eleanor in Rome. But by that time, too, he had got her letter about Luigi, Count Pirotta. Goddammit, he thought in sudden anger, did she think I had arranged all these postponements, these delays? Did she imagine I enjoyed waiting in New York, when she was in Italy? She knew I loved her, didn't she? My career was hers, too: didn't she know that?

"Oh, forget it," he told himself. "Forget Eleanor." But how?

The waiter had left, quickly and suddenly, as if he had decided the fifteen-per-cent tip on the tray was all that was forthcoming. Add to that the fifteen per cent that the management charged for all services rendered, and the waiter had a thirty-per-cent tip for one small jug of coffee, one small jug of tepid milk with skin on, two rolls (one stale), two transparent slivers of butter, and one small jar of dark brown strawberry jam.

I wish, Lammiter thought bitterly, someone would reach into a pocket and add thirty per cent onto all my royalties. Then, by God, I perhaps could afford to stay a summer in Rome, and argue Eleanor out of her titled dreams. Argue? That was a false hope: everything was beyond arguing now.

His annoyance with the waiter, he realized, was simply because the man had stirred up memories of his trouble with Eleanor. Wasn't it enough that his mind had gone blank of creative ideas, that the play he was about to begin when he arrived in Rome had vanished into thin air? How could he work? He could neither think nor concentrate. He could only look at ruins (for he was standing at the window again) and speculate about the past—a pleasant way of spending the present to avoid thoughts about the future.

He went back to his packing. It was then that he remembered his photographs. He had six rolls of film being developed and printed at the photography shop just off the Via Vittorio Veneto. He was to collect them just before eight o'clock this evening, when the shop closed. How could he have been so inept as to forget all about them? He'd have to stay one more night in Rome, after all.

He called down to the hotel desk, and told them that

he would not be checking out that afternoon, that he'd stay one more night. The voice replying to him was genuinely perturbed. It was sorry, extremely sorry, but his room had been assigned to someone else. All rooms were occupied. This was July, the busiest month . . .

A sudden revulsion seized him, a quick reaction to cut all losses. "The hell with it," he said aloud. He called the porter's desk, with instructions to get him a seat on a plane, any plane, any flight leaving Rome tonight for New York.

The chambermaid appeared as he ended his call. Without even seeing his suitcase and grip, she said smilingly, "The signore is leaving today?"

"Yes." How quickly the news got around! It was a matter of protocol in hotel work: Room 307 is checking out, get in line for the tips, pass the word along. But he had liked this middle-aged woman with the warm smile and kindly phrases. "I'm going home," he told her.

"To America?" She looked a little startled. She came from Perugia, and had known he meant to visit there some time. Then, quickly, "The signore likes Italy?"

"Yes, yes," he told her reassuringly. It wasn't Italy that was out of joint. It wasn't the times, either. It was himself. If the whole trip had been a mistake, it was simply that he had been unwilling to admit failure. He was admitting it now. He had been overconfident, too sure of Eleanor. He had let her slip away from him months ago, in New York. At last, he was really facing the truth. He had lost the girl, and he had deserved to lose.

"Just leave everything," he told the maid. "I'll be around until this afternoon, at least." He found a thousand-lire note. She was pleased by that, and more than pleased by the careful speech of thanks he made in Italian. Then he was left in his room to wait for word about his flight space to New York.

He sat down to write some letters. The first was to the man who had produced Lammiter's play and now was eager to read a second script. Provided, of course, it was the same as the first, only different. He doesn't want a playwright, Lammiter thought bitterly; all he wants is little Mr. Echo, who'll be a sure investment; he doesn't want a piece of creative work, he wants a piece of property. First, he decided, I shall write him the letter I'd like to write. Then I'll tear that up, smother all indignation, resentment, accurate descriptions of his mentality (I.Q. probably a high 80) and of his education (progressive to the point of being perpetually retarded). And I'll write a note saying his observations were interesting (he'll never know how) and that I'm sorry I cannot agree with him.

How did a man like that ever get into a position of power in the world of art? He had money. But so had cigarette advertisers and buttonhole manufacturers. At least, New York wasn't yet plagued by the problems of the London theater, where it was almost compulsory to belong to the esoteric clique if you wanted to be produced or recognized at all.

The telephone rang.

He glanced at his watch. Only half an hour since he had ordered his ticket. His ill temper vanished. Quick work, he thought approvingly. He picked up the phone, expecting the porter's voice. Instead, it was a woman who was speaking.

"Hello," the voice said in English. "Mr. Lammiter?"

"Yes," he said, puzzled at first.

"I wanted to thank you again."

There was no doubt who it was. The way she said thank you made him think of last night and a pretty face turned urgently, almost pathetically, to him under the cold lights of the Pincian Gate.

"Oh, it's you—" he recovered himself. "Glad to know you got home safely."

She laughed. "I have allies as well as enemies."

"So I saw. But I thought your friends were a little late in arriving last night."

"That's why I'd like to thank you."

"Oh, forget it. Glad I was there to shout at the nasty men. Who were they, anyhow?"

"I told you. The enemy." She laughed softly. He had to admit that he had rarely heard a more attractive sound. She said, "Please—could we meet?"

Startled, he blurted out, "Meet? Where? Here?"

"Oh no! That would be dangerous."

"At your place?"

"Still more dangerous. Meet me at Doney's. At noon."

"But I can't. I've got to wait here until—"

"Please. At noon. I must see you before you leave."

That made him suddenly wary. "Who *are* you?" he asked. How could she know he was planning to leave today? Did she or her friends have some kind of intelligence service working among the hotels? What was all this, anyway? "Who are you, what are you?" he asked.

"Someone who needs help. Badly." Her voice was low, fearful, but determined. Very quietly she added, "When you see me, pretend our meeting is accidental. Completely accidental." And with that tense warning, she ended the call abruptly.

After a minute's thought, he asked the hotel switchboard to inquire where that call had just come from—was it possible to trace the number, or had the operator any idea of the district in Rome from where the call was made? At first, he thought it was his Italian that created the confusion, and then—after several long outbursts of explanation ranging from the polite to the irritated (he must have sounded incredibly stupid)—he suddenly realized it was his question. Because no one had telephoned him.

He began to argue about that, and then (as he saw the futility of all this questioning) he broke it off hastily with a "Sorry, sorry. Please excuse me," disentangling himself from a conversation that was now beyond his powers to control. "And thank you, signorina. Thank you for your help," he added. Politeness in Italy, politeness was the key to everything—for the annoyance in the operator's voice vanished, and he could imagine the smile spreading over her face as she said, "Thank *you,* signore. And is it possible that another guest was calling you from his room?"

Yes, it could have been possible. Or the girl could have walked through the lobby to the row of house telephones near the elevator, and used one of them. But how had she known his room number? He might as well ask how she had known his plans for leaving Rome.

He went downstairs at a quarter to twelve. He hadn't quite decided if he were going to walk past the café called Doney's. Or not. It was just like that. He was interested, yes; and curious, definitely curious, but he was still wary. What was this girl? A confidence trickster, a prostitute as the police had suggested last night, a possible blackmailer? Somehow—perhaps he was too gullible—somehow he didn't believe any of that. He kept remembering the pleading note in her voice. "Someone who needs help. Badly."

The lobby, large, dark, and cool, shaded rigorously from the glare of the brilliant Italian sun, was filled with young people returning from their morning pilgrimages. Students clustered in groups: girls in cotton dresses with wide skirts and neatly bloused tops, flat heels, large hand-bags, and short white gloves; young men in seersucker jackets and crew cuts. It seemed as if half the college population of the United States was visiting Rome this summer of 1956.

He handed over his room key at the porter's desk. "Any word of a reservation?"

The senior porter shook his head. "Not yet, Signore Lammiter. We do not expect to hear anything definite until four o'clock."

Ah yes, Lammiter thought: now is the time for every-one to shut up shop for lunch. And after lunch, the siesta. Half-past four might be a more accurate prediction before any business would be done on that hot July after-noon. He turned toward the door, leaving an anxious group of schoolteachers from Ohio inquiring about seats for *Traviata* at the Baths of Caracalla. He halted at the entrance, hesitating behind the heavy curtain of white sailcloth which cut off the sunlight at the threshold. For a moment he watched the crowded hotel lobby; for a moment he listened to the bable of tongues. He could recognize at least six foreign languages being spoken in addition to occasional Italian—Spanish, Brazilian Portu-guese, French, English, Swedish or Danish (he wasn't quite sure), and Austrian German. Labels on neat piles of luggage near the doorway came from practically every country in Western Europe; from Egypt and Israel and Syria; from Ceylon, Hong Kong, Australia. For a moment, the noise and movement added to his indecision as if they hypnotized him. Then he noticed the large clock over the porter's desk. Five minutes to twelve.

He pushed aside the gently blowing screen and stepped through the open doorway into the brilliant blinding light. The light breeze puffed its hot breath into his face. He turned sharply left and entered the broad sweep of the Via Vittorio Veneto. He walked at an even pace on the sidewalk, as the other foreigners were doing. He was a man on his way to Doney's for a drink and a pleasant view of the world strolling by.

Three

THE VIA VITTORIO VENETO is the main promenade in Rome, a wide curve of a slowly descending hill, edged with trees, sweeping down from the old Roman wall to the more commercial streets of the modern city, covering no greater distance than half of a brief mile. But it contains much. It is the street of big hotels and sidewalk cafés, of small expensive shops for perfume and pretty shoes; of banks and imposing buildings; of lovely bareheaded girls strolling, breasts out, waistlines in, between the row of café tables; of the Capuchin church with its coarse-gowned tonsured friars welcoming visitors to view its crypts filled with dead brothers' bones—skull and ribs and pelvis laid out in patterns like a carefully arranged flower bed or a burst of fireworks. It is the street of thick trees giving dappled shade to broad sidewalks; of crowding taxis, smart cars, white-uniformed traffic policemen; of young men swerving on flatulent Vespas, foreigners on foot, young Italian soldiers on wide-eyed leave in ill-fitting uniforms; of crisp, khaki-suited tourist police with a protective air; of the United States Embassy sitting placidly among walled gardens and ornamental balustrades; of grave-faced, tall, handsome *carabinieri* with gold braid, black cavalry boots, and carefully held swords, pacing majestically in matched pairs; of the Excelsior, where Texas oil men and Hollywood stars scatter largesse and perpetuate the myth that every American is a millionaire; of neighboring Doney's, where the chic and the odd, the dramatic and the beautiful, the bad and the vicious, the known and the strange, the quiet and the flamboyant, the tragic and the farcical, the enchanted and the charming, all gather before the midday and evening meals to eye and be eyed.

The girl couldn't have chosen a meeting place more favored by foreigners, Lammiter thought as he reached Doney's. The pre-luncheon crowd had started to gather. The little round tables, which edged the wide sidewalk like a guard of honor, leaving a center path for the pedestrians (and it was surprising how many people would saunter past, not only once or twice but three times and more), were already half filled. In another fifteen minutes they would all be occupied.

He kept his pace slow, untroubled, his eyes seemingly looking for a table where a gay umbrella would provide sufficient shade. He had the sudden fear that she wouldn't arrive, that this little incident would end as a dreary hour of waiting, of false alarms, of fading hopes, and a sudden angry retreat to a lonely meal. Everything had gone so badly for him in the last four weeks that he had begun to expect nothing but disappointment. And then he saw her. He didn't have to try very hard to look surprised.

"Hello!" he said, stopping abruptly. She was alone at one of the tables that lined the grass edge of the sidewalk. Behind her was a row of parked cars, and then a stream of steady traffic. One table, to her left, was still empty; the other, on her right, was occupied by a handsome red-haired Italian, who was too openly interested in the girl to be anything but what he seemed—someone who admired a pretty woman. Pretty? She was beautiful. Lammiter stared down at her in amazement. "Well," he added, beginning to smile, "well—"

"It can't be!" she said, startled, smiling, delighted. It all seemed a natural succession of emotions. "But in Rome, everyone meets." she added. "Sooner or later, everyone meets."

"Are you waiting for a friend? Or may I join you?"

"Please do."

So he pulled round the other wicker chair to the side of the small round table, and sat down to face her. Behind him, he heard almost a sigh of disappointment from her Italian admirer.

"Have I changed so much?" she asked as he kept looking at her. She was wearing a sleeveless white linen blouse, low-necked. Her bare arms were tanned, rounded, firm.

"In a way, yes. Last time we met, you weren't so cool-looking."

"Cool? In this temperature?"

"It's hot," he agreed. "And I hear it's going to get hotter." Behind him, a chair scraped as it was pushed back. A waiter hurried forward to lift the money that had been left to pay for the Italian's Cinzano and to take Lammiter's order.

"Beer: Danish," he told the waiter, watching the Italian walk away. "Too bad. It spoiled his plans for a pleasant luncheon." And possibly a cosy siesta, he thought. He studied the girl's face, and he was smiling again. He hadn't felt as relaxed as this, or as little unhappy, for a whole month. Was he beginning at last to get over Eleanor? If so, this girl might be the pleasantest cure he could find. Her dark eyes were wide-spaced, richly lashed under excellently marked eyebrows. The forehead was broad and intelligent. Her features were classical, as Roman as one of the pretty stone girls in the Campidoglio museum. And, most startling against the honey color of her glowing skin, she wore no make-up on her lips. They were soft, natural. It was a current fashion among the Roman girls, he had noticed. With a white face, it would have had a drab effect. With their deeply tanned faces and skillfully mascaraed eyelashes, the natural lips were startling.

"At least we can talk now," she said, "and quickly. Before someone else sits down. Or perhaps the sun will discourage them."

He realized then that only their table was shaded at this time of day by the small tree behind them. Other tables had their sheltering umbrellas or awnings. But here, the three tables usually depended on the tree. He looked at the girl speculatively. It was always difficult to remember that anyone as decorative as this could also be clever. But it was necessary to remember that. More guardedly, he said, "Why did you want to see me?"

"To thank you."

He shook his head, smiling. "Try again."

"To warn you."

"Me?"

"We must keep smiling. We are talking about America —about Harvard in 1950—just before you went off to Korea."

"Look—" he said.

"Please smile," she urged, her voice low. The waiter brought a bottle of beer, opened it, poured it, and left. Lammiter said, as if there had been no interruption, "How do you know about Harvard? Or Korea? And who is watching us now so that we've to keep this bright and

breezy merriment stuck all over our faces? And why
should I be warned? I'm in no danger. I'm just a peaceful
guy who has been minding his own miserable business for
four weeks. I'm leaving Rome today, anyway."

"Yes, we know that too. And that worries my friends."

He looked at her, startled. "Friends" had been bitterly
spoken.

"They don't like your plan to visit Perugia, not after
your interest in me last night."

"Perugia? Your friends aren't quite up to date on all my
plans. I'm going back to America."

"Oh no!"

"You are forgetting to smile," he said. She stared at
him. She looked, suddenly, so young and defenseless that
he relented. "What's this all about, anyway?"

She shook her head.

"Come on, tell me," he urged gently. "You didn't come
here just to advise me to avoid Perugia."

"It was my friends who didn't want you to go there."

He noticed again the bitterness with which she emphasized the word "friends." "But you wanted me to go
there?" She was silent, watching him. It seemed better to
concentrate on her so-called friends. "Why did your—
friends not want me in Perugia?"

"They think you could very well be an agent, an American agent." He stared at her. But she was serious. "You
were in Army Intelligence, weren't you?"

He began to laugh. "Oh, I burned the bits of paper in
the trash basket for a month or two. Then the office caught
fire one day, and I was demoted. I held the door open for
the big brass when they visited my colonel."

She wasn't persuaded. And she wasn't amused, either.
She said slowly, "You've been in Rome for four weeks.
Without any apparent purpose."

"I am a writer. At least, that's what my passport says:
'writer.'"

"That is always a very good cover."

"Not since Somerset Maugham wrote *Ashenden*."

"You have friends in Washington. In Intelligence
work." She was trying to fight down some major disappointment.

"They stayed on in the service. Why shouldn't they
get promoted to Washington? You can't expect them to

live in foxholes or army tents forever." He looked at her with curiosity. "Did *you* hope I was connected with Intelligence?" he asked quietly.

She nodded. "Or the FBI. Or the CIA. Something like that . . ." She looked at him quickly, as if to surprise the truth.

"No," he could assure her frankly. "I've even lost touch with most of my old friends. I never seem to meet them nowadays." He frowned, as he suddenly realized that was not quite accurate. Three days ago, right here in Rome, Bunny Camden had thumped on his shoulder blade and practically given him curvature of the spine. But Bunny was probably in Naples right now, and you didn't talk about Bunny without Bunny's permission. Bunny was the type who knew what he was doing even if no one else ever did.

"Yes?" she asked quickly, noting the frown.

He said, "I'm puzzled. How did your 'friends' do all this research on me?—Just how did they learn—"

"They have a good source of information on you."

"They have?" He was suddenly annoyed. "And who are 'they'?"

"We must keep our voices low," she said. Her eyes flickered briefly toward a table under the café awning, where two men were seated. It lay opposite theirs, divided from them by the stream of passers-by. He noticed, now, that she always seemed to speak when people passed in front of them, as if their movement would hide her expression from the opposite table.

"All right," he said. "Who are 'they,' anyway?" He studied her face. "You don't really like them very much, do you? Then why call them friends?" She looked away, as if absorbed by the three American movie stars who were walking so slowly along the aisle between the tables. "Did they tell you to meet me here?"

She nodded.

"Then, if they expected us to meet, why were we to pretend it was all accidental? Who else is watching us?"

"I can't be sure," she said. "But it is likely I am being watched by other people, too."

"By the men who tried to kidnap you last night?"

She shrugged her shoulders, but she was worried. She took the cigarette he offered her with a strained smile of thanks.

"Weren't you afraid to come here?" he asked.

"I'm well guarded at this moment. And besides, the two men of last night are—" she hesitated "—they are dead."

"What?" He was incredulous, and then frankly disbelieving.

"Please," she said, "we must keep our voices low."

"Who killed the men who attacked you? *Your* friends?" He began to smile a little. What a story, what undiluted hogwash! Either that, or she'd better change the company she keeps, he thought.

"So they told me. This morning. But perhaps it may have been a lie—to make me feel all is safe. But—" She took a deep breath. Her lips trembled for a moment. Suddenly watching the fear she was trying to hide, he believed at least part of her story.

He said, "Do your friends know that you are working against them?"

Her face went rigid with surprise at his guess. Quickly, with a pathetic smile, she said, "Please—please pretend I'm finding out about you, instead of your finding out about me."

"And what do your friends want to learn about me?"

"Why are you in Italy? Are you dangerous to them?"

"Dangerous?" He was now amused. Her sense of the dramatic was more Italian than American, although her accent was practically regulation Miss Hewitt's Classes. She must have lived for a number of years in the United States, been to school there. Her manners were the recognizable pattern of the well-brought-up Eastern girl. "Wellesley or Smith?" he asked suddenly.

"*Please* take me seriously," she said sharply. "And my college was Radcliffe."

"Then we've got Cambridge in common." That was always a useful point of departure in any friendship. In a way, he thought, it was a pity that this one was going to be so short.

"Take me seriously," she repeated, her voice dropping. Her eyes were unhappy. Her smile was pleading.

"How can I? I don't know who you are. Or what you are really trying to tell me."

"*Don't* leave Italy," she said, turning her head to look at the traffic behind them in the busy street. If anyone had been lip reading her remarks, this little move would have defeated him nearly. "Please don't go. I need your help."

"I don't think your friends would approve of that suggestion. What's their line of business, anyway?"

She considered her answer for a long moment, and in the end she didn't give it. "The sun is moving around," she said, her voice as unhappy as her eyes. She pulled back her arm into the shade, and moved her chair a few inches into the narrowing shadows. "Soon we shall have to leave." She glanced over once more at the table with the two men. One was a middle-aged English-looking type: he still sat there, reading a book. The other, a handsome dark-haired Italian in an expensive gray suit, had left. But his drink was unfinished. He could be visiting another table. Lammiter found himself suddenly, unexpectedly, sharing the girl's tenseness. He looked at the reading Englishman—the thin haggard face and shadowed eyes seemed vaguely familiar, so did the lock of long wayward hair falling over the narrow upraised eyebrow—and then back at the girl.

"Something wrong?" he asked her quietly.

"I'll soon know," she said, watching the waiter approaching them. "Mr. Lammiter, can I say you've asked me to luncheon with you?"

"Yes, you can say that." But to whom? "And I hope you've accepted."

The waiter said, "Signorina Di Feo? Telephone for you, if you please."

"Ah yes," she said. "Thank you." She looked at Lammiter, and rose slowly.

"What comes before Di Feo?" he asked.

"Rosana," she said. She had a proud way of carrying her head, a most attractive and tantalizing way of turning to give a glancing smile over her shoulder.

"I'll wait here until you get back. Don't be long, or I'll get sunstroke."

Then, as he settled down to wait, he wondered whether she would come back. If she really needed help, she would. And yet, where did that place him? He was leaving Rome tonight. What help could he give? It would be kinder if he walked away, so that when she came back to this table —if she did come back—she would know that he couldn't give any help. Then she'd have to begin looking for some other obliging idiot. Yet he didn't start counting out money to cover the two paper tabs that the waiter had left under the ashtray on the table. He didn't make one move to leave. Instead, he leaned back in his chair, felt the warm sun play on his spine, and watched the parade of handsome Romans mixing with the eternal tourists.

Four

As HE WAITED for Rosana, Lammiter again noted the preponderance of young America: the college girls; and the high-school boys; and the young men just out of service, their hair still close-cut, their shoulders still squared away, and their GI savings in their pockets. There were older Americans, too, mostly family men shepherding their flocks back to their hotels: the gray-haired and bald-headed fathers, in button-down collars and the new drip-dry jackets posing as seersucker, patiently accepting a summer vacation spent in museums and churches while dissembling their worry about the low evaporation point of money; the wives, who had read the guidebooks and pro-vided the enthusiasm, now harried and hurried but still determined on culture in spite of the problems of food and drink for the children, of nylon laundry all over the bathroom, of the chore of keeping a family neat while it lived from suitcases; the children themselves, remarkably good-natured, who must have had better ideas on spend-ing a hot summer day than by breathing the gasoline fumes of a modern city. The English tourists were mostly middle-aged. The men wore high-waisted trousers held up by taut suspenders over transparent nylon shirts open and neatly folded back at the neck. And their choice in holiday shoes was odd: crisscrossed leather sandals dis-playing lots of heavy wool sock. Their women weren't what Lammiter expected, either: they didn't look like the Englishwomen he met in New York or Washington; these Roman tourists were more solidly constructed, sensible in shoes and ankles, more like Brussels sprouts than the well-advertised roses, nice and wholesome and all so very much alike. With some pepper and salt and butter, they'd probably taste alike, too. Once outside of the buses which had brought them across Europe, the English couples kept together, in tight phalanxes of four or six, as if they distrusted the friendliness of the natives. Perhaps they were new to travel, and were still worried about white-slave traffic, unmentionable diseases, and pick-pockets. The thin middle-aged Englishman sitting at the table opposite Lammiter seemed both horrified and fascinated by his own countrymen: he kept looking up at them in pained disbelief. Not one tie, far less an old school tie, among them.

If the English stiffened into set molds when they traveled, the French became as shapeless as a melted candle. Not for them was the clean shirt, and the trousers at least pressed under the mattress, or the dainty afternoon frock; they dressed for a comfortable journey (which usually meant five packed into a small beetle-like car with bits and pieces of luggage strapped all around): crumpled shorts and hairy legs, wrinkled skirts and soiled blouses, bare feet in equally dusty sandals. They sauntered slowly, carelessly, dropping into a ragged single file as often as not, like a column of Bedouins cautiously straggling into rival territory. If they were impressed, it was well disguised. And the worse a French tourist was dressed, the more contemptuously he looked at others. The carefully washed, brushed, and dressed Italians—even those who could afford only one meal a day—refused to be scorned. They ignored the tourists (after all, Rome had been invaded by barbarians for centuries) and watched the pretty Roman girls with national pride. From sixteen until twenty-two or so, they were beautiful, as beautiful as any Lammiter had ever seen anywhere. But what happened after twenty-two, he wondered? Then he saw Rosana Di Feo coming toward him at last. She was an exception to the general rule, he considered. She must be twenty-three or -four, and she was still a beauty.

"I'm sorry," she said, "to have been so long." But she didn't sit down.

So he rose. "I was watching the tourists," he explained.

Her voice was very low. "I've watched them for three days, watched and watched and wondered. Did you see anyone who looked as if he'd risk danger?"

He glanced at her curiously, and counted out the money and the tip for their drinks. "Shall we lunch now?"

"I can't." Her voice dropped almost to a whisper. She stood with her back to the other tables, to the café's windows. "They've learned you are leaving Italy tonight."

"Oh?" He hoped his face was under control. "So you're under orders to leave me alone now. I'm no longer dangerous?" He had spoken half jokingly. But she faced him, her back to the crowded tables, her face unguarded for a moment, and he suddenly realized that she was both afraid and hopeless.

"Yes," she said. "Those are the orders."

"And did the orders come by telephone, or by that handsome black-haired Italian in the gray suit? The one who sat opposite us for a while with the thin Englishman?"

"How did you know?"

"Because he is standing at the café door, watching you, right now." She said nothing to that. He said, suddenly serious, "Perhaps it would have been safer for you not to come back to this table."

"I told him it would be very suspicious if I left you without saying good-by."

"Who is he?" The Italian was a tall man, about thirty-five or so, with dark hair, thick, carefully brushed. He had a superior air, as if he were accustomed to behave correctly. He was obviously well fed, but also well exercised. He was most carefully dressed. Handsome, yes. Attractive to women, definitely. Now he was going forward to another table, to spend a few minutes in conversation with an aging beauty, exquisitely dressed, her white face sheltered from the sun by an elaborate hat, her vanity bolstered by the adulation of the two young men who kept her company.

Rosana hesitated. But she didn't answer his question. "If you change your mind about leaving," she said, holding out her hand to shake his, "it would be safest to keep it a secret." She pressed a small wad of paper into his palm. "Good-by."

"Safest for whom?"

"For both of us."

He shook hands solemnly, but the amusement quickened in his eyes. He was convinced that a good deal of dramatics had gone into persuading him to stay. There was too much emotion, too much play acting around here for his taste. He'd stick to the theater for that kind of thing, keeping it safely in a world of make-believe. But the day stretched out in its lonely fashion before him till he'd get on that homebound plane, and he tried to prolong the good-by."

"Have a safe journey," she said, a little bitterly, as if she had read his thoughts, and she turned away.

Quickly, he started after her. He raised his voice to normal "I'm sorry we can't lunch together."

She said urgently, quietly, "Don't follow me. Stay at your table!"

"Let me walk with you to the corner," he said. "Even acquaintances do that."

"There's no need."

"None. But I want to. Besides, if I didn't walk a pretty girl to the corner, it *would* look odd."

They were passing the table now where the aging beauty, her two young men, and the handsome dark-haired Italian were sitting.

"Oh, Rosana!" It was the older woman speaking, her white face cracking delicately around the lips and eyes. "You never come to see me any more," she said chidingly.

"I shall, Principessa," Rosana promised, halting unwillingly but politely as the three men at the table rose to their feet. Lammiter walked on slowly for a few paces, plunging his hands into his pockets as if he had nothing to do but wait. It was a relief to let the small wad of paper drop free from his palm into safety. Then he halted, looking at the traffic, while he lit a cigarette.

The princess's voice held Rosana. "We move soon to the hills. So come tomorrow, Rosana. The boys want to go to Ischia"—Lammiter could almost hear the flutter of their eyes and the pouting of their lips as they mimed their disappointment—"but I refuse to have anything to do with the Bay of Naples in August." And then there was a new inflection in the clear carrying voice, one of subtle sarcasm. "Luigi, do let me introduce you. Luigi Pirotta—the Signorina Di Feo." Lammiter almost swung round to face the dark-haired Italian. "But of course," the princess halted the introduction halfway, "you have met. How stupid of me! Wasn't Luigi a great friend of your brother's, my dear?" Her voice was elegiac now, hinting at disaster. Lammiter glanced casually around. The dark-haired Italian was very much at ease, sympathetic, regretful. Was it the charm of his manners that had caught

Eleanor Halley so surely? Or his profile, or his shoulders? They were all good. Lammiter threw away the cigarette, which had suddenly turned bitter. "How sad it all was, my dear, how indescribably sad!" the princess told Rosana, and then the girl, with a small bow and a fixed smile, walked on to join Lammiter.

He said nothing until they had passed the last table on the sidewalk. There was still something of shock and disbelief in his voice when he said, "Pirotta? Luigi Pirotta? . . . Or was she lying?"

"The princess may be tactless, malicious, even rude. But she never lies. Yes, that is Pirotta. He has a title, too, to impress his American fiancée." Rosana glanced at him swiftly. "I'm sorry," she added.

He didn't speak. He was still trying to accustom himself to the idea that the dark-haired Italian was Eleanor Halley's choice for a husband.

She said, "All right, I'll be honest. I'm not sorry. Except that the princess played my trump card. I was going to tell you his name, before we parted. So that you would stay."

"Why?"

"I am offering you revenge."

He began to smile, without much humor. He shook his head.

"You won't call it revenge, of course. That's too elemental. But Pirotta did steal your girl, didn't he? And now you begin to find out that, although he has a title and a distinguished family, and totally innocent friends with some kind of name or fame attached, and everything seemingly blameless, he still is not quite right, is he? He is not what Eleanor Halley thinks he is. Or what you thought he was."

"Would you tell me *what* he is?" he asked angrily.

"Only three people have known that. One was my brother Mario, and he is dead: a suicide, it was supposed." (How sad, the princess had said, how indescribably sad.) "One is Tony, my friend—" she glanced at him quickly "—my only true friend, and he is in hiding. And the third is I, Rosana Di Feo. Do you expect me to tell you the truth about Pirotta unless you stay here and help Tony and me? We don't want to be 'suicides' like my brother."

Lammiter caught her arm and prevented her from walking in front of a large American car feeling its way slowly out from the Hotel Excelsior's porte-cochére. He looked at the piles of luggage on the sidewalk, at the usual crowd waiting in front of the hotel, their cars edging in and out of the driveway. It was all so normal, so routine, that he told himself, This is fantastic. Here's the Excelsior, and women with diamond clips and tight silk suits; and that's the garden wall of the American Embassy down the street; and over there is the bookstall where I get the *Tribune* and *Time* and the *Rome Daily American* and anything else in English. I know this quarter backwards. The people look the same, the voices sound the same; the street is filled with sunshine and noise, with warmed spines and easy smiles, with pretty bare-legged girls in low-necked dresses. And beside me is the prettiest of them all, talking earnestly about suicide, glancing over her shoulder at that moment as if she expected we were being followed. Fantastic, the whole thing's fantastic. It just can't be happening. Not to me.

And yet, it was.

She hadn't even noticed the near-accident. Or perhaps she brushed it away as quickly as she freed her arm. "You pretend to be shocked when I offer you revenge," she said, intent on her own emotions, and her voice trembled as if she were on the verge of tears. "What else can I appeal to? Your patriotism? Don't you want to help your country? Or will you do less for it than I am willing to do?"

He said gently, trying to calm her down, "No, Rosie—ease up, old girl, or you'll be bursting into sobs. Wouldn't Pirotta find that interesting?" And as she took a deep breath, he went on, his eyes watchful, "Tell me—what kind of business is Pirotta caught up in? What is it?"

The moment of weakness was over. Her bitterness returned. Again she ignored his question. "What else must I say? Shall I fall back on the appeal to Sir Galahad? If you aren't a patriot, aren't you at least a romantic? You may not consider me much of a lady any more, but I assure you—I am in distress."

He persisted with his own questions. "What is Pirotta's racket? He *is* mixed up with something unpleasant, not honest, secret. Isn't he?"

She bit her lip.

"What is it?"

"Not here. They are still watching us probably."

"Must I stay in Rome—" he began angrily.

"But quietly, don't advertise it," she warned him quickly.

"—to hear what kind of a man Pirotta is?"

She halted at the corner of the street, her eyes on the red light which was about to change to green. She put her hand out to say good-by. He caught it and held it. "Rosana—look, if I stay in Rome, will you answer my questions?"

She looked up at him then. "Yes. All of them." Her voice softened. "So gladly, so very gladly."

Around them he heard the beginning of complaints. "What is wrong with those traffic lights?" someone asked angrily. Then Rosana laughed, and glanced toward the white-uniformed policeman who was in charge of the lights. Lammiter looked, too. The policeman was watching them both with a broad smile.

"Is he giving us time to say good-by?" Lammiter asked.

"He's a romantic. That's what Tony would call him," Rosana said, and took her hand away from Lammiter's grasp. "I want you to meet Tony. And he wants to meet you." The policeman pressed the switch, the lights changed, and Rosana stepped off the sidewalk. Lammiter watched her cross the street. Then he turned and walked slowly back to the café. He needed another drink.

She's got you, Bill, he told himself. And you agreed. Then he called himself a fool, an idiot, a moron, and larded the descriptions with imaginative adjectives. He might plead that he hadn't actually committed himself, yet he had been near enough to a promise to be irritated by a sense of guilt if he were to retreat from it. Then he swung away from his own emotions to take another look at Miss Di Feo. At this distance, away from those large dark eyes which could look so appealing and afraid at one and the same time, away from the best collection of physical attributes he had ever noticed gathered together around one spine, away from the soft voice and its gentle inflections (had a man ever fallen in love with a voice?), he could think of her more rationally. Miss Di Feo was a very smart little girl.

What facts had she given him?

None.

Nothing but a sense of danger threatening Eleanor—

as if he hadn't been too ready to believe the worst about
her God-damned count. Why should he go on worrying
about Eleanor, anyway? She was just about as smart a
little girl as Miss Di Feo, and as pretty, too, but don't let
him start remembering that. Anyone who could get engaged to a determined bachelor on the night of his first
play's success was not in need of much worry. And anyone who could manage to use her father's name (he was
a magazine editor when he wasn't busy worrying about
Eleanor) to find herself in Rome for Easter (just when a
fiancé was deciding he had to settle down to work and no
more parties and good-by to all the publicity and let's
hie me to a monastery—preferably Trappist) was not
in need of any worry at all. So there it was: Easter in
Rome, important friends of her father's who took her
around, a nice job as mixture of linguist and coffee-
brewer and decorative asset in the Embassy, and Eleanor
could write charming letters back to New York. Until
the last one. That was on the thirtieth day of June. . . .
"Dear Bill, I am sorry, but—" His name was Luigi Pirotta. A title, too. A very, very old family. Handsome
and charming. "In some ways, so very like you, Bill. I
know you'd approve of him. And this decision I've made,
however painful for both of us, is wise. You have your
work and all the people connected with it. There isn't
much room for me—and I was never quite able to fit
into the picture. So I shouldn't be surprised if this letter
was something of a relief to you. I know you'll understand." Understand? After the first angry shock, he broke
all engagements, including that visit to Hollywood, and
took the first plane that had a canceled reservation, the
new ideas for his next play already sifting away from his
mind like grains of sand scattering before a wind. The
weakness of determined bachelors was that they took
an engagement seriously. Once committed to the idea of
marriage, they expected it to stay with them for a life-
time. But take Eleanor—she was the kind who'd have at
least one broken engagement, three upset marriages, and
come out thriving on all the wasted emotions and bitter
recriminations. If he wanted to be sorry for anyone at
all, he ought to be pitying this fellow Pirotta.

Just as he had persuaded himself—using every unfair
argument, he would admit later—that he had no more

interest in Eleanor, he saw her. She was sitting with the princess who was so afraid of loneliness, the two simpering boys, Pirotta, and—back with him once more—the thin, vaguely familiar Englishman. And Eleanor had seen him, too. It was too late to change course. All he could do was to walk on. He'd drink his beer somewhere else.

But he didn't. For the old princess suddenly called out as he approached their table, "There's Rosana's young man! Eleanor, didn't you say you knew him? I'd like to meet him! Stop him, somebody!"

If only to save Eleanor embarrassment, he halted and smiled. "Hello, Eleanor, how are you?" Besides, it might be time to meet Pirotta. The Italian had risen to his feet. Yes, we're just about the same height, Lammiter thought: perhaps I could give him half an inch and he could give me seven pounds. He drew himself erect. Pirotta was holding his head pretty high, too. Over Eleanor's smooth crown of pale blond hair, their eyes met.

The princess laughed. "Isn't this delicious?" she asked, watching them carefully. "I adore Americans."

Five

THERE ARE some remarks at the beginning of an encounter that sound a warning bell: the wise man listens, takes heed, and makes off in the direction that will lead him most quickly out of firing range. So Bill Lammiter almost continued on his way, leaving the princess with her own special store of irony into which she would dip her well-sharpened darts. But Eleanor, quite unwittingly, changed his mind for him. "How *funny* to meet you here!" She smiled nervously at Pirotta. "Why, we were talking about you only this morning!" Then the smile trembled, and she bit her lip nervously, as if Pirotta's response had not been encouraging.

"I'm flattered," Lammiter said. And he remembered Rosana's words: *They have a good source of information on you.* Indeed they have, he thought as he smiled down at Eleanor. He hadn't really believed Rosana, not altogether. But at this moment, he began to believe a good

deal more of what she had said. And now Eleanor, her
thin delicate face turning to each of them anxiously, her
blue-gray eyes looking darker gray (as they always did
when she was nervous), her long slender body tense, had
begun making the introductions. She gave the appearance
of doing this very expertly, but Lammiter never managed
to catch the princess's name. It sounded something like
Zabaglione, which was most unlikely unless an ancestor
had spent his life whipping up Marsala and hot egg yolks.
But the thin middle-aged Englishman turned out to be
Bertrand Whitelaw, a journalist who spent much of the
year in Italy, visited America for lecture tours, wrote
weekly columns for a London paper and seasonal articles
for a New York literary magazine, and produced an occasional book on whither are we drifting, alack, alas. A
slightly younger version of his tired and troubled face
had occasionally peeked out from the glossy pages of
high-fashioned magazines, where American women were
now having their minds as well as their chin lines lifted.
For Mr. Whitelaw was an Authority. (Lammiter had
never been quite sure on what Whitelaw was an authority, but then writers have a healthy disrespect for one
another.)

The two boys embarrassed Lammiter by studying him
with open approval. He wasn't quite sure what nationality they were, didn't even listen to their names. They
now posed for him with heads cocked to one side, their
brown eyes so liquid that they threatened to pour out of
the large sockets and cascade over the beardless cheeks.
But no one paid any attention to them, and they gradually
grew disconsolate as the princess didn't even twitch their
leash. They became silent and motionless, as unnoticed
as the ashtrays on the table.

The princess had her sharp eyes on more entrancing
sport. In her white face, their strange amber color glowed
with anticipation. Her small red tongue ran its little point
across her thin scarlet lips, gathering distilled malice.
The dry ends of her russet-dyed hair seemed to spring
loose with the electricity of her emotions, as she peered
at Lammiter and then at Pirotta. She smiled. "How nice
this is! Luigi, isn't there a chair for Mr. Lammiter?
Find a waiter!" She turned to Bill Lammiter. "He's my

nephew," she said. "My only brother's only son. He's a dear boy. Aren't you, Luigi?"

Pirotta refused to be baited. He smiled and found a chair for Bill Lammiter. "What will you have to drink?" he asked amiably. The princess looked disappointed, but Eleanor relaxed for the first time, and all her old charm suddenly uncurled from its tight bud of worry, and blossomed. Yes, Lammiter decided, as conversation became general and harmless around him, Eleanor would make a very good countess. He could imagine her standing at the head of a marble staircase, extending a tight white kid glove to stiff white shirt fronts. She'd make a most attractive countess, he had to admit. And she was in love with Pirotta. She kept watching the Italian, silently, wide-eyed. Truly, as Eleanor herself would say, she was in love with her man, and not just with a marble staircase. What about Pirotta? He was in love, too. There was no doubt about that.

"But you aren't going? So soon?" the princess said as he rose. She stopped arranging her large gray straw hat (with its pink and blue flowers so carefully matched to the printed roses on her gray silk suit) and looked at him with amazement. "Why, you've been so polite listening to all our chatter that you haven't even told me what you've done with Rosana." She flashed a glance at his startled face. "What *have* you done?"

Bertrand Whitelaw said, "He has kidnaped her and is holding her for ransom. That is, after all, one of America's favorite indoor sports. Isn't it, Mr. Lammiter?"

Bill Lammiter studied Whitelaw silently.

"Now, Bertrand!" the princess chided, absolutely delighted. "After all, the Americans pay you enough for six lectures—or is it one lecture given six times?—to keep you living in Italy for the other forty-six weeks of the year. One shouldn't snap at the hand that feeds one. At least, not too obviously."

"Indeed I am not anti-American," Whitelaw insisted earnestly. "On the contrary, I'm the greatest admirer of America's contribution to civilization. A dry Martini, Principessa, is not to be sneezed at."

"Aren't you forgetting bubble gum?" Lammiter asked, too quietly.

The princess said quickly, "Ah, you must read Bertrand's column each week, Mr. Lammiter. Or don't you
read?—I mean, the London papers?"

"*Not* column. Heaven forbid," Whitelaw said reprovingly.

"No, indeed. It's a sermon," Pirotta said and gave a
genial laugh. Somehow, the tensions relaxed. Lammiter,
sitting very still, had to give Pirotta credit for his expert
diplomacy. The light laugh, applied at the right moment,
was always a solution. There were others. But then, Lammiter decided, I am obviously no diplomat. He looked at
Pirotta thoughtfully. It was disconcerting to find Pirotta's
handsome eyes quietly measuring him.

"The odd thing about Bertrand," the princess said,
"is that he lives so little in England and yet he is always
so clever about what England ought to do. Why, he
might be an American after all, mightn't he, Mr. Lammiter? By the way, I *am* curious. What *have* you done
with Rosana?"

Lammiter said stiffly, and he hoped he sounded a little
embarrassed and rueful and just a touch disappointed,
"Miss Di Feo had another engagement."

"She ran out on you, old boy? Too bad, too bad,"
Whitelaw said. Then, most unexpectedly, he added,
"What about lunch with me?"

"Splendid," Pirotta said quickly, and smiled over at
Eleanor. "We are just about to leave, too."

"Not yet, not yet!" the princess said sharply, seeing her
company suddenly dissolving. Her two young men
came to life at the anxiety in her voice. They cocked
their heads worriedly, like two very faithful and alert
French poodles. "First, we must decide what to do with
Rosana."

"Must we?" murmured Whitelaw. "And before luncheon?" He sighed.

The princess looked at him silkily. Heaven help him,
Lammiter thought. She went on talking. "Rosana runs
away from all attractive young men. She never comes
to see me, or any of her mother's old friends. She avoids
us, I think. Of course, her brother— Do you think she is
avoiding us all because of Mario?"

Lammiter, watching, suddenly saw anger in Pirotta's

eyes. But the Italian's voice was noncommittal. "Let us not talk about Mario."

"Of course, you knew him. And liked him. We all did. Poor Mario," the princess sighed.

"Poor Mario?" Whitelaw asked. "Now I am interested."

"Do you remember the scandal last year? Mario was found dead, naked, in his bedroom. Odd, wasn't it, to commit suicide without one's clothes on? People are usually so careful about appearances when they are dead."

"Oh!" Whitelaw remembered now. "Drugs. Am I right?"

"Yes . . . Drugs. So vulgar . . . And it concerned the sons and daughters of several well-known families. Horrid, wasn't it, Luigi?"

Pirotta was watching her. His face was controlled. He nodded.

"We were all *so* upset. One was afraid to look in the newspapers in case one knew the names. And of course, Bertrand"—and now the bright amber eyes were turned on the Englishman—"the Communists tried to make a festival of denunciation out of the whole sordid business. They began holding meetings, wrote editorials, organized parades. You know how they behave! And then—but don't you remember?"

Whitelaw said, "I was away lecturing at the time." He and Pirotta exchanged one look. To Lammiter, it seemed as if everyone had forgotten about him, as if there were a secret battle in progress. And then, suddenly, he began to feel that the princess was staging all this scene with a purpose. For his benefit? The little glance she flashed him now seemed to draw him into the center of it all.

"Then you missed *so* much fun," she told Whitelaw. "For some really clever journalist discovered that there were Communists, too, who were mixed up with all the scandal. So, of course, a great silence descended. But everyone knows that there are still some hidden drug rings. And with Communists running them, I hear."

"Oh, really!" Whitelaw exclaimed. He tried to hide his growing amusement. He smiled at the two other men. "Come, come—one doesn't believe everything one hears.

Especially in Rome." He turned to Lammiter. "The Romans are so nimble-witted that they supply the most delicious gossip to suit any situation."

Pirotta laughed. "If we didn't have the situations, we'd invent them."

"Besides," Whitelaw said consolingly, "you can't be afraid of your Communists in Italy. Now really, Principessa! They're such delightful people."

The princess said, disarmingly sweet, "I did *not* mean our *nice* Communists, who want to *help* the workers. I meant the real Communists—who *shoot* the workers. As in Poznan last month."

There was a little silence.

Eleanor ended it. "I just can't forget that photograph. You know—the one with the girl walking in front holding a flag all covered with blood. And the students and workers behind her." Her gray eyes widened, her lips trembled, her face flushed. She looked very beautiful, very touching, as Joan of Arc. Pirotta took her hand gently. Lammiter was glad to see that that comforted her.

"I think you must write my next article," Whitelaw suggested with a gentle smile for the princess.

"Would it be printed?"

"Why shouldn't it?"

"But would your newspaper trust me as much as it *trusts* you, Bertrand?" Again there was that little flicker of the amber eyes toward Lammiter as she lingered on the word "trust." Then she waved her soft white hands, the pink quartz and blue sapphires glancing with the sunlight on her long thin fingers. "Now we've all worked up a pretty appetite for luncheon." She began drawing on her silver-gray gloves. "And we have quite forgotten poor Rosana. Tell me, Luigi, did you ever hear the truth about Mario Di Feo? Did he *take* drugs? Or did he *sell* them?" There was again a brief silence. "Poor Rosana— she came home from America and found her brother a suicide, and nothing ever explained."

"How awful!" Eleanor said, all sympathy. "What is she like?"

"Young. Younger than you are, I'd imagine. And very beautiful."

"Oh!" Eleanor retreated.

"Wouldn't you say so, Mr. Lammiter?"

Bill Lammiter nodded. Eleanor was, strangely enough, watching him.

"No comment? Or did you find my story too moving? How splendid! Then I'll ask you to dinner tomorrow night along with Rosana. You and I shall cheer her up. Luigi, you must come, too, and bring your Eleanor. And you, Bertrand? We shall be six. How nice. I hate large parties."

"I'm sorry," Lammiter said, "but I'm leaving Rome tonight. So you see—"

"No, I don't," the princess said fretfully. "You can't leave Rome right now." She took a deep breath. "I want you to come to dinner tomorrow."

"I'm afraid I'll be in New York by tomorrow night."

"Really, Bill?" Eleanor asked. "Why, I thought you were going to spend the summer here, writing." She looked upset, as if she blamed herself for this change.

"I don't seem to get much work done in Rome."

"Does one *want* to work in Rome?" Whitelaw asked, with his amused smile.

"New York," the princess said, "will be as hot as Rome. Perhaps hotter. You won't work there, either. What are you writing? Another play? I know just the place for you in the Umbrian hills. I'll lend you a house. You may stay as long as you like."

Lammiter might have disliked trying to write in hotel rooms, but he distrusted borrowed houses even more. And then, just as he was about to refuse firmly, the look of disquiet that momentarily glanced over Pirotta's face made him hesitate. He looked vague, polite, uncertain.

Eleanor tried to help him. "Must you really go back to New York so soon, Bill?"

He made the mistake of not having a good excuse ready. The moment to make it came, and was gone.

"Then why don't you stay? You haven't seen a hundredth part of Italy. And there's so much to see, so much material for you to use in your next play. Don't you agree, Luigi?"

Pirotta made a polite murmur, quite unguessable but apparently friendly.

The princess suddenly tried a frontal attack. "Mr. Lammiter, what is making you *run* away?"

"Run?" Lammiter hoped he looked both startled and

stupid. Then he laughed, looking at the others for support. "I guess I just got set on the idea of leaving, that's all. I only decided on it last night." He was speaking slowly in a forthright manner trying to give the appearance of someone who was completely simple-minded. It was the kind of character they would all readily accept, because they believed in it. Except Eleanor: she had once or twice looked at him in surprise when he had sat silent and let the conversational ball slip past him; and now, when he was at last talking, she watched him with a small frown as he kept strictly to basic English. "I was standing on my balcony, having my last cigarette. I kind of like looking over that old wall. Makes a fellow think. Gives him a new viewpoint about a lot of things. I wasn't feeling too good, kind of down about everything. The weather, I guess; and not being able to get any work done, and all. Then this idea hit me. Just like that." He laughed again. He was holding the Englishman enthralled, at least. Whitelaw no doubt prided himself on imitations. "And then, a funny thing happened. Last night, or rather early this morning—you won't believe it, but it happened, all right—" He dropped his voice, and he noticed that Pirotta's interest in him had died away entirely. Pirotta would have been interested in him only if he hadn't mentioned the strange happening of last night. "I was standing—"

"I hate standing," the princess said, rising, "and there's my car. Mr. Lammiter, your arm, please." She put out a hand and let it rest on his forearm. They started walking toward the well-polished Lancia which had cruised slowly up the hill and was now stopping near the curb in front of them. He suddenly realized how slight and frail her bones were.

Very quietly she said, "I hope you understand what I was trying to tell you, Mr. Lammiter."

He nodded, noncommittally. He had reached the phase of trusting nobody. Only one thing had been decided about an hour ago. He was staying in Rome.

She went on, "At least I gave you a good excuse to change your mind about leaving. But you don't have to come to see me. I'm much too old. If only I had not been so tactful with Mussolini, I might have died while I was still attractive." She sighed. He looked at her in utter amazement, and now he wasn't acting any more. "It was thirty years ago, of course. I had gone to ask Mussolini a favor—my son and all his family had been arrested, ridiculous nonsense! Mussolini was standing behind the enormous desk in that gigantic room of his. He came round to where I was standing. He caught me and threw me down on the carpet. I slapped his face with the back of my hand—rings are so useful at times—and said 'Get up, you peasant!' And so he rolled off me, and I got up and smoothed my dress and walked out."

Lammiter burst into laughter. "You got away with that?" He helped her into the car, the anxious chauffeur watching each movement most critically, the two young men ballet-stepping around.

"But I had called him a *peasant*. That was what he liked to call himself. It won votes. Now, if I had called him what I *really* felt he was—a pig in the gutter—I shouldn't be here today." She sighed, settled herself on the car's white leather seat, and gave him her hand in good-by. "So I lived on. I don't really know who had the last word, though, the pig or I."

He closed the car's polished blue door carefully. Very small, quietly conspicuous was its minuscule coat of arms. He watched the car ease its way carefully into the busy traffic, before he turned back to the café. He was still smiling. Perhaps now he'd enjoy that drink he'd promised himself half an hour ago. But the little group at the table was not yet dispersed.

"My aunt amuses you?" Pirotta asked.

"She tells a good story." He began to laugh again. "I was hearing about her meeting with Mussolini."

Pirotta groaned humorously. "You really thought it was funny?"

"Don't you?"

"The first time, perhaps." He made a comical face, and yet lost none of his dignity.

Eleanor looked at them both with relief. This was the way she liked life: no jealousy, no dislikes, no animosities. "You *are* going to stay here and enjoy Italy, aren't you, Bill?" Perhaps she wanted to rid herself of all feeling that she had ruined his visit here.

"If one is offered a house," Whitelaw said, "one generally accepts." He was amused, interested, but not unkind. "You made quite a hit with the old girl, didn't you?"

"But surely," Lammiter said, "the princess didn't mean it."

They all stared at him.

"Now," he said, "don't tell me anyone can believe a word she says."

Pirotta's handsome eyes smiled suddenly with relief. "I'm afraid not," he said with regret.

"No dinner party tomorrow night?" Eleanor asked, in a strange tight little voice, the kind she used when she didn't quite believe what was said.

"If we went," Pirotta answered gently, "we might find that my aunt had forgotten to tell her housekeeper that she had suddenly invented a dinner party, here, at Doney's. She is getting old. Good-by, Lammiter."

They didn't shake hands.

"Good-by," Lammiter said, equally crisp.

Whitelaw's good-by was regretful. Perhaps, now that Lammiter seemed about to leave Rome, luncheon would be rather a waste of time and energy. "I hadn't noticed how late it was," he said, consulting his watch, "and I have an engagement this afternoon. It might be wiser to postpone our luncheon? One hates to rush coffee. Some other day?" He turned aside, then halted to exchange a few last words with Pirotta.

Eleanor took the opportunity to say, "I'll feel awful if you take the first plane home! Truly, Bill, I don't want to spoil everything." She looked at him pleadingly. "I wish you would stop thinking the worst of me. I'm sorry. I'm truly sorry." Perhaps she had seen Garbo in that recent revival of *Camille*, for now she was neither standing at the head of a marble staircase nor marching on the barricade of machine guns, but she was making the great renunciation.

"I know," he said, "it hurt you more than it hurt me." But he ought to have denied himself the pleasures of sarcasm.

She looked sharply at him, and her voice altered. "So it was all a little act."

"Eleanor!" he said reproachfully. He wondered if Pirotta's quick ears had been listening.

"I wondered—I never saw you so silent and wide-eyed."

"But I was so impressed. A princess, and a count! My, my, my . . ."

"Bill Lammiter! And I almost believed you had changed."

"Just the same old Bill," he said reassuringly. "I'm stuck with me. You know something?"

"No," she said quickly. "I don't want to know it."

"Then we'll make it a real good-by." He put out his hand. Quietly, he said to her, "I hope you'll be very happy."

She looked at him uncertainly, and then—as Pirotta came over to take her by the arm—she decided to accept that at its full value. "Thank you," she said, bowing a little.

"Madame la Comtesse receiving the good wishes of the local peasantry," Lammiter said with a little grin.

"Oh, Bill!" She was angry.

And suddenly, unexpectedly, he was sorry. But she was already leaving with her noble count. She was talking with vivacity and charm to emphasize how much Lammiter had lost. Oh, stop that! he told himself: it doesn't even make you feel any better.

At least, he thought wearily as he sat down for a delightfully solitary drink, she will not see me again, she won't invite me to her parties and try to find another girl for me and tell me how intelligent we are to remain such good dear friends. I'll be spared all that, thank God.

And then a most depressing thought struck him, suddenly, vehemently. At this moment, Eleanor might be angry with him, but she still liked him. She was still fond of him. But what would she feel when he discovered more about Pirotta? Hate, possibly. She's going to hate you, he told himself morosely. By God, and how! No one liked the man who unveiled the illusion. It would be easier if he cabled her father, got him to come over and save his darling daughter (and himself) from scandal. But that was too easy: ditching responsibility, escaping hate, was too easy a way out. Besides, the girl Rosana could be lying. Pirotta could be an honest son of a bitch after all. I'll have to find that out for myself, he thought. I'll have to stay in Rome, and find out the truth; and, if it's ugly, then calculate how it affects Eleanor, and then— And then?

His depression grew. He put the question away from him. He hoped he would never have to answer it.

Six

LAMMITER HAD another glass of beer, to let Eleanor and Pirotta put several blocks between them and Doney's. He resisted all temptation to pull out Rosana's crumpled wad of paper which had been burning a hole in his pocket for almost an hour: for now he was in a mood to listen to the need for caution. At last, and leisurely, he left the emptying tables and set off for a small restaurant he liked near the Via Ludovisi. To reach it, he crossed the Via Vittorio Veneto, its traffic now noticeably sparse, and he stopped at the paper stall at the corner of the two streets and bought himself *Time* and *Oggi*. So armed for a lonely meal, he walked on under the shady trees. And he wondered about several people.

He wondered about the princess, who must have postponed her escape to the hills this summer, for the weather was now hot and sticky and promised worse. Why? She hadn't run out of houses, obviously. The old Roman families (who never called themselves Italian) didn't usually spend the tourist months in the city. Nor did they make a habit of frequenting restaurants or cafés very much, and then usually in the late afternoon, when they'd quiz the foreigners' parade and store up some witticisms for dinner.

("Mr. Lammiter, to what do you attribute your percipient knowledge of the Roman way of life?"

"Talk with the waiters, son. Nice long conversations with waiters and barmen, the trusted friends of the lonely traveler."

"Waiters, Mr. Lammiter?"

"Sure. They are just waiting to tell you. Start them talking, son, and you cain't stop 'em. . . . They'll give you more to brood over than a carload of guidebooks. They're all strangers here, too. Did you know that people in the Abruzzi believe in werewolves? Let me tell you about the old waiter from the Abruzzi who once slept beside a werewolf.")

Werewolf . . . And I never did puzzle that story out,

he thought. The man had believed what he had seen with
his own eyes. In the waiters' dormitory, the young boy
who had just come from the Abruzzi used to start up
with a howl when the summer moon was full, while the
other waiters buried their heads in the sheets to smother
their breathing, and he would leap from his bed and out
through the door, to return with the dawn, calm, quiet,
unseeing, unhearing, already half asleep on his feet. "A
werewolf," the older waiter had repeated. "Such things
happen in my country." It's possible, Lammiter reflected,
that the boy was simply so homesick for the mountains
and forests of the Abruzzi that he'd lie awake on a hot
summer night crying to himself. Italians were a regional
people, their loyalty to the childhood places deep and pas-
sionate. And then there would come a moment when the
memories became unbearable, the strangled sob broke
loose into a howl of despair, and he'd rush from the room
where the older men (their memories now blurred by
city life) were lying awake, listening to him, watching.

Now, what made me start thinking about werewolves?
Surely not the princess. Nor Bertrand Whitelaw, even if
he was a tortured man. What troubled him, anyway? He
had the best of all his possible worlds: he was published
regularly; he had acclaim—and money, too, that nice
expendable stuff; he enjoyed all the prestige of a free-born
Englishman and suffered none of the tribulations of the
British climate. Presumably he was one of those types
who didn't need a wife, for he kept himself free from all
female entanglements. So what had he to worry about?
And then, Lammiter wondered, was Whitelaw's meeting
with Pirotta this morning something that had happened
quite naturally: Pirotta had been here to keep an eye on
Rosana as he waited for Eleanor, and Whitelaw had come
strolling along and joined him? Or had it been contrived?
If so, who had contrived it? Not Pirotta, Lammiter decided: Pirotta had many things on his mind, but a quiet
talk with the Englishman hadn't been one of them. In fact,
Pirotta had evaded any chance of a tête-à-tête with considerable skill. Pirotta, Lammiter thought now, was the
kind of man who usually got what he wanted.

Then why, if he were innocent of all Rosana's innuen-
dos, why had he sat at that table with Lammiter? The
American imagined himself in Pirotta's place: a difficult

moment with the princess heaving her variety of monkey
wrench into the works. But I, Lammiter thought now, I'd
have risen, taken Eleanor's arm, made a firm excuse (and
no one was going to refuse any lovers' excuses) and left
everyone to gossip to their tongues' content. Instead,
Pirotta had sat on, had listened and watched. He had
been extremely polite. Almost friendly. Disarming, was the
better word. Why?

Lammiter's lips tightened and he quickened his pace.
He knew one thing. He would like to spend half an hour
with Bunny Camden. Bunny, now one of the naval attachés at the Embassy—liaison work with visiting NATO
specialists, Bunny had explained vaguely when they had
met, by accident, outside the Embassy gates three days
ago—had the kind of mind that had been trained to add
up the facts and subtract the fiction from a puzzling situation. And Bunny Camden was a friend, a word that Lammiter didn't bestow lightly. Even if they only met at the
oddest intervals and in the strangest ways—and that, to
Lammiter, was part of the amusing aspect of their friendship which kept it alive through all the gaps between
their meetings—Camden was someone dependable.

He remembered Bunny's face when they had met outside the Embassy. His own had been just as delighted
and amazed—for the last time he had seen Bunny had been
in Korea, six years ago. Bunny was one of those Intelligence officers who had decided to stay in the service (in
Bunny's case, it was the Marine Corps), and now—a little
to his surprise and not altogether to his fancy—he had
been promoted to a quasi-diplomatic but completely
straight-forward job in the Mediterranean area. "Strictly
legitimate, now," Bunny had said, talking hard to cover
Lammiter's embarrassment at the meeting, for once the
delight and amazement were over, Lammiter was too conscious of the fact that he had been caught hovering around
the Embassy gates, hoping to intercept Eleanor on her
way out to lunch. Not that either Bunny or the friend
with him (quite definitely a friend, a classics professor
called Ferris from Pennsylvania, who was working at the
American Academy in Rome for the summer) could have
had any idea why they had found Lammiter waiting at the
entrance to the Embassy's driveway; but those who loitered were always sensitive about being discovered.

Especially when the discoverer was someone like Bunny Camden. "Hi there!" he had said, catching Lammiter by the arm. "And dammit if it isn't. Thought I knew that old bullet head and standout ears. What are you plotting now? If it's arsenic poisoning, we've already had it." And so Bunny could introduce and squash the current sensation about the Ambassadress and her bedroom ceiling, before he branched onto NATO, a prospective trip to Naples, and then suggested a party when he returned. "We must all get together," he said, including Professor Ferris in his smile, and Lammiter had agreed. Then they parted, and Lammiter hadn't thought much about Bunny Camden's old job or qualifications until Rosana had questioned him this morning. Now that he thought about it, Bunny Camden was just the type that Rosana needed.

Lammiter had reached the restaurant's entrance. He happened to glance back as he was about to enter its doorway. The heat was stifling now. The street was empty: the siesta hour had begun. Except for one man, who had halted near a tree on the opposite side of the street and was busily lighting a cigarette. Lammiter entered, paused, glanced back again over his shoulder. Yes, the man was looking in this direction. Lammiter went into the cool dark room. I saw that man at Doney's, he suddenly thought; just as I was leaving, I noticed him—a man of medium height and construction, thick-haired, dark, bare-headed like most younger Italians, wearing a blue cotton suit and white shirt such as a thousand bank clerks and office workers wore. Except that this one did not carry the usual thin black brief case, which seemed to be a necessary part of a white-collar worker's dress, the badge of his education.

The restaurant was almost empty. He chose a small table under the large ceiling fan. He agreed with the waiter that he was late, tactfully rejected a variety of pasta and hot bean soup, chose chicken *cacciatore,* to be followed by Bel Paese and fresh fruit. "Nothing to begin with, signore, nothing?" The waiter was desolated: like all Italians he enjoyed seeing people eat. But he brought a nicely chilled bottle of Soave Verona, and as he uncorked it, they talked about the vineyard from which it came: Romeo and Juliet territory, east of Verona. The waiter,

Lammiter guessed, came from that part of the country, too. (If he had been a Tuscan, Lammiter would have now been drinking Chianti.)

It was a pleasant little exchange, darkened by the shadow of another possible customer, silhouetted briefly against the sunlight outside as he pulled at the door's beaded screen to peer indoors for a moment. The screen fell together again with a shimmer of sweet sound, as the man turned away. The restaurant's owner, a stout motherly woman whose quick business sense missed nothing, called sharply to the waiter to take the new customer's order. "Outside, outside!" she indicated impatiently, so the man in the blue suit must have chosen one of the little tables on the sidewalk. He obviously preferred a table under the hot awning to the emptiness of a room. The waiter halted his graphic description of the two small pointed hills, lying like a maiden's breasts among the vineyards, where the Capulets and the Montagues had built their country castles.

Lammiter sipped the cool white wine, slowly. *I wish I had never noticed that man outside, or the brief case he didn't carry, or the cigarette he lit across the street but had thrown away before he looked into this room. I wish I had been left to enjoy my chicken* cacciatore *without the unpleasant thought that I'm being followed.*

He took up *Oggi* and pretended to concentrate on his Italian lesson for today. He smoothed out the small wad of paper which Rosana had given him and held it closely against the magazine's printed page. All it contained was a telephone number, followed by a brief phrase: *Before half-past four?* The question mark was a politeness: he wasn't being told, he was being asked. He could almost hear Rosana's voice adding, "Please listen to me, please. . . ."

He slipped the piece of paper quietly back into his pocket. He kept his eyes fixed on *Oggi*'s front page, but his mind was trying to decide on the most discreet way of telephoning. He wished he had had more training in this kind of work. Back in the army, he had taken a course on jujitsu and eye-gouging, like everyone else in his branch of the service. He had also learned to treat elementary ciphers with respect, and deal with maps. But that was all. His friends would never believe that, and they'd be amazed at the predicament in which he now found himself. For although he had always told them the truth—his actual experience in intelligence work had been boringly limited to routine security measures, nothing remarkable —everyone thought he was being modest about his work in G2. The more he insisted that he was on the lowest rung of the ladder, if he could be said even to have one foot halfway toward it, the more they nodded and fell into a discreet but respectful silence.

It was funny, though, to have this misinterpretation of his army service catch up with him in Rome, of all places. He could probably thank Eleanor for that: when Pirotta had questioned her about him, she had instinctively made him out to be a pretty important type. That's the way women were: anyone they had known well must be exceptional, brilliant. It depressed him now to think how Eleanor might have talked about him. He had rarely felt more depressed. It could have been partly hunger, though, for he began to feel more cheerful when a steaming dish of chicken and vegetables was uncovered before him.

By the time he had reached the stage of peeling a peach, he had decided to telephone Bunny Camden and arrange a quick meeting. There was a telephone at Madam's little desk, but that was too near the doorway and any attentive ears. Besides, it might not be wise to call Bunny at the Embassy; better to get in touch with him indirectly, better to play all this in an overcautious way, better to look ignorant, ineffective, and undangerous. The men who frightened Rosana, her so-called "friends," were just a little too quick in their suspicions. Better, much better, if he gave them no cause to speculate about him, to worry over his actions. And so, no direct telephone call to Bunny Camden. What was the name of the classics professor—the one who had been visiting Bunny at the Embassy three days ago? Ferris, Carl Ferris, now at the American Academy. That was a possibility, in fact the only one he could think of. A visit to the American Academy on the Janiculum Hill was an innocent way to spend the next hour. Quickly, he drank the small cup of bitter coffee, paid his bill, made the correct good-by with its necessary compliments, and braced himself to see the blue suit sweltering outside. But the man had gone. Perhaps Lammiter had eaten too slowly, or the sidewalk table had been too hot, or the man had simply resigned his job in disgust. Anyway, Lammiter enjoyed his walk to the corner of the Via Vittorio Veneto, where he'd find the bus that would take him across the Tiber to the Janiculum. It was only on the bus itself, almost empty at this time of day, that he realized that the man in the blue suit had probably only given way to another. He looked carefully at the three passengers who had got on board along with him. Then he began to smile. "This has gone far enough," he told himself, thankful that he still had enough perspective left to see the ridiculous. "Half of Rome is *not* following you. Stop worrying, stop imagining. Just go to the Academy, find out from the porter where Carl Ferris is staying, and then move on to the next item on your little list."

Ferris received him with some wonder on his thin tanned face. But he was both cordial and pleased to see Lammiter, even at this odd calling-hour. "Come in," he said. He was hastily dressed in shirt and trousers. "Sorry, we were just finishing a siesta." He looked a little embarrassed. He raised his voice, to keep his wife safely wherever she was. "Okay, honey. Just a friend. We'll be in the living room."

"I shan't keep you long," Lammiter said, following Ferris from the little hallway into a high-ceilinged room. "And I'm the one who should be sorry. I didn't realize what time it was." His watch told him it was half-past three.

"We've been here long enough to adopt the Roman habits," Ferris explained with a grin.

"All of them?"

They both laughed. Lammiter was looking round the room with interest. It was furnished in the usual Italian way, but Ferris had added a lot of his own things: books, as you'd expect, plenty of books, on archaeology, Etruscan art, history; large photographs of columned temples, a sculptured torso, a typewriter, and a desk piled with notebooks and manuscript.

"We like the view," Ferris said, pointing to the window, and quickly picking up a black lace brassière lying over the arm of a chair, he retreated toward the bedroom. He came back, fastening his cuffs, and trying to assume control of the interview. "Writing a new play?" he asked.

Lammiter said, "I keep trying to settle down to work. But I've had a bad attack of distraction. Today—well, I've decided to clear up the current batch of problems, and then, perhaps, I'll have some peace to settle down to a hard job of work."

Ferris lit a cigarette and dropped the match carefully into a pot of flowers. "What's on your mind?"

"I want to get in touch with Bunny."

"Well—go ahead!" Ferris pointed. "The telephone is in the hall."

"Would you call for me? I'll wait here. I don't want to call and then find he isn't there."

Ferris glanced at him with a slight look of surprise, followed by amusement. "And then have someone insist that you leave your name? It is odd, isn't it, how a reasonably honest man feels impelled to answer truthfully on the telephone?"

Lammiter grinned. It was pleasant to be judged an honest man, even reasonably so. "You were in OSS?" Ferris looked as if he might have been World War II vintage.

"No. Navy. But I enjoy a good Hitchcock."

"Oh—I'm not on any hush-hush job. Nothing like that."

"Of course not." Ferris smiled broadly. "You sound like a real pal of Bunny's. He's always engaged in some quip or merry prank."

Lammiter liked Professor Ferris's flexible use of language. He also liked the prompt way Ferris moved into the little hall and put the call through. He had to make two calls: one to the Embassy, one to a private address. In both cases he left his own name, a sure sign of failure.

"Bunny's said to be in Naples," he reported when he returned, "but he's expected back some time today. I left word for him to phone me fastest. Where can I have him reach you when he does get back?"

"I don't know. I've practically checked out of my hotel. There's just the luggage to collect and the last bill to pay."

"You're leaving Rome?"

"Well—no. Not actually." He hesitated. "I just want to keep some people guessing."

"Oh?" Ferris would make a good dean of students. Lammiter found he was clearing his throat nervously, almost ready to tell the whole story.

"Oh, just some people. Some people who seem pretty eager to have me leave." He grinned suddenly. "Don't ask me why. I'm staying to find out the answer for myself. But I'd like it to appear that I really was going back home—and when I do stay, I'll make it look like a sudden impulse."

Ferris nodded. He was bewildered but polite.

"So—" Lammiter rushed on, "I'd like to keep telephoning you here, to see if Bunny has been run to earth. I'd like his advice on something. What's your number?"

Ferris scribbled it down on a piece of paper. "I'll be here most of the day," he said, pointing to the books opened on his desk. "I'm finishing a paper to deliver this weekend at the opening of the summer school in Perugia." Then he noticed Lammiter's gradual edging toward the door. He smiled, "Well, I shan't keep you now."

"Good-by," Lammiter said, restraining his eagerness. "And many thanks. In fact, many many thanks." He added truthfully, "Hope we get together some day."

"I'll give you a ring when we come up to New York for Christmas shopping. Perhaps Bunny will be on leave then, and we can make it a party. You knew him in Korea, didn't you? He makes a good story of the time you met."

They shook hands. A clatter of high heels on a marble floor suddenly made Ferris snatch the cigarette from his lips, nick its burning end with his fingers, and then jam the broken stub into the cuff of his trousers. "Gave up smoking months ago," he said cheerfully as he opened the door. "Doctor's orders. Sure you won't stay for coffee? That's one thing our small gas ring can cook around here."

"Some other time. Oh, by the way, you are a historian, aren't you? How long did that Roman wall—the Aurelian Wall—how long did it keep out the barbarians?"

"More than a hundred years."

"Then they might have managed it?"

"The Romans? Yes. If only they had invented gunpowder." Ferris was delighted by the effect this produced. "Or a United Nations. Or both." He smiled. "Yes, they might have been here yet. Frankly. I don't know whether it's better that they aren't still around. They'd be too clever for the rest of us, by this time." He smiled again. "Good-by."

"See you in New York." Lammiter ran lightly down the flights of shallow stairs, his hand sliding down the smooth stone banisters. Once this house had been a villa standing in its own grounds; now, the various floors were broken into small apartments. Someone moved on the landing above; a small hard object, a pebble, a nail, grated under a cautious shoe. The little sound was silenced so quickly that Lammiter knew that someone regretted it and was now standing motionless, not even daring to breathe. For a moment, he wondered if he should retrace his steps just to spread more alarm and confusion. But he continued on his way, whistling cheerfully. Nothing that had been said either near or actually at the door of Ferris's apartment could possibly be interesting to anyone else.

In the hall, he stopped to look at the eighteenth-century ceiling, now peeling here and there, fading in patches, a little scabby. But there was still plenty of opulent draperies, pearly arms, pink chins, sofalike clouds, and a sunburst over all. A young man came out of the ground-floor apartment, leaving the sound of a piano, *fortissimo brillante*, behind him, and caught Lammiter craning back his neck to admire the painting. "Hits you with a splash, doesn't it? You'll get a better view from the top floor," he suggested.

"I've had my quota of stairs for today."

"You at the school?"

"No. Just visiting an old friend before I leave for home." From above, there came no sound of movement.

"Thought I hadn't seen you around much. Like a lift into town?"

"Thanks, I would."

"Most people do. There's a long wait between buses."

They left the villa with its curlicued trim around the front door, stepped onto the half-acre of sparse gravel which formed the garden along with clusters of rhododendron bushes, and passed through the elaborate gate, broad enough to take a coach and four. The young man started his motor bicycle. "Hold my books, will you?" He thrust a small pile of learned-looking objects into Lammiter's arms. "All set?" Lammiter, perched behind, could only nod and grip with his knees.

They roared down the Janiculum Hill toward the river. Lammiter laughed. His driver half turned his head, and the bike swerved sharply.

"Nothing, nothing!" Lammiter yelled. And then he thought he ought to offer a plausible explanation. "I just thought of the people waking up from a siesta and cursing our noise."

"Noise?" The young man looked perplexed, listened for engine trouble, and then took the bridge over the Tiber at full throttle.

But even after Lammiter, temporarily bowlegged, had dismounted and said good-by to his benefactor (nameless and asking no name, just one of the friendly souls who offered a lift in the same spirit they'd accept it), he was still amused by the vision that had suddenly burst upon him as they roared down the twisting Janiculum road toward Father Tiber. It was a vision of someone most serious, who had indeed followed him into the villa, who must have come hurrying out too late, only to see Lammiter, complete with schoolbooks, perched on the rear of a motor bicycle, careering down between the Janiculum trees. He would very much like to see the written report on the Afternoon of Signore William Lammiter.

Seven

AT THE HOTEL, the porter's desk announced with quiet triumph that there was space available on the midnight plane. Lammiter paid his last bill, told the porter he'd collect the ticket himself, and found his luggage in the entrance hall, where it had already been deposited. No doubt there was some new American in his room, standing on his balcony, smoking a cigarette, wondering about the Aurelian Wall which he overlooked, admiring the giant crowns of the huge pine tree beyond the Gardens. He wished he could have had just one minute to say good-by to that view. It had cheered him up on many a night in these last few weeks. He hadn't been happy. But he had liked that balcony, the sunset, the moonrise, the flight of the swallows. It would have been pleasant just to have had one last look around from the balcony. But life wasn't a playwright, drawing everything neatly into a final scene and last act. Life had a way of surprising and not explaining and turning you out into the street without one moment for sentiment.

Perhaps just as well, he thought: he hadn't much time to waste now. It was just after four o'clock. And what would be the safest way to telephone Rosana? He was taking not the smallest chance that his movements weren't of interest to Pirotta and his organization— Rosana's hated "friends." As for his own role in this strange fantasy, he'd find out when he saw her. He'd find out a lot of things. That was the end purpose of the telephone call as far as he was concerned. Then he decided how he could both telephone and evade anyone following him. He made his way through the crowded lobby, and signaled to the doorman for a taxi from the cab rank across the street. "To the airport," he told the doorman. He was conscious of a man who, circling vaguely around, now stood within earshot.

He had come prepared for a touching farewell. His pocket was bulging with hundreds of lire notes (he'd be glad when it was empty of the tattered scraps of paper sticky with age: handling them, he began to understand the Wyoming cowboys who wouldn't touch dollar bills; they weren't real money. Silver dollars might need leather-lined pockets but at least they felt and sounded like something) and his progress through the hall to the doorway was triumphant but embarrassing. Everyone, even the second *facchino,* who had once taken his shoes to the cobbler's, had gathered nonchalantly along his route of dispersal. A taxi was waiting—and within one minute of his last good-by, he was being driven down the Via Vittorio Veneto, past Doney's where the postsiesta crowd was already on view (all washed and perfumed and powdered, bare heads shining and carefully dressed, fresh low-necked dresses with wide skirts swirling over tanned legs and barefooted sandals), down into the business section of the city, past the fountains, the buses and jammed cars, the narrow sidewalks encrusted with human beings, to reach the American Express Office near the Spanish Steps.

"The Signore is going to the airport? Then I wait?" the driver asked as Lammiter prepared to climb warily out of the small green taxi—legs got trapped by the up-and-over step at the door of every Roman cab. Lammiter looked sharply at him. But then he realized it was only the Italians' magnificent communication system designed to make a traveler's life as well served as possible: it was amazing how thoughtful an Italian could be for other people's comfort. Anyway, one always had to take the first taxi in the waiting rank: this man had come to him in his right and fair turn. There was a protocol about being hired that would defeat any planted cab trying to pick up a special fare.

Lammiter relaxed. "Too long," he said tactfully. The Italian gestured that that didn't matter, he could wait. "Too much money," Lammiter added with a sad shake of the head. The Italian looked regretful, but he understood that.

"The signore speaks good Italian," he said wistfully. *"Molto bello!"*

"I know about four sentences," Lammiter said with a grin, pleased and modestly untruthful, "and you've heard two of them." They had the usual attack of conversation. The driver came from the province of Calabria, which explained *his* accent—and then, with good wishes to the driver's wife and two *bambini* and the canary that wakened them too early every morning (better be careful, that one, Lammiter thought: the early bird in Italy was apt to end up grilled for lunch), and pleasure expressed in the success of the immigrant brother in Schenectady (*that* was something to hear pronounced) who grew his own grapes in his back yard and made his own wine, they parted. Lammiter carried his two cases, with his typewriter uncomfortably gripped under his arm, into the cheerful bedlam of the American Express offices. The noise was overwhelming: the afternoon mail was being collected and the crowd was enormous, mostly American and very young. It was odd how you instinctively raised your voice the minute you started talking to a foreigner, as if you thought that loudness would make you clearer. The Italian English-speaking clerks behind their counters listened with tolerant good humor.

Lammiter looked round for a free corner where he could unload his luggage before his arm cramped up. He found one beside a girl who was tearing open a letter she had just picked up at the mail desk. She was on the young side of twenty, a blonde, with her hair caught back at the crown of her head by a perky blue bow, smartly dressed (how did girls, traveling, keep themselves so crisp and neat?), cool, capable, confident, and—judging by the way she was opening her letter—as homesick as a six-week-old puppy dog shut up in the baggage car. "Telephones?" he asked her, as he set down his cases.

She looked up wide-eyed from the letter's first lines. "Telephones? Upstairs, I think."

"Upstairs?" He looked at his baggage and then at the crowd.

"Do you want me to look after these things for you?" she asked patiently, eager to get back to her letter.

"Would you?"

"Sure. Don't be long, though. I'm meeting some friends." And they'd all troop out with their letters to the Spanish Steps; and there they'd sit, while they read and discussed the letters from home, on the long long flight of old stone stairs, the flower stalls and the fountain at their feet, the old church raising its towers above their heads. It was the daily ritual.

"Don't worry," he promised her. She nodded, sat down on one of his suitcases, and went back to her letter. He eased his way through the tight crush. It wasn't possible that everybody knew everybody else, and yet, bumping against a quiet young man and exchanging an understanding grin for their common predicament as they made way for each other, he felt they might have all belonged to the same town. Suddenly he felt ancient, although actually he was only about ten years older than most of them.

He managed, after two false starts, to call the number Rosana had given him. "Hello there," he said. "Ready or not, here we are." Just when he began to wonder if he had been cut off, he heard Rosana's voice.

"Where are you? Not at the hotel?"

"No," he said, amused at her concern for his lack of caution. "No. Nor at any place where I'm likely to be known. And I have my luggage with me."

"Take a taxi to the station. When will you get there?"

"In twenty minutes, possibly fifteen."

"Can you delay that a little? Make it five o'clock."

"At the station? Where?"

"Just get out at the main entrance. Giuseppe will meet you. You saw him today."

"Did I?"

"He drove the princess's car."

"Oh! Well, that should be easy."

"Perhaps. I hope so. But don't be rash. Please." She sounded worried.

"Five o'clock?" he asked soothingly. He heard the telephone go dead.

Funny, he thought, all foreigners believed Americans were rash. If they only knew us properly . . . Then he smiled as he descended slowly (he had time to waste) into the crowded room. How many of the young Americans here could talk or understand Italian? How little money had they in their pockets, how few traveler's checks to last their ambitious journeys? How many thousands of miles traveled, how many still to go? Rash? Ambitious, perhaps. But not rash, if you remembered the months of planning, the budgets calculated to the last dollar, the guidebooks studied, the maps memorized in private. His thoughts halted abruptly. Near the door, he saw the man he had noticed in the hotel lobby. Coincidence? Anyway, the man was leaving.

"There you are!" the blonde girl said in relief, and rose from his suitcase. She stuffed the letter pad she had begun to use into her outsize handbag. "Are you really William Lammiter? The one who wrote *Home Is the Hunter?*"

Cursing inwardly, Lammiter glanced down at the labels on his suitcases. She had looked so childlike and unnoticing with her candid blue eyes and her pretty little bow. He smiled. "Did you like it?"

She was frank, at least. "I haven't seen it yet. I live in Burbank. That's California," she explained carefully. Californians were always so helpful. "Mr. Lammiter, would you do something for me? I'm writing to Mother and Dad. Look—here it is." She drew out the pad of paper from her handbag. "You see, I'm answering this letter I got today. Dad fusses. So I'm writing to tell him I look fine—got all my teeth and both eyes. Look—would you bear witness to that? Right here . . ." She pointed to a small asterisk in the margin of her letter.

He had given enough autographs in the last six months to have stopped hesitating at signing his name. (At first it had troubled him.) But still he glanced at what he was going to sign. He said with a grin, "I always read the small print." It was a harmless letter home, gay and affectionate. "Are you traveling alone?" he asked her. No wonder her father was worried.

"Yes."

"How long have you been here?"

"In Rome? Oh, just five days. But I've been traveling since school ended in June. I went to England first, and I saw Scotland, too— I loved that; and then I went to France, and then Spain—oh, it was wonderful in Seville. Four days there. I went out every night to hear the gypsies sing. They live in caves. Have you heard them?"

He shook his head, and began to write.

"They're the most," she said dreamily.

"You've run into no trouble?" Heavens, he thought, I'm going paternal.

She eyed him frankly. She smiled. "I've met nothing but gentlemen, except for one fat slob of a middle-aged—" She brushed that aside. "I laughed so much, I thought I'd go into a fit or something. He was furious. Funny, isn't it? —It's always the ugliest and oldest who think they are irresistible. He—" She broke off. "Hi—Tommy!" She waved to a tall young man in a shirt with a buttoned-down collar.

"Hi, Sally! See you on the Steps!" Tommy said, with a searching glance at Lammiter.

Sally confided, "I met him in London, and then again on the bus from Naples. That's the nice thing about traveling—you always keep meeting up with people. What did you write there?" She wrinkled her brow as she read the closely written lines.

All descriptions of your daughter endorsed. Wherever she has landed, the situation seems well in hand. At least half the college students in America are having their school picnic abroad this summer. Like

Sally, they're healthy, still solvent, and completely cheerful. You ought to see them, though, lining up for a letter from home.

"Why, that's genius!"

"*Thank* you."

"But it is!" She gave him a wide, even white teeth gleaming, smile.

"Needs cutting," he said, rereading his composition. "I always write too much. Get carried away, I suppose. Good-by and good luck. And thank you for taking charge of my luggage."

"Thank *you,* Mr. Lammiter. I'll let you know what I think of your play."

She would, too. They shook hands solemnly.

In spite of these delaying tactics, he arrived fully five minutes early at the station. Fortunately, he had scarcely time to step out from the hot small cab onto the hot wide sidewalk before a porter arrived, which gave him something to argue about. That was better than standing alone before a modern railway station, with its vast stretches of windows and glass doors to make a man feel both observed and vulnerable.

"No, thank you," he told the porter, looking around the open square in front of the station.

"*Si, si, signore,*" the man insisted. "Your friend waits near the wall. His car is there." He hoisted the suitcases and led the way to the side of the station building, where an ancient wall—a collection of giant squared-off boulders—lay outcropped against the station's glass and concrete.

Here was another open space, cars, some moving, some waiting. A small gray Fiat edged toward the porter and then stopped. "*Ecco!*" the porter said, swinging a door open and the luggage inside. He didn't even count the money that Lammiter held out to him. Then all this probably *was* right, Lammiter decided, in the sense that it was arranged. But the Fiat troubled him. Not its size, nor its color: he had noticed a hundred small gray Fiats since one of them had waited for Rosana beneath his hotel window last night. It was the license plate that bothered him: its three last numbers—all he had been able to see from his hotel balcony—were identical with those on the

abduction car. He hesitated. Then he thought, this is interesting, this is very interesting. He moved to the car door.

"Hurry!" said the driver impatiently.

The car was so compact that Lammiter could only see
the man at the wheel properly as he stooped to enter. Yes,
he verified as his memory kept on stirring, it could be the
same man who had driven the princess's noble and aged
Lancia. A dark-eyed man, about thirty-five or so, with
coarse black curling hair, combed, long and thick, back
from a broad brow whose permanent wrinkles looked
more like furrows, giving him a constant look of surprise.
His skin, sallow and coarse, was like untanned leather. He
had given up his chauffeur's dark blue uniform, and wore
a white short-sleeved cotton shirt open at the neck. His
arms were brown, muscular, well covered with strong
black hair. His teeth were white, his smile infectious, his
American strongly accented but completely fluent and
assured. "I'm Joe," he said. "Giuseppe is too much to say.
Call me Joe. What the hell kept you?"

Ah, we're being informal, Lammiter decided. "I thought
I was early."

"Sure. That, yes. I mean when you followed the porter.
You were slow. What's so funny about the car? Got a
bashed fender or something?"

Lammiter made his voice as offhand as possible. "I
was wondering whether I ought to buy a Fiat."

"What for?" Joe's furrows were marked.

"To take back home with me. Doesn't use much gas."

"What do you want a Fiat for?" Joe asked, shocked.
"You could get a Chrysler or a Caddie."

"Or a Lancia like the princess?"

They both laughed. "That's some car!" Joe said.
"Almost thirty years old. It's a—a—" he searched for
the word.

"A period piece?" Lammiter suggested.

Joe's furrows deepened, trying to understand all the
possible meanings, before agreeing.

"It matches the princess," Lammiter added.

"It sure does. It's period, all right. I'm nursing it through
traffic and it comes to a full stop. Period. Get it?" He
laughed uproariously.

"Where did you learn your American?" Lammiter
asked.

"I drove for an American colonel."

"World War II?"

"Sure."

"Where are you from?"

"Sicily. Came up with the Americans, all the way."

"And you never went farther than Rome?"

Joe's face became absolutely blank. He concentrated on winding his way through traffic. At last, noncommittally, he said, "I liked Rome. It never got hurt by the war. I had enough of bombed-out buildings and ruins."

"Ruins—that reminds me. What about that wall back there?" It seemed a safer topic than Joe's life.

"Wall?"

"The huge chunks of stone, just outside the station."

"Oh, they're good and old. Older than anything else you see around this town. You like that kind of thing? What are you—a professor or something?"

"No, just curious."

Joe studied his face. "I guess you are," he said quietly, "or you wouldn't be in this car." Then he laughed and turned the conversation back to classical remains. "If you want ruins, you come to Sicily some day. We got older ruins than anybody else. Older than the princess."

"But she's better preserved?"

Joe's smile was real now. "She looks better by moonlight, too." He thought about the princess. *"She's* something, isn't she?" There was a mixture of admiration and dislike, mixed with a grudging respect, in his voice.

"She certainly is." Lammiter noticed with interest that the car had made a long detour, almost back to the Spanish Steps, before it now swerved southwest, by busy narrow streets, toward the Tiber. "How long have you worked for her?" he asked casually.

"Since Signorina Di Feo's brother died." Joe's face was blank again, but there was a new grim note in his voice.

"You worked for him?"

Joe nodded, and seemed now to be concentrating on this busy section of the city. Down here, near the river, the narrow streets crisscrossed and twisted, passing yellow walls with plaster peeling, baroque churches, small piazzas, ancient fountains, Roman pillars, posters on every wall, a ruined temple, a busy trolley-bus terminal, a hodgepodge of twenty centuries. Lammiter had the feeling that they had already doubled and then redoubled back on their tracks. It was a part of Rome that always gave you that feeling, anyway, even if you were walking as straight as the flight of a bullet. But Joe was being cautious. He had a quick way of looking into the rearview mirror, of glancing left, then right, as the car was halted at a street corner. And the only sign that he was as impatient as Lammiter to reach their destination was the way his hand, as he waited for the lights to turn green, would smack several times on the gearshift as if to say, "Let's go, let's go!"

Lammiter wasn't quite sure, but he had an idea they were approaching the Piazza Navona. (He had dined several times down there, in what had once been a Roman emperor's stadium—the Piazza was actually the long oval where the chariots had raced.) Yes, they were entering its gateway now. The three Bernini fountains were spaced down the center of the long oval where the crowds of children now played and women gossiped as they watched them. All these people lounging around, enjoying the early evening sun which turned the yellow plaster walls into a soft gold, couldn't possibly live in the houses, numerous as they were, that edged the Piazza: some did belong to these flats and rooms in the old converted eighteenth-century houses, but most must come from the dark narrow streets, cobbled lanes, which led off on all sides. It baffled Lammiter trying to think of how many families could live in the square mile around the Piazza. For once, all those pigeons looking for love and bread crumbs would be outnumbered.

"You get out at the church," Joe said. "See that red-haired guy at the fountain opposite? That's Salvatore. Call him Sam. I always do. He'll take you from there."

"To where?" And then, "What about my luggage?"

"I'll keep it safe."

"Look—" Lammiter began. But the car had already stopped.

"Quick!" Joe said, reaching across Lammiter to open the door. There was no time to argue.

"Don't lose that typewriter!" Lammiter said sharply, and got out. The car drove on. He was left at the steps to the church, a contorted variety of baroque with just one adornment too many. Architects should beware of their afterthoughts.

"Hello!" a quiet voice said, and a friendly hand was slipped through his arm. "This way," the red-haired man said.

Lammiter glanced down at the hand on his arm. He had been told, and had believed until now, that Italians disliked and even avoided personal contact with strangers. Unless, of course, the stranger was a pretty woman with a fine pair of hips. Lammiter himself didn't particularly enjoy being arm in arm with a man whom he didn't know. He twisted round to look again at the church commanding the Piazza Navona, and the man's hand had to drop away from his arm.

"I agree that the church has a certain fascination," the amiable voice said. "A horrible sight, isn't it?"

"It isn't as bad as all that. It could have used a little restraint, perhaps."

"You must visit it some other time. But now—this way, Mr. Lammiter."

And then as Lammiter hesitated, looking at the narrow street, no more than eight feet wide, toward which his new guide had turned, the man said, "Dear me, I always forget the formalities. I'm Salvatore, although Joe insists on calling me Sam. I find it simpler not to argue with Joe. He is a Sicilian." The pleasant smile broadened. "Now, have I identified myself sufficiently? I am sorry I am such a rank amateur. I ought to have carried a broken eggshell which would fit into the one you should have in your pocket." Then the voice changed, becoming impatient and authoritative. "Come. We are not here to enjoy the view."

He led the way into the narrow street, darkened by the high buildings edging its worn cobblestones.

Salvatore was one of the red-haired Italians, a type with gray eyes, thin-cheeked face, hawk features. His head was noble, if a little out of proportion with his body, for he was short and slightly built. Yet, Lammiter remembered, the grasp on his arm had been firm and decided. But polite. As polite as the pleasant voice. The man was a superb linguist: he kept up a constant chatter in his excellent English. He never hesitated for a noun, searched for the correct tense of a verb, or failed to produce the conversational phrase.

"Yes, indeed," Salvatore was saying, now back on the subject of the church where they had met, "Bernini would have agreed with you. You know Bernini, of course? He designed the fountains in the Piazza—oh, and many more, all over Rome. Churches, too. But these fountains in the Piazza—did you notice how Bernini arranged the figures in the central one that faces the church? He made some look away and others shield their eyes with their hands from the awful sight." Salvatore laughed. "Delicious, simply delicious. And very naughty. Don't you think so, Mr. Lammiter? Or what *are* you thinking?"

"You didn't learn your English driving an American colonel around Italy." And, Lammiter thought, am I the only one around here who has a second name?

"Ah—you've been listening to Joe." He shook his head. "Those were his happiest days, driving colonels into shell holes. Actually, I was an interpreter during part of the war, with the English. Now, of course"—the gray eyes were briefly amused, and the thin mouth smiled gently— "I am a guide. The old ladies' tours love me. My historical dates are always reliable, my anecdotes pure. This way, Mr. Lammiter." Salvatore halted, looked quickly back over his shoulder, looked again ahead, and then side-stepped into a dim doorway filled with cats. "Quick!" he said, and Lammiter found himself following without argument this time. But he had plenty of thoughts as he stood in a dark stone hallway. If anything happened to him, anything unpleasant, then—well, it was too late now. He had begun walking into this hallway when Rosana Di Feo had persuaded him to meet her at Doney's. He had also the thought that Salvatore had talked in order to baffle his sense of direction. Could it be possible they had almost retraced their steps to the Piazza Navona? He had felt they had been circling around, gently but definitely.

"Where—" he began. Salvatore made a signal for caution so determined that Lammiter found himself obeying it. In any case, having come this far from a table at the Café Doney, he might as well continue without asking where he was going. He would find out, soon enough. He did allow himself to comment on Salvatore's maneuvers. "Very professional—for an amateur." Salvatore shot him a keen glance, smiled, too, and murmured, "Thank you." Then in silence they began the ascent.

The stairway was of stone, with every tread hollowed into a drooping curve by two hundred years of footsteps. Enough light filtered down from a window in the roof to let him see the cats, in the corners of the landings, scattering angrily from the crumpled sheets of newspaper which held something that looked very unappetizingly like cold pieces of spaghetti.

Salvatore stopped at the last landing, leaned over the staircasewell to check on the shadows below. Here, in the far corner of the landing, one cat was so hungry that it didn't run away. It stood looking over its shoulder, hostile, suspicious, curious, hopeful. Then, as Salvatore knocked gently on a door, the cat relaxed its taut muscles. It turned back to gulping down its cold pasta, while, in silence, they waited.

Eight

THERE WERE two people in the room: a seated man, bald-headed, who didn't rise, but turned his chin over his shoulder to look at the stranger much as the cat had done; and Rosana, standing behind the door, now closing it quickly.

It was a quiet room, shadowed at the threshold, but opposite the door—over by the wide-open window—it glowed in the warm light of a Roman evening. There was a pot of red geraniums on the broad window sill, with their clear spicy scent; some books, papers, and a small radio on the desk near the armchair where the man sat; a wardrobe highly varnished, cheap; a wooden table with wine and food—bread and cheese, a bowl of peaches; a narrow bed neatly made. Children's voices from below came soaring up along with the noise of falling water. The evening breeze, touched with unexpected coolness, flowed past the heavy shutters which were folded back to let every breath of fresh air enter and swirl round the room. The geraniums, the fruit, the scent of roses and jasmine which Rosana wore, all emphasized the freshness of the clean air, so great was the contrast between this pleasant unpretentious place and the staleness of the sour-smelling mysteries on the staircase outside.

"Here he is," Salvatore said as if he were a conjurer producing a lighted cigarette from his ear. "A little dazed, I think, but still curious. See?" For Lammiter had moved quickly over to the window and stood at his side, as he looked down.

"Thank you, Salvatore," the girl said. "I hope we didn't make you late for your own appointment. But Giuseppe is on duty at six."

"And the princess can't be kept waiting, while my flock of Swedish schoolteachers can? Now, now, Rosana, that was only a joke. I'll be in good time for the schoolteachers."

"You ought to leave now," Rosana said worriedly. She came over to the window, too.

Lammiter had been right. He was looking down at the Piazza Navona. He had been guided carefully in a wide arc, by a maze of narrow alleys, to the cobbled street that backed the buildings along this side of the Piazza. Was all the precaution to impress him? Or perhaps these people were really afraid.

"Satisfied?" the bald-headed man asked. He didn't sound either welcoming or particularly friendly. Lammiter looked at him, and saw why the man sat immobile. His right leg was out of action, its ankle bandaged, stiff, propped up on the footrest before the armchair. He was probably in some pain. That might explain his bad temper, or the fact that he had a large fiasco of Chianti too near his elbow.

Rosana said pleadingly, "Tony—please!" She tried to explain to Lammiter. "This is my friend Anthony Brewster, an Englishman who—"

"All right, all right," Brewster said. He must have been fond of the girl, for he looked as if he would have bitten off anyone else's head and chewed it into little pieces. He took a deep breath, and studied Lammiter gloomily. Lammiter was in no mood to be outstared.

The Englishman was about forty years old, with a powerful body now beginning to run to fat. His legs seemed short, so he probably was only of medium height when he stood on his feet. He wasn't completely bald. Once he had had fine reddish-fair hair to match his eyebrows and lashes; now, he had only a slight fuzz of thinned-out pinfeathers, beginning in a line over his ears and stretching back in longer strands to the nape of a weather-reddened neck. Normally, his blue eyes might have been both shrewd and merry above a shapeless clown's nose and a friendly mouth in a brick-complexioned face. He was intended to look both round and genial. But this evening he was neither. He was sharp and bitter. His general good nature had vanished. He looked angry, worried, suspicious, sullen, stubborn. "I didn't want you here," he told Lammiter abruptly.

"Then I'll leave," Lammiter said equably. He looked at the door where Salvatore still stood. On guard? Salvatore had been turning the key in the lock, slowly, carefully. For a moment he looked startled, as if he hadn't expected Lammiter to leave so suddenly. And then, it was Lammiter who was surprised; hadn't Rosana locked the door after they had entered? "If you didn't trust me, then why did you have me brought here?" He took a few steps over to the door.

"Oh, stop being so thin-skinned," Brewster said. His voice was slowing. "Come back. Over here. And stop towering over me. Sit down. Rosana insists you can be trusted." He paused. When he spoke again, his words were uttered with considerable effort. "She has a weakness for Americans, particularly when they are tall and not—not—unprepossessing." He smiled around him, as if delighted with his victory over that word. "I hear you're famous, too. And rich."

Lammiter's face had hardened. "I don't have to stay," he reminded Brewster. He didn't sit down.

Rosana said, "Please—don't leave." She looked toward the Englishman unhappily. "Tony's ill. He's had no sleep for three nights."

He's drunk, Lammiter thought. It's useless staying here. And somehow, he felt a crushing disappointment. He had expected too much from this interview. He looked at Rosana, then at Salvatore, who had come forward into the room. Brewster's eyes had closed. The hell with this, Lammiter thought, and took a step back toward the door.

Salvatore said quickly, "We never like to leave by the way we entered. Let me show you another way, Mr. Lammiter, much simpler."

Rosana was upset. "No, no—not yet."

Salvatore pointed to Brewster. "He's had no sleep for three nights. Now he wants to sleep. And you want to waken him?" He shook his head, and then he smiled gently, as he looked at the Englishman. "Let him sleep. Then he will be more himself when we have the meeting tonight. Mr. Lammiter can come back then. This way, Mr. Lammiter." He had opened another door, a small door in a side wall, which Lammiter had, until this moment, imagined as leading into a closet; now he saw it led into a small hall used as a kitchen.

Lammiter hesitated. Salvatore seemed almost too anxious to get him to leave. Perhaps Salvatore hadn't approved of his orders to conduct the strange American to Tony Brewster's rooms. He was saying now, "Come, Mr. Lammiter, I know this is all most disappointing, but I've an appointment at six. I'll have to hurry."

Rosana broke into a rush of Italian. "You brought him here. It would be better if you weren't seen with him again. I'll show Mr. Lammiter the way downstairs. I'll watch at the window until you cross the Piazza. Then he and I shall leave, too."

"Is he coming back here for the meeting tonight?" Salvatore was speaking in Italian, too.

"I suppose so."

"Then why did Tony want to see him now? Couldn't that have waited until tonight?"

"Tony wanted to brief him about our meeting."

"When is it?"

"Eleven o'clock."

"If Tony is awake," Salvatore said doubtfully. He looked down at the peacefully dozing Englishman, and his taut face relaxed into a fleeting smile of sympathy. "Better if we postponed our meeting until tomorrow morning. He needs sleep."

"But we have little time—" Rosana's voice was sharp with worry.

"Is it really so important that we meet here tonight?" he asked impatiently. "I thought our job was almost over. Is there something new?"

Rosana said firmly, "We meet tonight. Tony wants our final reports."

He shrugged his shoulders. "All right, all right." He

turned toward the kitchen, and then paused. Casually, he asked, "How much does the American know?"

"Nothing at all."

"Then that's about as much as I do." He looked at Lammiter speculatively. "What is he, anyway? Our special envoy to the White House?" He laughed briefly. "You never can tell what Tony will think up next. And, Rosana—take away that bottle from him before you leave. He's had more than enough. And you'd better set the alarm clock for a quarter to eleven, or he won't be awake to let us in." Then he turned to Lammiter. "Goodby," he said in English. "I'm sorry your first visit turned out to be such a waste of time—for both of us." He made a wry grimace.

"Give me a hand to stretch Brewster on the bed," Lammiter said. "He will sleep better."

"We might only waken him again." He looked searchingly at the American. "You understand Italian?" he asked unexpectedly.

Lammiter smiled. "You mean I was listening to you and Rosana? I just liked the way she talks, that's all." It was an evasive answer, but it was all that Lammiter felt like giving, somehow.

Rosana's laugh was unexpected.

"Don't get too interested in Rosana," Salvatore said with heavy good humor. "Tony would not approve of that. *Arrivederci*." He entered the narrow kitchen, opened the door in its end wall, listened, and then stepped quickly into the hallway outside. The door closed behind him, locking itself with a decided click.

Rosana's eyes were angry. "Salvatore makes such silly jokes—" She crossed over to the side of the window to look down on the Piazza. "He's always like that. He's too clever, too bitter."

"Perhaps he needs a bigger job than he has."

"That," Tony Brewster said, and his voice seemed brisker, "may be the explanation of Salvatore which I've been seeking for years." He opened both eyes and looked at Lammiter almost approvingly. "You see—" he said, now raising his chin, too, "I am not so drunk as you all thought me. I may need sleep, but I'll get that in its proper time." He eased his bandaged leg. "Dammit, perhaps I'll *have* to go to some bloody hospital after all.

Rosana, get me another bottle of wine and two more glasses. Quick, we may have even less time than you think."

As she obeyed, he went on talking. Brewster was not yet drunk. But just as certainly he was not exactly sober. Rosana brought a fresh bottle of wine unwillingly to the table. She exchanged a quick glance with Lammiter. "Tony—" she began, as Brewster poured wine for all.

"Get back to the window, Rosana," Brewster said. "You promised Salvatore. Remember? Don't worry about me. Wine increases my eloquence. You know that."

Rosana crossed to the window. Worry made her angry; she was frowning.

"I like Salvatore. We are good friends," Brewster told Lammiter, handing him a glass of wine. "But there have been developments in the last three days that go far beyond the work that Salvatore and Joe and Rosana and I have been doing for the past year—our official work, you might call it. There is no need for either Salvatore or Joe to be concerned with anything except that official work."

"I see," Lammiter said, and relaxed. "I was beginning to think you didn't trust Salvatore."

"Didn't trust him?" Brewster asked, annoyed. "We've been together, off and on, since 1944. He led a partisan group that did a very good job against the Nazis, a very good job indeed."

"What's his name?"

"Didn't he tell you?" Brewster was amused.

"I don't know him well enough to be on second-name terms with him."

Brewster's smile deepened, but he seemed to have forgotten Lammiter's question. He had one of his own. "Why did you come here?"

"Rosana—"

"Yes, yes. But why did you listen to her?"

"I want to know more about Pirotta."

"More?" Brewster was watchful now. "How much *do* you know?"

This is the moment, Lammiter suddenly felt when Brewster either becomes interested in me or bored with me. In one case, he will talk; in the other, he will simply chitchat, and I'll learn nothing about Pirotta. He made a wild plunge. "Pirotta is connected with some narcotics ring."

"Oh?" Brewster seemed unperturbed, but he flashed a quick glance at Rosana.

"She told me nothing," Lammiter said quickly. "I've been listening to the princess, that's all."

Now Rosana and Brewster looked at each other. "And what does the princess know?" Brewster asked, very quietly.

"That Count Luigi Pirotta belongs to the same organization to which Rosana's brother belonged. There were also hints that Communists are backing this narcotics ring—certainly they're mixed up with it somehow. According to the princess, that is. There was a good deal of hinting. In fact, I'd say she was needling Pirotta, and his friend Mr. Whitelaw. That's possibly her way of being angry." He looked at Rosana for confirmation, but the girl was watching the Piazza. She waved to someone down there.

"Whitelaw? Bertrand Whitelaw?" Brewster asked.

"Yes, Whither-are-we-drifting Whitelaw. I had the feeling he was one of the princess's targets, too. Why? Where does he stand?"

Anthony Brewster's shrewd blue eyes studied Lammiter. At last he said, "Your princess is meddling with dangerous things. I wonder how she could have learned about the Communists' control of the drug ring?"

So it's true, Lammiter thought, and does knowing the truth make you feel any better? It did not.

Rosana turned quickly away from the window. "Tony —I didn't tell her. I haven't been seeing her. I've avoided her for the last three or four months."

"But no one knows about the control of the drug ring except—" Brewster's voice was worried but unaccusing. He frowned down at the table.

"Except me and you and Giuseppe and Salvatore."

"And now Mr. Lammiter," Brewster reminded her. "But who told the princess?"

"She has the quickest ears and the sharpest tongue of anyone in Rome."

"Seemingly." Brewster's brow wrinkled into red folds.

"And she also doesn't give one good God-damn for anyone on two legs," Bill Lammiter said. He looked at the Englishman. This might be a ripe moment to press his question. "What is Pirotta's connection with this drug ring?"

"He organized it. He's in control."

Lammiter felt the blood drain from his face. The truth was worse than he had imagined. Eleanor, he thought, my God, what is going to happen to Eleanor?

Brewster was watching him. "No more questions?" he asked mockingly.

Lammiter brought a chair to the table for Rosana. He pulled up one for himself. He said, "The quickest way to answer all my questions is to tell me the full story."

Rosana sat down, looked at him gravely with her large dark eyes, and then at Brewster. She smiled.

Lammiter said, smiling back, sharing her unspoken joke, "You don't see Brewster telling any complete story to anyone?"

Brewster said, "There never *is* any complete story. There are always a dozen developments, each with its own importance to different people, always a dozen possibilities for the end, and none of them conclusive. Unless someone dies. Then that *is* final—as far as he is concerned."

Rosana shivered as if she had felt a cold draft on her bare arms. The laughter had left her face. She brushed her short dark hair away from her forehead with a nervous gesture.

"Rosana doesn't like me to talk of death," Brewster said. "Don't worry, Rosana." He tapped his bandaged leg, gently but markedly. "This won't kill me. It is just one of the hazards of our game." He looked now at Lammiter. "If I tell you any part of the story, you'll have to face hazards, too. You can't just walk in here, find answers to your questions, and then walk out again, saying, 'How interesting. . . . Some day I must write a play about Rosana, the girl who was helping Brewster to find out about the Pirotta narcotics ring, the girl whom Pirotta trusted enough to make his secretary.' No, Lammiter, if I tell you anything, you are one of us."

Lammiter's grave eyes looked at Brewster steadily. He nodded, controlling his impatience. He'd have to let Brewster take his time; no doubt Brewster was still deciding whether he could be trusted.

"I just wanted to warn you of the hazards," Brewster said. "This leg of mine, for instance, is a good example. Three nights ago, I was coming back here—about eleven o'clock—walking along one of the old streets. I heard a car behind me. At first, I thought nothing about it. And then, as it almost reached me, I had a sudden odd feeling. I made a leap for a doorway and fell, twisting this leg badly. But I was lucky. The car mounted the narrow pavement and just scraped past me. It ripped my sleeve. If there hadn't been three young men walking in the street, I think the car would have reversed and tried to run me down again."

"It was aimed at you?"

"Straight for my spine."

Rosana said, "It's bad luck to talk this way. Death is quick to hear it. The wise man does not attract his attention." She tried to laugh. "That's what Giuseppe tells me."

"Yes, it was an attempt to dispose of me," Brewster said placidly. "Just as there was an attempt to kidnap Rosana last night: kidnap her, question her, and then kill."

Rosana stood up.

Brewster told her sharply, "I'm only reminding you how stupid I was three nights ago. And how stupid *you* were last night. Next time you have a message from Pirotta, to keep an appointment after midnight, you will remember to develop a high fever or a blinding headache or even an aunt's funeral."

"Pirotta didn't plan last night. I *know* he didn't. He arrived late, yes, but he didn't plan it that way. Tony, believe me: he was upset, too upset and worried, when I told him what had happened."

"And you believed him? You still can believe him?" He turned to Lammiter. "She's too much of an innocent for all this business. Are you?"

Lammiter said, just as abruptly, "I wouldn't know." He waited for another unexpected, probing question, but Brewster went on talking about Rosana as if she had left the room. "She's too intent on her own discoveries, she never thinks the enemy has *his* own discoveries: he's finding out about her just as she has found out about him. She must learn to be careful, cautious, distrustful." He looked at Lammiter shrewdly. "I still don't know if I think you are distrustful enough to keep her safe in Perugia."

Perugia? Lammiter looked sharply at Brewster. He frowned. He didn't want to go to Perugia. Pirotta wasn't in Perugia.

"A pair of bloody romantics, if ever I saw one," Brewster said bitterly, surveying them both as if they could neither see nor hear him. "But with this damned leg— what am I to do?"

Rosana said, "You'd better start trusting Mr. Lammiter. You will have to send him with me to Perugia. Because, Tony, there is no one else to send."

"What about your friend Joe, from Sicily?" Lammiter asked the girl. "You like him. He's a nimble-looking type. Why don't you take him to Perugia?"

"The less you mention Perugia, the better," Brewster advised.

"Or Salvatore," Lammiter said, turning to the Englishman. "Why don't you send him with Rosana? He's your friend, isn't he?"

"Yes." Brewster's eyes narrowed as they studied Lammiter.

"You said you trusted him."

"I do." The voice was icy.

Never question Brewster's judgment, Lammiter reminded himself.

Rosana said quickly, "Both Giuseppe and Salvatore only know about the narcotics ring, nothing beyond that."

"That's all they need to know," Brewster said. "If I had been able to walk about, Rosana wouldn't have been told any more, either. And you wouldn't be here."

"Why choose *me?*" That was the question that had puzzled Lammiter ever since he came into this room.

A slight smile hovered round Brewster's eyes. "Because you have such helpful friends."

Lammiter looked both amused and puzzled. "I'm flattered."

Brewster's voice became bitingly precise. "Such as Edward Tillinghast Camden."

"Bunny? You know him?"

"We've met."

"Surely you can do better than that for understatement," Lammiter said with a grin, remembering the kind of tangles into which Bunny could get. Anyone who had worked with Bunny was not only light-footed but sure-witted. "Why not tell Bunny about Perug—" He halted. "Sorry. Anyway, why not tell Bunny?"

"We've been unable to reach him in these last three days."

"He's been out of town." That was a mistake: to admit knowing Bunny Camden's movements was tantamount to saying he was in Bunny's confidence.

"Ah—" Brewster smiled now as he looked at Lammiter. His interest rekindled visibly.

"Look—it's just an accident that I know he isn't in Rome." Lammiter protested earnestly.

"Of course, of course. And I suppose it was just an accident that you were loitering near the Embassy three days ago and met Captain Camden so innocently?"

Lammiter said nothing.

"Rosana saw you. She was trying to get in touch with Camden, much as you did. Only, she wasn't successful. So she waited to telephone him at his apartment. But he never did go back there. Do you know where we could find him?"

Lammiter shook his head. "Let's get this straight. Bunny is no longer working in Intelligence."

"But he knows what to do, whom to contact, in an emergency," Rosana said. She looked nervously at Brewster.

Lammiter went on determinedly. "And it *was* an accident meeting Bunny. We are good friends. That's all. In fact—" he smiled, to ease the shock in Brewster's eyes —"if Bunny and his Marines hadn't adopted me on the way out from the Pujon trap, I'd have been either dead or a prisoner. There wasn't much future for me, either way, until this Marine platoon came stumbling along." He paused, sensing their complete disappointment. To fill the embarrassing silence, he rushed on. "You know the Marines: they can't bear to leave anything behind them. So they picked me up and joshed some life into me, and got me stumbling along with them." And a damn long stumble it had been, cold on the white-gray snow, over the frozen mud and the ice-glazed rocks, down that winding path to the cold white-gray sea. He could still remember the wind that cut through his shoulders, the

cruel numbness in his hands, his feet weighing half a ton
and every ounce packed with pain.

"I see," Brewster said. He looked at Rosana, shaking
his head. She had put both her hands to her mouth. "And
last night, Lammiter, you weren't keeping an eye on the
car that tried to kidnap Rosana?"

Lammiter shook his head.

"Oh!" she said. "Oh!—And I thought I was so clever,
so clever. . . ."

"So romantic," Brewster said. He heaved a deep sigh of
weariness and reached for the bottle of wine. He had limited
himself all through this conversation, so far, to one glass.
Now he poured generously, drank, and poured again.
"Two bloody romantics." He was neither bitter nor
amused, this time. This time, he was almost philosophic;
and completely depressed.

Lammiter said sharply, "The surest way to make a man
useless is to keep telling him he's useless."

Brewster grunted.

"And I'd like to add that you aren't much use, right
now, yourself."

Brewster looked up angrily. Then, just as quickly, his
mood changed. He even laughed. "The trouble about the
English," he said, "is that even when they are beggars
they like to be choosers." He looked at the American carefully, and then he decided. "All right. You'll do. You'll
have to."

"Thank you," Lammiter said wryly. But he also thought,
this man and I could become friends. Good friends.
This sudden thought, summoned by instinct, both surprised and pleased him.

"You want to know more about Pirotta. I want help.
We'll exchange services, *quid pro quo*. Right?"

Lammiter nodded. *"If* I can be of any help to you—"
He was still doubtful.

"I'm the judge of that. One thing is at least in your
favor: I think, after your experiences in North Korea,
you don't trust a Communist."

"That's one fact about me you have got straight."

Brewster pushed aside his glass of wine. "Thank God,"
he said, "that I don't have to convince you about the
miserable realities of political life before you'll even let
yourself listen." He was easing his leg, hiding the pain of

it, altering his hips' position, in his chair. He rubbed his thigh. He gave a sudden smile that was both honest and warmhearted. "Now," he began, selecting his words with care . . .

Nine

BREWSTER, once he had decided to give out information, talked without pause. Either the wine had increased his eloquence or his subject was one that had haunted him so constantly that he could repeat a list of facts as calmly and impersonally as the multiplication table. Lammiter listened in shocked silence. He was quite aware he was not being told everything, just the necessary outline to establish confidence and enlist his help—but it was enough. And it was startling. Lammiter sat frozen in his chair.

It was not the fact that a powerful narcotics ring could be selling drugs from Rome, as if it were a reputable business, which was so startling. After all, the world newspapers had been reporting for months on another drug scandal in Rome. (A young girl's body had been found on a beach at Ostia, resignations had followed in high places, and several explosions had been touched off that were still reverberating round some well-known heads.) But it was the scope of this narcotics business that was news to Lammiter, news both astounding and horrifying.

The poppies for the drugs were grown in the drab fields of Asia Minor, processed by some obliging Middle Eastern countries, shipped to Italy and France, where there were even factories and well-organized salesmen and (in France) a sizable market. But the main target was America. The shipments of drugs were constantly being steered through western Europe toward the United States. There was no doubt about that. And across the Pacific, the direction of drug trafficking was still more blatant. There, in recent years, the agrarian reformers of Red China had increased production of opium, heroin, and morphine to staggering totals—all for the smugglers' trade out of Hong Kong and Thailand and Japan to San Francisco.

Lammiter looked both uncomfortable and angry, as

men do when they don't quite want to believe something that they instinctively feel may be too true for comfort. "You make it seem as if western Europe were all under a constant barrage of narcotics. My God, Brewster—"

"I'm not exaggerating. I've only time to give you the barest details now. Later, if you're interested, you can trace down many more. They're all in print."

"In print?"

"Ever heard of Interpol?"

"The International Police Force? But I thought the war had killed it."

"It's been resurrected. Headquarters are now in Belgium. You must read Interpol's recent report on the narcotics business. You'll find all the facts and figures about each country's contribution to this ugly mess—who grows the stuff, who processes it, who sends it traveling, what ships have carried it, what seamen have smuggled it. They're all named. My dear Lammiter, the whole thing is a campaign against the West, planned and carefully subsidized by its enemies, aided and abetted by men whose lack of morality is amply compensated by their cupidity. Those who grow opium, or process it, or ship it, ask no questions about why it is being brought or where it is being sent. They just keep their eyes fixed on their bank accounts."

"They are monsters!" Rosana burst out.

"Yes, yes," Brewster said calmly, pulling the conversation back to cold reason. "The United Nations Narcotics Commission has also issued its reports. The facts have all been gathered and noted down. Believe me"—he was becoming a little impatient—"I am neither exaggerating nor lying. America *is* the chief target."

Rosana said, "And what is more, it is your young people who are the center of the target."

"At this point," Brewster said, "Rosana always bursts into tears with indignation and helplessness. But cheer up, my softhearted Rosana: at least one drug-exporting firm is going to be out of business within a week. Thanks to you, Rosana. And to me. I may as well admit I've had one success in my life: Luigi, Count Pirotta." He said the name with relish. He smiled benignly.

"There are a lot of people to be thanked," Rosana reminded him. "There was Bevilacqua over at the Questura." She turned to Lammiter. "Bevilacqua is the detective who has been working on the Pirotta organization ever since my brother's death. He's *very* good. He's clever, truly. He did more than anyone—" She bit her lip and smiled. "And then the two nice Americans—narcotics agents from Washington—they are now in Bari and Trieste waiting for two ships to arrive."

"They're always so interested in catching the *supplies*," Brewster said irritably. "Opium, heroin, cocaine, marijuana. You puts in your penny and you takes your choice. But I'm interested in *people*. Such as our handsome count, who is making hay, with a nonny, nonny yea." He cocked his head and looked at Lammiter. "Does my levity shock you? Good. I need something to shock you into taking me seriously."

"It's all very well for you to see Pirotta as a comic character, but it isn't your country that's getting the treatment," Lammiter reminded him grimly.

"Oh, some of the treatment blew off on us. The American bases in Britain are naturally of interest to Pirotta's friends. His salesmen found them difficult, so they couldn't resist trying to make some customers among the young and foolish in the local population. I think we caught them in time."

"It is strange," Rosana said, "how all people who take drugs try to convert others to be like them. They pretend it's nothing at all, something normal and natural. They need company, I think."

"That's how it spreads. Worse than smallpox," Brewster agreed. "Anyway, the British are definitely interested in this. Or else I shouldn't be here." He looked suddenly at Lammiter. "I'm a journalist, by the way."

"You are?" Lammiter smiled.

"Yes, indeed. The London *Echo* is hoping to get an exclusive story when it can all be told."

"When is that?"

"Next week—as soon as the two new shipments arrive and are consigned to Pirotta's warehouses."

"Something in Brewster's voice caught Lammiter's attention. He said slowly, "I think it isn't the sale of narcotics that really interests you. I think it is Pirotta himself."

"You may be right."

"Why?"

"Because Pirotta is not in the narcotics business for money. He's in search of power, political power. He's a Communist."

"What?" Lammiter looked at Rosana. She was quite calm, as if she had long accepted the idea and could no longer be surprised by it.

Brewster went on quickly, "He has set up, during the last eight years, a remarkably efficient organization, international in scope, with its key men all Communists. It can be turned to political uses when necessary. Meanwhile, it adds to the Communists' secret funds, helps to corrupt their enemies, and gathers a list of future traitors—drug addicts can always be bribed by heroin, or blackmailed with threats of exposure. They'll be quislings, every one of them."

Lammiter was still thinking about Pirotta. "But he's the fellow who has everything," he said, almost to himself.

"Pirotta? Not in modern terms. What power lies in an inherited title today? What money?—Possessions now mean taxes. So what does an ambitious man do? He knows Europe is changing. He chooses the most ruthless force in the struggle for power. He sees the Communists as the wave of the future. And he is determined to stay on its crest. His family has managed to swim there for years."

"For three centuries, to be accurate," Rosana said. "They've switched sides for three centuries, always choosing the winners. Until Mussolini." She laughed softly. "His father chose wrong, there."

"So he thinks he'll regain the family's power by supporting the Communists?" Lammiter asked.

"He'll give up his title willingly, in exchange for being a leader. What's in a title? Power is the thing. And then there is another practical consideration. When the machine guns are turned against the innocents, he and his friends have determined which end of the machine guns they'll be facing. Astute characters."

"Yes," Lammiter said with marked distaste. He looked at Rosana again.

She returned his look frankly. "You are wondering why I am friendly with such people?"

"Was it your idea, or did your clever policeman suggest it, when you and he were discussing your brother's death?"

"Bevilacqua?" She laughed with relief. "See, Tony, Mr.

Lammiter trusts me. He doesn't think I really belong with them."

"I see," said Brewster. "But I also think that Pirotta, too, is beginning to see. Look at last night—"

"But Pirotta said they were 'business rivals'—men from Naples who were trying to take over—"

"Did you believe him? Last night, what was the number on the car's license plate?"

Rosana looked suddenly anxious, as if she instinctively knew some bad news was about to be given her. "I *told* you the number, Tony," she said.

"And now I shall tell you that the car that tried to run me down was a fourteen Fiat, gray, with the same number-plate you noted."

There was a moment's silence. Lammiter took a sharp breath. I wish, he thought unhappily, I wish to God I had seen the whole license plate last night. Then I'd have known whether the fourteen Fiat, gray, which brought me to the Piazza Navona tonight was the car they are talking about.

"Yes?" Brewster asked him.

Lammiter shook his head. He had nothing to add: the three last numbers on a license plate were not enough.

Brewster turned to Rosana again. "You will have to be extremely careful for the next week. I'm taking no risks with you, Rosana. Lammiter looks like a well-built young man to me. He has strength enough for the journey to Perugia by himself."

"But I could help him—there's so much I know and he doesn't—"

"I shan't ask too much of him. All I need is a pair of good eyes in Perugia, who will report back to me what I myself would like to have seen. And that—" he turned now to Lammiter, "you will do at once. At once, so that the necessary steps can be taken—"

"Look here," Lammiter said, genuinely puzzled, "if you and Bevilacqua and the two men from the Narcotics Bureau in Washington have this Pirotta organization all ready to blow apart, what need is there for anyone in Perugia? The case is practically closed, isn't it?"

"Nothing is ever closed. One thing leads to another. But I told you that before, didn't I?"

"All you have to do now is to start blocking out your special story for the London *Echo*."

"There is another story, too. And every bit as important. It could be even more so."

Lammiter said, with a sudden anger that surprised himself, "I don't think there's any business more contemptible than drug-smuggling, unless it's pimping or slave-trafficking. What's more important than catching people like that?"

"Rosana—would you hand me my file?" As she reached for the pile of books, carelessly jumbled together, and selected one ordinary-looking volume of medium size, Brewster looked at Lammiter. He had become bitterly serious. "What's more important? Not much. Unless it is catching the men who support a system of forced labor, of torture and secret police—the men whose chief business is to bring that kind of existence to your country and mine and Rosana's. I am talking about the professional Communist, Mr. Lammiter. *Not* the workman who votes Communist because he wants a better deal, a bigger share; *not* the woman who thinks that if the system were changed, men would be changed, too. I'm talking of the professional Communist. He's just another kind of narcotics smuggler, perverting minds instead of bodies. He's a liar and a cheat and a betrayer. He's the man who makes slave-labor camps possible. What's more important than catching that kind of man?" He took the book from Rosanna. "To spread his empire around this world, he will plot dissension, destruction, and hate. *He* won't do the fighting or risk the dying. Oh no! He must stay alive, in order to control the peace that follows. To the professional Communist, people are always expendable." Brewster took a deep breath. "Now I step down from my soapbox."

He opened the book. It was hollowed out in its center, a bogus book, as in one of those antique leather objects that coyly display cigarettes. In the space where cigarettes usually lie, there was a small Manila envelope. Brewster opened it, searched inside, and drew out a snapshot. He studied it. He gave a strange smile, acid, contemptuous. Then he looked up, speaking casually, seemingly at random. "Pirotta was a friend of MacLean's."

"MacLean's?"

"Don't you remember two men called Burgess and MacLean?"

"Oh—them!"

"Yes, them. Now we're getting to the *real* issue," he

said with sudden relish. "All that briefing on the narcotic ring was only the first slices off the roast. But now we are getting to the real meat and bone."

"You mean all that information about narcotics was only an introduction?" Lammiter's voice was both surprised and a little dismayed.

"It was both necessary and important. I hope you forget none of it. Because it all links up. If I hadn't been interested so much in Pirotta as the head of a drug syndicate, I shouldn't have tried to find out whom he was going to meet in a *trattoria* over on the unfashionable side of the Tiber. I went, expecting to find some new face to add to our rogues' gallery. Instead, I saw him meeting a man called Evans." The sharp blue eyes were watching. "You don't recognize the name?"

Lammiter searched his memory. He shook his head.

Brewster looked delighted. "I suppose not. His case was kept pretty quiet. He happened about a month later than MacLean and Burgess."

"Most unfortunate. Don't tell me he was a Foreign Office type who specialized in America, too."

Brewster glanced quickly at Lammiter. "His job didn't seem of much importance. Not until one began to study the people he met. They were all influential."

"And," Lammiter said bitingly, "they all trusted him."

"Indeed, yes. He was an expert confidence man."

"How did you get onto him?"

"You flatter me. I wasn't quite so suspicious then as I am now. Otherwise he wouldn't have left the country."

"For Moscow?"

"Of course."

"What is he doing now in Rome? Can you guess?"

"Nothing to do with drugs," Brewster said firmly. "Evans deals with power politics. He is a diplomat's diplomat. And he was always an excellent persuader." Brewster half closed his eyes as if he were trying to see the occasion for Evans's visit to Italy.

"Do you think he has brought instructions from Moscow to Pirotta?"

Brewster shook his head. "Pirotta is only the go-between."

"But he's head of the narcotics ring, isn't he?"

"That's how I know he is only the go-between. In Com-

munist undercover work, the really important man is
rarely the head of anything. Don't worry about the ambassador—look at his chauffeur; or a cipher clerk; or an
undersecretary. Pirotta takes orders from someone quite
outside the narcotics ring. Evans wouldn't meet the head
man directly—"

"You sound pretty definite on that." Lammiter was not
quite so sure.

"I ought to be. Once, I was something of an expert on
people like Mr. Evans."

"That used to be your job? Before you branched into
drug-smuggling?"

"Before I branched—?" Brewster began to laugh. "My
God—branched! I was kicked—and no pretense of upstairs, either—into a minor job, outside my own field. It
was the biggest hint to resign a man ever got."

"But why?"

Brewster said impatiently, "Does that matter? What
matters is that I've spotted Evans in Rome. I was given
the job of uncovering a little company of spoiled brats
who were playing around with heroin and opium. But—"
he was laughing again, "—but I found more than anyone
expected. By God, I'd like to see their faces next week
when the news reaches them."

Lammiter wanted to ask, "Whose faces?" But he felt
he had already asked more than his allowance of questions.
Brewster talked cryptically, partly because he expected
any intelligent person to grasp the full meaning of his quick
allusions. He wasn't the sort of man who paid any attention
to those whose wits couldn't follow his. Even drunk—for
he was beginning to show the effects of this last bottle of
wine—he was a formidable opponent. He must have once
made a relentless enemy. Once. Lammiter watched Rosana take away the empty bottle with a shake of her head.

But Brewster had noticed it, too. "Rosana—you'll find
another fiasco in the kitchen," he said angrily, as if
to prove that his voice was not thickening. "Wine makes
me think. You know that. It's food and drink."

Rosana went, even if slowly, toward the kitchen. Tony
Brewster was a man who seemed to get his own way. It was
then that Lammiter understood how fully the damaged leg
must have hurt the Englishman. For once, he had become
dependent.

"Yes," Brewster said, relaxing back into his chair, "I'd like to see their faces when they hear about Evans. Rosana!—"

"Coming," she called back.

Lammiter was watching Brewster. Once he must have been good at his job as an Intelligence officer. Then he had gone stale, worried too much, and been transferred. And now he was drinking too much cheap Chianti, brooding about "them," who had transferred him, sobering up to get the necessary information which would damn the "spoiled brats" like Pirotta, thinking mostly of the work he had once done ("the real meat and bone"), and remembering Evans.

"So you saw Evans," Lammiter said appeasingly. "You recognized him."

"And he recognized me. Which explains *that!*" Brewster pointed to his leg, but he was watching Lammiter carefully. Suddenly, he held out the photograph. Lammiter had the feeling that until this very moment, Brewster hadn't quite made up his mind to show him the snapshot. "He still looks very much like this. Just in case you run across him in Perugia."

Lammiter, startled, looked at Brewster, and then at the snapshot. Evans was strolling along a London street with some park trees and a bus sharing the background. He was elegantly dressed, bowler hat in hand, light gloves folded, rolled umbrella, dark suit of conservative cut. He was the very perfect gentleman. He was tall, thin, with his head at a slight angle as if he were listening politely. (One could see how he had earned quiet popularity.) Fair hair; a prominent brow; a thin high-bridged nose; a tight-lipped mouth; not a particularly strong chin.

"That was taken five years ago by a street photographer. Very lucky picture. Caught his general attitude. Of course he has changed a bit. His hair is now grayish, his skin has gone sallow. He is still wearing English-cut shirts and ties, though. Just won't give them up."

"But what do I do if—" Lammiter bit off the rest of the sentence. (He had been about to say, "What do I do if I see Evans in Perugia?" But suddenly he was wary, embarrassed by the situation he had created for himself: he had started making promises that might be impossible to keep.) "I'm not the man for this job," he said frankly, holding out the photograph to Brewster. "It's an emergency, obviously. Don't waste valuable time with me. Get someone like Bunny Camden. There must be people at your own Embassy who'd like to catch up with Mr. Evans."

"I tried that," Brewster said, slowly, bitterly. "But I'm a drunk who's got persecution mania and a complex about Communists, didn't you hear? No one would see me at the Embassy—I'm an embarrassment. That's the reason I sent Rosana to find Camden." He took the photograph at last. "You'll remember this face?"

"Why don't you get the Italian police—the man with the odd name . . . Bevilacqua? He's at least friendly, isn't he?"

"I'm afraid the Italians have nothing against Evans. Except the fact that he's using a false passport. But before we can find out enough about that, Evans will have attended a most secret meeting in Perugia and be gone, as quietly as he came." Brewster considered something, and then decided to add, "Besides, some of my informants are a little nervous if you mention a policeman. No, no, Lammiter, I can't risk frightening away future sources of information."

"You trust them?"

"After I prove their stories," Brewster said with a smile. "This week I heard three very interesting pieces of news, dribbled to me in a frightened whisper. First, Pirotta was to have a quiet talk, four nights ago, with a most important man. That, as I proved, was true. Secondly, a meeting was being most secretly arranged in Perugia for this important man. That may also be true. I think it is. My informant, a very careful customer, was found knifed to death two nights ago in a back street in Tivoli. A café brawl."

"But you doubt if your man was in it?"

"It has always been a useful diversion."

"Yes," Lammiter agreed. "As poor old Christopher Marlowe found out. Which proves that playwrights should stick to writing plays."

Brewster looked at him with some surprise, and then smiled. "He made a bloody good secret-service man."

"Until he got knifed in a London tavern."

"You're nervous?" The smile was mocking.

Lammiter grinned back. "Perhaps. Or perhaps I know I'm not a bloody good agent. Frankly, I'd be of no use to you in Perugia."

"I don't expect you to do any *thinking*."

"Thank you."

"All I want you to do is to find out if Evans has actually gone to Perugia. If he turns up there, telephone me here. That's all."

"And you'll get the Embassy to listen to you then?"

"Or someone," Brewster said grimly. "At least, we'll know that second piece of information was accurate. It will no longer be in the category of rumor. It will be a fact, proven and true."

"But where will I look for Evans in Perugia? My God, Brewster, it's a sizable town."

"I'll tell you where you can look for him."

"Was that the third piece of information you received?"

"You can count, I see," Brewster said. "I'll have a map of Perugia ready for you tonight, all the details. . . ." He was tiring now. "Once Joe and Salvatore leave here, you and I will talk a little more. The final advice . . . You'll have to rent a car. No, better still, I'll persuade Joe to lend you his. Three hours, four at the most, and you'll be in Perugia."

And then, as Lammiter still looked worried, Brewster's voice broke into anger. "You're backing out! But you can't. You'll *have* to go! Just as you had to stay in Rome. When the trouble breaks, you want to try to keep as much of it away from Miss—Miss—" He looked at Rosana.

"Eleanor Halley," she said.

"From Miss Halley as possible," Brewster finished. Suddenly he was completely exhausted.

Lammiter said nothing. He rose. Brewster slowly put the Evans photograph back into the envelope, and the envelope into the hollowed-out book. His fingers, like his voice, were now overcareful and slow. Lammiter turned away, so that Brewster could not see the pity in his eyes: it was pathetic to see anyone as good as Brewster becoming a man with a mania. Evans, Perugia . . .

"What are you afraid of in Perugia?" he heard his own voice asking.

"The three-sided chess game," Brewster said abruptly. He reached slowly for the new bottle of wine. "Go and have some dinner," he added testily. "Put some sense into your thick head. Come back and listen. I'll—I'll tell you—enough to make your ears pop. And you"—he wagged a thick forefinger at the American—"can tell it some day to old Bunny. I wouldn't have to argue with him like this, damn you. He's the only one who believes me, the only one—" His voice had begun to drone into an undertone. "The only one," he said, rousing himself for a brief moment. He actually put down his half-finished glass on the table, and pushed it away. It upset.

"I'll help you to stretch out on the bed," Lammiter said. He put an arm around the thick waist and started to heave.

"I'm all right," Brewster said, pushing all assistance aside. "Where's my damned crutch? Lost again." Rosana found it where it had slipped under the table. He took it, and began moving across the room, heavily, with difficulty and considerable pain. He dropped it at the bedside, flopped down with a sigh of impatience, and eased his bandaged leg onto the mattress.

"Tomorrow," Rosana said, "Giuseppe and I shall take you to the sisters."

Brewster looked at Lammiter, as if defying him to laugh. "Nuns! That's where I have to go. Hear that, Lammiter?"

"It's safe. And quiet. And pleasant," Rosana said. She had wiped up the spilled wine and taken away the bottle. Now she was setting a small alarm clock, and putting it within reach of the bed.

"So is here," Brewster said, his eyes closing. "I think I'll sleep. At last." Brewster began to laugh, gently. "Hie me to a nunnery. . . . This old Protestant?" His eyes closed.

"But Santayana went—" Rosana began. Lammiter motioned toward the door. The girl nodded. She looked round as if checking everything. She replaced the hollowed-out book in the pile of innocent volumes. She straightened a chair, lifted the empty glasses, and then went toward the kitchen.

Lammiter looked at the man stretched out on the bed. He was already slipping into sleep. The pool of deep

golden sunlight near the window had shifted on the floor,
moving slowly toward the bed. The chorus of children's
voices rose into a permanent happy chatter broken by
loud ecstatic shrieks. On impulse, Lammiter closed the
shutters, cutting out light, muffling the sounds. "No,"
Rosana whispered. "He likes to breathe." She opened the
shutters again. The man on the bed grunted gently, and
let sleep drift over him, a soft gray mist of forgetfulness.

Ten

ROSANNA WAITED for Lammiter to join her in the
kitchen before she opened the back door that led onto
another flight of stairs.

"When does the alarm clock go off?"

"Salvatore said a quarter to eleven, but I set it for
half-past ten. I thought I'd give Tony time to awake
thoroughly. He must let us in." She closed the door carefully behind them, and shook it gently to test the auto-
matic lock.

Lammiter suddenly remembered something else. "Didn't
you lock the other door after Salvatore and I arrived?"

She nodded, made a gesture for silence, and listened.

He lowered his voice. "But I saw Salvatore locking
it. . . ."

She looked at him and smiled. "Testing it. He doesn't
trust women." Then she motioned to him, and they began
to descend the narrow staircase. In this house, the back
had become the front: on this kitchen staircase, the light
was warm and sunfilled; people lived behind these doors,
breathed this air, flavored it generously with the meals
they cooked and ate. But at this moment, these flats
seemed all deserted. There were no voices, no scolding,
no laughter. Two doors even stood open, showing walls
needing plaster and paint, too many random pipes, a
crush of wooden chairs round littered tables.

"Where is everyone?"

"Taking the air in the Piazza. It is the evening ritual."
For a moment she hesitated, glanced back up the staircase, frowned. But she went on, without saying something she wanted to say.

Wasn't it safe to talk here? Lammiter wondered, as they descended the worn stairs. Safer than the Piazza. He glanced at his watch. It was after seven o'clock. Only an hour since Brewster had begun to take him into his confidence. An hour was a long time in some ways, short in others. In an hour, you could smoke half a dozen cigarettes, or read a newspaper, or write a letter, or just sit and dream. You could travel four miles on foot, sixty in a car, a hundred in a light plane. You could make a friend (or an enemy) who might last you fifty years. And in one hour, you could make decisions that would change the entire course of your life.

Rosana put her hand on his arm as they reached the last short flight of stairs, so that he halted, too. She looked up toward Brewster's door. She was still troubled.

"He will be all right," Lammiter said encouragingly. "A little sleep, and he will be biting all our heads off with his usual gusto."

She smiled. Then quickly she leaned over the worn balustrade, its eighteenth-century carvings of conch shells and triumphant Tritons partly washed away by a sea of passing hands. She decided it was indeed safe enough: the entrance, just below them, was quite empty. She faced him. She looked extremely unhappy. She said, "He *is* only a journalist."

"What?" He stared at her. "You mean Brewster wasn't sent here officially on any mission?"

She shook her head.

"He wasn't transferred to this job?" Kicked downstairs was the way Brewster had described it.

Again she shook her head.

"Was he kicked out entirely? Why? Drunk?"

"Oh no! Not then!"

"For making mistakes?" Such as letting Evans slip away from England.

"Tony says that he made only one mistake." She halted, listening. Reassured, she hurried on. "After Evans had escaped, Tony kept searching for the man who had warned Evans. The man who had helped to place him when he began his career, and promote him into the right department. For there *has* to be such a man."

"Yes," Lammiter said slowly, "there has to be such a man." It was a disquieting thought. "Did Brewster find him?"

"Tony says he must have been close, very close, to finding him. For suddenly—for no reason he or any of his friends could understand—he was given quite another problem to solve."

Lammiter couldn't see Brewster taking that lying down, not that old protestant upstairs. "So he made several biting remarks and lost his job altogether?" Then he frowned, wondering if secret-service agents ever did get discharged. If they were of no more use, what happened to them? Given less and less important work, until they were so bored they just faded away? In more ruthless countries, they fell out of trains.

"He didn't complain, make any protests. I wish he had. I think it was then that he began to—began to drink more than he should." She looked anxiously at Lammiter. "You see how it is?"

"I see," he said gently. He was a little touched by the way she had tried to make him understand about Tony Brewster. He watched her eyes. "You believe all this?"

"But of course! Tony does not lie."

Yet it was only Brewster's word. . . . "People could say that he brooded too much over his disappointment—exaggerated the situation."

"That's what the Communists did say. It spread around. In the end, even most of his friends stopped believing him. So he threw up everything, took a journalist's job, and came to Rome. He used to be a journalist long ago—before the war."

"Tell me one thing. What did he mean by 'three-sided chess'? Wasn't that what he said?"

"It's his theory that the Middle East and the West and Russia are all playing a chess game. Russia is standing to one side, supervising the moves. Tony says 'jogging the pieces.' Making the others take certain moves that are bound to cause countermoves—and *always* trouble."

"But—no one can make nations move except the nations themselves. Governments listen to their own advisers."

"What if one of them is another Evans?" She looked at him solemnly, letting him fill out the rest for himself.

What if such a man, trusted as Evans had been, could influence opinion? Or delay an important document? Or misinterpret a piece of urgent news? One small move like that might start a whole chain of events.

"He will not be working alone," Rosana said. Anxiously she watched him. "He could begin trouble. And he will have help to make it spread."

Yes, Lammiter thought, if someone in the foreign ministries of other Western countries were working along with such a man, the trouble might well spread. Lammiter tried to muster a counter-argument. This was the kind of crazy theory he might have expected from Tony Brewster. "But—" he began.

Rosana seemed to guess something of his doubts. She jumped to Brewster's defense. "Tony does not say that Russia is winning this chess game. He does not even say that the Communists have men like Evans still in our governments. What he says is—the Communists have *trained* for this kind of game. They have tried to get their men in position. That, we all know." She took a deep breath. "It frightens me."

He looked down at Rosana's dark eyes, the gentle curve of cheek, the finely molded features. She pushed back the ridiculous fringe of short dark hair which had fallen onto her brow.

"Yes," he said, "they have tried. We all know that. But don't let Tony's theories worry you. Things are looking pretty peaceful just now. Why—Malenkov was even passing out boxes of chocolate in England, and patting babies' heads. What did one woman say?—'Ow, *isn't* he nice? He's just like my uncle!' "

"And four weeks later, when the workers were shot down in Poznan?" Rosana asked angrily, her eyes widening. "What did she say?"

At the entrance they heard a quick footstep. They looked at each other. Lammiter slipped his arms around Rosana, drawing her closer to him, back against the wall. He whispered, "What else would we be doing here?" She half smiled. And as the man came upstairs, Lammiter kissed her. He could feel her sudden gasp, ending in a little laugh of embarrassment as he ended the long kiss. The man, returning home from his work earlier than most (the usual hour was eight o'clock), was probably hurrying upstairs to wash and change his shirt before joining his wife and children in the Piazza. He looked at them curiously as he passed. But there was a smile on his dark face, a good-natured understanding of why two strangers should be sheltering from the world inside his doorway.

Bill Lammiter tightened his grip around Rosana's soft waist. And this time, when he bent forward to kiss her, she did not gasp. They stood in silence for a long minute, looking at each other as if they were searching for an answer to their own questions. He let his arms fall to his sides. He said, "We must go." What was wrong, he wondered? If any girl could help me forget Eleanor, here she is. And yet— Sharply, he told himself he was an idiot, a fool.

Overhead, the footsteps ceased, and a door banged shut.

"He accepted us," Lammiter said.

"Yes," she replied. She began walking down the last short flight of stairs. He followed more slowly, watching the way her graceful neck met her shoulders in a clear smooth curve. Why had that kiss been such a damned anticlimax?

Rosana said quickly, "Will you be able to find your way here at eleven o'clock? Knock three times quickly on Tony's door. And then a pause. And then a fourth knock. And then speak, when he asks you who is there, just so that he will know who it is."

"What if he is still asleep?" He had a ridiculous vision of a small line gathering outside Brewster's door.

"The alarm is the kind that keeps ringing until he does answer it."

"He'll be in a filthy temper." He hesitated. "And suppose he falls asleep again. What do I do? Wait until you and Salvatore and Joe are all there to start pounding?"

"You must be serious," she told him, horrified by such an idea.

"I'd prefer to meet you somewhere. Couldn't we have dinner together, around nine?"

She said, "If you don't want to go up by yourself, then —But why don't you?"

"I'm out of my depth here," he admitted. "Have dinner with me, and you can put me more in the picture, and we'll climb the stairs together. We've worked out a good alibi, anyway, for any stranger who comes along." He slipped his arm around her waist again. I'm a man who keeps trying, he thought. "Dinner?"

She shook her head. "Too dangerous. I'll meet you across the Piazza, at the church steps. I'll walk on, and you can follow."

"That's one thing I can always do—follow a pretty girl."

"You *must* be serious," she warned him gravely. "Eleven o'clock." She slipped away from him, and stepped out of the sharp black line of shadow, across the bright threshold, into the golden Piazza.

It's odd, he thought, as he watched Rosana disappear from sight, it's odd how I have kissed the prettiest girl in Rome, and there's so little to remember. No joy, no excitement . . . He might as well have stolen a kiss from his prettiest schoolteacher. He stopped thinking about Rosana and concentrated on his own exit.

Around the three fountains, the children swarmed, thick as ants around three sugar bowls. On this, the eastern side of the Piazza, the buildings were drenched with warm light, but the doorways were now in shadow as the sun slipped lower in the western sky. Opposite, the buildings lining that long side of the Piazza Navona were in complete shade from the hot evening sun. There, not far from the church, was the *Tre Scalini,* where he had dined before. It looked inviting, cool, and empty at this time. But it was too early to eat in Rome. He would look as conspicuous as the few hungry tourists, their stomachs geared to half-past seven, who were making their appearance by horse and cab. Tonight, he decided, it was better not to be seen hanging around this district. And there was a taxi driving into the Piazza by its northern entrance, the old gateway to the Roman circus, where the chariots had raced. He smiled suddenly at the strange quirks of memory, at the odd facts he had assimilated in this last month of wandering round the city, at the peculiar moments they would keep returning to the surface of his consciousness.

He watched the taxi curving around the Piazza toward the restaurant opposite. He timed it carefully. Now, he told himself just before it reached the restaurant, and plunged away from the dark doorway over the hot glaring sidewalk, across the cobbled street which edged the central island, among children learning to walk, children on bicycles and in baby carriages, children carried, children running, laughing, crying, children holding other children, children. This was obviously a district central enough to let the men return home for a midday dinner and a pleasant siesta.

The taxi was emptied, paid off, and about to be driven away. Bill Lammiter raised one hand and left the crowd. "Via Vittorio Veneto," he said, out of habit. But in a sense that had become his own *petit quartier*.

As the cab circled round the long island of fountains and children, he glanced out of the window. He had been reasonably certain as he had crossed the Piazza to reach the taxi that he had not been followed. And now, nothing followed him out of the Piazza. Good. And yet strange— for he had been followed this afternoon. When had it stopped? About the time he had met Giuseppe, or Joe, or whatever Rosana's Sicilian friend called himself. No, even earlier than that. About the time he had telephoned Rosana from the American Express office? It wasn't a question he liked.

One thing he did know: interest in him had faded. Or —and this thought was less comfortable—or interest in him was merely pushed aside for a certain space of time in which "they" knew what he had been going to do. One didn't need to follow a man whose movements were known in advance.

This thought, as he looked at it from all angles, became definitely ungainly. He could wish he had never conjured up this particular little monster.

He looked at his watch: it was a quarter to eight now. . . . Eight o'clock—what had he to do before eight? There had been something. Oh yes—photographs! He almost laughed aloud with relief: it was pleasant only to face such a tourist occupation as collecting photographs. By all means, let's go and collect photographs.

But he kept wondering about Rosana. Could she actually be in love with Tony Brewster as Salvatore had hinted? That was difficult to believe. Yet women were so damned unpredictable. And men, he told himself, were so damned vain: she let you kiss her, but you didn't measure up, and that's the part that really annoys you. Or perhaps, and this was less wounding but more distressing, her ideal woman was the Venus of Cyrene, classically pure, noble as marble, cold as the tomb.

The photography shop, just off the Via Vittorio Veneto, was about to close. The last customer was leaving, and two of the assistants had already gone. An elderly white-faced man in a white cotton coat looked increasingly depressed as Bill Lammiter entered. But he took Lammiter's receipt, and while he searched slowly through an immense collection of envelopes for the prints, Lammiter used the shop's telephone to call Carl Ferris over at the American Academy. It was a brief call, and a careful one. (Lammiter mentioned no names.) There was no news of Bunny Camden except that he was reported to be on his way back from Naples. Professor Ferris sounded a little glum, as though playing guardian angel over a telephone was beginning to pall. "I'll keep calling," Lammiter promised. "Sorry. But it's an emergency."

He turned to the envelope of prints, which the man had at last found. The photographs weren't particularly good. After all the fuss he had made about collecting them, they just were not any good at all. Color was, of course, the trouble. He would have to use a light meter as carefully as an amateur. But that was the kind of thing that took all the fun out of photography. To have to measure and calculate made picture-taking too serious a business.

"How much?" he asked the tired face behind the side counter. "And there's that telephone call to add to the bill." He counted out the cost in soiled and sticky lire notes that felt no longer like paper but almost like thin velvet. Behind him, a woman's high heels came clacking through the narrow door. (The tired-faced clerk had, hopefully, already pulled an iron trellis partly across the entrance, leaving only a small space for this late and slender customer.)

"Are these ready?" she asked in good Italian. She was standing at the main counter, holding out a numbered receipt. So eager was she to have her snapshots that she hadn't even looked at the other side of the shop. But Lammiter would know the sound of these heels anywhere, apart from the clear light note of her voice. He didn't have to turn around to see the supple figure in its simple dress, or to watch the way her fair head would be tilted to one side a little pleadingly, as if she could cajole the clerk into finding her photographs. It was Eleanor.

The clerk took the receipt she handed him. He searched, slowly but politely, among the bundle of envelopes. "Not here, signora." He looked at her sympathetically.

"Are you sure?" She was upset. "Please look again. They ought to be here. And I must have them."

Lammiter started toward the door quietly, quickly. You said good-by to all that, he told himself: only today, this early afternoon, you said good-by definitely. Get out of here, Lammiter—

He was at the door, about to push aside the iron gateway to let him ease his way onto the sidewalk, when he heard her say, "You see, I'm leaving Rome. For America."

He nearly said, "What?"

She was saying, "Oh, thank you. Thank you very much. I knew you'd find them."

He pushed the iron trellis a little more to one side. It scraped harshly, shivered a little, and stuck. He pulled at it impatiently.

"*Signore, signore, uno momento, uno momento!*" said the clerk, leaning into life as he rushed round to salvage his precious gate.

"Bill!"

He came back into the shop. For once, he had absolutely no idea of what he would—or even should—say. She had been crying. She had been crying a great deal.

"Oh, Bill!" She put out a hand to touch him as if to make sure he was real. "I tried to reach you by phone this evening. I didn't know—" Her voice strangled: she was crying again, quite silently. And her sudden tears distressed her still more. She bit her trembling lip and turned her head away from him and the curious clerk.

"How much?" he asked the man, pointing to the envelope Eleanor held in her hand. He paid for that, too. Quite like old times, he thought as he took her arm and steered her through the gateway. "Now where?"

"My apartment is just round the corner."

"Oh?" he said, as if he hadn't known that. How many nights had he passed by its windows and wondered— Hell, he thought as he tried to jam on some brakes: for a man who had buried his past so determinedly, he was helping it out of the grave too damn quickly.

"Please," she said, "please would you come up and

have a drink? I—" She looked at him with her large blue-gray eyes. Her lips trembled again. "I—I can't trust myself in a public place. And I need—I want to see you." She looked down at the envelope of photographs which she held in her hand. "I was packing, I wanted these to put in my case. The last memory . . ." She tried to laugh.

"Ah—careful!" he said, taking her arm. "Come on, Ellie, or you'll have me in tears, too. How would you like me standing on the Via Ludovisi crying my heart out?" She managed to laugh, this time.

The old name had slipped out. Ellie . . . How long do we stay vulnerable? he wondered. "All right. Let's go."

Eleven

THEY WERE BOTH SILENT, making their way for the short distance along the sidewalk, narrow here with trees, past the very small café with its three small tables outside for those who wanted a glass of wine. Round the corner, on a side street, quieter than even the quiet Ludovisi, was the house where Eleanor Halley shared an apartment with two other American girls. Like Brewster's house in the Piazza Navona, this place had once held a large private household. Now, its floors were divided into flats. Here, the ubiquitous dentist lived and worked, a designer had his carefully balanced name plate on display, a Swiss textile firm announced its Rome headquarters, and people like Eleanor paid overlarge rents. But in Rome, one had to add privacy and quiet to one's cost of living. The staircase had marble veneer, intricately worked. The elevator was venerable, limited (it held two people only), slow, quivering with its efforts.

"We'd have done better using the staircase," Bill Lammiter said.

"I'm on the top floor," she said warmingly.

That was all they said during the whole journey to her apartment. He wished he had never agreed to come: conversation was going to be difficult, now that the first surprise was over. She was calmer, too. It looked as if perhaps she didn't really need him around, after all.

The apartment was rambling, with large rooms leading off a dark central hall. She led him through double glass doors screened with lace into a dimmed and elaborately furnished room, everything exactly arranged in patterns of tables and ornate chairs. There was a good deal of glass and marble and gold-tipped wood, of silk brocade and net curtains carefully draped and puckered and folded.

"We share this room for everything except sleeping," she explained. "Hideous, isn't it? And I can't move a thing—there's a maid who goes with the apartment, and she won't let us alter the position of one ashtray. The awful thing is, there's a lot of good stuff in this room, and it could look beautiful." She moved over to the two huge square-shaped windows, which began at high waist level and stretched almost to the carved and painted ceiling. She pulled them wide open, after a brief battle with yards of lace, and flung apart the outside shutters. "It's cool enough now," she said, in her peculiar way of half-explanation. Eleanor had always talked to people as if she expected them to be thinking along with her, keeping a kind of silent conversation going, so that her mental jumps needed no explanation. What she was telling him was the fact that she had adopted, along with the Italian furniture, the Italian habit of shutting windows as well as shutters while the sun was up.

She glanced at him. He had barely entered the room. He stood quite still, watching her. "Am I talking too much?" She tried to laugh. "Someone *has* to say something. The silence in the elevator nearly smashed my eardrums. Don't look at me like that! I'm all right, Bill."

"Are you?" he asked quietly, listening to the nervous edge in her voice, watching the anxiety in her wide-open eyes. Why had she brought him here? The reason had been real enough, he felt now, but she was backing away from telling it to him. "Then perhaps you don't need anyone." He turned toward the glass doors.

"But I do. I need *you*."

"Why?"

"I've never felt so—so lost in all my life. Honestly, Bill—" She gestured helplessly. "I tried to call you twice this evening."

"So you said." His voice was quite neutral. He caught a

glimpse of himself in one of the several mirrors strung around the walls. He didn't look neutral, though. He looked like a man who had been strung out on a rack.

"Don't hate me, Bill. Please don't hate me—"

"I don't hate. I don't—" he took a breath and finished lamely, "—anything." He must put on a better show than this. He looked around him, thinking he would stay for five, polite, agonizing minutes; and then get the hell out. And stay out of Eleanor's life forever. He chose a chair that would be the least comfortable. "Where's everyone? All out to dinner?"

"Dorothy and Maymie are in Amalfi on their vacation. I sent the maid home this morning. I thought I had an engagement for tonight. With Luigi."

He reached in his pocket for a cigarette. "This allowed?"

She nodded, saying "sorry" as she found a cigarette box to open in front of him, and then searched for matches. Suddenly she remembered the drink she had offered him. She must indeed have been upset to have forgotten all these politenesses. Eleanor was the kind of girl who always remembered a man's little comforts: a good geisha, he used to joke. She brought him a well-mixed Scotch and soda with ice, and a large saucer to replace the Venetian glass thimble of an ashtray which he was balancing on his knee.

"And I thought," she said wryly, still following the pattern of thought that he had interrupted with the smoking ceremony, "that I was going to visit some friends of Luigi's this weekend. In Umbria. Luigi was going to join me there when he could."

He said nothing, nothing at all. Did she really enjoy hurting him like this? He even managed to look at her quite candidly. And then he saw she was not thinking of hurting him; she was too engrossed in hurting herself.

"But it's all off," she said. "All off."

"Well, you can see Umbria some other time, when you get back from America. The hill towns won't run away. They've been there for a couple of thousand years, at least."

"It's *all* off, Bill!"

"Off?" He rose.

"Luigi—I—we aren't getting married."

"What?"

"I'm going home for good." The words rushed out, ending her attempt at self-control. She turned her back on him. "I handed—I handed in my—"

He took a step toward her. But she was fighting off this attack of emotion by herself. She said, in a tight, strained voice, "I handed in my resignation at the Embassy this afternoon. They took it, too. Without one question. As if —as if they were glad I was going back to America. Suggested I leave as soon as possible."

"Thank God for that."

She swung around. "Why do you say that?" she asked sharply. "Why?"

He temporized. "What else would you expect me to say, Ellie?" he asked gently.

"You're just like the Embassy. Too quick—" Angrily, she brushed the tears from her cheeks. "They were too obliging about letting me go; no questions asked. Nothing. Bill—what's wrong? What are they trying to protect me from? What—"

"I suppose they saw your mind was made up." Not a brilliant remark, but the best he could muster at this moment.

"But it *wasn't*—not really. I could have been persuaded to stay."

"Why?" he asked. "To plead with dear Luigi?"

"Bill!"

He didn't apologize. But at least he had driven the tears away. "The sooner you leave, the better," he said curtly.

She faced him, angry, a little frightened, but determined. She quieted her voice. "You're like the Embassy," she repeated, "pushing me off on the first plane—" She hesitated. "I think you know something," she said slowly, "something I should know. What is it? Have you heard some rumor? Some—"

"Ellie," he said very quietly, "what are you going to imagine next? I'm a stranger here. Where would I hear rumors?" He walked over to the window. The evening sky had changed from gold to apricot and orange, and now —even as he watched—the flaming colors were streaked with violet-gray. Soon it would be dark.

"You heard the princess today. . . ." She sounded worried, puzzled.

"I just don't get this." He swung round to face her. "You

and Pirotta looked pretty damn well pleased with yourselves at Doney's, this lunchtime." He could have been more tactful. She flinched.

And then she said, the lines at the side of her lips suddenly drawing down so that her mouth seemed frail and miserable, "That was a pretense."

He looked at her sharply.

"Luigi didn't want his aunt to see that something was wrong—she would have been delighted: she never did think I was the right girl for Luigi; and we were hoping we could get everything straightened out. That's why I met Luigi for lunch." She took a long, deep breath. "But everything got worse instead of better."

"Look—" he began, and stopped. If ever he had seen a man in love, it had been Pirotta. "I just *can't* believe it. That guy just doesn't give up so easily."

Eleanore said, shaking her head, still hardly believing it herself, "We had some trouble two nights ago. Last night we had another quarrel—no, that isn't the right word—it wasn't a quarrel exactly. It was worse than a quarrel. Just—" She dropped her hands helplessly to her sides. "Just trouble. Which I can't understand. I just don't know what is wrong, Bill."

"Then why break off an engagement? Or is this getting to be a habit?"

She flinched again. She said quietly, "I didn't break it off. It was Luigi who—" She stopped, facing him. Abruptly, she turned away and sat down. She lit a cigarette very carefully. "He broke the engagement this afternoon," she said at last.

Involuntarily he said, "That was the only solution. I mean—it was the right thing—for your sake. But I'm sorry. It's a hard blow. Even if you sensed trouble coming, it is always hard to—"

She was staring at him. "What do you mean—'right thing'? Or 'for my sake'?" She was angry. "Look, Bill—I wanted to tell you all this just because I—well, I felt you were the only person I could trust."

"Trust with what?"

"With what?" she echoed blankly. She looked at him, utterly bewildered now. She shook her head. "Bill, what *did* you expect from me? I just wanted to tell *someone*, to have them listen, to have them understand. Someone I—I like very much. Someone who likes me, so that any advice I get will be honest."

"But why choose *me?*" he asked angrily. Why cut open healed wounds?

"I don't know, I don't know," she said, and her voice slid into tears like that of a child who is frightened. "I just wanted—I just wanted to see you."

Or perhaps, he thought savagely, the wounds had never healed. His, at least, were as raw as on the day they had been inflicted.

"Please stop teaching yourself to hate me," she said sharply, her tears changing to anger. "I watched you at Doney's today. You really had cast me for the role of villainess, hadn't you? Nothing I could have done or said would have been right. Nothing." There was a long silence. Her voice became calm, sad. "Don't, Bill! One can always sneer at people—one can always find something to laugh at. But you don't *have* to do that with me. I know how wrong I was. And how I hurt you. I'm sorry. I've said that before. And I meant it. I didn't need to lose Luigi to know how you felt when I treated you so— so badly. You don't love me any more, but you don't have to hate me."

He watched her as she spoke. It was all as painful for her to say as it was for him to listen to. But she was right about some things. He might as well admit it honestly, as she had. Today, at Doney's, he had been twisting every memory of her into a caricature, every thought about her into a bitter criticism. He had been trying to teach himself to hate her. Why? To stop loving her? Damn those big gray eyes, soft and shadowed, watching him so unhappily across the darker shadows of this room.

"I always told you I was a mean son of a bitch," he said gruffly. He finished his drink quickly, and rose.

She rose, too. "And I never believed it. Or I wouldn't have telephoned you this evening. I wouldn't have asked you to come up here." She held out her hand for his empty glass. "Let me mix you another."

"I hate Pirotta's guts," he admitted. "I'm glad you are leaving him. Glad. But I'm sorry, too. Sorry this had to be . . ." He put out a hand and touched hers. They were two shadows, facing each other in a darkened room. The deep dusk blotted out all expressions, all memories.

She didn't move. He tightened his hand round hers, and took a step nearer. "Ellie—"

She came to life. Her arm and her voice were taut. "No, Bill! No—I'm selfish and vain and stupid, but I didn't ask you to come up to—oh, Bill, I'm not as cruel as that! Have you got all your memories of me so twisted?"

He dropped her hand. She didn't step away, though, not at once. She touched his arm, gently, as if to soften the sharpness of her refusal. And then she moved quietly, without haste, over to the wall and switched on the light.

"You know," he said, making his voice as natural and easy as possible, "I think we both need some dinner."

She smiled suddenly, with relief. "Do you mind if it's simple? The larder didn't expect company. Eggs, cheese—that kind of thing? And there's Valpolicella."

"Good," he said. "Hemingway characters always drink Valpolicella. Lets them get things straight." He managed a laugh. "I'll help with the omelette. Where's the kitchen?"

"As far down the hall as possible," she said, almost laughing, too. "Who wants an old kitchen near any old dining room?" She led the way into the hall, switching on lights.

He noticed a telephone. "By the way, why did you have to phone me twice? Didn't the hotel mention I had checked out, the first time?"

"Yes. But they expected you back."

"They did?"

"You had left your raincoat."

"My Burberry?" And as he stared at her incredulously, he suddenly could see it, hiding on a hook behind the opened inner door to his bedroom. His much prized, over-priced Burberry. "Darn! So that's how I found room for my camera in my suitcase."

"You should use a Minox," she said, "and carry it in your pocket. That would solve a lot of problems."

It was the old argument between two camera addicts, each trying to convert the other to his own particular love. Lammiter had always preferred the full-sized print he could get with his Rolleiflex.

He halted at a doorway, and looked at suitcases on the bed, evening dresses over the top of a trunk, clothes pulled out of a wardrobe, jars and bottles and lipsticks all pushed into a group beside a large handbag on the dressing table. "Now I begin to see why you always depended on a Minox. But have you room even for it?"

"I can always ditch my cigarette lighter. Most of this stuff will be sent after me. I'm taking just one bag."

"When do you leave?"

"Tomorrow, early." She bit her lip, looked at him uncertainly. "Bill, am I doing the right thing?—Running away like this?"

"I think it's the right thing."

"But I've nothing to be ashamed of. Why should I run?" Her gray eyes, blue when she wore blue, green when she wore green, looked obliquely at him from under the fringe of dark lashes. "Luigi is, of course, going to say that it was all my decision. Noble of him. He's telling that to his relatives, right now, at that dinner party we were going to attend tonight. Can't you see them? Horrified and angry. Shaking their heads. Saying 'I told you so, my dear boy. These Americans—' " She broke off.

"Now, Ellie," he said, and searched for a handkerchief. "Look—" he spoke sharply, to switch her mind away from the dinner party, "you didn't leave your name, did you?"

"Where?" She stopped wiping her eyes, and stared at him. "At the hotel."

"But why not? I wanted to *reach* you, Bill. I thought you could call me when you— Bill—what's wrong with that?"

He looked at the floor, black and white marble. He looked at the walls, arsenic green fading to yellow; at the carved ceiling, the bogus Corinthian plasterwork; then back at the disarrayed bedroom.

"Look at *me*, Bill," she said gently. "What's wrong?" She looked as if she might smile.

You women, he thought, God damn it, you women, you are truly impossible.

Eleanor said, "I brought you up here to listen to my troubles—and now I think I have to listen to yours." She did begin to smile.

"No," he said sharply. "I've no troubles. But I sure as hell wish you hadn't left your name at the hotel in connection with me. I just don't want you tied up with me at all, at the moment."

That made her serious. "Why? Luigi wouldn't object."

"His friends might." He spoke jokingly.

She looked at him, startled. She said bitterly, "His friends certainly would. They object to everything I am and do." She tried to laugh. "Why don't they like me? What have they to do, anyway, with choosing Luigi's wife?"

"His friends?"

"Yes, his friends. They didn't approve of me, so he let me go. Yet, a month ago, when some of his relatives objected to an American girl who hadn't a millionaire father, Luigi laughed. Ludicrous, isn't it?"

"Who were these friends of his? Italians?"

She shook her head. "Italians are never rude—not to a woman. One had a French name, Legros. The other— well, he talked English, but he wasn't English."

"I can't see any man disliking you," he said, half smiling. "Ellie, don't hurt yourself imagining things—"

"I'm not imagining. In these last few weeks, I've had too much experience of being inspected by Luigi's family *not* to know when I am being carefully considered. Honestly, Bill— Two nights ago, Luigi took me to dinner. We drove out into the country—to a house at Tivoli, not a restaurant, a private house. I never knew who the owner was. I never met a host or a hostess. There were two middle-aged servants, men who looked as if they were made of wood: cubical faces, broad cheekbones, square-shaped bodies, and shoulders that looked like a high plateau. We had *apéritifs* on the terrace, the Frenchman, the bogus Englishman, Luigi, and I. There was a lovely view of the gorge and the waterfall and the old Greek temple up on the hill—do you know it? Thank heaven for that view: the conversation couldn't have been more boring. The men just didn't make any pretense of being sociable. They talked with Luigi and sort of watched me as I listened. They didn't like me to begin with, not even before they met me, I guess." Her voice had calmed down: she was disguising the hurt in it; she was even making a brave attempt to be amused. "Ridiculous? Yes, I know it sounds ridiculous. But it all happened just like that." She turned away. "I'll tell you the rest over dinner." She moved toward the kitchen.

"Tell me now," he said, catching her arm.

"Here, standing in the hall?"

"What happened next? You were bored. . . ." Suddenly he saw the whole picture developing in front of him. "Don't tell me you started playing around with that Minox of yours."

She looked a little startled. "How did you guess?"

"You always did play around with it."

"Yes," she said, smiling now, perhaps remembering how they had first met in New York, two strangers alone in the Romanesque garden of the Cloisters, two amateurs trying for a good camera angle, a significant view of the George Washington Bridge soaring high over the Hudson. "And you weren't always sure whether I was lighting a cigarette or taking a picture of you."

Yes, he thought a little bitterly, I almost imagined you must have liked the look of me. "So you took some pictures on the terrace of the house at Tivoli."

"Not exactly like that. I wanted to see the view from the edge of the terrace. Luigi and his friends were busy talking. So I rose and went over to the balustrade. The light was still good enough—with luck I could get some pictures. I took out the Minox. And I wandered a bit— you know how it is—the view is always better on the other side of the garden."

"No one paid any attention?"

"I suppose they didn't think I'd wander far. But I explored round some shrubbery and saw a man sitting there, all by himself. He was reading. He made a very nice composition with the Greek temple on the hill across the gorge behind him."

"So you photographed a man sitting in the garden? He didn't notice?"

"He looked up, of course. But you know how quick a Minox is. I'd already taken two photographs." She paused. "You know, he was furious. He rose and took a few steps toward me, saying, 'And what are *you* doing here, may I ask?' And I just was speechless."

"Did he see the camera?"

"I don't think so. My hands had dropped to my sides. And before I could explain or anything, he turned on his heel and walked away."

"So you went back to the terrace?"

She nodded. "Luigi was coming to meet me, and the others were standing at the balustrade. They must have heard the sound of the man's voice. Luigi saw the Minox in my hand. 'For God's sake,' he said. 'Hide that damned thing!' So I slipped it into the pocket of my skirt."

"The others heard?"

"Impossible. He spoke under his breath. It was the first time I'd ever heard him use strong language, though."

"I shall try to reform," Lammiter said gravely. "Well, that was quite a party you had."

"Oh, that wasn't all! The Frenchman wanted to know who had been talking to me. And I said, 'A very rude Englishman. He didn't even give me time to explain.' Because that really annoyed me, Bill. I hadn't been slipping through shrubbery to spy on him."

"He was English?" Lammiter asked quickly.

"I know a genuine broad A when I hear it. Besides, he *looked* English—he had that kind of thin drawn face and very neatly brushed hair—"

"What color?"

She looked at him in surprise. "Grayish."

"Tall?"

"Definitely. And thin. Almost concave." She looked at the suddenly thoughtful Lammiter. "I am *not* making this up. It's true."

"I believe you. Tell me, did he appear at dinner?"

"No. Seemingly the villa and garden had been divided into two houses. They told me he was an eccentric who rented the other one."

"And no more was said about him than that?"

"I tried to make conversation about eccentrics, but it was switched away onto Korea, of all things. And Luigi was no help at all. In fact, he excused himself for a moment, just before the dessert arrived, and he stayed away for half an hour at least."

Visiting the English eccentric? Lammiter wondered. "He was probably as bored as you were," he said.

"He came back looking worried, not bored. We left then. Very quickly. And that's when our trouble really started. Apparently I had behaved badly." She tried to smile. "That made me as mad as *he* was. And right in the middle of our quarrel, when he was absolutely white-lipped—I had never seen him like that—he snapped out, 'He is right! You're totally irresponsible, hopelessly immature.' "

Lammiter, who had been both amused and puzzled, stared at her. "He? Which he?"

"That's what I asked."

"What was the answer?"

"No answer. Luigi switched right over to my walk in the garden. Why had I explored so far, what was I doing, anyway?"

"You told him what actually had happened?"

"Why not?"

"That silenced him, I bet."

"As a matter of fact, he burst into a stream of Italian. Words that I don't even know. He only stopped when he was out of breath."

"So you said you were sorry, you must have been mistaken, let's forget everything."

"Anything for peace," she agreed.

"My, my—you did have a first-rate quarrel, didn't you? But at least you managed to keep hold of your photographs." He smiled.

"The trouble with you, Bill, is that you are not only understanding, but that you understand me too well." Then she smiled, too. "I wasn't too honest about them. I—I was so mad when he demanded the camera, I clenched my fist around it, and—well, I said I had taken the film out of it."

"Then he asked you for the film."

"No. He grabbed my purse. There were two rolls of film there. He took them both."

"Quite the commissar, isn't he?"

She looked at him searchingly. "Yes," she said slowly.

"And yesterday he had the films developed, and found—?"

She bent her head. Her voice was stifled. "People at Ostia. People at Doney's. People . . ."

"He came back for the Tivoli film?"

"Last night. But it was being developed and printed."

"Did you tell him where the film was being printed?"

"Why should I? What *right* had he to behave like that?"

"Jumping Christopher!" he said. "You must have been really angry."

"I was. That was our worst and final quarrel. Bill—what made Luigi behave like that?"

He looked at her, wondering how much she had begun to guess about Luigi Pirotta and his friends. A future commissar didn't have freedom of choice in a wife. He had two categories that were safe: he could choose a woman who was as deeply involved as he was or he could choose a placid mooing creature who turned tail to the wind like all the other cows in the field. But never could he choose anyone who asked questions and expected truthful answers. Worse still was the woman who—if she didn't get the answers—searched for them by herself. If Luigi Pirotta hadn't known all the rules of the game he was playing, he knew them now. That was the trouble about power politics: you never knew all the rules of the game until you were too far involved to be able to draw back.

"Because," she was saying slowly. "Something did make him react that way. He—he panicked." She said the word with distaste. "Most of his anger was really fear. But why?"

Lammiter said savagely, "The man's in love with you, that's why. He's afraid for you. Is that the answer you wanted?"

"Oh, Bill!—" She made a peculiarly pathetic picture, warding off this last lunge of bitterness, the frown of worry still on her brow, the dried tearstains till smearing her cheeks.

"Men are brutes," he told her cheerfully, trying to laugh away his own fears. "Perhaps you'd better feed this one. How about that omelette?"

"I never know what you'll say next," she said, completely baffled. But she turned toward the kitchen.

"May I use your telephone?"

She looked back at him, surprised again. "Why yes, of course."

"And do you mind if I look at the photographs?"

For a moment, as she hesitated, his excitement turned to worry. Suddenly, angry with everything, she said, "You can burn them if you want to!" And then she was in the kitchen, banging out her sudden temper with pans and mixing bowls, more like a volcano in brief eruption than a ministering angel.

Twelve

QUICKLY, Lammiter examined the numerous prints before he went to the telephone. On Eleanor's orders, they had been enlarged almost to a two-inch square from their usual postage-stamp size and the roll of film had been cut into individual sections. Only about two-thirds of the film had been printed, indicating that the rest hadn't been worth spending the extra money on. But two-thirds wasn't a bad average for Eleanor's technique; and they were good prints, very good prints indeed. The girl could take pictues. Better than I can, he admitted to himself.

He riffled through the prints nervously. There were many studies of people. What if the Tivoli pictures hadn't come out? After all, it had been late in the day, and the light would be difficult. Then, in two photographs with darkish corners—either underexposed or taken by failing light—he saw a white circular temple on a rugged hill, and, in the foreground, a man. In one picture the man was reading, his head bent. In the other, he had looked up, but not yet turned to face the photographer. His profile was sharp and clear. It could very well be a side view of the man in Brewster's photograph, the ex-Englishman called Evans. Brewster would know, most definitely.

Lammiter laid the photograph on a table under a lamp. Then, quickly scanning the negatives against the light, he matched one with the print. He wrapped the negative and the print together in his handkerchief; the others he slipped back into the envelope. The angry clatter from the kitchen had been replaced by a pleasant smell of sizzling butter.

Brewster's humor would have appreciated the scene, Lammiter thought as he waited by the telephone. Then he wondered, why do I keep thinking of Brewster? The

man has invaded me. Do I believe him? Few people
would, and I'm as wary as any New Englander. . . . Yet
why else should he be standing here, in Eleanor's apartment, waiting once more for a professor of Latin to answer his call? As for his own immediate life—it had vanished into thin air: the plane reservation to New York
(damn, he'd have to call the airport and cancel) might
have been waiting for him in outer space; his raincoat
might have been left in a hotel on Mars; and he had
even stopped worrying about his typewriter and camera.
The real world had become a shadow play of half-remem-
bered dreams; and Brewster's nightmare world had become the reality. Even Professor Ferris, now speaking,
was—quite unwittingly—a part of this new strange
fantasy.

Ferris had a pleasant voice on the telephone. His Italian was beautiful, sonorous, spoken with care but overwhelming accuracy. You could easily tell he was a foreigner: he had learned the language abroad, away from
the incredible variety of regional pronunciations and inflections. And, inexplicably, Lammiter was reminded for
a brief moment of Salvatore's voice. Then he pushed
that idea aside, and answered Ferris. "I bet," he said
admiringly, "the cab drivers ask you to recite Dante.
Have you ever discovered why they are such special
connoisseurs of the first lines of the *Divine Comedy?
Nel mezzo del cammin di nostra vita.* . . . Is that what
makes them drive in the very middle of the road?"

"Oh, it's you!" Ferris said, in English. He sounded too
annoyed to join in any fooling. "Where the hell have you
been wandering?"

"Not too far. Sorry, though. Did I keep you from going
out to dinner or something?"

Ferris softened a little. At least, he laughed. "Don't
give that a thought. It's only half-past nine."

Lammiter glanced at his watch in surprise. Nine fifteen.
when a man called that half-past nine, he was really annoyed. "I *am* sorry."

"We've been waiting here—" Ferris began, his hunger
now dissipated a little by excitement.

Alert, Lammiter said, "We? Is our mutual friend
around?"

"Yes. He's returned. Thank God. Now I can pass you

over to him, and go back to a normal existence."

"He's *there*—with you?"

"Very much so. He's eaten all the nuts, finished the olives, and told us his stories twice over." Bunny Camden's voice cut in. "And how is my elusive friend? Carl thinks you're in need of some dinner yourself."

"I'm as sober as a Presbyterian elder. I'm just suffering from a touch of euphoria." Lammiter glanced down, approvingly, at the envelope of photographs in his hand. "I must see you."

"Where are you visible?"

"At Miss Halley's apartment."

There was a brief silence. Then Camden said, "Aren't you complicating your life unnecessarily?"

"Not unnecessarily, I hope. Where do I see you? I've an appointment later this evening. At eleven."

Behind him he heard the sound of wheels. Eleanor was pushing a trolley, arranged with food, down the hall toward the living room.

"Remember where we bumped into each other a few days ago?" Bunny was saying.

"Yes."

"Walk past there. Around—let's see—around ten. And keep on walking. I'll catch up with you."

"My feet are in good condition."

"That's fine. But don't trip over that euphoria."

They parted, as usual, with a grin on their faces. I ought to see more of Bunny Camden, Lammiter thought: he's good for my morale. But life had a peculiar way of dealing out agreeably mad companions only in little snatches. It was much more generous with the bores.

"All ready!" Eleanor's voice called from the living room. She sounded quite normally cheerful again. The room looked more cheerful, too, with all its warmly shaded lights switched on. She had cleared a round table and set out the supper, and she was studying the bottle of Valpolicella. "You'd better deal with this." She handed over a corkscrew. "Good news?" she asked, noticing the expression on his face.

"I think so. When are you leaving?"

"Tomorrow morning."

"You know—I shouldn't be surprised if I joined you." She looked a little embarrassed, as if she were nervous about that idea. "I'll try to get a seat—damn, I've got some more phoning to do—the airport."

"Let's eat the eggs first. I'm afraid I scrambled them."

"That's the way you felt, I guess." He laid the photograph near her. She paid no attention to them.

"I imagined the eggs an English eccentric," she admitted.

"They taste better than he does, I'm sure." He put down his fork abruptly.

"What's wrong? Aren't the eggs—"

"They're fine," he told her. "But I just remembered a joke I could have made on the telephone. Dammit—why must I always be witty five minutes too late?"

"Is that why you write plays?"

"You sound as if you—" he looked at her quickly "—as if you didn't like playwriting as a profession."

"What was the joke?" she asked, dodging a straight answer.

"Oh well, I was talking to a hungry man with a beautiful wife."

"How do you know she's beautiful?"

He thought of this afternoon. "By the way she inspires him."

"Oh—he's a sensitive type?"

"Knowledgeable," he conceded. "And I ought to have quoted Max Jacob's advice to a starving lover looking at his mistress's bare shoulder. That would have silenced even a professor."

"Now," she said, "I'll just let you soar. I don't even pretend to be able to hang on to the tail end of the kite."

"Jacob was a surrealist poet—kind of 1910 vintage—before we were born, anyway."

"Just a dear old dotard," she agreed. "But what did he say?"

"Oh—" he tried to get out of this now "—wit never seems so funny when you serve it up cold."

"He was starving. He was looking at his mistress's shoulder. And what did he say?"

"*Une escalope de vous, ma divine.*"

She looked at him blankly.

"I will *not* explain," he warned her.

"You don't have to. I know my French." She shook her head. "The truth is, it isn't funny."

"Ellie—it is! It's the funniest poem—"

"If you are a man, perhaps. But it makes all women's shoulders feel nervous. Are all men cannibals at heart?"

He grinned. "How often has a man told a girl he could eat her up? Or called her honey, cookie, sugar, peach? Or even—no, I never did like tomato."

She had truly the most delightful of smiles. "Look—" she said in sudden surprise, "I'm all cheered up! I almost laughed."

"I'm glad I'm good for something."

She removed the empty plates, offered him cheese, helped herself to a peach. "Two hours ago," she admitted, "I wouldn't have dared to laugh because I'd have ended in hysterics. Two hours ago, I couldn't think straight. I couldn't even pack. I'd pick a dress up and then drop it, and lift a pair of shoes and then I'd find myself at the dressing table, looking for lipsticks and Band-Aids. I was sort of disjointed, mentally. But now I'm beginning to think, not very well, just a little. . . . Bill, won't you explain what all the trouble is about? There is something very far wrong, isn't there?"

"I think so. But I don't know very much. You probably know more than I do."

"Why should I?"

"Because Pirotta seems to be the storm center."

"Is he in danger?" She stopped peeling the peach on her plate, and pushed it aside as if all appetite had suddenly closed down, like a shop front at noon. "Is that why he picked a quarrel—to send me away?"

"Perhaps."

"But if he's in danger, I should warn him—"

"Warn? Don't look so God-damned worried about an utter, first-grade, one-hundred-and-twenty-five-per-cent heel." Perhaps he had let his own emotions carry him away a little.

She flushed. "Bill! I must say—"

"Don't!" he advised her. "You've been pressing me all evening for the truth. Well, here it is—as I see it. Think of all the decent guys walking along the streets of Rome, and you had to pick a prize like Pirotta. If he is in trouble, he's earned it. Save your sympathy for the decent guys who don't make so much money, but at least make it honestly. They're the ones Pirotta thinks he's going to boss."

NORTH FROM ROME   119

"Honestly?" she repeated. She gulped and was speechless. Then, "Bill, how can you, how dare you—"

"I'll dare more than that." He was ominously quiet. "The only honest thing Pirotta has done, since he kissed Mamma and went off to school at the age of nine, was to fall in love with you."

She rose and began clearing away the last remains of supper onto the trolley. He let the silence last for at least two minutes. "How many photographs did you take out at Tivoli?" he asked.

"Five or six." The temperature was glacial, touching zero.

"Only two came out."

"Did they?"

"I took one of them along with its negative. Do you mind?"

That caught her by surprise. She shook her head, looking at him. "There *is* trouble. Isn't there?"

He nodded. "Don't take sides, Ellie, neither Pirotta's nor mine. Please just get on that plane for home. Please . . ."

"And ask no questions?" She half smiled. Perhaps his concern for her had touched her a little.

It was the moment to apologize. "I'm sorry I was so crude. But you wanted the truth from me. I gave it."

"As you saw it," she added.

"Sure. And we're all fallible, I know that."

She looked at him, "I'm sorry I was angry," she said in a low voice.

He became brisk, made a show of glancing at his watch, rising. "I'll wheel this double-decker along to the kitchen, and then I'll have to leave. Can you take care of yourself?"

She nodded.

"What is this gadget called, anyway? A super-deluxe push-me-around?"

"It's a laboratory cart. I wanted something bigger than the usual little trolley. I got this from a hospital-supply firm—one of those drug-supply houses—"

He jerked to a stop. The peeled peach rolled off its bed of Bel Paese rind and Camembert crust, and splashed like a bomb on a black square of tile. "Help!—Help!" He searched for a napkin.

Eleanor began to laugh. "Now, this *is* funny," she said.

"Very funny," he agreed glumly and set her giggling again as she mopped up the tile.

"Your face—" she tried to explain. "You had such a sudden look of horror. Now what were we talking about? Oh, yes—this laboratory cart and the drug-supply house. It's a very big medical firm, and a well-known one."

He wondered a little at all this elaborate build-up.

"Highly reputable," she said. "And honest." Her voice sharpened. "And that's how Luigi makes his money."

Fortunately, they had reached the kitchen, a dark cell lined with wooden cupboards. The cart was safely still. He walked back into the hall.

"Well?" she asked. "Or do you think it is dishonest to be a director of a firm that supplies medicine to cure people?"

"How many directors are there?"

"I've met four. They are the most delightful men." She smiled mischievously. "*And* honest."

"I'm sure they are." And he *was* sure about that. Pirotta needed honest men and an honest firm for his support. The more reliable the firm, the less government supervision. How much opium and heroin had he diverted from the company's warehouses? He wondered if the Italian detective with the romantic name was now studying Pirotta's falsified lists of imports. All Pirotta needed was a handful of well-paid and efficient clerks in key positions to baffle any honest board of directors.

She walked along the hall with him. "Don't you believe me about Luigi?" she asked suddenly, pathetically.

"Do you want a nice comfortable answer, or the truth?"

"We had that," she said, a little bitterly. "The truth as you see it." She shook her head wearily. "I wish I'd stop asking myself questions. I wish I knew what to do."

"Pack," he told her, "and get all ready to leave. Will you do that for me?"

She nodded. But she was still trying to answer her own questions.

He said, "Keep the door locked and bolted. I'll call you around midnight, just to hear how the packing is going."

"Look, Bill," she said, "aren't you worrying about me a little too much?"

"No," he said firmly. "And don't start thinking I'm
judging Pirotta badly because I don't like him." He took
her hand and gave it a most formal shake. "Good night,
Ellie." He hesitated. So did she. Her moment of bitterness
had gone. She had banished her anger. She smiled, not
too happily. Perhaps she was wishing that everyone would
give up dislike and prejudice and make this a world fit for
heroines to love in.

She mustered her gratitude. "Good night, Bill. And
thank you for—for rallying round."

But not for giving advice, he thought. "Good night," he
said again, and turned away. Behind him, the door was
locked. And then bolted. She might not believe him, but at
least she had listened to him. He wondered, with a stab of
pain, whether good night might not mean good-by; and
then, with a stab of fear, whether he might never get free
of this girl even if he never saw her again.

"What's wrong with this damned elevator?" he said
angrily as he heard it shivering and groaning so slowly up
toward him. He glanced at his watch. Seven minutes to
ten. He began to run down the staircase, lightly, easily,
round and round the pivot of an elaborately carved
stone column decorated with plaster acanthus leaves. You
should have taken a hint from the builder of this place,
Lammiter now thought; he didn't know when to leave well
enough alone. Everything was fine until you had to start
telling her the truth. That was the odd thing about truth: it
wasn't a variable; truth was hard cold fact, and yet it
varied, it could seem a prejudice, an unjustified attack,
almost a slander, if the moment were wrong. Your timing
was miserable, he told himself angrily.

Upstairs, Eleanor Halley didn't move away from the
door. She stood there, looking along the empty hall,
seeing nothing. She wished desperately that he hadn't
said what he thought about Luigi Pirotta. But perhaps the
fault had been hers: why had she gone on and gone on,
asking Bill questions? Because she wasn't satisfied with
any of her own answers?

She didn't like the thoughts that suddenly confronted
her, but she didn't push them aside as she might once
have done. She left the door, walking slowly down the hall,
considering them from a variety of angles.

Yes, she decided, the fault is all mine: if Bill has become a jealous man, suspicious and exaggerating, I'm the one to blame. But I never thought that was the way it would turn out when I ran away from him. Ran away? Perhaps. But not from him. From Broadway and the life that would turn our own life together into something no longer ours. Rehearsals, rewrites, tryout in Baltimore, more rewrites, short tour in Boston, Philadelphia, more rewrites, a chorus of darlings echoing through dressing rooms and after-theater parties, a pantomime of meaningless kisses from almost-strangers.

"Don't you see," Bill used to say worriedly, "these things mean little; it's just their way, it has nothing to do with our life."

Nothing? It took Bill away from me, using up the weeks, the months that never could be replaced. If I had been in the theater it would have been different. But I don't want to go to bed at four in the morning and rise at noon; I don't want to live in hotel rooms and furnished apartments and have mobs of people always around me. Because that's the way it was going to work out. If only his play had *not* been a success, then we could have planned— Oh well, what's the use? Even when I ran off to Rome last April, was he free to follow me and persuade me back? Oh, no! The play was a success, but Miss Whosis wanted a new speech written and Miss Whatsis objected to the cuts in her lines and Mr. Wicher needed a few more aphorisms to bring out the texture of his character, and weren't the changes made in Boston and re-worked in Philadelphia perhaps a little unnecessary for New York? And on top of all that, Hollywood, six weeks dragging into months . . .

The awful thing was that if I had told Bill all this, he would have listened. He would have worried over it. He would have given up playwriting and concentrated on short stories or editing news reports. But he is a good playwright—most promising, said even the bitterest of critics. So that is that. What woman is going to spend the rest of her days remembering she has killed off a promising playwright?

And now?—Bill will recover: he was on the way to recovery until I brought him here tonight. My fault again, my fault . . . And yet he did help me; he will never know how much it helped me to hear his easy voice and his silly

jokes and even his biting remarks. He made me normal
again, able to face the journey home. And he will go
home, too, and he will write more plays (if I keep away
from him), and the only difference in them will be
that they'll be less amused by life and more acid about
women. The critics would like that. But every time I go
to see one of his plays, I'll be hearing what he thinks about
me, she thought unhappily.

And Luigi—what about him? But this will get no clothes
packed, she decided abruptly. She crossed swiftly over the
threshold into her room. She was folding her favorite
evening dress and looking round for some tissue paper
when the doorbell rang.

Could this be Bill, back again? What had he forgotten?
Or perhaps—perhaps he had decided that he owed her a
little explanation, a sort of half-apology for his attack on
Luigi.

"Who is it?" she called through the door, her hand on
the key. She was half smiling, remembering Bill's sense of
humor, wondering what excuse he had concocted to dis-
guise the apology.

A young voice, a boy's voice, replied. "The raincoat of
Signore Lammiter. Here it is."

"But *he* isn't here."

"He will come to get it later."

She was a little taken aback. She would have understood an apology, even offered sideways. But this bare
excuse for Bill's return later was something that angered
her. "Leave it there, outside," she said sharply. How silly
could Bill get?

There was a brief pause. Then the boy said, *Si, si,
signora.* As you say." He must have dropped the coat on
the mat, for she heard his footsteps retreating. And then
the elevator door closed, and the usual rattle began as
the boy descended. There was only silence outside.

She let her hand drop away from the key. I suppose I
am to telephone the airport for him, too, she told herself,
and reserve that seat for him. Oh, really, Bill Lammiter!

Then she knew she was unjust. Bill wasn't really like
that. He had left for some appointment, hadn't he? Perhaps
he hadn't enough time to go back to his hotel: perhaps he
had telephoned the hotel and got a bellboy to bring the
coat round. And he'd collect it here, coming to say good-

by (*and* to offer that explanation and half-apology, she was sure of that) on his way to the airport tonight. After what had happened, he would not wait until tomorrow to catch a plane home, not unless she was going to suggest it. And she wasn't. She wasn't going to run into any more dead-end streets. But she kept thinking of the raincoat lying abandoned.

I'm the one who is being silly, she thought now. She unlocked the door, swung it open, her eyes on the mat outside. There was no coat. Only Luigi.

"Oh no!" she said, and tried to close the door. He grasped its handle, holding it ajar.

"I must see you, Eleanor—I must—" His voice was as distraught as his face. "Please, Eleanor. Please—" As she hesitated, he stepped inside, closing the door behind him, locking it.

Thirteen

BILL LAMMITER slackened his pace as he reached the Via Vittorio Veneto. Now it was a curving river of brilliant lights, surging with pleasure traffic, pouring its people in a continuous current of smooth bare heads along the crowded sidewalks. Up the hill to his left, the outdoor tables on both sides of the street had multiplied and still were not enough. The chatter of voices sounded like the constant rush of a waterfall. And above all the noise and the glitter was a Roman night sky, an ink-blue silence scattered with diamonds.

He crossed the street with difficulty, for the Vespas were out in full force. The cooler air, which had blown in on the city with sunset, was almost too fresh for the suntanned shoulders. But for the men—and most were properly dressed in jackets—the fallen temperature was perfect. One of the joys of Rome was the pleasure of the late evening stroll. He turned to his right, following the Embassy's garden wall. Here, without benefit of cafés and crowded tables, the sidewalk was quiet and normally lit. Most people he met were on their way up the street, preparing to plunge into the endless parade. No one paid him the least attention.

Bunny Camden was standing talking to another man just outside the Embassy gates—just a couple of Americans in slim-shouldered light jackets and dark flannels of narrow cut, collars buttoned down, tie ends free, well-polished brown leather shoes, heads hatless, hair crisply cut, well-shaven faces, and a look of having stepped straight out of a shower not so very long ago.

We're developing a new type, Lammiter thought in amusement as he walked on. Gone are the Scott Fitzgeralds and the Babbitts of the twenties; gone the horn-rimmed glasses and the conscious tweeds of the thirties, gone, too, the Hollywood shoulders and Florida shirttails of the postwar forties. The relics of these eras look odd, now, like Aunt Lavinia's marcel wave or Cousin Kitty's pompadour.

Behind him, he heard Bunny's voice saying, "Well—good to have seen you. We must get together soon." That was also the new formula of good-by—willing but not too definite, leaving a pleasant escape route for all concerned —and then Bunny's brisk heel-to-toe stride was echoing behind Lammiter.

At this point in the street, the Via Vittorio Veneto branched off on its biggest curve to the foot of the hill. It was noisy, down there. So Lammiter kept straight on as he was going, following the street that was closer to the Embassy grounds, dimly lit and quiet. He didn't want to have to shout to make himself heard when Camden caught up with him.

"And how's the euphoria?" Camden asked, falling into step. He was shorter than Lammiter, but solidly built with plenty of hard muscle and no spare fat. He had a remarkably open, ingenuous face—he looked younger than his thirty years. His neatly brushed hair was dark; his brown eyes were cheerful; his wide mouth relaxed easily into a broad smile, showing strong even teeth, very white against his deeply tanned skin. Only the decided jut of his jaw line and the marked eyebrows gave any clue to the real Camden.

"Oh!" It wasn't a beginning Lammiter had expected; but it was a cue to take things easy. "I tripped over it. By the way, was that another college professor you were talking to, back there?"

"A textile manufacturer. We did our basic training together. Why?"

"Just trying to sort out types. They're all mixed up these days."

"Very difficult for writers. How's your new play coming along?"

"It isn't," he said curtly.

"Sorry," Camden glanced curiously at him, and retreated tactfully from the danger area. "Thought you writers always had something in the works. Or perhaps you've been too occupied? I gather you've been *very* occupied." The smile in Camden's voice disappeared. The introduction was over, the mood of friendly helpfulness established. He became impersonal and businesslike. "By the way, where is your eleven o'clock appointment?"

"At the Piazza Navona."

"Then we'll walk in this direction, and circle around. All right?"

They were reaching a district of luxury offices. At night, this small quarter closed down early. It was almost too empty.

"You don't think we are being followed, do you?"

"I watched you coming out of Ludovisi into the Vittorio Veneto. No one crossed the street after you. No one followed you down the street on its other side."

"I'm getting the jumps, I guess. I had a feeling in the Via Ludovisi that someone was standing under one of the trees, back in the shadows, just across the road from me. I stopped and lit a cigarette. Then a girl moved out of a dark patch into the light, and pretended she wasn't waiting, jiggled her white handbag, gave me the profile. They're so damned pathetic, they embarrass me. So I walked on and pretended I hadn't seen her—one snub less for her to count. Now I wish I had gone over and searched along that row of trees."

"And what good would it have done you? If you saw a man in the shadows, how do you know he wasn't keeping an eye on one of those girls? And what could you have done, even if he had been waiting for you? Catch him by the lapels, and say, 'Hey, you, tough guy, want me to bash your face in?' I doubt it. I very much doubt it. It's only in the movies that people behave like that." He touched Lammiter's arm and guided him across the street. They entered a narrower one, running obliquely away from the quiet offices. "This all right?" he asked, as he noticed Lammiter's quick glance back over his shoulder. On either side, closing them in, were silent and darkened houses.

"Sure. Just so long as we don't get a car aimed at our spines."

Camden looked at him sharply. "Say—you've been mixing with some peculiar people."

"It all began last—"

Camden said quickly, "Before you start telling me anything, you ought to know that I'm just a very minor attaché—no more, no less. I'm not an undercover type, or one of those cloak-and-dagger characters."

"Since when?"

"Since away back. I got out of the business before I got into it. I'm a bright boy, don't you know?"

"What did you do in Washington?"

"Bill, all I did was to sit at a desk and evaluate. That's the solid, unpainted truth. I sat at a desk until everything except my brain—and maybe that, too—was going flabby. I screamed, 'Let me out, let me out of here!' And I got this job eventually. Liaison mostly—NATO—Naples. At least I get some fresh air and a sun tan." He looked at Lammiter. "God damn it, you tell people the truth and they won't believe you!" He was exasperated enough to be believed. "I'll listen to your story, Bill. But, frankly, that's perhaps all I can do."

"You can always evaluate," Lammiter said with a grin. "And your liaison work nowadays may come in useful, too." Camden might know someone who would be interested in Brewster's story. "I'm only following the best advice my father ever gave me. When a picture fell off the wall or a drain clogged up, he'd yell 'Get an expert, get an expert!' And whatever you say, Bunny, you're the expert. I'm just a man who was curious."

"And now I'm curious," Camden admitted. "Go ahead."

"Where was I, anyway?" He was flustered by Camden's casual approach.

"Expecting a car to aim straight for our spines," Camden said cheerfully, but he looked as if he were prepared to listen.

So Lammiter began. He began with Tony Brewster. That wasn't the way he had intended to start his story.

But sometimes an apt cue is a better starting place than the first fact of a chronological account. And there was no doubt that the very mention of Tony Brewster's name startled Bunny Camden into complete seriousness. He listened to Lammiter's story with full attention, and—what was just as important—real interest. It was obvious that Lammiter was telling him something that was much more than he had expected.

They walked at an even pace, two men out for an evening stroll like so many others through the quieter streets of Rome, seemingly following no pattern of direction. By the time Lammiter had told of Rosana and her connection with the Pirotta narcotics ring; of the men around her—Bevilacqua the policeman, Joe the Sicilian, Salvatore the guide; of the princess and of Bertrand Whitelaw; of Eleanor Halley and her photographs, they had swung in a large arc of crisscrossed streets to the Piazza dell' Esedra. It was half-past ten. They could have walked the direct distance from Vittorio Veneto to the Esedra in an easy ten minutes.

For a few moments, Camden stood looking at the vast circle of the Piazza. Traffic swirled around the enormous central fountain, brilliantly illuminated to turn the high jets of water into golden plumes. Beyond them, on the other side of the Esedra, was the giant stretch of ruined walls and arches of the Baths of Diocletian, the enormous broken piles of bricks watching, from their withdrawn shadows, the bright lights of the modern arcades that curved round the other half of the Piazza.

"I like this fountain," Camden said, as if they had been discussing only the beauties of Rome. "Hear it? Falling water lighted. Helps one to think, just looking at it, listening. . . . Let's have coffee, and a seat."

"This isn't the Piazza Navona," Lammiter reminded him in a low voice.

"Plenty of taxis here," Camden said. "One will get you there in five minutes at this time of night." He led the way into the arcades and found a table that sheltered beside one of the giant pillars spaced around the half-circle of buildings to support the high curves of their arches, two stories high. Above these arches, each with its central ball of light, rose three more stories of large windows. So wide was the circle of the Piazza that the buildings didn't seem the giants that they were. Only the people, so miniature, and the cars, swirling round the fountain's pool like little water boatmen, put the scene into human proportion. The Italians, like the Romans, built for the gods.

Camden had chosen a table not too near the band that played in front of one of the cafés. For there, most people had gathered, either to sit at the crowded tables, or to stand, hundreds deep, as near the music as possible. Lammiter put away his mild protest, and settled comfortably to listen. It was his favorite aria from *Tosca,* and to judge by the silence of the crowd, oblivious to the steady hum of traffic, one of their favorites, too. Art is long, life is short. The buildings of stone looked down and approved.

Camden had ordered coffee in crushed ice for them both. He drank slowly, watching the play of the fountains. Then, quietly, he said, loud enough for Lammiter, not loud enough for the nearest strangers to hear, "I had known, of course, about the narcotics trouble. Recently, I met one of our people from the Narcotics Bureau in Washington: he's only one of several top men who've come over here. That's how serious it is. And Interpol also has men on the job. And there was a man I met, just last month, from one of the United Nations committees. The Italians are worried, too. So are the French. It isn't any secret in official circles. It's one of the undersurface battles that Russia has been waging since the end of the war."

He looked casually around the tables. So did Lammiter. No one was near enough to overhear. Beside the vast pillars of the enormous arcade, the people seemed small and distant like figures in a Piranesi landscape.

Camden went back to admiring the fountains. "So I knew some of your story. But I didn't know the part Pirotta was playing. Your detective, Bevilacqua, didn't tell us all that when he visited us at the Embassy last week."

"He went to the Embassy?"

"To advise us that one of our people might find her name caught up in a mess of publicity. Nasty for everyone."

"Eleanor?"

Camden nodded. "I bet there was a sigh of relief when she asked for leave today. Solved the problem of finding an excuse that wouldn't upset Bevilacqua's investigation. Tricky."

Camden looked around again. He said, "We're out of luck. Bevilacqua usually comes here in the late evening for a quiet half hour on his way home."

Lammiter looked startled. He had forgotten that Bunny always had a reason behind his actions. Bevilacqua had been his reason for coming here.

"Oh well," Camden said, "let's pay and go to a movie." He picked up the check and counted out the money.

"Look—"

"Now, now . . . You've still got fifteen minutes." Camden rose. And Lammiter followed. Under the arcade, side by side with shops, now closed, and the innumerable cafés and some third-class hotels, were several movie houses. Camden led the way quickly into the nearest large opening lined with the still photographs of an American gangster movie whose title and actors were complete strangers to Lammiter. "Part of our cultural exchange," Camden said with resignation. They paid, and entered a stone-floored passage, bleakly lighted, bare of furnishings or decorations, which twisted around behind the backs of the arcade's shops, with the booming sound of giant voices drawing nearer and nearer. Suddenly, Camden and Lammiter were inside a large open-air theater entirely enclosed by high buildings.

They stood for a moment, to accustom their eyes to the darkness of the sky overhead. Apart from the ghost-light from the distant screen stretched across the back of high houses, and a few shaded windows up in the buildings, and the stars above, there were no lights. The rows of collapsible wooden chairs were well filled, but most of the audience preferred the center and even the front seats. (The better to hear everything, Lammiter thought, as the booming ricocheted from wall to wall.) This left the back rows, sheltering under a pergola of vines overhead, almost empty, except for a scattering of couples.

Camden groped his way carefully to two seats at the far corner of an empty back row. Here, even the loud voices from the screen (two men fighting over a loose-haired, loose-mouthed blonde) were cut down in volume and in clarity. It was possible to talk, guardedly, and to listen. It would certainly be impossible for anyone to overhear.

Camden came straight to the point. "Now we'll discuss Mr. Evans. What does Brewster want us to do?"

"He wants to see you."

Camden let that pass. "But what can anyone do about Evans? There's no law against being a Communist. No law against a man visiting Italy from Russia."

"Unless his papers are false."

"Yes. That's why I'd like Bevilacqua to hear that part of the story. He could set something in motion."

"Brewster says there isn't enough time for that. What about the British? They'd also set something in motion, I'm willing to bet."

"Extradition? I don't think Brewster wants that—not just yet."

Lammiter felt stupid. "I guess not," he said lamely. No quick answers, he told himself: think, you lummox, think before you open your big mouth.

"It would be interesting to find out who the men are Evans is going to meet at Perugia, and what countries they've come from. That would give us the direction of Evans's mission here."

"I don't follow," Lammiter admitted frankly.

"We might learn from their identities where trouble is being planned. Supposing it is somewhere in the Far East, then the top-level agents infiltrated into that part of the world would need last-minute instructions—certainly a co-ordination of instructions—before any crisis was launched. Evans would be good at that. He has worked with both British and Americans. He knows where they are strong, and where they are weak. He's just the man to place the charges of dynamite, correctly, to start a landslide."

"But if the Far East is going to have more trouble, why did he come to Italy? I'd have thought Bombay or Karachi or Hong Kong would have been a better center for a meeting." He stopped. Camden hadn't said it was the Far East; he had only said "Supposing. . . ." Italy was a nice central meeting point for what? Western Europe and the Middle East? "If I were you, I'd contact the British Embassy right away," Lammiter said grimly.

"The trouble is, Brewster isn't exactly popular in diplomatic circles."

"So he told me. But if he has something new to say, won't someone at least listen?"

"Listen to a man who is a drunk?"

"Now—" Lammiter said quietly "—don't *you* start believing that! He likes his Chianti, but he can talk and think. He is still in control."

"I believe you, but thousands wouldn't."

Lammiter fell silent. He glared at the screen, where loud arguments had given way to gaping kisses, and the actors' faces had swelled up to the alarming size of twenty feet. He wondered what had happened to all the excellent movies he had seen last winter. Had they been torpedoed, crossing the Atlantic?

He lit a cigarette and let the match flare near his watch for a moment. "I've six minutes left," he said. "What have you decided?"

"Tell Brewster that I'd like to warn two men about Evans's appearance here. One of them is a Canadian, another is English. They are good Intelligence officers, in Rome at the moment on another job. Then, when the time comes for Evans to be picked up, England and the Commonwealth can do it together." Camden grinned. "That's diplomacy, son." Then he was serious again. "Secondly, tell Brewster I think he should let Bevilacqua in on the full story, too. He knows more experts in this kind of business than all the attachés in Rome put together. Between us all, we'll have Perugia well covered."

"Perugia— Why is Brewster so insitent on Perugia?"

"Why was Pirotta so insistent on keeping you out of Perugia?"

"That was when he thought I might be an agent—" Lammiter cut himself off. "I see," he ended.

"One last thing—ask Brewster to give you as much information for me as possible. After all, he's only given us one real fact, so far: that Evans is in Italy. That isn't much to go on."

"Why don't you come and see him yourself? I still think that makes good sense."

"I told you before—this is not my kind of business. The experts will push me out of the picture by tomorrow."

"Will they indeed?"

Camden ignored that. "But meanwhile I'll start interesting them. That shouldn't be difficult. Then, after you've seen Brewster and got his go-ahead signal, they'll be ready to move. Right? Here's a number where you can leave a message for me at any hour." He slipped a card into Lammiter's pocket. "Call me as soon as you leave Brewster. Then you can relax and concentrate on your girl."

"That suits me," Lammiter said.

"Which girl?" added Camden softly, and rose.

They made their way out. The loose-mouthed blonde was now in full scream as her true love smacked her jaw. "You can see why our cultural attachés develop stomach ulcers," Camden said as the shrieks hounded them into the corridor. "They spend half their dinner parties explaining that all American children don't pull knives on their teachers because their hypodermics have been taken away from them." He stopped to search for a cigarette. "Keep your visit to Brewster short. Don't let him start making speeches." He seemed to remember something pleasing. "Or quote Shakespeare. Not tonight." He struck a match. "Keep moving, pal. Stay with it."

Lammiter recovered sufficiently to say, "Well, good to have seen you. We must get together soon," and walked away. Behind him, Camden had difficulty with the sulphur matches. He took a long, long time to light that cigarette. Lammiter was well alone as he came out into the Piazza.

The golden jets of hissing water rose into the dark sky and fell, rose and fell, bathing the nymphs and their sea monsters with spun silk spray. The music was gay and happy, a joyful rendering of *Oklahoma!* The people liked it. Their applause drifted over the sound of engines and brakes and horns. A city of contrasts, he thought: a sense of peace mingled with constant noise, the day's warm air and the night's cool breeze, stone and flowing water, shadows of giant buildings and the brilliance of delicate light. And the people, relaxing from their own troubles and worries, enjoying this moment, accepting this feeling of well-being as their due and proper right. He wondered if Bevilacqua was sitting among them now, relaxing, too, from the grim knowledge of his police work.

He had let two taxis pass him. Now he signaled. "To

the entrance of the Piazza Navona," he directed. "As quickly as possible." A smile of delight answered him. He would reach there in possibly less than five minutes. But Providence protected children and drunks and Italian drivers.

He was still thinking of Bevilacqua, the man deep in the background whom he would probably never meet. And then he thought of Bunny Camden's other background friends—the Canadian and the Englishman who weren't diplomats. He'd never meet them, either. Nor the unknown men who had helped Brewster gather the small bits of information that made the whole pattern. Nor the Federal agents from Washington, now waiting at Bari. Nor the man, so deep in the background that he'd never even know all our names or nationalities, who would watch Evans's friends in Perugia and track them back to the countries where their hidden poisons were at work.

Camden had said, ". . . leave Brewster. Then you can relax and concentrate on your girl."

He had answered, "That suits me."

But now, he wasn't so sure of his answer. It wouldn't be easy to sit at a café table, even with Eleanor, enjoying the little world around you, when you kept remembering the background people. How far did they ever relax?

He looked at his watch again as they neared the Piazza Navona. Eleven o'clock. He'd be a few minutes late. Not bad, considering everything. He hoped Brewster's temper had not been too jangled by the alarm clock that kept ringing; but once he heard what had detained Lammiter, he would probably simmer down, then Lammiter began to wonder what Brewster would tell him tonight, once the others had left and they were alone.

One thing was certain: whatever Brewster could tell would be stranger than Lammiter could ever invent.

Fourteen

THE TAXI JOLTED to a sudden halt beside the massive blocks of stone that marked the remains of the gateway to Domitian's stadium. By night, they were dark and grim.

As Lammiter walked quickly through the entrance and saw the lights and shadows of the Piazza Navona before him, he wondered how many chariots had come thundering into this enormous circus and drawn up at the starting gate, horses quivering, drivers tense. And how many men had looked up at the waiting faces and felt a moment of fear, before the mask of pride and readiness was slipped into place again? What made them risk death? Money, imperial favor, or the roar of the crowd?

The crowd . . . the crowd was strangely silent this evening. And then he noticed they were mostly clustering together, toward the east side of the Piazza, as if the wide pavement had tilted and poured them into a massed semicircle. The foreigners dining at the *trattoria* were still sitting over their coffee cups and wine-glasses, but as he passed the hedge that shielded them from the Piazza, he saw that the waiters, at least, were curious. In the intervals of serving, they would group together, talking, watching the other side of the Piazza.

He was opposite the thickest bulge of the crowd, at the center point of all their interest. He looked, casually, hiding his sudden worry. He was looking at the house where Brewster lived. But everything was quiet, peaceful. Lights were in the various windows, in Brewster's, too, up there on the fifth floor. He checked his impulse to cross the Piazza and mix with the crowd. The church of St. Agnes was just ahead of him, and Rosana would be waiting.

But she wasn't there. Not yet. He thought it wiser to cross over to the central fountain in the square and admire Bernini. The church steps felt too naked. He walked slowly round the elaborate sculptures of the fountain. A few children still played, unheeding. An old woman sat slumped on a stone ledge, too old to go running to see or even to care about seeing. A few tourists were wandering around the other fountains; he didn't need to feel conspicuous here.

But his nervousness increased.

When Rosana came, she'd have to lead him round by the side street, as Salvatore had done this afternoon, and they'd enter Brewster's room from its back staircase. A pity he hadn't his pocket flashlight with him, so that they wouldn't trip over the cats. Women were always late; he should stop this worrying. She'd better come soon, though:

he had spent a full ten minutes admiring Bernini's work, and the typical tourist was not as sculpture-conscious as all that. Was she over in that crowd? It was stirring now: people were moving around, talking. What had happened, anyway? Stop worrying. Thirty people or more lived in that house over there. The lights were on in Brewster's window. The curtains were open, and he could see the pot of geraniums on its window sill. Then he saw a man pause at the window for a moment, turning as if he were talking to someone behind him. The man's black silhouette retreated back into the room. There was left only the square of yellow light, and the pot of geraniums, and the strangely curious crowd far below. He felt not worry now but actual fear: Rosana had been punctual enough at noon.

He looked toward the church. Only a couple of middle-aged tourists sat on its steps and studied their tired feet. Was the church open? Was Rosana waiting inside? Perhaps she had seen the crowd and retreated, perhaps she had taken refuge inside. If so, she'd expect him to have enough sense to go in. Only, he thought as he came nearer the church doors, they look very, very closed. He turned, hesitated, and then started toward the crowd, wondering if this was the best thing to do, thankful that his Italian was good enough to find out what was wrong. Everyone in the Piazza seemed to know what was wrong, except the tourists. Rosana might be in the crowd; she *had* to be somewhere.

Now people were drifting away from the crowd, singly or in small groups. They would drift, and stop to argue, then drift again. Except one man who was cutting smartly across the center of the Piazza. Two men broke from the crowd and followed him. It was such an open maneuver that Lammiter halted in amazement. The first man, walking briskly toward the church, seemed unaware of any trouble. But his ears must have been quick, for he heard the hurrying pace behind him and he glanced briefly over his shoulder. His short stride almost became a walking run. He had reached the place where Joe had let Lammiter out of the car this afternoon and driven away with all the luggage; he looked round again. This time there was no doubt that he was being hunted. He suddenly swerved, away from the church, and headed at an open run for the cobbled pavement of the narrow *calle* near him. The two following men were running, too, lightly easily. They were quicker.

Lammiter came to life, and set off after them. He had lost five seconds, there, staring in amazement at the man who had looked around. For it was Joe himself, Joe with his mop of black curling hair and his furrowed brow, looking more surprised than ever.

The narrow street, eight feet wide, a paved dark lane between dark houses, bleakly and scantily lit, was empty except for the three men. The two pursuers had almost caught up with Joe. He turned quickly to face them, his back safely to a wall. He held a knife in his hand. Its blade snapped open. He half crouched, waiting. His lips drawn back from his teeth, he made two sharp jabs at the air. The two men halted.

One of them had something in his hand, ready to strike. He hesitated as he heard Lammiter's running footsteps, jerking his head round for a split second. He said something. His companion was watching the waiting Sicilian, circling round as he, too, brought his gun out of his pocket. He, too, was going to use it to strike. They weren't going to shoot. Why? Lammiter wondered.

Then he understood. Noise. They didn't want noise. So he stopped running, opened his mouth, and with all the breath left in his lungs, he let out a rebel yell. A flutter of pigeons came from the roof tops. Board shutters were flung open from a window above his head, unexpectedly revealing a lighted room, and a stream of angry words in a shrill soprano voice poured down on him before the shutters were banged together again. But, more surprising, an answering rebel yell came from the Piazza behind him. And then the clatter of racing feet and laughter, girls' laughter echoing into the dark canyon of the little street.

The two men looked at each other. The one who gave orders spoke again, as the clatter of feet behind Lammiter suddenly scraped to a halt and a young man's voice called a warning. The girls' laughter changed to an excited squeal. Lammiter was too busy keeping his eyes on the gun now pointing at him to look round and welcome his unknown friends. Then another angry command was spoken, the gun was lowered, and the two men suddenly

took to their heels. They disappeared round the curve of
the street into the night.

They didn't want witnesses either, Lammiter thought.
He walked toward Joe, whose knife had closed and vanished as quickly as it had snapped out. He glanced over his
shoulder. The little group behind him—three girls and a
thin young man—was clustered together as if they didn't
quite know what to do now. "Thanks a lot," Lammiter
called back to them. "Good night."

"I thought you were kidding," the young man said
awkwardly. "That yell—I just thought you were kidding. Was that for real—the gun, I mean?"

"Why," one of the girls said, "I've never seen *anything*
like that in Rome! Why, you just can walk down any old
street. I've never seen anything like *that!*"

"Good night," Lammiter said.

"If I had known," the young man said angrily, "I
wouldn't have brought the girls chasing in here—"

"You would, too!" said another of the girls. "Did you
ever see anything like that! In this setting—it's medeeval,
completely, utterly medeeval."

From above, the shutters banged open again. The four
young faces turned upward in amazement as the stream of
eloquence now emptied over them.

"Come," Joe said, his hand grasping Lammiter's wrist
urgently.

"I'm looking for Rosana—"

"She had to go to the country."

"To the country? But—"

"She's all right. Come—" His impatience grew.

"I've got to see Brewster . . ."

"Later, later. Keep moving." He turned abruptly away,
dropping Lammiter's wrist, and walked on. "Come on," he
said impatiently.

Behind them, a girl's clear voice said, "Isn't she won-
erful? Oh, *how* I *wish* I could speak Italian like *that!*"

Then the young man's voice called to Lammiter,
"Everything okay?"

Lammiter looked back. He waved reassuringly. Then
he caught up with Joe's short quick steps.

Joe said nothing more. He was too busy being cautious. They were, after all, following the same route that
the two men had taken. At the curve in the street, he

paused, keeping close to a wall, studying what lay ahead. There were no recessed doorways. And, just as important, there were witnesses available here, too. Six, in fact. A couple of elderly Italians walking slowly with their dog; four middle-aged foreigners, two husbands, two wives, looking completely frustrated. "Well, *ask* someone, Geoffrey," one of the women was saying impatiently. "We can't wander on these streets forever. Why don't you *ask* someone? There's an American, isn't it?" She quickened her pace toward Lammiter. "Can you tell us where is the Peeasa Navoena?"

"Straight ahead."

"Thank you *so* much." She looked back at the lagging Geoffrey. "See, darling, it was perfectly simple. . . . All one needs to do is use the tongue in one's head. Coming, Betty?" The women walked on, annoyance still quivering. The two men followed. They gave Lammiter a brief nod of thanks and a bitter look.

Lammiter said, "I guess I deserved that. Why hadn't I enough sense to say I was lost, too?"

Joe glanced at him sharply. He said quietly, in control of himself once more, "I parked the car about two blocks away from here. We can talk when we reach it. Now, we use our eyes and our ears." Then he fell silent. He looked like a man with several problems on his mind, all of them grim.

The two blocks stretched nearer to eight before they reached the car, parked beside others in a small square. It was Lammiter's guess that they had skirted round the Piazza Navona, almost to its other side. Or hadn't they? He was certainly as lost as poor old Geoffrey had ever been. The feeling increased as he looked at the car's license plate. "Get in! Quick!" Joe ordered in a low voice.

Lammiter hesitated. Then he got in.

"Where are we going?" he asked. He was too tense. He tried to look less worried than he felt. It was not easy. He kept his eyes ready for the slightest movement from Joe.

"Away from here," Joe answered curtly.

He headed straight for the busiest street, the Corso, with its narrow sidewalks packed with strolling people, overfilled trolley-buses, cars, the eternal Vespas and Lambrettas. They twisted west. They crossed the Tiber briefly, and then came back again to the Via Flaminia. They drove north, then east, then south a little, climbing a hill. And at last, Joe drew up at the edge of a road, where couples in parked cars were far from conspicuous. On one side of the road were gardens, on the other a walk with seats for the view, for here the ground fell away abruptly to a lower level of streets. Lammiter could see over the roof tops, far beneath, across the whole city with its domed churches and lighted monuments.

"We'll keep the windows closed, and we'll talk," Joe said, taking out a twisted pack of cigarettes and offering one to Lammiter, "and *then* we'll know where we are going."

Lammiter said, "Keep it short." He was thinking now of the telephone call he must make to Camden. Nothing was working out the way they had expected. "What's gone wrong?"

Joe was silent.

"I saw a man at the window. Was it Salvatore?"

"That was Bevilacqua. Sam was down in the Piazza, with the crowd. We were both worried about you. Couldn't see you over by the church. Rosana told me to look for you there."

"I was staying well out of sight behind the fountain," said Lammiter, lamely. It had seemed an intelligent move, at the time. Now it seemed frankly silly. "I arrived late." He saw that Joe was watching him even more carefully than he had been watching Joe. And suddenly, too, he realized that Bevilacqua's visit was not just a friendly call, that the crowd gathered in the street was not grouped round a traffic accident. "What has happened to Brewster?" he asked tensely.

"He's dead."

"Dead?" The shocked word was jolted out of him. For several moments, he could say nothing. "How?" he asked at last. "A fake suicide?"

"Not this time. He was lying stretched out on his bed with the fiasco broken at its neck and dropped beside him. He had been struck a blow on the head."

"Was there no struggle? Didn't he shout? Did no one hear anything?" He was frankly incredulous. "A man was murdered in a room with a window wide open on a piazza crowded with people. . . ."

"Men like Brewster don't shout," Joe said abruptly. "They are trained not to shout. And there was no struggle in the room. The bed—disarranged a little." Joe was watching Lammiter very carefully now, but the American was too troubled to notice. "It had been smoothed down again, perhaps?"

"I don't get it." Lammiter was following his own thoughts. "If there was no struggle, then he was asleep. If he was asleep, who let anyone get in? And one blow from a bottle—a fiasco padded with straw—that was enough to kill Brewster?" His face showed complete disbelief. "It must have been a hell of a blow."

Joe took a deep breath, almost of relief. "You talk like a policeman, my friend. All these questions . . ."

Lammiter stared at him. Guilty men didn't bring up the dangerous questions, guilty men didn't search for answers. Was that what the Italian was thinking?

Joe said very quietly, "You were right to have doubts. They smothered him first, with a nice soft pillow."

Lammiter rolled down the window, and threw away his half-finished cigarette. He took several deep breaths to steady his nerves. He felt sick, half stifled. A crippled man, lying helpless, perhaps asleep . . . He rolled the window up again, leaving a couple of inches open for fresh air.

"I felt that way myself," Joe agreed. "I can usually run faster than I did tonight." His eyes, watching Lammiter carefully, had lost their grim look of suspicion.

"But how—"

"Let the police find the answers. That's what they're paid to do."

"And that's another thing! How did the police get there, anyway? Who told them?"

"There was an alarm clock that kept ringing. A neighbor went to complain. She found the door unlocked, and then Brewster. She started screaming. That brought a couple of policemen up from the Piazza."

"The door had been left unlocked—and we were to walk right in?" His voice was bitter. He was beginning to understand why the unnecessary blow from the bottle had ever been struck. Rosana had handled that bottle. And there were fingerprints on the glasses, too. Fingerprints everywhere, his own included. This was much better than any faked suicide. Rosana and he would have to be questioned, perhaps held by the police. Perhaps? Most certainly. And for how long—a day, two days, three? "They made sure we weren't even going to reach Perugia," he said with rising anger.

That was a mistake. He knew it the moment it had slipped from his tongue. He remembered, too late, that Brewster had told neither Joe nor Salvatore nor Bevilacqua about Perugia, or Evans, or Pirotta's main interests.

Joe was watching him again. There was a new gleam of interest in his eyes.

Lammiter said quickly, "How did you learn all this about Brewster, anyway?"·

"I reached Brewster's door just before eleven o'clock. As you said, it was open, and I walked right in. I walked right into the police."

"And did you want to meet them?" Lammiter was sarcastic.

"A Sicilian wants to meet—?" Joe laughed that off, briefly.

"The crowd could have told you there were policemen up there. But you went on upstairs." Lammiter paused. "And then the police let you go. How obliging of them, how very—"

"And thanks for helping me, after that," Joe said, branching off. "If you hadn't, I'd probably be in the Tiber right now, or dumped from a fishing boat off Ostia tomorrow. You know—it's a pity you don't trust me more."

"I trust you enough to ask you to take me to a telephone. And quickly." He touched Camden's card in his pocket to reassure himself it was still there, and brought out his cigarettes. "Have one of mine?"

"Thanks." But Joe made no move to start the car. "Why did you come running after me tonight?"

"I wanted to make sure I'd see my typewriter again."

"Save the jokes until I feel more like laughing."

"To tell you the honest truth," Lammiter said, "I just didn't think. I saw a couple of men on your heels, and I started running. It was just as simple as that."

"You just didn't think." Joe could be sarcastic, too.

"Not at first. When I started thinking, I let out a yell."

"Who were those men?"

"I don't know."

"Nor I," Joe said. He heaved one large and weary sigh. "It's a pity you don't trust me more," he repeated very gently. "I've got some questions that keep bothering me."

"Look, Joe, drive me to a telephone. You'll get your answers quickest that way."

"But I don't drive so well with questions on my mind," Joe said sadly. "Now why should those two men have been looking for me tonight? I've never seen them before in my life, and I thought I knew most of these boys. They aren't connected with any narcotics ring. Nor is Perugia."

"Who would be interested in my answers as well as you? It couldn't be Bevilacqua, could it?" And for the first time in this fencing match, Lammiter felt he had pierced through Joe's guard.

Joe started the car. "Don't guess so much," he said sharply. "That could lead you into real trouble."

"It already has." It was midnight now. Lammiter would never make that plane, even if he had wanted to. He wouldn't make any plane tomorrow, or the next day either. He glanced at Joe, who was both silent and angry. "Don't worry, Joe. My guess was all my own. I don't think any of the men you are hunting would even notice."

"Notice what?" Joe tried to be casual. But no one likes hearing his own mistakes.

"When we met, this afternoon, you were talking tough American. You were a man who had knocked around, done odd jobs, driven cars, become attached to the Di Feo family, then to the princess, part-time handyman, personal retainer, and probably black marketeer on the side. With a heart of gold, of course. But now you aren't talking that kind of language. Because you aren't thinking in that kind of language."

Joe glanced at him sharply.

"I'd say you were now a detective, an agent of some kind, one of Bevilacqua's bright boys, who's got several problems to solve. Where did you go to college in America?"

Suddenly, Joe laughed. It was a real laugh. "I like you," he said, keeping his eyes determinedly on the traffic. "You've got a sense of humor. Me, Ginseppe Rocco, one of Bevilacqua's bright boys . . ."

"Yes, that's what I'd say," Lammiter went on quietly, "except for one thing."

Joe was guarded now. "What's that?"

"The license plate on your car. Its last three numbers are the ones Rosana noticed last night when a car tried to pick her up. It's the number Brewster noticed when a car tried to run him down. Who could have borrowed your car, Joe?"

"Mannaggia!" Joe stared at him. For a moment, his face showed alarm; then it became blank again. "So," he said at last, "the laugh is on me, eh?" He fell silent. But Lammiter noticed that the car's speed had increased as much as the traffic would allow. Whatever Joe was, he certainly knew how to handle a car.

Fifteen

ONE OF THE greatest charms of Rome is the fact that it is still a living city—not just a collection of office buildings, business headquarters, and stores which all close down at night, leaving bleak lights in their windows for cleaners and watchmen. There, the streets are not suddenly emptied after the working day ends, to let the tourists wander around like dispirited ghosts searching through a graveyard. There, the people not only work but live. Round the corner from the main streets are always the little streets and little squares, with apartments and flats and rooms and houses. There are trees, and flowers, and gardens surrounding great villas, the green touch to keep a city from turning into a suffocating blanket of stone and plaster.

Now, as Joe swung it away from the noise and light, the car turned into a street where most people had already gone to bed. They abandoned the car there, leaving it beside others equally nondescript. For a moment, Lammiter had the impulse to run, to get to a telephone. But he wasn't sure where he was, or in which direction to run, and a running man would attract attention. Besides, Joe's quick eyes were expecting a little trouble. He nodded, as if congratulating Lammiter on his wisdom, as the American waited for him while he locked the car. Then, at a brisk pace, they cut through a small square, walked across a busy intersection where a large movie house was still open, and entered a long street of high-walled gardens surrounding large villas. There was little stirring, a few pedestrians, an occasional car. The noise of the city's late pleasure traffic became a distant background to the peace of the night. It seemed warmer here, as if the trees and the flowers had trapped the hot sun and still fondled it in the moonlight. The air was heavy with the fragrance of jasmine and gardenias.

They passed two villas, standing far back from the street, dark and mysterious in their nest of trees. (They looked quite empty, as though the owners had left for their summer places among the hill towns.) As they approached the third garden, Joe pulled a ring heavy with keys from his pocket. Ahead was the entrance to this villa, an enormous double gate of elaborately wrought iron, set into high stone walls, a polished brass bell at one side and a shield with a coat of arms above. They were passing the gates. Joe glanced into the gardens. He swore softly and his pace increased. Lammiter glanced, too.

In that brief moment he saw a gatehouse, dark and empty, and then a villa, standing well back from the street, commanding a circular driveway. Its rooms were lighted, its handsome portico a blaze of hard brilliance. And he saw, too, the coat of arms over the gate, a wolf's head quartered with three beehives. Wasn't that the same coat of arms he had glimpsed in miniature today on the door of the princess's car?

Beyond the main entrance lay a small narrow gate, chained and padlocked, partly overgrown by a tangle of leaves and branches climbing along the wall. But someone had oiled the padlock and the hinges of this unused gate, for Joe unlocked it easily and swung it open soundlessly. Quickly, with a last glance along the quiet street, he pulled Lammiter inside the villa's garden. Carefully, he closed the gate and secured it once more. They were standing in a stable yard at the back of the gatehouse. The building, Lammiter now saw, was a garage, politely turning its honest utilitarian face toward the yard away from the painted elegance of the villa. (Once it had been a stable and coach house, for he passed a disused horse trough and pump as he followed Joe across the paved yard.)

Joe unlocked a panel of the garage door soundlessly,

swung it open a few feet, and beckoned him in. He stood in complete darkness as the door was closed. He could hear Joe fumbling against a wall. A click, and a bare light glared down at them from a high beam. In front of him stood a venerable and highly polished Lancia.

"Quick!" Joe said, pointing to a rough flight of wooden stairs at one end of the garage. "And when you get to the top, wait. Or you'll break a leg."

Lammiter left Joe at the light switch and passed three horse stalls, a heap of tires, neatly stacked oilcans, an ancient carriage, bridles and harness hanging from hooks. Then he began climbing. At the top was a dark recess. He waited there. He had to. The light didn't penetrate as far as that. Now Joe switched it off, and the blackness was complete again.

The minute seemed interminable. And then a wooden step gave a faint groan, a more solid piece of blackness stood beside him, and Joe grasped his arm. "One moment," Joe said, edging past him, opening a narrow door. Beyond was an attic: a floor of bare boards cluttered with islands of trunks and boxes, all striped with the pale white light of stars and moon that came through the slatted shutters of the windows.

"Quiet!" warned Joe angrily. For the pale light was deceptive: Lammiter, on his way over to the nearest window, had misjudged a shadow and stumbled against a pile of harness. There was a smell of dry leather, the feeling of grit under his feet, the sound of a bat's steady whir as it circled under the low rafters. He reached the window. It was, more accurately, an oblong for ventilation, tucked into the shade of the pink-tiled roof, with only the slatted shutters for covering. But the view was excellent. He could see the driveway, with the villa far to his right; slightly to his left, almost below him, were the front gates.

"The princess goes to bed late," he said softly. Joe had no need to tell him to keep his voice almost to a whisper. From the garden the gentle splash of water in some hidden fountain came so clearly into the attic that he needed no reminder that all noise was amplified by the stillness around him or that these ventilation windows were unglazed.

Joe began talking, very quietly, in Italian. Lammiter

swung round, almost falling over a couple of leather bags and a typewriter. He stood staring at Joe, who had not taken leave of his senses but was using all of them, in a long complicated conversation over a telephone. In this attic of ancient and abandoned possessions, the small black telephone was a strange intrusion. It had been installed in the wooden frame of the door itself, inside a panel cut in the jamb.

Joe had been talking about his car, probably (he spoke too quickly for Lammiter to be sure) giving its location. There was something about number plates, and a change; something about watching a garage. And then Joe began talking about Lammiter, for he looked across at the American for a quick moment and then dropped into a dialect, Sicialian possibly, which was completely unintelligible. This part was brief. Very unflattering, Lammiter thought with a smile. It was the first smile he had felt like giving for a long time. A telephone was a great help to morale.

Joe hooked back the receiver into the inside of the panel and swung it shut.

"My turn," Lammiter said.

"I must wait for a call."

"I must make one! Or shall I start heaving a few trunks around and give an Apache scream? That's worse than a rebel yell. I've all kinds of sound effects ready to use."

"I believe you would," Joe said. But he was almost smiling, and he swung the panel open again. So Lammiter at least had been declared friendly. He stepped carefully over the typewriter case, looked down and exclaimed, "Hey, that's mine!" but kept on moving as quickly as possible to the telephone. Joe might change his mind.

"I told you they'd be safe," said Joe. "You should trust me more."

"I trust as much as I'm trusted." Lammiter reached in his pocket. "I need some light," he said angrily, trying to make out Camden's writing. Was that an eight or a three? He felt for a match.

"Shield it," came Joe's quick warning.

Lammiter obeyed, put through the number, and waited. "I gather you aren't supposed to be here."

"Only when I'm working on the Lancia. I lock up, hand the key in at the house, get the gates locked behind me. There was a burglary at the villa last year, so now everything is locked and—"

"Sh!" Lammiter said. It was an American voice speaking at the other end of the line. "Camden, please. Bill Lammiter speaking." Joe had moved across to the ventilation slats. He seemed to be watching the villa, but he was listening. Lammiter was sure of that.

"Oh yes," the voice said as if that was no surprise.

"There's been trouble tonight. Can I reach Camden himself?"

"Just a moment. Here is where he can be reached meanwhile." A number, vaguely familiar, was rattled off. "Got it?" It was repeated. It was Eleanor Halley's number.

"That's enough!" Joe's urgent whisper came across the still attic. But Lammiter had already got the number. "Shut up!" he said, to silence Joe's steady stream of fine Sicilian curses. "Bunny? There's bad news."

"So I've just heard." Camden's matter-of-fact voice was a real slice of comfort. "It's breaking fast. Must be more of an emergency than we guessed." He paused. Then he said, "There's trouble here, too, Bill."

"Something has happened to—" He couldn't finish. He hadn't expected that news. And he hadn't expected the news to hit him this way, either.

"Take it easy. She isn't here."

"Isn't there?" he asked blankly. And then, savagely, "Where the hell is she?"

"*Zitti!*" Joe warned from the window. "Sh!"

"Take it easy, Bill," Camden was saying. "She left a note for the maid. She says she'll be back on Monday."

"Monday—" Today was Thursday. No—Friday now. "And where has she *gone?*"

"She didn't say."

"Did she take any clothes—any—"

"It's difficult to judge. The bedroom's in a state of eruption."

"She was packing. Going home tomorrow. Look, Bunny, stay there. I'll be right around."

"You stay *here!*" said Joe, looking angrily over his shoulder.

"No, don't come around," Camden's voice said. "That gains nothing. The case is in good hands."

"What happened? For God's sake, Bunny, tell me what's been going on?"

"I got in touch with that Englishman I mentioned. He was definitely interested. He wanted to talk to Miss Halley. We telephoned. No answer. I thought we'd better go round to her place and see her. We kept knocking at her door. No answer. So I telephoned the police, they wakened the porter downstairs, and we all got in. There was a lot of packing interrupted and dirty dishes. But no girl. No photographs, either."

"But—"

"Have you still got that snapshot?"

"Yes."

"Good. Where are you?"

"In a loft, guarded by a watchdog called Giuseppe Rocco." There was a quick rush of light footsteps behind Lammiter.

"Giuseppe Rocco?" Camden's voice repeated. Joe's hand forced its way between the receive and Lammiter's mouth. It was not a happy gesture. Lammiter was never in a mood to be gagged, least of all now. He kicked sideways and aimed the hardest blow he could manage with his free hand at Joe's chin. "Don't do that, don't you ever do that to me!" he said in sudden fury as Joe's grip was forced off his lips.

Joe's hand was in his pocket, his balance regained, his knees slightly bent, crouched, ready. His lips were narrowed with an anger that matched Lammiter's.

"What's going on there?" Bunny's voice was suddenly alarmed. "Wait—put Rocco on the phone—here's a friend of his—Bill, put Rocco on the phone!"

"For you," Lammiter said, holding out the receiver. Joe straightened his body slowly. His right hand was still in his pocket. His eyes were wary and never left Lammiter, but he took the receiver.

Lammiter sat down on a trunk. There was sweat on his brow. He took out his handkerchief, and inside it he felt the small negative and its print. There was still one piece of identification left about Evans, still one photograph. But Eleanor could identify the man even better. Eleanor . . . Now a cold sweat broke over his brow.

Whoever was talking to Joe had authority, information, and—finally—instructions to give. Whatever he was saying had a noticeable effect: Joe's face was astonished, but it was no longer troubled. He even smiled and nodded encouragingly over to Lammiter. Now, thought Lammiter wryly, all I have to worry about is Eleanor.

He waited impatiently for the first sign of the end of Joe's instructions. But Joe gave his own brief report, in his very best Italian, before the call seemed near an end. Probably he had been on the telephone no more than five minutes all told, but to Lammiter they seemed an hour. He signaled as Joe was giving his final *"Si, si, capo,"* and held out his hand.

"The American wants to speak to his friend," Joe said into the phone and handed it amicably over to Lammiter. Then he walked back to the window.

Camden's voice said, "I think that's settled a lot of things."

"Where can I give you that snapshot?"

"Rocco has all the instructions."

"But, look—"

"This isn't our country, fellow," Camden said gently. "Let Bevilacqua and his boys handle this."

"And we do *nothing?*"

"Oh, we'll help when and if needed."

"Bunny—" he tried to talk calmly, "any guesses about Eleanor? Any evidence—any—"

"Not yet. But Bevilacqua is definitely interested. Brewster's murder makes all these problems very much his business."

"Where's Pirotta?"

"Seems to have left town."

"When?"

"I'm told he left his house around nine thirty, with luggage. He was driving. Just before ten o'clock his car was seen outside Rome, on the Via Flaminia, heading north. Looks as if he's the advance guard for Perugia."

Lammiter didn't speak. Just before ten o'clock he had been saying good-by to Eleanor.

"Take it easy, Bill," Camden's calm voice said once more. "We'll get all these bastards, every God-damned one of them. See you tomorrow. Follow instructions." He hung up.

Lammiter swore and tried to recall the number. Joe,

at the window again, said quietly, *"Basta basta*! Finish!
Stop!" He beckoned urgently.

Lammiter took a deep breath, a slow deep breath. He
hung the telephone receiver on its cradle, and closed the
panel back into place. Slowly, he went over to the window. He felt suddenly tired, tired and defeated. Joe, on
the contrary, was a man full of restored confidence, a
man who looked as if he were sure of the road he was
following. Lammiter asked bitterly, "How about that
phone call you were expecting?"

"Oh, forget it," Joe said, friendly now and smiling, too.
So it had been Bevilacqua whom Joe had wanted to contact. Lammiter's wishful guessing had been right, after
all, but that fact gave him no comfort at the moment.
"How good is Bevilacqua?" he asked. Good enough to
find Eleanor long before three days were over?

"Look, will you? Look!" said Joe. Lammiter looked.

In front of the villa, slowly descending its steps, was a
man dressed in a dinner jacket. Beside him, a white scarf
over her shoulders, was the princess. Their voices carried over the garden in the still air, but they were still
too far away to be clearly understood. They were speaking in English, the man protesting politely ". . . no
need. . . ." The princess was equally polite, ". . . no
trouble at all. . . ." An elderly woman, short and fat,
dressed in unrelieved black, came hurrying after them
with a cloak for the princess. Then they began walking
toward the gate, the woman in black keeping a discreet
distance behind her mistress and the departing visitor.
The voices became clearer. And now, too, Lammiter
could recognize Bertrand Whitelaw. The Englishman was
no longer quite so amused or amusing as he had been
yesterday at Doney's. He even looked uncomfortable, ill at
ease. He was trying to explain his late visit, and a man
who makes excuses is vulnerable.

The princess, of course, was enjoying herself. "It's
always delightful to see you, Bertrand. Even at midnight."
She had lost little of her incisive charm. "Now don't
apologize again. I *like* to walk by moonlight. It's so good
for one's memories. At my age, Bertrand, that is what I
live on."

"Principessa—" He glanced back at the maid, and
hesitated.

"Maria and I have been together for fifty-four years. Nothing surprises her. Besides, most conveniently, she knows not one word of English. You were saying—?"

"Principessa—where is Luigi? I've been trying to find him, but he has left Rome."

Lammiter, at the mention of Pirotta's name, stopped watching the scene with a casual eye. He was really listening now.

"Ah!" the princess said with drama to match the moonlit garden. "So you came to ask about Luigi, and all the time I was flattering myself that you were worried about me."

"But I was. When you didn't appear at Sylvia's dinner tonight—"

"Oh, I was suddenly tired of enormous dinner parties. And of Sylvia. She is *so* correct. How did she like my telegram?"

"She didn't read it to us."

"How very disappointing! Of course, telegrams aren't the politest forms of refusal. Don't you want to know what I said?"

"Of course," Whitelaw said patiently.

"Impossible to be with you. Lies will follow."

"It sounds much better in its original French."

"Bertrand, you know everything! Yes, I suppose it does. But I've always wanted to use it. The French have such a knack for the cynical phrase. Don't they?"

At the window above, Lammiter shook his head. The princess had such a knack for confusing an issue. Not much was left, now, of Whitelaw's simple question about Luigi Pirotta.

But Whitelaw had not given up altogether. "I heard tonight that there seems to have been some kind of— trouble between Luigi and Miss Halley."

"Trouble? Oh, he and his little American have decided not to get married. Young people are *so* changeable."

"I can't understand it."

"Who has ever understood people in love! But I'm sure our friends at dinner did their best to find an explanation for everything. What did they say—the American has had five husbands, and Luigi likes young boys?"

"No one was being malicious."

"How odd! Or perhaps they hadn't had enough warning."

"Tivoli was blamed, however. It seems the trouble started there, two or three nights ago."

"Now really, Bertrand—how completely ridiculous!"

"One of the guests at dinner was a friend of Miss Halley. She lunched with her on the day after Tivoli. She insisted that the quarrel was not at all serious. And certainly, today at Doney's, I didn't notice anything wrong. It really is so—so inexplicable. I'm a little troubled. After all—" He hesitated.

"You *are* Luigi's friend," the princess finished for him, with a touch of amusement.

Upstairs, Lammiter stood rigid. His anxiety was rising as steadily as a bead of mercury at noon. How many people had been at that dinner party? How many servants? Ears listening, tongues repeating. Tivoli . . . Tivoli. Throw one small stone into a pool, and the ripples spread out and out.

The princess had moved to the gates. In Italian, she gave Maria the command to unlock them.

"Would you tell Luigi I'd like to get in touch with him?" Whitelaw asked.

"Why do you keep thinking *I* shall see Luigi?" The princess's voice was sharp with annoyance. "He never asks my advice."

"Perhaps not. But he always takes your help."

"Why should I give it?" she demanded. "This morning, I wished he were—he were dead. That shocks you?"

"If you want me to be shocked—yes."

"Good night, Bertrand."

He still hesitated. "Principessa—I don't want to alarm you, but as I rang at the gate tonight for Maria to let me in, I noticed two men in your garden—walking around the side of the villa."

"Servants."

"They seemed to vanish so quickly when they saw me."

"Naturally. They know very well that they are not supposed to walk in the garden. Good night." She offered him her hand in a very final gesture.

He kissed it. "If you need help, do call on me. At any time. And I'm sorry I troubled you so needlessly—"

She laughed again. "I do believe you want to protect

me, Bertrand! I am touched, indeed I am.——Maria, open the gate!—No car, Bertrand? Did you *walk?*"

"I prefer to walk," Whitelaw said stiffly and went into the street. Maria locked the gates behind him.

"Come, Maria," the princess said clearly in Italian. "Let us look at the gardenias, and so to bed."

Lammiter straightened his back and stretched his shoulders. What had brought Whitelaw visiting at this hour? Some talk at a dinner party? Or had the Englishman heard something more than gossip? Then Lammiter began wondering about Whitelaw himself. He ought to have asked Camden about Whitelaw, but he had forgotten. Or, rather, other questions had pushed that one to the back of his mind. "Joe—" he began, but Joe made a sign for caution. Something in the garden was holding his attention.

The princess had not gone to look at the gardenias. She was standing quite motionless in a patch of moonlight on the driveway, looking toward her house. Waiting? Suddenly the lights over the door of the villa were switched off. A man hurried from its steps, cutting across the paved garden which the driveway encircled. Lammiter's body stiffened abruptly. The running man was Luigi Pirotta. He was now reaching the princess. He said, angrily, "I thought he'd never go! What did he want?"

The princess lifted a hand in warning. "Voices carry," she reminded him.

"What did he want?" he repeated, more quietly.

She said coldly, "You cannot leave yet. Bertrand is on foot. Walking slowly. And the street is very long." She looked away from him, wrapping the cloak around her more closely. It was a gesture of separation.

"I have still some things to explain," he said gently. "Maria—"

"She will not listen."

"No? Come into the garage. She can't hear us there." He entered the courtyard. She hesitated. "Maria," she called softly to the woman still at the gate. "Keep watch!" Then she followed Pirotta.

As the garage door scraped on the cement floor, Joe moved swiftly away from the window toward the door, using the sounds below to cover his own light footsteps. Lammiter had not moved quickly enough. He was caught halfway across the wooden floor. He didn't trust either its loose boards or the treacherous light. He tested a trunk lying flat on the floor beside him. It seemed solid enough. He sat down. That way, there would be no danger of any sound from him. Joe had opened the attic door about two inches. He looked across at Lammiter and nodded; then he bent his head, listening.

The voices came up to Lammiter faintly from the dark garage. The lights had not been switched on down there. The garage door must be open. The voices were hushed, talking in Italian, sibilant and energetic, but too quick for Lammiter to understand. And somehow, he was relieved. He did not have to listen. He had had enough of the uncomfortable feeling of eavesdropping. He would be no good at this kind of business, he thought as he watched Joe. He rested his head in his hands, trying to get his own problems balanced. He had to fight hard to keep down a rising impulse to walk right downstairs, confront Pirotta, and drag him to the nearest police station. Yet it wouldn't solve anything. Joe would be doing exactly that, right now, if it was the answer. Joe was in command here. "Follow instructions," Camden had said. Yes, sir, I'm following instructions, sir, Lammiter thought. He was sitting on a battered trunk in a disused attic, sweating out instructions. Had Camden thought of that? Or of the sound of Pirotta's voice, so gentle and suave? The princess had been sharp and angry at first. No longer. Pirotta was a persuader.

Then he suddenly thought, Pirotta is here; he hadn't been leaving Rome just before ten o'clock, traveling north on the Via Flaminia. He was in Rome when Eleanor vanished. Had she gone with Pirotta?

Lammiter rose to his feet, but even as he moved to the door, the car's engine started. Joe's look of warning changed to amazement and his signal for silence froze in the air. Caution was unnecessary, anyway, at this moment: the Lancia's drone smothered all sounds.

Lammiter stood in the recess at the top of the stairway, looking down into the empty garage. He was too late. Or Pirotta had been too quick. The car was already in the yard, swinging toward the driveway. The princess was standing very still at the door of the garage. Maria was beside her, anxious. "I opened the gate," Maria said. The princess said nothing. "The gates are open," Maria repeated, raising her voice. In the driveway, the car's engine was running smoothly, softly, then faded to nothing.

"Yes, yes," the princess said wearily. But she did not move away. "Maria, did I do right? Did I?" Her voice broke, and her head drooped. Her hands went to her face to conceal it.

Lammiter heard a light rustle of movement behind him. Joe had moved away from the door, back to the window. What had drawn his interest there? And now Lammiter heard the car once again: it was still there in the grounds. It hadn't left, not yet. As he reached the window, he saw it start from the front door of the villa to sweep down the driveway. It slowed for a brief moment at the open gates. Then it was through, turning left, traveling fast.

"No one drives that car but me." Joe's low voice was bitter. "How do you like that, eh? That's one thing I'd have sworn—Why, she's always worrying about one little scratch, and he drives like a crazy man." Then he looked at Lammiter. "Don't worry, my friend," he said gently. "I heard all their talk. It's in here." He tapped his forehead and grinned widely. "The princess said she would telephone Alberto to expect Pirotta. There's only one Alberto she would telephone. He's the caretaker of her house up in the hills. Don't worry, we know where he's taking the girl."

"Girl?"

"Sure. His girl. He picked her up at the villa. That's why the car stopped there. What's wrong? Don't—" His voice changed and his arm shot out. But Lammiter dodged.

"That's my girl, too, Joe." And he started downstairs.

Sixteen

LAMMITER SLIPPED into the courtyard. Maria was coming away from the front gates, heading in his direction as if she would now attend to the garage doors. She didn't catch sight of him until he had reached the corner of the building. She gave a hoarse little scream; and the princess, walking very slowly toward the house, halted and turned round.

Lammiter stepped into the driveway. "Good evening," he said to the frightened Maria. "Or good morning, perhaps."

"Oh!" the princess said. For once, she had nothing else to say. But as Maria rushed to her side (whether to defend or to be saved, Lammiter was not quite certain), the princess took command. "Quiet, Maria! Go to the house." And then, as Maria retreated unwillingly, the princess said, "Good morning it is, Mr. Lammiter." Maria, more reassured, covered another ten feet toward the villa, but there she stood, loyally disobedient, her face masked in pleasant suspicion.

The princess looked at him searchingly. She was angry. "All gates are locked. Am I to believe you climbed over my wall?"

He looked down at his blackish-gray trousers liberally streaked with dust. He tried to brush it off. "I'm sorry—" he said awkwardly. "I just had to see you." He hoped he sounded like a man who had indeed climbed a wall.

"The usual way to enter is to ring the bell at the gate," she said.

"I didn't want to waken everyone at this time of night."

"Most thoughtful of you." She was still acid. "And why were you determined to wake *me?*"

"I saw your car drive off."

She hesitated. "Indeed? And so you came to warn me? How *very* kind," she said mockingly. She obviously believed that attack was the best defense.

He tried a little attack of his own. "Pirotta was driving."

"Oh?" She stood very still.

"And Eleanor was with him, wasn't she?"

"It's very late for questions, Mr. Lammiter. Come and see me tomorrow." She smiled, almost kindly, and turned away.

"You have one habit I like," he said. "If you can't tell the truth, you don't tell lies."

She halted and faced him. "Why are you here?"

He said, "Yesterday at Doney's you invited me to stay in Italy. I've decided to accept. That's all."

"I gave you more than an invitation. I gave you warning." She suddenly burst out, *"Why* didn't you talk sense into Eleanor's head and make her leave?"

"She was leaving today."

"Too late, too late," she said angrily. "Why, why did she ever come to Rome, why did Luigi have to fall in love with her? Why didn't he marry Rosana, and there would have been none of this trouble?" She halted abruptly and controlled her emotions. "Stop glaring at me like that! Do you think I'd ever have let Luigi take my car if I didn't believe we could still save Eleanor?"

"From what?"

The princess hesitated. "I only know that there is danger. She knows too much about matters that do not concern her. She must be hidden. For her own safety. Just a few days, that's all. *Please* believe me, Mr. Lammiter. Do you think that I shall ever have let Luigi take her away if—"

"Was she all right?" he interrupted quickly.

She looked at him with astonishment. "But of course!"

"Did she go of her own free will?"

"Really, Mr. Lammiter! One would imagine—"

"It's too late for imagining. I want to *know*. Did she go of her own free will?"

"Yes." She watched his face. "I'm sorry," she said more gently. "She had to go. There was no other solution. She will be safe, I assure you."

"No other solution?" he asked. "You could have telephoned the American Embassy if Eleanor was in danger. You could have called the police."

"Impossible!"

"Why?"

"Because we want no publicity. There is danger in publicity. Danger for Eleanor—and for Luigi. We must keep everything discreet: no scandal, no disgrace."

"That's going to be difficult."

"Not so difficult. Luigi has resigned from his company. You see, he, at least, took my warning at Doney's."

"Do you actually believe that resigning from a company—an innocent company at that—is going to have any effect on evidence?"

"What evidence will stand up without witnesses?"

"His firm would know from its books that he had

been up to mischief. What about the shipments of drugs he has sidetracked?"

"But its directors may not want such publicity, Mr. Lammiter. As you say, their firm is a good one, solid, respectable. It took too long to build up that reputation. Do you think they want it destroyed overnight? One touch of scandal . . ."

"Sure," he said bitterly. "It would empty their pockets, too." So honest men would form a solid wall of respectability around Pirotta. And the princess would cover up Pirotta's guilt for the sake of the family name. What about the crooks who had worked for him? But criminals rarely talked: they wouldn't give evidence against him. They would cover up for him, more than anyone, in order to save their own skins.

The princess was watching him with marked displeasure. She said coldly, "Must Americans always think of money?"

He looked at her, equally coldly. "But dear Luigi never thought of money, indeed not. I suppose he was only dedicated to the noble cause of spreading dope addiction?"

For a moment, her eyes blazed with anger. For a moment, he thought she was going to turn on her heel and walk away. But she did not. She dropped her eyes. Perhaps that was as near to an apology as she could ever come. "It's all over," she said in a low voice. "All that degrading and evil business is over. He has given me his word." She faced Lammiter again. "Don't think that I am excusing anything he has done," she said almost fiercely.

"Has he promised to drop all his political ambitions, too? Or at least change them to open, honest politics?"

"Politics?" She clearly did not understand what he was saying.

"If Eleanor is in danger, it doesn't come from the men who worked in narcotics."

"Do not underestimate them. They are vindictive and dangerous. Believe me, Mr. Lammiter, the danger is very great."

"We're talking at cross-purposes," he said impatiently. "What I meant—"

"Do you know what you really mean? Why, you don't even know what you've *done!* You are to blame for all this, Mr. Lammiter. And you stand there—"

"*I'm* to blame?"

"If anything happens to Eleanor, you will be responsible. You instigated, persuaded her to—" She made a gesture of distaste. "No doubt you had the most patriotic motives for acting as one of your country's agents. But why draw Eleanor into—"

"But that's nonsense. Who told you this, anyway? Pirotta? Surely you don't believe—"

"Why was she trying to reach you this evening? Why did she want to see you before she left Rome?"

"She was trying to reach me—where?" And then suddenly he remembered Eleanor's telephone calls to his hotel. "Just let me explain," he began quietly. "It was—"

"How *could* you have drawn her into all this hideous mess?" The princess was glad to scold someone. "I hold no brief for Luigi, but he, at least, is trying to protect her."

"Does Eleanor believe that?"

The princess shrugged her shoulders. "She is a very strange girl. She kept quite silent all the time she was with Maria."

"You were not with her?"

"Luigi had a great deal to tell me. After all, he did owe me some explanation."

"And a very good job he made of it."

"That is quite enough," the princess said sharply. "Maria, let this man out at the gate."

"This man will go when he is good and ready," Lammiter said.

"I shall call the police."

"You should have called them an hour ago." He had scored a point: she must have had that impulse and then smothered it. Or been persuaded out of it. He pressed on. "Better still, you should have had an honest talk, alone, with Eleanor. Then you would have found out that she doesn't know one thing about the narcotics racket. She is in no danger from that."

"But—but she *is* in danger."

"Yes," he said very quietly.

"From what?" she asked quickly.

"I tried to tell you."

"From what?" she repeated. And now, the doubts that

had troubled her and been silenced were stirring again.

It was a good time to leave, Lammiter decided. "Ask Mr. Big," he said.

"Mr. Big?"

"Mr. Big the Second. Dear Luigi. Oh, he isn't anywhere near that, yet. But that's the direction he is taking. Not fascist, of course. That's been tried. And there won't be any march on Rome, this time. His friends without faces have more subtle methods than that."

She said haltingly, "Friends—without faces?"

"Yes, his friends at Tivoli, who don't like being photographed. Good night, Principessa." He bowed. To the maid he said, "Don't trouble about the gates, Maria. I can go out the way I came in." He smiled for her. She had not understood what he said, for he had been too tired to face any Italian verbs. It had been a mistake, after all, he thought wearily, for him to try to talk with the princess.

He made an effort and walked smartly down the driveway. He was more than tired: he was exhausted. The gate was near, and the wall beside it looked higher than he remembered. His exit line had been good theater, but a damned silly idea. He had enough sense still left to keep well away from the garage. Would the princess watch? No, probably not. She would never be caught watching anyone. But she would have no objections to Maria's watching and telling her what the crazy foreigner did.

He refrained from looking round. And then, almost at the gates, he noticed how the bushes and flowering trees had been planted partly to screen the entrance to the yard, partly to soften the bleak stone. He plunged through this mass of shrubbery, and behind its shelter made his way slowly and carefully along the wall. It took some time. He reached the second gateway by which Joe and he had entered, and there was the path to lead him back to the courtyard. He couldn't be seen here from the driveway. He halted, and waited. If Maria didn't come round the corner of the garage in the next few minutes, he'd risk that bare and vulnerable courtyard. Everything seemed bleak and purposeless. What am I doing here, anyway? he asked himself angrily. Eleanor had gone of her own free will. That was all he needed to sink him into this cold pit of despair.

Seventeen

MARIA DID NOT APPEAR. Perhaps she was too busy offering salts of ammonia to the princess. Anyway, the garage door was forgotten. It still gaped open. And still Bill Lammiter stood, making up his mind to cross the courtyard and climb the stairs. And then? Sleep upstairs in that attic, while each minute took Eleanor a full mile farther away? She had gone of her own free will. Had she? What was free will worth when she had not known the full truth? He could blame himself for that. He hadn't told her much tonight. And yet, he hadn't been free to talk. It always came back to the same old frustration: the eternal pull between what you wanted to do and what you had to do.

He turned and measured the wall behind him with his eye. Difficult, but not impossible. And once over? Try to find out which of the princess's villas in the country had a caretaker called Alberto. And then? Hire a car and find his way—hell, one man was useless. In trouble, one man was not enough. He heard a light step from the courtyard. Quickly he glanced over his shoulder.

But it was Joe. The garage door was left open behind him for Maria to find exactly as the princess had left it. He was carrying one of Lammiter's suitcases, and in the other hand he held his keys ready.

"What, no typewriter?" Lammiter asked as he took his bag.

Joe gave him a strange smile, looked up at the wall, and shook his head. Then, in silence, he opened the padlock of the gate and urged Lammiter through. The long street was quiet, except for a few people in the distance, where it ended in some kind of boulevard, a brightly lit *corso*. Joe set off toward the lights at a quick pace. Apparently, it was all right to talk now, for he said, "You worried me, you worried me." Suddenly he grinned. "You know, I thought you might even be climbing that damn wall. Here, let me carry that bag. You're all worn out

162

making decisions. Just leave them to Joe, eh?"

"I'm all right," said Lammiter curtly.

"We'll get a lift."

"Not on this damned street, we won't."

"I phoned for a taxi." Joe's smile was broad. He was in bright good humor.

"Sure," Lammiter said gloomily. Joe's little jokes were even worse than his own.

Joe said, "Hope I grabbed the right suitcase. You have to look pretty when you walk down the main street of Perugia."

Lammiter looked at him.

"But first, we'll find your little American. You stay with me now, eh?" Joe was amused.

"Well, this is better than sleeping on an attic floor."

"After what happened? Look—it took me a long time getting that place fixed up. I don't want to have it discovered now."

"Sorry if I altered your plans," Lammiter said more cheerfully, "but I like them better this way."

"Yes," said Joe, "I noticed you were getting kind of restless. Come on, then. Let's keep moving. Another block, that's all." And as he quickened his pace still more, he went on, "Want to know what's happening back at the villa right now? The princess is mad. She's good and mad. She's ordered all the servants out to search the grounds, the garage, everywhere. That's my guess, but I'll bet on it. She's getting angrier every minute. With Pirotta. But she doesn't know that yet. She thinks it's you that is making her mad."

I hope she will branch onto Pirotta, before it's too late."

"She will. She will. She's no fool. How did you know she hated Mr. Big so much?"

"Mussolini wouldn't be her idea of God's gift to Italy. He built the biggest railway stations and the biggest shell holes, too. And he divided her family: her brother on Mr. Big's side, the princess and her son against him. What happened to her son and daughter-in-law?"

"They were banished to Lipari. Died there." Joe looked at him curiously. "You've stirred a lot of memories tonight. Good! The more she is mad, the better. For then she starts thinking. And after that she acts." Joe's admiration was unbounded.

Lammiter did not share his enthusiasm. "Perhaps. I heard her at Doney's. But it must have taken her weeks to act on that gossip about Pirotta."

"Weeks?" Joe laughed. "She heard that news yesterday with her breakfast tray. Maria tells her everything. And the cook tells Maria everything. And I'm a good friend of the cook. See?"

Lammiter looked at Joe's broad grin. He had to smile, too.

"That's good," Joe said with approval. "And from now, we tell each other the truth, eh? That makes our lives much simpler, my friend. And one more thing, don't call me a policeman. And never call Bevilacqua that, either. If you meet him."

"If . . ." Lammiter said, and changed his suitcase to his other hand. He was feeling better now. In every way. It was strange how depression could slow up the body, too. "Good for you, Joe," he said as he now noticed which bag had been chosen. It was the one that had clean shirts, shaving kit, and a suit. "How did you guess? You certainly hadn't time to look."

"Not tonight," Joe admitted. "Your talk with the princess was too interesting. And then, afterward, I had to telephone."

"Next time I go traveling, I'll have special locks made."

"But you had nothing to hide, my friend," Joe said soothingly.

"I bet I disappointed you when you looked inside."

"Sometimes Rosana trusts too easily. She liked you. So—I was suspicious."

"Where is she now?"

"Pirotta sent her north."

"Pirotta?" He couldn't hide his alarm.

"He telephoned her about nine o'clock. I was with her when she got his call. He wanted her to meet his car— and drive north. We thought she was traveling with him. Now, it seems he just sent her ahead."

"You let her go?"

"Look, she's the one who gives orders. I'm only a chauffeur," Joe said angrily. "Besides, we had a chance to have someone in Pirotta's car, going to his destination. Do you think we would let that chance slip?"

"But Rosana's only a girl. My God——" He broke off as he noticed a car coming toward them.

"Girls can deal with Pirotta better than——"

"Watch out!" Lammiter interrupted. "That car is traveling too slowly." It was a gray Fiat. A Perugia license plate, he noticed. A long quiet street of sleeping houses, a few people walking, the lights and traffic nearer now but still a full block away. The car was slowing down still more.

"Take it easy," Joe said. "Don't you recognize the old bus? We've changed the plates, that's all. Now, in! Quick!"

The car barely stopped. A thin little man in a blue suit stepped out from the left-hand door as Joe slid across the front seat to take over the wheel. Lammiter was closing his door even as the car moved forward again. He leaned over to drop his bag on the rear seat. Through the window he saw the little man strolling toward the bright lights of the *corso*. "Neat!" Lammiter said with approval.

"We practice in the long winter evenings," Joe said. He pointed happily to the princess's house as they passed the gateway. The lights were still blazing, and there were two servants on the driveway. "What did I tell you? She's nobody's fool, that old girl. Nobody's." And then, as the car made a right turn and Lammiter was still silent, he added, "But what she'll do to Pirotta is one guess Joe does not make." He thought about that. "What would I do if my nephew, my only remaining relative, was a man like Pirotta?" He shook his head. "It would take courage, much courage. That worries you, my friend?"

Lammiter shook his head. He could only think about Eleanor. No good, no good to keep his mind paralyzed like this. Much better to think of other things, to fill in the gaps and learn what and why. Problems were never solved blindly. First, he must know whatever Joe could tell him, and only then would he begin to see what lay ahead. Whatever Joe could tell him . . . He glanced at the serious-faced Italian. "I'm glad I'm on your side," he said with a sudden smile.

Eighteen

THE CAR HAD TURNED into the upper stretch of the Via Vittorio Veneto. The cafés were still bright, the tables crowded. There, just over there, was where Lammiter had sat with Eleanor and Pirotta. And here, at this table so near to the roadway, he had met Rosana.

"Tell me," he said quietly, "was Pirotta ever in love with Rosana?"

Joe shrugged his shoulders. "It would be natural. She is beautiful. She was seeing him every day. That was the job we gave her. She did it well."

"Perhaps too well."

Joe gave him a quick look.

"Is she in love with him?"

The car swerved. "That was nearly an accident," Joe said angrily. "Stop these worries. Let me drive. She hates him, doesn't she?"

They had reached the top of the Via Vittorio Veneto. Joe was intent on the streams of traffic still converging on the Pincian Gate. As they passed through, Lammiter glanced back at the long rows of hotel windows overlooking the Aurelian Wall. There was someone on his balcony: a man standing, smoking a cigarette, looking out over the wall into the Borghese Gardens, and no doubt cursing Joe's sudden blast on the horn.

"Just there last night," said Lammiter, "Rosana came to meet Pirotta. Does a girl go out at three in the morning to meet a man she hates?" He thought for a moment. "Does any girl, brought up as carefully as Rosana, go out at three o'clock in the morning unless she's in love?" People in love did fantastic things.

Joe was silent. He seemed only to be concentrating on entering the broad highway through the Borghese Gardens.

"Or perhaps she was acting on your orders, last night?"

Joe shook his head. The car, freed from cross-traffic, now sped along the avenue of trees. The dark peace of

166

the park surrounded them.

"What are you trying to say?" Joe asked suddenly. "Rosana has betrayed us?"

"No."

"That's better, my friend." Joe relaxed a little.

"But she may have betrayed herself. At least, she has been removed. That was tried last night, and it failed. Tonight, she went of her own accord. And all because she still can't quite believe that Pirotta would ever harm a woman. What did she hope to do, anyway—convert him? My God—women!"

Joe's brow was deeply furrowed. "Did she know about your Mr. Evans?"

"Not mine," Lammiter said quickly. "I want no part of him." Then he looked at Joe carefully. "Who told you about Evans? Bevilacqua?" Was that the news Joe had heard over the telephone?

"She knew about Evans?" Joe persisted.

"Yes."

"*Mannaggia!*" Joe took a deep breath. "If I had known that, she'd never have met Pirotta tonight." Then, suddenly angry, "Why didn't Brewster tell us about Evans? Why?"

"Evans was not your business."

Joe brooded over that. At last, very quietly, he said, "I don't think they will kill her. Or the American girl. They will hold them, yes. Until the meeting in Perugia is over. Then—perhaps it does not matter what Rosana or the American knows."

"You don't believe that," Lammiter said bitterly, and fell silent. Joe said nothing. "What will happen, once the meeting is over?" That was the question that had paralyzed Lammiter for the last half hour. His mind could not, or would not, let itself think beyond it.

Joe said, "That is always the trouble with men who do violence. There is no point where it is easy to stop. The men who killed Brewster find they have to crush me out, too, just in case I knew about Evans. And Rosana must disappear so that the police will think she ran away from Rome. And you are to be held by the police for questioning. And the pretty American must not be allowed to speak."

"And Salvatore? What's happening to him?"

Joe shrugged. "So it goes on," he said softly. "Step by step the violence spreads. But not always in the form of open murder, my friend. Too many dead people make too many headlines."

"I wonder where you would have ended?"

They had left the Borghese Gardens now, and cut through a vast and imposing square. Piazza del Popolo, Lammiter noted. Joe concentrated on swinging the car into a brightly lit street, now fairly quiet but obviously a main artery of the city, before he answered. "In the Tiber. One body in the Piazza Navona is enough for one night's work. The man who planned Brewster's killing knows that. He is not a stupid man."

"*One* man?"

"He has plenty of help from people who are willing to take orders and ask no questions. And you, my friend——" Joe's voice lightened "—ask too many questions. That is how I know you are not one of them."

Was that a polite hint to stop being curious? Lammiter wondered. He didn't take it. "Evans—is he this un-stupid man?"

"Violence is not his business. He has his own problems, his own mission. What his bodyguard will do to protect him is their business. The NKVD keep their own secrets. Evans will keep his."

"But he must sense that they will commit any violence to protect him."

"And he will pretend to himself that they don't. He always has. Do you think Brewster was the first to die so that Mr. Evans could complete his mission?"

No, not the first . . . There had been Brewster's informant, knifed to death at Tivoli only a few nights ago. . . . Then Lammiter looked quickly at Joe. "Did you know anything about Evans before tonight?" It had been a pity, he thought now, that Brewster and Joe had not got together for a frank exchange of bits and pieces of knowledge. Yet, in their kind of business, allies could be as difficult to identify as enemies. In their world, danger and disaster stood at each man's elbow, ready to strike. Suspicion was not something ugly or uncharitable, it was a necessity to keep them alive. Where had Brewster made his mistake?—Then Lammiter realized that Joe had never answered his last question.

Nor did he now. "Pirotta—" Joe was saying "—there's another who lives with pretense. He organizes narcotics smuggling, but does he ever let himself think of the human beings he has turned into animals? He is helping men like Evans, but does he let himself think of the people who are murdered or abducted? No, he looks the other way. The thugs and the murderers are around him, but he persuades himself he is different: he has ideals, he is a rebel, a man in advance of his time. He is a very great persuader. Like your Mr. Evans. They have persuaded so many innocent people all their lives. But most of all, they persuade themselves."

"If it is not Evans, if it is not Pirotta, who—"

"No, no. They have their own jobs. They may not even know the man who directs them to this meeting in Perugia, watches over them. His job is security." Joe frowned. "It is—how do you say?—divide the labor?"

"Division of labor."

"Division of labor," Joe repeated, memorizing, as he increased speed. They were traveling fairly fast now, although the street, stretching so straight in front of them, was still lined with apartment houses. "We're going north from Rome," Joe said with satisfaction. "No one following us, so far." Then he nodded at the blocks of modern buildings they were passing. "The Roman legions would never believe me, but this is the Via Flaminia. Yes, this is where they marched, all the way to the Adriatic."

"That's a long haul." It was two hundred miles or better, right over the spine of Italy. And the spine was all mountains, with hills on either side. Lammiter glanced at his watch. It was just after two o'clock now. "What's the driving time on that distance?"

"We only go halfway," Joe reassured him. "As far as the hills of Umbria. Perugia is the capital, and—"

"I know, I know," Lammiter said impatiently. "But where does the princess keep her country cottage?"

"In Montesecco, not far from Perugia." Joe was amused by something. "Cottage . . ." He let his amusement burst into a broad grin. "And questions, questions . . . You like them, eh?"

"Dammit all, the only information I get out of you is prised out with a question mark."

Joe said softly, "And I think you ask the little questions to keep yourself from thinking about the big one."

Lammiter was lighting a cigarette. He wasted three matches, three thin little sticks of wax that snapped too easily. The fourth attempt was successful.

"Don't worry," Joe said. "We'll find the American girl. At Montesecco." He had been constantly watching the rear window. Now he relaxed. "We're clear. Not one car behind us for the last half hour. Light me a cigarette, too." He stretched his shoulders, took a new grip on the wheel. The car leaped forward at full power.

Around them, there were vast stretches of black countryside, occasionally broken by small clusters of farmers' cottages standing together at the side of the road, in darkness and silence. The road was straight and long. And very quiet. "Now," Joe said, "we will be able to hear the march of the legions' feet and the songs they sang." Then, brusquely, "We'll stop each hour to stretch our backs. This car is too small for your legs, I know, but try to get some sleep."

"No. I'll spell you at the wheel."

Joe shook his head. "I know this road. Get some sleep."

"It's better if we talk."

"So that *I* won't fall asleep?" Joe was amused. "I like you, my friend, I like you very much. I'll even answer some questions. Or shall I tell you the story of my life?"

"Which life?"

Joe laughed. "Well," he admitted, "there's the one in Sicily. There's the one in America. There's the one in Rome. Take your choice."

"In which did you meet Salvatore?"

There was a sudden moment of stillness, only broken by the steady hum of the smooth-running engine.

Tactfully bridging the silence, Lammiter added, "Salvatore . . . What's his second name, anyway?"

"Salvatore Sabatini," Joe said slowly. "And what made you think of him?"

"He's been at the back of my mind most of this night."

"Now *I* start asking the questions. Why?"

"Oh—just a lot of little things," Lammiter said vaguely. But he was remembering more than was comfortable.

"Such as—?"

"Well—he knew Rosana and I were in Brewster's flat

this evening. He knew we were to meet again at eleven."

"So did I know."

"He tried to get me to leave with him, as if he didn't want Brewster to start talking to me. In fact, he only left me behind when Brewster seemed to be falling asleep. He checked the locked door to the cat staircase, and he did that carefully. Then he looked at me as if he were afraid I had been watching him. Now I think he may have been unlocking the door."

"Sometimes a man remembers things to suit his thinking," Joe reminded him quietly.

"I'm not suiting my memory to anything. I felt uneasy at the time. But Rosana and Brewster trusted Sabatini. So I trusted him." Never play down your instincts, he told himself: listen to them, Lammiter, listen.

"And when did you start distrusting Sabatini?"

"Since I started adding up all the little things. He spoke to you in the Piazza tonight. When you told me that, I didn't think much about it. But Sabatini isn't an amateur like me. He knows the rules. When he spoke to you, he broke them. Didn't he?"

Joe made no comment.

"It was almost as if he were identifying you to the two strangers who started hunting you. How else did they know you?" He watched Joe's face.

Joe gave him a sudden smile. But his voice was quite serious, almost grim. "Yes, I thought of that. I thought of that when I thought of a man who could have used my car."

"Sabatini?"

Joe nodded.

Lammiter tried to straighten his stiff legs. "I might have guessed you——" he began. He could laugh now at his worries about Sabatini. The man was the reason Joe had been sent north. Sabatini was Joe's own particular division of labor. "You were ahead of me, Joe."

"Not me. Bevilacqua."

"No one has seen Sabatini since he spoke to you in the Piazza Navona——is that it?"

"That's just about it."

"Well," Lammiter said with some relief, "my guesses weren't so damned stupid after all, not if Bevilacqua is——"

"Bevilacqua has no guesses. But he is taking no chances."

"Then he must know something. Why else would he send you chasing north?"

"In this business," Joe said, "you do not always know. If you wait until you know, it can be too late. So you act on the greatest probability. If Sabatini is the man we want, I shall find him near Perugia. That's all in the pattern. *If* he is the man we want . . ."

"You make him sound more important than I thought he was." But Joe added nothing to that. "He isn't an Italian, is he?"

"So now *you* are telling me something? I, an Italian, don't know he isn't an Italian!" Joe was annoyed. He tried to be amused.

"Look, Joe—I make my living listening to people speak. I listen to actors up on the stage, I——"

"In America, yes. What's that to do with Italia?"

"Look, Joe—" he tried again, "I thought I could speak Italian when I came to Italy. Once—before a war in Korea—I took a degree in Romance languages—Italian and French. So when I arrived here, I thought this is a breeze, Lammiter, my boy; what's a rusty subjunctive or a forgotten pluperfect conditional between friends? But every Italian I've met—you included, so why the hell do I have to tell you all this?—has been politely amused by the way I speak his language. I'm a walking grammar book."

Joe looked somewhat mystified, but unpersuaded.

"Every city, every town in Italy, every village perhaps, has its own little tricks of language. Not only with the words and phrases, but even with the way they are spoken. Right?"

"But you hear all kinds of accents in Rome," Joe argued. He was still on the defensive.

"Sure. It's like New York. It's the meeting place for the rest of the country. But what regional accent does Sabatini have?"

"He comes from the north."

"Are you sure? Or is that what he tells you because you come from the south? Don't you see, he'd have to meet someone from his supposed home town before he could be pinned down as a liar." But no doubt Sabatini, if he ever had met such a man, would then come from a little town a hundred miles east, or west, whichever seemed safer. Then Lammiter was suddenly shocked by his own eloquence: it had led him farther than he had meant to go. "I can be wrong," he said. "I guess I was carried away. Forget it, Joe. Let's stick to what we do know."

Joe was silent for a full minute. "Now all that could be very interesting," he said at last, half lost in his own thoughts. "If it is true," he added, still a little on the defensive.

"I told you to forget it."

But something had made contact in Joe's mind. Lammiter could almost feel him thinking. "Very, very interesting," he said at last, furrowing his brows at the dark stretch of road in front of them. "If your guess is right, then Sabatini could be more important than any of us thought."

"But he's only a guide—" Lammiter began. He stopped short, remembering Brewster's warning: never look for an important agent in an important position; never look at the ambassador, look at his chauffeur.

"It would be a perfect cover," Joe conceded with grudging admiration.

Lammiter said slowly, "I don't like this, Joe. I don't like it."

"You began it."

Lammiter said nothing. For the second time that night, he forced himself to play down what women call instinct and men, more modestly if less elegantly, a hunch. Stick to the facts, Lammiter, he thought grimly.

But Joe was not going to let any deductions wither in the bud. "You still think Sabatini isn't a real Italian?"

"Yes. But what does that matter?"

"Then he's not only told one lie, he's living a hundred lies. *That* matters." He waited, but Lammiter was keeping quiet. "So I'd like to learn why you say he isn't an Italian. Sure, sure, I know we've all got our different ways of speaking. In Venice, Giorgio is always Zorzio." His voice sharpened. "But in Italy, there are people who speak as well as you do."

"Hey there!" Lammiter said quickly. "I speak bad Italian, Joe. That's my point. I speak like a God-damned book. I've no background to my voice. That's what I mean—no background. Why, even the principessa has that. She's a Roman, isn't she? She's educated and traveled, but you wouldn't say she came from Milan or Naples or Florence."

"Background . . ." Joe said thoughtfully. His feelings were less ruffled now. "You've got a quick ear, eh?"

"If I hadn't, I wouldn't try writing plays."

"Sabatini comes from around Milan. You say that's impossible?"

"I'd say you should get a Milanese to check on his voice."

"Simple, isn't it?" Joe said, sarcastic now. "But I never met any Milanese who talked with him."

"How long has he lived in Rome?"

"Eleven years. Since the war."

"He and Brewster were in the underground together. Right?"

Joe nodded. "We checked back to the day he was born. Near Milan."

"That's definite?"

"We didn't take Brewster's word for him alone. What do you think we are?" Joe still had some hackles rising. Then he calmed down. He even gave a brief laugh. "Want me to recite for you?" he asked suddenly.

Lammiter glanced at him quickly.

"Salvatore Sabatini, born 1917, Milan, father a lawyer, only child, bright boy. Won prizes at school. Did his military service in the *carabinieri,* student at Milan University. The Germans came, father was killed, mother died. He left Milan, joined some underground fighters around Como. Met Brewster. Later, joined a British battalion as interpreter. After the war, he came to Rome, worked for a travel bureau, became a guide. He did some black marketing for a while—small-scale stuff. And a little smuggling—nothing big. Just a small operator. But he got to know a lot of small operators. People on the fringe. Brewster found that useful: your best information can come from people on the fringe." Then he looked at Lammiter. "Well?"

"I was thinking his father would be kind of disappointed."

"Oh—some people drift."

"Some do."

"You are not buying?"

"Are you?"

"You heard what I told you. It all runs straight, as straight as this road."

"But it's a poor showing for such a good start." And, Lammiter thought, Sabatini hadn't given him the impression that he was content to be a man without a future.

"The war changed people. Made them——" Joe paused. He frowned again at the road ahead of them. Then he said, and his voice had altered, "The war killed some people, too. Killed them and left no trace."

For a moment, Lammiter didn't follow. "You mean, the man who took to the hills around Como could have died up there?"

"Died? He could have been killed in cold blood." Joe took a long deep breath. "Underground fighting was not always a brave story. Sometimes, for politics, a good man was murdered. Yes——that could have happened. You take a man's life, and then his name."

"But what about his friends? A murderer couldn't take them over, too."

"Often the groups of those partisans were small. Sometimes they were wiped out, killed or captured. Sometimes there was only one survivor. He would join up with another group. Who would question him if he was a fighter who hated fascists and Nazis? These were the only necessary credentials, my friend."

Grimly, Lammiter said, "We've built up a pretty picture between us. I don't like it, Joe. Less and less."

"It may be false. Perhaps Sabatini *is* the student who went into the hills. Perhaps he didn't play with the key of Brewster's door. Perhaps he was so frightened, down in the Piazza, that he spoke to me. Perhaps he wasn't the one who borrowed my car on those two special nights. You see, my friend, there's an explanation for everything. Sometimes false, sometimes ture. The main thing is that we know what we are meeting if we find Sabatini walking down a street in Perugia. Because, if he's innocent, he won't be walking down a street anywhere: he was one of Brewster's little group, and it is being——eliminated."

"If he's innocent, he's dead. Is that it?"

"Or in hiding, so that he will not be dead. Certainly, he will *not* be walking around as if nothing had happened."

"What does he know about you?"

"Just what Tony Brewster or Rosana knew."

"He could have checked on your story."

Joe laughed. "Sure, he could."

"You don't sound worried."

"Giuseppe Rocco has lived a simple life. He's just a dumb Sicilian who got into trouble in Syracuse over a girl. When he got out of the prison hospital, he followed the Americans. But now he lives in Rome, and all he wants out of life is a bigger and better automobile. He went to work for Brewster, because Rosana persuaded him, and he'd do anything for Miss Rosana. Also, he hopes there will be some cash as a reward. Also, he keeps buying lottery tickets. Dumb as they come, that's our Joe."

A prison hospital, thought Lammiter, might be a good place to pick up a recently vacated identity. But it seemed indiscreet to speculate openly about that. So he gazed out at the dark fields. They had begun to slope, to rise and fall. Far-off shadows against the sky were hills. The road was beginning to meet twists and turns. They passed through a small town, with its new buildings looking square and bare among the older houses with their cracked and peeling plaster.

"A dump," said Joe, with all the scorn of an adopted Roman.

They passed other small houses, always in little groups, as if people preferred to live as close together as possible. As in the town, the new buildings replaced war damage. Brightly painted in greens and pinks, they were startlingly picked out by the car's headlights. So were the bullet holes on the older houses, pitted and pock-marked by bursts of machine guns between the cracks and stains of age. In the distance, a heavy truck changed gears. Here and there, headlights swept over the fields, and a few cars hissed past.

"Any chance of overtaking Pirotta?" Lammiter asked suddenly. Joe could drive. They were making excellent time.

Joe shook his head. "I worked too carefully over that

old Lancia," he said regretfully. "She could drive from here to Geneva without a complaint."

"I still think we ought to have stopped it back at the gates."

Joe shook his head again. "We couldn't have stopped them, my friend. I had a knife, you had no weapon at all. The gates were open, the engine was running. And there were three men in the car."

"Three?" That startled him. Then amazement changed to irritation. Joe did not need to measure out his information like this.

"Pirotta, and two men who work for him. He was taking no chances."

"But—" He stopped, annoyance giving way to fear. Joe was preparing him. For what?

"I did all we could do. I telephoned. The alarm is out. The Lancia will be noticed." Then, as Lammiter said nothing, he added, "If we had tried to stop them, they'd have changed their direction. Then we wouldn't know where to follow them." Again he glanced quickly at the American. He said harshly, "Stop thinking they will kill her. That—not! I have already told you."

"Whom are you persuading? Me—or yourself?" Lammiter asked angrily. "If Sabatini is the man in control, he didn't stop at killing Brewster, his old friend, his old comrade. Did he?"

"But he has more of a problem with the American girl. She has a lot of important friends. The Embassy—what will they say? Her father and his newspaper friends—what will they keep printing? The principessa—she won't be silenced."

"The princess!" Lammiter said in deep disgust.

"She's your ally by this time. She has heard how they took the American girl from her house."

"How they took—?"

"Sure. Do you think your girl walked into the car? Take it easy, Bill, take it easy," Joe said worriedly.

"Go on," said Lammiter. "You'd better tell me it all. All."

"She came out of the villa slowly. She stood at the top of the steps and looked down at the car. Maybe she didn't like Pirotta's two men on either side of her. Maybe she had expected to stay at the villa. Maybe the car frightened

her. She turned, and tried to run back into the house.
But the two men were ready for that. They caught her.
One had a hand over her mouth. They carried her down
the steps. She was struggling. And then she didn't struggle." He hesitated. He glanced at Lammiter. "They didn't
hurt her. They put her to sleep, maybe. With a needle—
that's the quickest way. It would make the journey easier."

Lammiter took a deep breath and steadied himself.

"The princess saw nothing of that," Joe reminded him.

Lammiter nodded. The princess had stood in the courtyard. Maria had been walking to the gates. Neither of
them had seen.

"But the princess will hear. The servants in the house
would be watching. I know them. By now, she has stopped
being angry with you. Now she is your ally."

And what did that matter?

"You don't think that's important?" Joe asked quickly.
Then he smiled, shaking his head, and concentrated on
the road. They were swinging around a large church and
a group of small houses. "Past this village," Joe said,
"we'll stop. Stretch our legs."

"I'm all right. Keep on going."

Joe was watching the road, now running straight again
for half a mile or so. His eyes were on the far-off lights
of an approaching car. The lights blinked. Joe answered
with his, as he began to slow down. So did the other
car. It stopped under some trees and its lights were
switched off. Joe stopped and switched off his lights.
"Out," he said. "Stretch your back. Get some air in your
lungs." He opened his door, and crossed the road to the
other car.

Bill Lammiter did as he was told. He stood looking
across the fields to the east. There was a faint pencil
stroke of lightened darkness along the horizon. In front
of him was a little vineyard, over there a patch of corn
thrusting its strong stalks toward the sky, and flowers
planted wherever there was a spare corner of earth. The
air was cool and sweet.

Behind him, Joe called to him softly, and he climbed
back into the car. The other was already leaving.

Their car started forward. "The Lancia is keeping to the
road," Joe told him. "That is one fear you can drop out
of the window, my friend."

Lammiter tried to smile. Joe was doing his best to give him some encouragement. And it was true: the car that had reported to Joe made Lammiter feel better. The numbness was leaving his mind. They were not alone, two men on an endless road stretching over limitless fields.

"Next stop," Joe said, "we'll get some gas. And coffee. And more information, too. And then, the hills. And after that, Montesecco. Right?"

"Right."

"Now I tell you the story of my life," Joe said.

Nineteen

THE DAWN ARRIVED as they turned off the Flaminian Way and branched to their left. For some time they had been traveling among spreading hills and deep woods. Now the road ran along the side of a valley so broad that it seemed more like an immense plain rimmed by steep small hills, each complete in itself, sharp-pointed, almost symmetrical, drawn by an artist with an exact eye and a sure hand. Behind the hills were more hills, their peaks peering over each other's shoulders. And every hill had its neat terraces of carefully spaced olive trees; its crest was sometimes forested, sometimes crowned by a walled miniature of a town. Down in the valley, a vast patchwork quilt of cultivated fields and trees was flung over the land, the neat squares stitched together by a very small river curving its way slowly back to Rome.

"The Tiber," Joe said, and rubbed his right shoulder and neck. They were the first words he had spoken in the last hour. Since their last stop, in fact.

That had been at a small house, solid and square, with a large number painted on its dark-red walls, standing quite alone at the side of the road. It was the house of a road-repair superintendent, numbered according to the section of the highway for which he was responsible. In the small garage built into the house, Joe had found some more gasoline, not that he needed it, but it was wise to keep the tank as full as possible. And there had been some more information, too. Pirotta's car, with Rosana presumably, had passed just before midnight, driven at a reasonable speed. The Lancia had passed two hours later; its speed had been furious.

"Crazy," the superintendent had said sadly, thinking of possible accidents to his fine road. He was a middle-aged man, thin and wiry, intelligent as good workmen are who take a pride in their jobs. At the moment, he was tired with his vigil, but he gave them a cup of hot coffee and a sandwich of sliced sausage slapped on a torn hunk of hard-crusted bread, and as he moved quietly around his little kitchen next to the garage—"The wife and kids are asleep upstairs"—he talked in a hoarse whisper with Joe, and threw Lammiter a friendly nod and a gap-toothed smile every now and again, as if to make him feel he was in this conversation, too. Then, with last instructions about heavy repairs on a bad hairpin bend of the road (a mile farther on, hard frosts last winter, the worst winter within living memory), they left the man telephoning his news of Joe's arrival back to headquarters.

That stop had only taken nine minutes—Joe and Lammiter were still finishing their sandwiches as the Fiat started from behind the shelter of the house and turned onto the road again. But instead of being reassured, Joe was worried. "Rosana can't be alone in Pirotta's car," he said. "She would have checked in at that house if she had been alone." He didn't have to add his biggest fear: that Rosana might no longer be in the car; her body, stripped of identification, might have been thrown into a ditch. But five minutes later he said, "They'll keep her as long as she can be useful to them." Then he lapsed into silence and concentrated on the road, for there were more trucks now to be passed, enormous and thundering. The road-repair superintendent would be stifling a yawn to curse their weight, as he slipped off his half-buttoned trousers and unlaced boots and climbed into bed with his wife and children.

Bill Lammiter kept himself awake, but he had not offered to drive. A strange road, climbing between broad-shouldered hills and woods, in the half-light between night and day, was better left to Joe's memory. Even when they came into the Umbrian plain, and the day was born, Lammiter did not suggest he would take the wheel. For now there were other hazards: cumbersome, slow-moving farm carts, pulled by pairs of gentle white oxen with formidable horns and amiable eyes.

"And here is the way to Montesecco," Joe said, swerving past a team of oxen, cutting ahead of them before they started blocking up the narrow dusty road, which climbed up its own neat hill. The white oxen looked after them reprovingly; their driver yelled what he thought of cars and dust. "Yes, yes," said Joe, almost to himself, "I agree. But it would take you half an hour to reach the town. We'll do it in three minutes."

The road twisted among trees up toward the walled town. Beyond the trees, on either side, the terraces of olive groves rose step by step. They seemed dead. The silver-green leaves were black and hard. Last winter's frosts must have been bitter.

Joe noticed the look on Lammiter's face. "Yes," he said, "it's tough on the people. This is the way all the hills are this year. But give the olive trees three good years, and they'll come alive again."

"Three years. It's a long time to wait." Lammiter could see the town more clearly now: a mass of roofs and towers behind an encircling wall.

"People have lived here for nearly three thousand years. That wall was first built by the Etruscans. Then the Romans came and built on top of it. What's three years to a wall like that?"

The wall, massive and high, of light-colored stone, rose abruptly before them. But they did not enter its arched gateway. Lammiter had just time to glimpse the hill inside the gate, the narrow cobbled street lined with stone houses, before Joe turned the car into a track running toward a two-storied house with yellow plastered walls and a red-tiled roof. He had not noticed it, coming up the hill. The roadside trees had obscured it. And then, almost immediately, they were in a small farmyard, scattering chickens, avoiding two men and a wooden cart, passing three giant haystacks, and coming to rest around the corner of the farm side of the house, under a rough arbor of vine leaves.

"This," Joe remembered to say as he got out of the car, "is the farm where Alberto buys most of the food for the princess's house. I used to come here on my free time. Have a look at the view." Then he left, walking toward the farmer and his son, with arms outstretched and real laughter in his voice.

Well, we're among friends at least, Lammiter thought. He stood beside the car, trying to get the cramp out of his legs. American cars might be bold and brassy, but they didn't tie your muscles in knots like this. For a few minutes, he watched the farmer and his son. Like the other peasants he had seen on the Umbrian roads, they were of good height, straight-backed, decently dressed in a clean rough shirt with sleeves rolled up (and only one button open at the neck, no expanses of manly chest advertised here), a waistcoat for warmth, work-stained trousers, and heavy boots. Their faces, turned curiously toward him for a brief glance, were tanned and high-colored. Battered felt hats were tilted over their eyes, more from habit than from sun, for the early morning light was bright but kind, and the cool night air had still no warmth in it.

Lammiter turned up the collar of his thin jacket and closed his lapels. He walked, stiffly, past a wooden yoke and a harrow, over to the haystacks. From there, the land dropped steeply downhill, and he could see all the vast sweep of valley and the neatly outlined hills. By this pale gold light, the trees down on the plain stood sharply etched, each shape clear in its long row. And over all, lay a stillness.

He turned to look at the little town enclosed in its strong wall. Over the blighted olive trees he could see the crest of the curve of wall nearest him—he was too near it to see its whole encircling arm flung round the tightly packed yellowed roofs and ancient stone towers. He heard a dog bark; somewhere a cock crew; a man was singing an endless song. Even sounds seemed as etched as the rows of trees and the folds of the hills.

The boy moved over to the car, and Lammiter joined him. He was about sixteen, with good bones in his face, blue eyes, light hair. He looked at Lammiter gravely, noting his jacket and trousers, his shoes; then he looked back at the car.

"*Molto bello*," Lammiter said, pointing to the panorama beyond the haystacks.

The boy took his eyes away from the car. He looked

now at the view he lived with. He was quite silent. Then suddenly, he said, *"Bellissimo!"* A smile of happiness, of sheer joy, illuminated his face. Lammiter found he was smiling, too. *"Bellissimo!"* he agreed. The boy looked at him again, but he was no longer a stranger.

"All right," Joe said, coming back to the car, "we go inside and get us some food and sleep." He pulled out Lammiter's case. He gave a wave to the boy, who was already picking up a wooden yoke for the two white oxen his father was leading toward him. "Come on, Bill. We've made them late enough."

Lammiter left the world of golden light and followed Joe's quick steps.

"Any information?" he asked.

"Pirotta's car arrived first. Then the Lancia about an hour ago. And don't start worrying about my car. If anyone asks questions, we are just a couple of guys from Perugia, buying some extra supplies for a restaurant. You know what's happening in Perugia this weekend? The university begins its annual summer school for foreigners. Sure, for foreigners. It's packing them in. Name any nationality, and Perugia's got them. Isn't that just dandy?"

So that's why poor old Perugia was chosen for Evans's meeting place, Lammiter thought. He had a feeling that the town could have done without the honor. "Clever," he said. "Clever little bastards we're dealing with." He looked at Joe. "Can you see the princess's place from here?" he asked.

"Why?" Joe asked, suddenly suspicious.

"You're dropping back into character," Lammiter said with a grin. "That's why."

"Well, you can't climb over *that* wall, that's for sure."

They entered a dark kitchen, clean but careless, only lighted by a barred window overlying the wide door. There was a bed against one wall, three hard chairs, a table, an old chest of drawers with traces of elaborate painting, a dresser, some paper flowers on one cracked plaster wall under a woman's faded photograph.

"His wife's dead?" Lammiter asked, looking around at men's comfortable disorder. There was soup in a deep pot at the side of the low fire, cheese roughly set on the wooden table with a loaf of bread, a jug of Chianti, two earthenware plates, two wooden spoons.

"Four years ago. And three other children, too. Flu epidemic." Joe rummaged around and found two cups, and as Lammiter served up the soup, he took out his knife, picked up the loaf, held it against his chest, and cut toward himself into its hard crust. Then he tapped the thick slice of bread on the table and watched the ants fall out. "If I may step out of character again for a moment," he said with a smile, as he tapped once more to make sure that the ants had gone, "this is symbolic of our kind of work." He swept the back of his hand over the table and the ants fell to the floor. Then, as he handed the slice of bread to Lammiter, "Okay, bud. Philosophy class is over. Eat. And listen. And don't start telling me you don't need any sleep. We all do: Pirotta, his men, you, and me. Only I'm going to scout round for half an hour first; and you're staying here. Upstairs." He finished tapping his own slice of bread.

Lammiter ate. The warm soup took the chill out of his blood. And as he had time to think over his initial objections to Joe's plan, he saw they were stupid, and he was glad he had kept silent. Joe was right. A foreigner walking in the early morning through the streets of Montesecco would only rouse questions. And questions made talk. And talk carried. But Joe was known here: no one would be surprised to see him; the Lancia had arrived, hadn't it? Why not its chauffeur, too? Joe must have friends in this town. And Pirotta?

He put that question to Joe after their quick meal was over, and he stood ready to climb the stairs to the room above. "Sure," Joe said, "he's popular. Always got a smile and a kind word for everyone." He looked shrewdly at the American. "He's an attractive sort of fellow. Sweeps in here in his car, gives a wave of his hand, and everyone feels happy that a man can have some good fortune in this hard world."

"Even the local Communists feel that way?"

"You noticed the posters plastered on the walls?" Joe asked quickly.

"Couldn't miss the hammer and sickle."

"That catches the eye," Joe agreed. "But the Communists here—" he paused, shrugged his shoulders.

"They're mostly anti-clerical, that's all."

"There's poverty, too."

"It isn't always poverty that makes politics. Sometimes it's pride. Ever read about Umbria? The Pope's army besieged this town ninety years ago, and when the troops got inside—well, there was a lot of raping and killing. Same thing happened in Perugia. People round here remember these things. And they remember the days of their greatness, back in the fourteenth century, when each town in these hills had its commune and its captain of the people elected to govern. Then they remember how that freedom was destroyed—the big families seized it first, then the Church seized it from the big families. A real mess of power politics."

"But the Church is not a temporal power any more. Those days are over."

"Do the people in the south of your country forget the war against the north? There are people here, many of them, whose mothers saw the mercenaries break through the cannon holes in the walls of this town and what they did. It is no use pretending that such evil things did not happen. They are important in politics, even ninety years after."

"So evil lives longer than good. . . . That's depressing."

"The good is remembered, too. Garibaldi came and freed them. They remember that day, most of all." He smiled suddenly. "Don't worry so much about these posters. There are others on the wall, if you looked closer. This is still a free country. A few years ago, we gave away that freedom. Sure, Italy may be poor, but she is rich in memories. And they all teach us something."

"Yes," Lammiter said gloomily. "If we only remember all the lessons and not just the ones that suit our theories."

"Here, take this upstairs with you." Joe pulled off his crumpled blue jacket, stuffed his tie into his pocket, and handed them over. He rolled up his sleeves, unbuttoned his shirt at the neck. "The room at the left is yours. Don't leave it. I'll be back soon. Got to see some friends."

"I'm glad to hear they do exist," Lammiter said, still worried.

"Sure," Joe said cheerfully, "sure we have friends. Get some sleep and you'll feel better." He chased away some chickens which had come exploring from the yard into the kitchen, and then shut the wide door behind him.

Upstairs, Lammiter entered a small dark room. He dropped his suitcase, and Joe's jacket on top of it. Quickly, he went over to the solitary window and half opened its shutters, letting the early morning sun stream in; so this room faced east toward the wall of the town, while the kitchen downstairs had opened to the west. People around here, whatever their politics, were unanimously against windows, or perhaps solid walls gave shelter from cold winter winds and the blaze of summer. He pushed the shutters farther apart, cautiously, and looked out.

From this height, he had a good view of the road as it presented itself before the entrance to the town. From here, too, he could see a wider sweep of the wall, and the rippling tiled roofs, and even—where the hill rose inside the walls—the top-floor windows of the houses, with shutters now opened and balloons of bedding already billowing on the sills to air. To his right, there were trees, perhaps a large park, standing just within the walls where they curved round out of sight. But he couldn't see any sign of Joe.

Down at the gate, two women in light cotton dresses balanced loads of washing on their heads while they exchanged a word and a laugh with a man holding a horse by a rope halter. An old woman in black, long-skirted, came plodding up the road. But there was no sign of Joe.

His eyes searched the olive grove that stretched beneath him. It ran, to his right, along the wall for some distance and then gave way to a field and trees, trees that matched those just over the wall where the park lay. Was there some other entrance over there to the town? Or was the park a large private garden? Was that where the princess lived?

He looked back again at the main gate. The women were leaving, taking a rough trail to the left that must lead to other farms outside the walls. The horse was being led into the town, clattering over the solid paving stones. The old woman was hurrying out of sight. From one tower, a bell sounded, gentle and melancholy. And there were other sounds, too: the rattle of iron wheels over rough stone; occasional voices—distant and merging; someone calling out; someone laughing; and from the grass under the olive trees, the first chitter of insects, tuning up for their noonday concert. And then, far over to the right, in the field with the trees, he saw a man herding two goats.

In spite of himself, Lammiter laughed. It was Joe. Where did he get the goats? Lammiter wondered. Perhaps he had found them tethered among the olive trees, and had taken them along to give local color to his walk across the open field. He was herding them toward the wood which lay outside the park. So that was the direction where the princess's house lay?

Satisfied, Lammiter turned away from the window. There wasn't much in the room—a narrow bed with a mattress that looked as old as the town itself, a low carved chest, a brown-spotted piece of looking glass, and some wooden pegs on the wall. Two flies had come in from the open window, large black country flies circling slowly around the naked electric bulb hung from the ceiling.

All right, he thought, I'll play it Joe's way. I'll stay here and count those damned flies.

But first, he investigated the other room upstairs. It was innocent enough. It was used now as a storeroom. And then he stood at the top of the stairs, listening. Again he fought down the impulse to follow Joe. He went back into his room and closed the door. He took off his jacket, loosened his tie, sat down on the mattress, and lit a cigarette. Sleep? He couldn't. He had too many thoughts pounding through his brain. Play it Joe's way, he told himself again: sweat this one out. But if ever he had to learn how much he loved Eleanor, this was a hard way to do it. He ground out the cigarette under his heel. If I ever do meet Pirotta, I'll kill him, he thought suddenly.

He stretched out on the bed and counted the flies—five now—and watched the pale sunlight deepen, and listened to the cicadas beneath his window. Sewing machines, he thought drowsily, sewing machines stitching away, stitching, stitching. . . .

Twenty

Hᴇ ʜᴇᴀʀᴅ a distant voice saying, "Bill." A hand was on his shoulder. He came quickly out of sleep, sitting upright so suddenly, making such a wild grab for the hand on his shoulder, that Rosana cried out. He stared at her unbelievingly.

"Yes, it's Rosana," she said. "I did try to wake you gently."

"Eleanor?"

"No, she isn't here. She's at the Casa Grande. She's all right, Bill. So far, she's all right. She's in a locked room upstairs—one of the princess's own rooms." She looked at his face. "She's all right. She's by herself."

He suddenly noticed he still grasped her wrist. He let it go. "Sorry." He glanced at his watch. He had been asleep for almost an hour, a deep dreamless wonderful hour. "How did you get here?"

"Giuseppe sent for me."

"Joe?"

"He came in by the gate at the woods, where the gamekeeper's house stands. Jacopone—that's the game-keeper—came up to the big house and passed the word to Anna-Maria to get me downstairs." She touched her very loose cotton dress of pink and green checks. "How do you like it? Anna-Maria lent it to me. She's Alberto's wife."

"How many servants are at the big house?"

"Just Alberto and Anna-Maria meanwhile. The princess always brings the others with her from Rome."

"And just Jacopone at the gamekeeper's cottage?"

She nodded. "Two old men and one old woman," she said as if she had guessed his thoughts. "Not much help, except in good will."

"Are you sure of that?"

"Yes. The princess telephoned and gave Alberto her orders. She woke the operator at three o'clock in the morning. It was quite a sensation. But so were the cars."

She moved to the window, looked out, and then drew the shutters closer together.

"Where's Joe? Tethering goats back into place?"

She sat down on the wooden chest. "He was going to follow me, I thought."

"Ready for rear-guard action?" Or Joe might have other friends to visit. "Well—I'm glad you're out of that place, Rosana," he said awkwardly. "What has been happening up there?"

"I'll tell you when Giuseppe arrives. He will have to hear most of it, too. I only saw him for a minute at Jacopone's cottage." She looked down at her hands. And she began to cry, very quietly, just sitting there on the chest in her shapeless dress, her head bent, the tears slowly running down her pale cheeks. She didn't want him to notice, so he sat still and looked now at the floor.

She said, "So they killed Tony Brewster." And she took a long shuddering breath. But she had stopped crying. "And Joe told me that Sabatini—" She paused. "Could it be possible? Could he have betrayed us?"

"It's possible." He remembered Joe's words last night. "If he didn't, then he is in hiding—if he's still alive. First, your brother. Then, Brewster. Who's next?"

"Not any more of us, if I can help it," she said with a sudden burst of cold anger.

Lammiter said nothing to that. He had his doubts.

"Don't look so worried, Bill," she said gently. "No one saw me come here. You see, I lived at the Casa Grande for almost two months after I came back from America. The princess was the only one of my mother's old friends who stood beside me when my brother died so—so badly. The princess knows what disgrace is—her only brother blew his brains out when he saw what his politics had done to Italy—oh well, anyway—she sent me away from Rome until the scandal died down, and I stayed up here. I know every inch of the house and the garden and the woods outside the walls; my only friends were Alberto and Anna-Maria and Jacopone. So this morning—it was easy. You see?"

She rose and went over to the window again. She turned back. She moved around, restless, not sitting down.

"It was here," she said, "in this room, that I first met Bevilacqua."

"Joe brought you here to meet him?"

"Oh no! It was I who persuaded Giuseppe to join Brewster's group. He was to be my watchdog. And he has been very good. Only—I'm difficult to watch, I think."

Indeed you are, Lammiter thought.

"It was Jacopone who brought me here," she went on. "You see, Bevilacqua had heard that the men with whom my brother had been connected were going to ask me to join them. Oh—not an important job, of course. I was just to be a sort of secretary." She was embarrassed.

These friends of her brother's had created a job for her, Lammiter thought. "Very considerate of them."

She missed the irony in his words. Earnestly she explained, "No—just very clever. I had no money, I needed a job, and then—if I ever did learn more about my brother's death, I wouldn't be free to speak out. I had become one of them. You see?"

"And Bevilacqua asked you to accept the job, if it were offered to you."

She nodded.

"That was a hard assignment," he said quietly.

She nodded again. She hesitated, and then she decided to finish her story. "The job was offered to me. And I took it. And I found that I was Luigi Pirotta's secretary."

She paused again. But Lammiter, watching her in silence and sympathy, seemed to give her courage. "That was a shock," she admitted. "I knew he was my brother's friend, but I hadn't known he was in the same horrible business. But then I persuaded myself that he had been drawn into that mess just like my brother Mario. Because—" she swung round lightly to face him, her dark eyes almost pleading with him to understand her "—if I ever admitted that Luigi Pirotta knew what he was doing, had chosen such a way to live, then I would have to condemn Mario, too. You see?

Lammiter saw.

"I kept hoping that Luigi, like my brother, was only a—a—"

"A front man, dupe," he finished for her.

She said, "Tony was absolutely right: I trusted too

easily. Because I—well, perhaps I was a snob. Our families—" She looked away. She said proudly, "Luigi and Mario never were educated to behave like that."

"Didn't Pirotta's father—the man who blew his brains out—didn't he go off the tracks?" He had spoken bluntly, purposefully. And it had its effect. She dropped her half-sad, half-excusing little piece of snobbery, and became the girl Brewster had liked.

"Yes," she flashed back at him. "But that was open politics. He chose Mussolini's side. He was wrong. But he hid nothing. He didn't deceive people, pretending one thing, doing another."

"Not like his son, dear Luigi."

She looked at him. "No," she admitted, "not like his son." She moved back to the window. "What is delaying Giuseppe?"

"You always call him Giuseppe."

"Do I? Perhaps I prefer Giuseppe to Joe."

"How did you come to choose him as your—your watchdog?"

"He drove for my brother. I couldn't afford a chauffeur, so I recommended him to the princess, who needed one. Then later, when Bevilacqua introduced me in Rome to Tony Brewster—well, Giuseppe seemed just the kind of man Tony needed. And he was devoted to my brother. Giuseppe is a Sicilian, you know. He wanted to find my brother's murderer as much as I did. So I—recruited him." She tried to smile, as if she were happy about one wise accomplishment in her life. "That's the technical word, I believe."

Poor Rosana, Lammiter thought, caught in such a web of disaster that not even those who are loyal to you have been able to tell you the whole truth. He looked at her beautiful face, strained, white, pathetic. She had changed in the last twenty-four hours: she had lost her self-confidence; something had crushed hope out of her heart. He felt a sudden cold shiver touch the nape of his neck. "Rosana," he said softly, "when all this is over—"

"Over?" she broke in. "But when? And how?"

"When it's all over," he said, with an optimism he did not feel, "then—" He stopped, listening to the footsteps entering the room below, and rose.

"It's Giuseppe," Rosana said.

Joe came upstairs whistling. Was it an act? Lammiter wondered: Joe liked to encourage people. Here were two who needed all Joe could give.

"Had a nice walk?" he asked Joe as he entered the room. Joe was more like a peasant than ever. He had borrowed a battered felt hat, and stuck a field poppy's frail stalk through its grease-stained ribbon.

"Had a nice talk?" Joe said with a grin. He took off his hat and turned to Rosana. "The signorina got here without trouble?"

"Of course," she told him severely. "We were beginning to worry about you, Giuseppe."

Lammiter looked at them in surprise. Then he remembered that Rosana believed that *she* was in authority. "Look," he said, "let's keep everything simple. Joe—Rosana—Bill. We're in this together." He gave them both a smile. There was a brief gleam of answering amusement in Joe's eyes. "Joe was on the scene last night more than either of us," he told Rosana. "So he has a better idea of how things stand. I think we'll elect him boss around here. We'll play it his way."

Rosana seemed a little startled, and then a little doubtful as she studied Joe's furrowed brow and ingenious grin.

"He can outthink both of us put together," Lammiter answered her thoughts. "He's a Sicilian, isn't he?"

Rosana smiled suddenly. "He's a Saracen, you mean. He will have us storming the castle with knives out. Thumb on the hilt, and strike up. Wasn't that your father's last piece of advice to you, Giusep—Joe?" But she settled herself on the wooden bench, and her smile was no longer teasing. "All right. What do we do?" She looked at Joe.

"First of all, we'll learn a few facts. Who drove you here in Pirotta's car?"

Rosana's eyes opened still more at the brisk voice. But she obeyed it. "A mechanic—one of the men at the garage—Poggioli's—where Pirotta has repairs done. He knows nothing. He was just hired to do a job. He is following instructions, though. He wouldn't let me out of the car, except at one café just beyond Terni; and then he came with me to the lavatory, and waited outside, and took me back to the car, so I couldn't telephone anyone."

"Did he talk much?"

"It's a long journey. He began to talk halfway."

"About himself?"

"His name is Giovanni. He was worried about not being able to say good-by to his girl except by a telephone call. She was angry. They were going to a party tomorrow night."

"He expects to be away from Rome, then?"

"He wouldn't answer that question. But there were three of Pirotta's suitcases in the back of the car. It looks as if he is going on a vacation."

"Did Giovanni talk about his girl?"

"Constantly. It seemed a safe subject, I think. Her name is Margherita. She works at Stefano's—that's a shop for making artificial flowers. She is seventeen. Very beautiful. Dark curls and good figure. They are getting married next month. That's about all, I think." She frowned, trying to recall anything else.

Joe took out an old envelope from one trouser pocket and a stump of pencil from another. Lammiter, sitting beside him on the bed, saw what he was jotting down. *Stefano—fiori artificiali—Margherita 17, tipo Lollobrigida —Giovanni, mecanico—Autorimessa Poggioli.* "It's good enough," Joe said. "It will be simple to track down the girl. She will know where her Giovanni is going."

Lammiter stirred restlessly.

Joe looked at him. "This is not useless," he said gently. "All we have to do is to wait for the next few hours. No one is leaving the Casa Grande until two o'clock, when the two men who forced Eleanor into the car are taking the bus. At present, they're on guard: one in front of Eleanor's room, the other at the telephone. Pirotta wants to be wakened at noon, and his car is to be ready for him at three. Signorina Halley is to be kept in her room until he returns this evening. Dinner for two." He looked at Rosana. "And one dinner on a tray in Miss Halley's room. And the mechanic eating with Alberto and Anna-Maria. Right?"

She nodded. "Anna-Maria asked how much food she must buy. The princess keeps an eye on the bills. And Pirotta said, 'Oh, enough, enough until tomorrow night. We'll be leaving then.' So it's my idea," and she glanced with a little smile at Joe, "that the important meeting at

Perugia will be over by tomorrow afternoon. Is it possible?"

Joe said with a grin, "I think Tony Brewster taught you a lot of things."

"Or perhaps," she said softly, "I learned a lot of things from Joe without knowing I was being taught." She stood up. "That's about all, isn't it? I had better get back now."

"Going back?" blurted out Lammiter. "Into that place?" Dinner for two, he remembered bitterly. "Are you still hoping you can influence Pirotta?" he asked angrily.

She shook her head. "That's one idea that died last night, when I kept my appointment with his car. He was there, waiting with the mechanic. When I saw he wasn't going, I knew he had tricked us again." She turned to Joe. "*You* know he had said over the telephone that he wanted to finish some work in the country, and that I was to bring along the papers I had on the Galante correspondence—that was an honest business deal he was arranging for his firm."

Joe said soothingly, "That's what he told you."

"But when I saw Pirotta wasn't going, I stepped out of his car. I was scared, and angry. Then he said that Eleanor was in danger, that he had to persuade her to leave Rome that night. He said that he needed me to be with her, to look after her, to keep her company. Do you know—I do think he told the truth then. Perhaps," she added bitterly, "it is the only time he ever told me the truth."

"So you got back into the car?" Lammiter asked.

"I got back into the car." She looked up at him. "You helped me when I needed help. So—" she shrugged her shoulders "—I help you. I'll get into Eleanor's room when she wakens. She was still half drugged when they arrived this morning. But she has to eat. And a tray must be carried into her room."

"You won't be allowed near her! Look, Rosana, Pirotta never told you the truth once in his life, except when he said you were beautiful. Last night at his car?—The same old confidence trick. He wanted you out of Rome. Brewster's been murdered and you've run away. See what he's building up around you? Suspicion, a wall of

suspicion as big and thick as that wall out there." He
caught Joe's eye. "How much evidence have Pirotta's
friends planted, how much fabricated? I bet, right now,
that Brewster's diary is being found."

"He never kept a diary. He *wouldn't!*" she said derisively.

"Of course he wouldn't. But either a diary or a letter
will be found saying he was becoming suspicious of you,
that he thought you were working against him, that he
had challenged you yesterday afternoon, and you had
been frightened. Joe—I ask you: am I talking nonsense?
Or is all that in the pattern?"

"Pattern?" Joe said and was as stupid as possible.
"Well, maybe . . . You write a play about it, eh? You
have a real good plot there." He said to Rosana, "Glad
we've got a writer fellow with us to show how plots are
made."

Rosana avoided their eyes. "Yes," she said haltingly,
"that could be true. It's in their—pattern." Then her
voice became bitter. "But I shall be allowed to see
Eleanor if I am willing to make her listen to Pirotta's
story. He needs me for that— I've already had the first
hints. He will persuade me, and I have to persuade Eleanor, that right is wrong and wrong is right. His story will
seem very, very good. Yes—that is also in the pattern."
Suddenly, her face was emotionless, and her voice reminded Lammiter of the princess. "I'm going back to the
Casa Grande. Now. At this moment. Is that agreed?"

Joe agreed.

"Bill," Rosana said, "you know someone has got to
reach Eleanor. She *must* know she is not alone."

"Yes," he said. "But—"

"Oh, you Americans! But—but—but! I shall come to
no harm." She began walking over to the door. She
looked down at the loose pink-and-green checked cotton
dress, and laughed as she pulled it in, for a moment,
against her slender waist. "How thin I have grown!"

"Tell Eleanor—" Lammiter began, as he followed her
to the door, and then he was silent.

"That you are here? Those will be my first words to
her." Then she was looking at him, most serious with her
large dark eyes. "Good-by, Bill."

He took her hand awkwardly. "Good-by, Rosana. Take

care of yourself." He kissed her cheek, on an impulse he could not explain. Or perhaps hand kissing was not his line.

"I shall, I shall," she said reassuringly. She touched his arm for a moment.

"I go with you part of the way," Joe told her, picking up his hat.

"More questions? But I told you *everything!*"

"What did the princess say on the telephone?"

"I couldn't talk to her. The mechanic wouldn't let me."

"What did she say to Alberto?"

"He wouldn't tell me."

"He wouldn't?"

"It upset him too much. But one thing I do know: the princess must be against Pirotta. For Alberto wouldn't even speak to him when he arrived in the Lancia. Anna-Maria had to do all the talking." She gave a last smile to Lammiter; and a cheerful wave of her hand. Then she started downstairs. Joe was about to follow her.

"Just a minute," Lammiter said, and caught Joe by his arm. "There's a limit to everything. Do you expect me to stay up here all day?"

"I'll be back soon."

"I'd like to stretch my legs, look around, get a feel of the town."

"I can't risk you——"

"What risk? None of Pirotta's hired men know me. I'll take no chances. I won't even try to climb the Casa Grande walls."

Joe relented. "Wait until the morning bus arrives. Follow it in. Look as if you could have come that way."

"I certainly won't try to look as if I had just buried my parachute."

"Okay, okay. Keep to the narrow streets. Pirotta's car has to travel along the main one."

"When does the bus get here?" Lammiter looked at his watch. It was now a quarter to eight.

Joe shrugged. "Depends on its business at the other little towns. You'll hear it, all right."

Rosana's voice called from downstairs: "Coming?"

"Coming!" Over his shoulder, to Lammiter, he said quietly, "If it makes you feel better, I'm going to telephone. We keep in touch with the big world, eh?" He gave a cheerful salute and ran downstairs.

"You're so *slow!*" Rosana scolded him gently in Italian.

"We'll be quick now. And careful?"

"*Very* careful." You could hear the smile in her voice. "What a mess you two have left in this kitchen! Someone ought to wash these dishes, put things away—"

"Yes, yes." He closed the kitchen door firmly.

Upstairs, Bill Lammiter stood at the window and waited until he saw Rosana in her borrowed dress—it looked pink at this distance, and far too noticeable—cross the field toward the wood. Then she vanished from sight. But once more, he couldn't see Joe. Then he looked at the gate to the town. For a moment, he was startled: a girl in a pink cotton dress was standing talking to two thick-waisted women in black. Other women joined them, all with bundles of laundry on their heads. Then they scattered, shouting good-naturedly in their strong hoarse voices to each other. Some followed a path across the road, to houses that must lie outside the walls. He counted three pink dresses altogether. He relaxed then.

He took off his tie, rolled up his sleeves, opened the top button of his shirt. He studied himself for a moment in the scrap of looking glass on the wall. That buttoned-down collar was straight from Madison Avenue. He took out his penknife and with its small blade carefully cut through the threads that held the buttons. Strange how laundries could remove buttons so easily, he thought as he sawed away. But he admitted the finished effect was more in local color once he had crumpled the collar still more.

Then he remembered the jacket which he would have to leave in this room. He went through its pockets and removed the handkerchief with the Evans photograph. Cigarettes and matches, too. And his keys. But passport, traveler's checks, his wallet? The checks could be left here, in his suitcase. The passport was another matter. He hated to part with it. It could fit into his trouser pocket and probably stay there if he didn't have to run, but he couldn't always be clamping one hand to his thigh to make sure the passport was still safe. Then he found he was smiling: in a play, a character would probably make a grand exit without giving a passing thought to all the damned documents he had to stow away about him; everyone bulged when he traveled nowadays. But he wasn't writing a play. All right, he decided, and opened his suitcase and stowed away his passport, his checks, a notebook, his heavy wallet, and his jacket. Then he locked the case and carried it into the storeroom along with Joe's discarded jacket. He laid them behind an open sack of down feathers. Someone hoping for a new mattress? He closed the door and returned to the bedroom, looking around him carefully, picking up the cigarette stub. He was leaving as little noticeable sign of his stay here as Joe had. The farmer wouldn't run into trouble from any prowlers. As Joe would say, you never could tell in this game.

He pocketed the neatly folded handkerchief and some lire notes he had taken from his wallet. No bulges, at least. He looked at his watch again, and wondered when the bus would come. He was ready to go.

Twenty-One

INSTANTLY, there came the bugling of a bus horn, and then the muted drone of a powerful engine pulling up the hill to Montesecco. Bill Lammiter, lying on the bed, fallen into that strange state of waking dream when the body accepts sleep but the mind holds it a short distance away, roused himself and swung his legs onto the floor. The drone was louder. It could be a truck, but it might be the bus. He glanced at his watch once more. With a shock, he saw that it was almost noon.

He went to the window and waited there. At least he felt rested. And less depressed. Joe hadn't come back, but that didn't worry him very much: Joe had left with several purposes and he had told Lammiter only one of them. He wondered now what commands the princess had given old Alberto on the telephone at three o'clock in the morning. He could imagine the operator, roused out of bed, cross but curious, forgetting about cold feet as she listened to the princess. But the princess would imagine that, too: perhaps her directions to Alberto had been so cryptic that Alberto was still puzzling them out. What had she thought Alberto could do, anyway? Lock Pirotta in his room like a disobedient schoolboy?

Impatiently, he watched a boy cycle out of the gates, an enormous bundle of dried twigs on his back, and then veer well in to the side of the narrow road. A farmer with two yoked oxen, pulling a cart laden with barrels, looked back downhill over his shoulder and hauled the beasts off the road close to the trees, to give safe passing-room. The loud engine throbbed, changed down to an extra low gear to cope with the last hill outside the gates, and then the bus came into sight. Briefly. For behind it there was raised a cloud of dust from the loose surface of the road. The bus eased its way through the gates and gathered a spurt of speed from the rough pavement now under its wheels.

Bill Lammiter started downstairs, a little impressed by the bus. It was not so large as the CIT or Europabus giants, which he had seen so often leaving Rome for destinations as far off as Venice or the Swiss border, but it looked new and shining. The people of the hill towns were better served than he had imagined. Good, he thought: they must be tired of watching well-fed, well-dressed tourists who could afford to spend four weeks without working. And yet, as he opened the kitchen door and stepped into the cool shadows of the yard, he couldn't remember any signs of grudge or hostility or hidden jealousy from any of the people in the month he had spent among them. "Enjoy yourselves; smile: we only ask for politeness," they seemed to say to the visitors. "If we had your money, bless it, we'd do the same. And perhaps we shall, someday. Who knows? There's the lottery, there's my uncle in America, there's that job I may get if the typewriter factory opens near my home." They were a concentration of optimists—how else would they have survived so many centuries of invaders and looters?

Borrowing some of the Italians' perpetual hope, he crossed the shadows of the farmyard and entered the white blinding sunlight of the olive grove. Above, the sky was cobalt blue and cloudless; from the dry grass, came the cicadas' constant chorus. Round the gate, activity had died away. The meal of the day was approaching, and the women were in their kitchens. Only an old man stood there, a lonely sentinel leaning on a stick, squinting in the strong glare, supervising the plain below. *"Buon giorno!"* he said to the passing stranger, and looked back at the view. *"Buon giorno!"* Lammiter said, and stepped into the town.

The street ran straight up from the gate for no more than three hundred yards, and entered, at the top of its hill, into the beginning of a piazza. He glimpsed three or four tourists waiting for someone. They must have arrived with the bus. He dodged into the first small side street leading to the right, so narrow that one car would only scrape through at considerable risk to its paint work. He didn't imagine Pirotta would drive down here, with a bright smile and a wave of his hand to children who played in the shade. Neither the children, nor the old men sitting at the doors, nor the women who had come out for a moment to make sure their street was still there, paid much attention to him after the first all-over glance. He noticed two girls, foreigners, taking photographs of an old doorway a little ahead of him. So he dodged again, into the first street on his right, and hoped it would bring him near the wall. His plan was to walk all round the town, following the inside of the wall wherever possible. He was curious to see not only the layout of the town, but how many entrances Montesecco had. When he found Eleanor again, a knowledge of this little town might mean the difference between entrapment and escape.

He had entered by the west gate. When he reached the south gate, he saw that it led nowadays only to a road that had degenerated into a rough track leading out to fields and trees. This couldn't have been the entrance Rosana and Joe had used: it would only have led them into the little street where he now stood. He walked on, toward the east. And then, suddenly, he saw he had reached a high-walled garden of some size, adjoining a three-storied house, dominating everything else on this street. A house? It was a small fifteenth-century palace, built to withstand an army. This wall of the house, rising blankly from the cobblestones, was formidable:

stopped in front of the town hall. A woman with a large basket and a small boy got out. Three people, soberly dressed in their Sunday clothes, rose from their seats in the shade and climbed on board. That was the local bus, all right. Now it was swinging around the piazza to leave by the way it had entered, bugling its horn gaily at two young girls who had suddenly emerged from one of the side streets. Americans, he decided as he noted their clothes and cameras. He gave up all idea of taking a short cut along this side of the piazza to reach a south exit to the town wall.

Just as he was turning to retrace his steps down the alley he saw the two American girls stop as they looked across at the church, grasp each other's hands, and then run toward the nearest street. They were laughing. He glanced over at the church. Now he saw what had driven the girls away: a flutter of tourists, of all shapes and sizes, was coming slowly out of the church with the anesthetized look of those who had just swallowed a lecture, while their guide still talked as he shepherded them toward the little café-restaurant. He had his amusing moments, too, to judge from the sudden gust of laughter that blew across the piazza. He was a small man, thin, neatly dressed in a gray suit with a panama hat worn at a jaunty angle. Something in his movements, a quick grace, caught Lammiter's eye.

For a moment, Lammiter froze, staring at the man across the square. Then, instinctively, he turned on his heel and retreated down the alley, no longer cursing its curves and twists. Salvatore Sabatini . . . that had been Salvatore. Or have I just got him on the brain? he wondered. He wished now that he had waited to see the guide's face more clearly, or that the man had taken off his hat to mop his brow and show the color of his hair. But the guide had not been so obliging. He had only walked with a light step, made a dramatic gesture toward the town hall, raised a laugh with some merry quip, and then led his flock relentlessly toward the restaurant.

But I couldn't wait, Lammiter thought: once he was near enough to be identified, he could have seen me, too. Then Lammiter put aside all speculation and concentrated on his direction. His only aim now was to get back to the farmhouse. He hoped to heaven that Joe was there, waiting.

He had some more trouble, for he must not appear to be a man who was in a hurry. Or a man who was going anywhere. He tried to look like a tourist who was wandering around by himself. It took him ten minutes to fight his way out of the labyrinth of small streets and alleys, twice retracing his steps, once almost back on the piazza itself. But at last he came to the main street of the town, which would take him down to its entrance gate. Carefully, he made sure there were no tourists in sight. No, they must be back at the restaurant, settling down to plates of heaped spaghetti. And there, thank God, was the gateway itself.

He passed under its huge arch and a blast of heat engulfed him as he stepped onto the dusty road that led down the hill of olive trees to the plain beneath. The farmhouse dozed among its warm terraces. The cicadas were starting the ninety-fifth movement of their daily symphony.

"Mr. Lammiter!" The voice was young, surprised, and soprano. "Why, Mr. Lammiter!"

If only to silence a third "Mr. Lammiter!" ringing out over the countryside, he halted and looked around. The two American girls he had avoided in the town had been standing to one side of the gateway, studying the posters plastered up on the old wall. Now they ran toward him, bare feet sure in flat-heeled sandals, their wide skirts and crisp blouses looking cool and uncrushed even in this wilting heat. They had broad smiles on their pretty faces, flashing sets of very white and even teeth at him in delight. He didn't share it. Who the hell are they? he wondered.

The blonde one said, tossing back her horsetail of hair like a young colt, "Mr. Lammiter—don't you remember me?" Her voice, fortunately, had dropped back to normal.

"Sorry," he said, "I'm not Lammiter." He tried to walk on, but her child's blue eyes looked at him so accusingly that the moment of escape was lost.

"But you are, too," she said, hurt. Her friend with the Italian haircut was fixing the strap of her camera most tactfully. Then the blonde suddenly smiled again. "Oh—you're traveling *incognito!* I see—" She looked at the red-haired girl with relief. "He's traveling incognito, Julie. They always do that. I *told* you."

"Goodness," said the soft puzzled voice of Julie, "all my friends spend all their free time writing novels and things. But I don't think *any* of them know they'll have to travel incognito. I don't think any of them know *that*. Or they wouldn't be writing. I mean, why do you *get* famous if you don't want to be known?"

"Oh Julie!" the blonde said, taking charge. Then to Lammiter, "We saw you before. I *thought* it was you. I waved, but——"

"Was that in the piazza?" he asked quickly. He hadn't noticed any waving.

"No. In a little street, about half an hour ago. Just after the bus arrived."

"Did you point me out to the others from the bus?" He was smiling, playing it as easily as he could. But, again, his stomach muscles knotted and tightened.

"No!" the little blonde said most decidedly. Then she laughed. "We aren't speaking to *them!*"

"We're isolationists, temporarily," Julie said with a giggle.

"We've been abandoned," the blonde said, "abandoned on the doorstep of a little hill town. And it's *frustrating*. Because over there," she waved to the north section of the wall, "you can look out of a gate and *see* Perugia on a hill of its own."

"Look—this sun's pretty hot," Lammiter said. The approach to the town felt more open with every passing minute. His eyes searched for the nearest adequate cover. And it lay, unfortunately, in that row of trees at the edge of the road almost opposite the farmhouse. He looked in despair along the trail that circled the outside of the wall. At some distance, there was a patch of trees and another farmhouse. "What about walking along here?" he suggested. "There's shade among those trees." He pointed northward.

"Too far," the blonde said, shaking her head. "These trees here are much nearer," and she set off down the main road, Julie following her, handbags and cameras swinging blithely. Lammiter hesitated, debating whether it would be possible to steer them away from the direction of the farmhouse and onto the subject of the guide instead.

"Could you give us a lift to Perugia?" the blonde girl asked suddenly, turning around to wait for him.

"I haven't a car. Sorry."

"Then we really are stuck here until the five o'clock bus," she told Julie.

"Four hours!" Julie said in despair. "And we've photographed *everything* already. Except the white bulls. *Where* have they all gone? They *were* here. I saw two beauties just in front of the gate as we arrived—and a wooden yoke—and bells on the ends of their horns—and now there isn't even *one* in sight. It's *maddening!*"

She stopped and opened her camera. "Just a moment! This might be something interesting."

Lammiter walked on quickly, veering toward the opposite side of the road from the farmhouse. "Why don't we sit here for a few minutes?" He stepped onto the grass, and then behind a tree. "Did your guide tell you what happened to the olives last winter? It seems that—"

"You *don't* remember me," the blonde said in a low voice, giving a quick look over her shoulder to make sure Julie was far enough away. "But it was only yesterday, and I sat on your suitcase and you wrote—"

"Of course I remember," he said quickly. He did, now. "Today you've got a green bow on your hair instead of blue. Very mixing."

"I'm Sally—Sally Maguire." She looked around again. But Julie was still on the road, her head bent over the camera's view finder.

"Burbank, California."

"Now I feel much better!" She smiled delightedly.

He wished he did. He'd have to wait at least three minutes before he mentioned the guide again. "Have a seat," he suggested.

She looked at the sparse dry grass doubtfully, but she sat down, gathering her wide skirts tightly and carefully around her legs. "Where are you stopping?"

"Oh, I just walked up here for exercise."

"You *walked?* From the valley?" She was horrified.

"I'm walking back for lunch, right now."

"Goodness!" she said. That prospect didn't rouse much enthusiasm. "Do you know Italian, Mr.—Mr.—?"

"A little," he admitted. "And Smith's the name at present. Original, isn't it?"

"If you could do some talking for us—I mean, could you come back to the town with us? I hate to ask you to do any extra walking, but—"

"I haven't very much time," he said awkwardly. "What's the trouble anyway?"

"Transportation," she said gloomily. "You see, this guide— Oh hello, Julie! Any luck?"

Julie came over to where they sat, closing her camera. "The light is wrong or something," she said ruefully. "All that scenery and nothing to take . . . The hills just flatten out like split peas. It's—"

"Maddening," Lammiter said abruptly. "Now, Sally— what about this guide?"

Julie didn't sit down. Perhaps she didn't like hearing herself quoted. She stood, looking around her. "I can see a farmhouse over there," she said, suddenly pointing across the road. "Haystacks . . . Why, there may be white bulls, too. And there's the farmer! Hi, there!" she called, and began to run toward Joe.

Lammiter rose quickly as Sally scrambled to her feet. She said, "So it is! Perhaps he will know!" And she began hurrying after Julie.

Joe had been crossing the yard when Julie called out, and he stood now, facing her, a jar of water in his hand, trapped. He made the decision to accept this complication, seemingly, for he set down the jar of water and came forward a few steps to intercept the girl and keep her away from the open kitchen door. From where he now stood, the Fiat could not be seen.

Lammiter lit a cigarette. Keep out of this, he told himself. But it was not easy. "He can't speak English," Julie called back to Sally. "Hurry—you've got the phrase book!"

Sally had a better idea. She halted and looked back at Lammiter. "Mr. Smith— Please, would you help us?" She waved to him frantically, and then ran on. So he followed, crossing the road quickly, deciding, as Joe had decided, that the sooner this was over the better for everyone.

The girls' heads were bent over the phrase book as he joined the little group. Joe had somehow managed to edge them away from the open yard toward the shelter of a tree. For a moment, his eyes looked at Lammiter, half amused, half angry. Lammiter had only time to give one small helpless gesture before Sally looked up.

"Would you ask him if there are any other buses? *Before* five o'clock?"

Julie said, "Here it is! *Toro. Toro.* And *bianco*—that's white, isn't it?"

"I don't think the animal is a bull, exactly," Lammiter said. "Is that what you want to ask—permission to photograph his white oxen?"

"The bus," Sally said, "don't forget the bus."

Under Joe's critical eyes, Lammiter's Italian failed him. It degenerated into disjointed words and phrases.

"My!" said Sally, listening to Joe's flowing reply, "doesn't he make it sound so *easy!*" She looked at Lammiter. "Did you get all that?"

"Some of it. He says the oxen are mostly down in the fields with the men. You'll find them all dozing under the trees. It's siesta-time."

"*Siesta,*" Joe said, and nodded vigorously. "*Siesta.*" He looked as if he were about to leave.

"What about the bus?" Sally asked.

"It leaves at two," Lammiter said, definite about that. The afternoon bus left at two: the men who had forced Eleanor into the Lancia, their job over, were leaving then. It was the best news Joe had brought back that morning. Two o'clock, and two less to deal with at the Casa Grande.

Sally shook her head. "Two o'clock? But that's the bus that just *won't* take us any farther than here! It's a chartered bus, a tour, with a guide and all. Tell him that!"

"They put you off the bus?" Lammiter asked, in genuine amazement.

"Well, you see, we really weren't supposed to be on it. The guide was angry—"

"Oh, but he was nice afterward," Julie said.

"Not nice enough," Sally told her firmly. "We could have stood, couldn't we, to Perugia? Or sat on our suitcases in the aisle, or something? Couldn't we?"

"It's against the law, he said."

"Phooey!" said Sally. "If the peasants can stand in a bus, so can I. I've two legs like them, haven't I?" Then she turned to Lammiter. "Tell him *that* bus is all full. Two people are getting on here in—in—*what's* the name of this town?—Montesecco—and that's another thing, the bus wasn't even scheduled to come here. Assisi for lunch, we were told. And then Perugia. But we just rushed through the churches in Assisi, and here we are in Montesecco."

"He said this place was less crowded for lunch. I'll say it is!" Julie interposed.

"Tell him," Sally repeated, nodding toward Joe.

"Let me get it all straight first," Lammiter said. "You got onto this chartered bus in Rome—"

"Because there was no room, not a single seat, on any other of the buses. We hadn't any reservations—just decided last night we were going. So this morning we went along to the Esedra piazza, you know—the one with all the fountains and buses and things—and we couldn't get a seat *any*where. It was *frustrating!* Then this nice young man from the CIT offices—"

"*He* was very nice," Julie said.

"—tried to help us get to Perugia. He found these two seats on this bus, empty, no one in them. So he popped us and our luggage on board. The driver didn't say anything, just took our money. No one paid any attention— they were all too worried because the guide hadn't turned up. Then when we were almost out of Rome, the bus stopped at a little café, and this guide came on board, apologizing like mad. Then he saw us, and was absolutely furious. He wanted to put us off the bus right there. But we just sat and smiled. *No* one was using the old seats, anyway."

"But he was nice, afterward," Julie conceded. "And he could talk *five* languages: French, German, Swedish, Dutch, and English. That was for us—the English, I mean."

"And now," said Lammiter firmly, "the two seats on the bus are needed for two people boarding it at Montesecco. But why are you in such a hurry to get to Perugia?"

"Our friends are all there," Julie said with a smiling glance at Sally, "for the summer school. And by Saturday we'll have to leave Perugia to get to Genoa in time to catch our boat. It's maddening."

"It certainly is," Lammiter agreed gravely. "What is the guide's name, do you know? He could be reported."

"Oh, we wouldn't want to get him into trouble," Julie said. "He was an Italian. And the old ladies loved him, didn't they, Sally? It was Signore Samarini this and Signore Samarini that, all the way."

"Sabatini," Sally corrected. "Signore Sabatini."

Joe had been a very patient Italian, polite if not comprehending. But for one brief fraction of a second, his eyes looked very directly at Lammiter.

"Sabatini—you're sure?" Lammiter asked. And I was right, he thought in a quick moment of jubilation. That *was* Sabatini I saw.

She laughed. "I couldn't forget it. Once, my favorite novel was *Scaramouche*. I asked Signore Sabatini if he was any relation to the author, but he wasn't, and he didn't have time to read novels, either. Squelch!"

Julie said, "But I don't think you should report him. We don't want to get him into trouble. After all, it was a *chartered* bus."

"Where is it going?" Lammiter asked, casually. "Perugia, and then?" Beside him, Joe was standing very still.

"Florence tomorrow. Next day Venice," Sally said with the scorn of the tourist who has spent two months instead of two weeks on her travels.

Lammiter stared across at Joe. "They aren't having much of a stay in Perugia, are they?"

"Not much," Sally answered Lammiter. "They're leaving Perugia at the crack of dawn, practically. They'll just have this afternoon, that's all when you come to think of it. I bet they're in bed by nine o'clock."

"Wish I had the afternoon there," Julie said regretfully. She opened her camera and kneeled to look up at a haystack, symmetrically wound round a center pole that pointed into the sky. "Well, this will just have to do instead."

Sally said, "Ask the farmer if there is no one in Montesecco who could give us a ride to Perugia."

Lammiter translated. Joe, watching Julie carefully, was edging away. "Get them back to the road, for God's sake," he said, "and don't let them photograph you." He turned his back on Julie. "*Buon giorno!*" he said to Sally. Quickly, he lifted his water jar and carried it toward the farmhouse. Its doors closed firmly.

"No ride. No bus. What's happened to our luck?" Sally asked, finding a smile somehow.

"Well, he's got to catch up on his siesta." Lammiter began walking back to the road.

"If *only* he had waited," Julie said, "he'd have made *such* a good study. All those wrinkles and furrows—"

"The light's all wrong, too many shadows here," Lammiter said quickly. "Hey, don't waste your film on me, Julie."

She lowered her camera, frowning, calculating how much film she had left, and then sighed in agreement.

"Come on," he urged them, "there's another farm over there—along that trail under the wall." He pointed toward the north side of the town.

"They'll be having a siesta, too," Sally said gloomily. "I don't see it—this business of going to bed in the middle of the day."

"And there are some others who don't see it, either," he said thankfully. Three young boys were playing outside the gates: or, to be exact, they were having a wonderful time tearing large strips off all the posters. "There's a study for you, Julie. You can call it *And a little child shall lead them*."

"Look, look, look!" cried Julie. Coming along the trail that Lammiter had pointed out was a farm cart drawn at a slow ceremonial pace by two stately white oxen. "And they've got hats on!" she added in delight as she ran past him, past Sally, racing over the rough ground without one thought of a sprained ankle.

"Perhaps," thought Sally out loud, new ideas popping into her bright blue eyes, "perhaps he's going down to the main road—and if he'd only wait until we got our suitcases—then we'll find a passing car in the valley—perhaps?"

"I don't think you'll need me as a interpreter this time," he said, as he listened to the mixture of broken English and one-word Italian that drifted over toward them. The driver was young, smiling, delighted with this break in boredom. "Good-by, Sally."

"Can't we give you a lift?"

"No, thanks. I'll cut down over the oliver terraces and make good time."

"Thanks for *everything*. 'Bye."

"Thank *you*," he said, as he watched her run toward Julie. The cameras were out. The children were gathering around. The driver beamed from his seat on the edge of the car and straightened his hat. The oxen stood placidly. Everyone was happy.

Twenty-Two

FOR APPEARANCE'S SAKE, although he didn't expect any further interest in him now, Lammiter climbed down through three terraces. It was harder work than it had looked, and the heat among the olive trees was blistering. So he veered to his left and circled cautiously back to the farmhouse.

The kitchen door was open. Joe was finishing a hasty meal. He looked up at Lammiter, shaking his head slowly.

"It's all right," said Lammiter. "They've met some friends up at the gate."

Joe pushed back his chair abruptly and went to the stairs. "Where can I wash?—I'm filthy," Lammiter asked, helping himself to Chianti. Then he saw the water Joe had carried in, and a basin beside it. He ripped off his damp shirt. He was drying himself with it when Joe came downstairs. "Well, did you see them for yourself?"

"They're loading the suitcases onto the cart. But don't give me any more shocks like them." He sat down at the table. "Come on. Eat!" Then, as Lammiter helped himself to cheese and bread, Joe said, "Sabatini . . . There couldn't by any chance be another man using that name? Someone who was sent to take Sabatini's place?" Joe was arguing it out with himself. "He did not leave with the bus from the Piazza Esedra, remember. He got in much later, outside Rome. Why? To avoid all the guides and drivers who were gathered at the Esedra, perhaps?"

"Or the police," Lammiter said with a smile. "Stop kidding yourself, Joe." But it must be difficult for Joe to grant that someone had played the old confidence trick on him and on Brewster, and played it well: no one likes to admit he has bought the Brooklyn Bridge, or that someone he thought was a friend turns out to be a traitor. "No one has taken Sabatini's place to cover up his murder. He's alive. And in good spirits. I saw him."

"Where?" The word shot out like a bullet.

"In the piazza. He was taking his tourists to eat at the

restaurant." He glanced at his watch. "Just three-quarters of an hour ago. They'll still be there."

Joe had risen to his feet. "But Sabatini won't eat with them. He didn't come to Montesecco to enjoy its cooking." He took a step toward the door, and then paused. "Sabatini—" he said, softly "—alive and walking around as if nothing had happened." His lips tightened.

Lammiter remembered last night in Joe's car. "At least," he said quietly, "we know the kind of man we have against us."

Joe nodded, grim-faced. Slowly, he said, still puzzling out the reason why Sabatini should have come to Montesecco, "He's making a check, making sure that everything is going well." Joe's eyes suddenly gleamed. "Or is there some change in plans, some last-minute instructions?"

"He doesn't trust Pirotta?"

"That kind of man trusts no one." Joe took some more steps toward the door. *"Mannaggia!* If only we had a telephone in this house!"

"You aren't thinking of walking into the town, now? My God—you are likely to run into Sabatini on the prowl. Wait until two o'clock comes, and the bus leaves."

"I want to see him with my own eyes."

"He's got eyes, too. And if he is making a last-minute check—" Lammiter stopped short. "Joe!"

"Some risks can't be avoided," Joe said angrily.

"Joe! Listen, will you? If this *is* a last-minute check, can the meeting be in Perugia today? He leaves tomorrow for Florence, remember?"

"He won't attend the meeting. That is not his job."

"What is his job? Security, isn't it?"

"If you are right and he isn't an Italian," Joe said, "he could be a member of the NKVD working in Italy."

Lammiter pushed aside his plate of bread and cheese. He tried not to think of Eleanor. He forced his mind back to Perugia. "Sabatini won't leave Perugia until Evans is safely out of there."

"You have only the word of two girls that Sabatini leaves Perugia tomorrow. He may not go with that bus. He may stay behind, rejoin the tour tomorrow night in Florence. What would be a safer way to travel to Venice?"

Venice—Lammiter thought. Why Venice?

Joe was saying, "You're putting more trust in your two maniacs than in Rosana."

"I'm putting more trust in them than in Pirotta. Rosana only repeated what he told the housekeeper. 'Tomorrow night—we'll be leaving then.' Very obliging of him to announce his departure so frankly." He rose. "The meeting is this afternoon. Pirotta takes Eleanor away with him tonight. Is that it?"

Joe looked at him. Slowly, he said, "Could be. Could be . . . I'll report it anyway. If you are wrong, Bill, then I'll come asking you for a job." He pulled a watch out of his pocket. "Half-past one."

"Half-past one it is." Lammiter timed his watch exactly.

Joe was calculating. He said, "I wait until ten minutes before the bus leaves. I make sure that Sabatini and his two men climb on board. Then I telephone. Then I see a couple of people. Then I come back here for you."

Lammiter shook his head. "I'll wait, too, until Sabatini leaves on that bus. But then I'm heading for the Casa Grande."

"No!"

"Yes! Don't worry. I'll keep out of Pirotta's sight. And as soon as he drives off for the meeting in Perugia, I'll bring Eleanor and Rosana out."

"No, Bill. There's too much risk. I don't want any alarms being telephoned to Perugia."

"But that mechanic—Giovanni—will be the only opposition left. He's harmless enough."

"Not as harmless as you think. He's already done a stretch in prison: assault and robbery. Now he's got a job to do that no honest man would take even for a million lire. And that's his price. We traced his girl this morning. She got scared and told us."

"A million lire?" That was less than seventeen hundred dollars, but it sounded better in lire. "What's the job?"

"She didn't know."

Lammiter said, "Joe—what are you trying to hide from me? Last night we talked about a lot of things. We gave ourselves a pretty clear view of the kind of man who had Brewster murdered. He is ruthless, cold-blooded, and as wily as they come. You told me he might think it

wise to get rid of Eleanor, but he couldn't risk any publicity. Yet there's one kind of publicity he could risk.
Eleanor could disappear with Pirotta, couldn't she? An
elopement, Joe, an apparent elopement. Anyone would
accept that story."

Joe was silent.

"Did the mechanic's girl tell the police where he is
going? Didn't she know that?"

"Venice." Abruptly, Joe moved into the yard. He
turned quickly to his left, toward the side of the house
where the car lay.

Lammiter gripped the back of his wooden chair.
Venice, he was thinking again, Venice . . . the place for
lovers and elopements. But a gondola on the Grand Canal
by moonlight was only one-half of Venice, the enchanted
half. There was the workaday half, the quays where the
ships of all nations lay and loaded and unloaded. Venice
was an Adriatic port. You could take a ship there, in
sight of the Grand Canal, and you could sail out through
the lagoon to Greece, to Turkey, to the Black Sea.

He looked down at his hands, knuckles white through
the deep tan. He swung round as a shadow fell on the
oblique stream of sunlight now spreading over the
threshold. It was Joe. Lammiter took a deep breath and
relaxed his grip on the chair.

Joe said, "Ugly thoughts you were thinking. Here!" He
held out a revolver. "That will keep them company." He
looked at his watch. "Time to go. How do you plan to
get into the Casa Grande?"

"By the gate down at the woods. There's a gamekeeper's
cottage. His name is—Jacopone?"

Joe nodded. "I told him he might expect to see you."
He half smiled. "I had a feeling you might get restless
and do something damned stupid."

"Thanks," Lammiter said, "thanks, friend." He slipped
the revolver into his pocket. "And here's something for
you." He took out the folded handkerchief and passed
it over to Joe. "It's the photograph Eleanor took of
Evans, up at Tivoli. Perhaps you could send it to Perugia?
It isn't very clear; but it's better than nothing."

Joe took the handkerchief, checked inside it but wasted
no time in examining the photograph. "You took a long
time to trust Joe," he said as he pocketed the handker-

chief, and he smiled. "Oh well, now I can stop worrying about you."

"I forgot about that photograph." And that was true. He had forgotten, until he put his hand in his pocket.

"Sure, sure. Good luck!"

"Good luck to you. When do we meet?"

"Chi sa?"

Yes, Lammiter thought: who knows?

Suddenly Joe put his arms round Lammiter's shoulders, gave him a brief embrace and a thump on the back. Then he moved to the door, slipped quietly into the farmyard, and was gone.

Lammiter closed the door, ran upstairs, found his case and opened it. First thing needed was a shave. That cost three careful minutes in front of the fly-spotted glass. Quickly, he put on a clean shirt, a new tie, and a fresh jacket. He jammed the passport and wallet and checks into his pockets. If his plan failed, if he were to be discovered wandering around the princess's Casa Grande, he was going to look exactly like what he was: Bill Lammiter in search of his girl. That way, he wouldn't have to explain what he was doing in Montesecco. That way, Joe wouldn't be connected with him. He would make his story clear, and he would make his story hold.

When he was ready, the suitcase hidden once more, the bed smoothed down, nothing forgotten—he clamped a quick hand to each of his pockets and checked their various bulges—he crossed over to the window. He closed the shutters as he had found them when he first entered the room, leaving only a small crack of light which still would give him a glimpse of the entrance gate of the town. He glanced at his watch again. Two more minutes, and the bus would leave the piazza. He wished Joe luck, wherever he was.

As he waited, he perfected his story. The princess had told him Eleanor was at Montesecco. So he had come here. By bus—to Assisi—yes, that could be true: the buses stopped at Assisi for lunch, Sally—or was it Julie?—had said, bless both those inspired and amiable maniacs. And then, in Assisi, he had hired a taxi to the gates of Montesecco. His driver had pointed out the Casa Grande to him. He had got into the grounds by exploring along the outside of the wall and convincing the game-keeper that the princess had sent him. Yes, that was the story. If he ever got time to explain it, he thought grimly.

Then he heard the heavy drone of the bus, lumbering cautiously down the street toward the gate. It came slowly out from under the heavy arch like an elephant testing its way cautiously at the edge of a water hole: and then its brakes were eased a little and it started to gather more speed down the road, leaving a large cloud of dust swirling around the torn posters. Signore Sabatini was no doubt pointing out and explaining the withered olive groves.

He closed the shutters and went downstairs. The table needed clearing. Then he decided to leave it littered. Two men had eaten there: that was all right—two men lived here, didn't they? Only, neither of them would have wasted any food. He dropped his unfinished piece of cheese back onto its platter, and pocketed the half-eaten crust of bread: the chickens in the yard would dispose of that evidence. Then he saw his damp and discarded shirt. He bundled it up and threw it under the bed. He smiled when he saw it was not alone. Someone else had the same idea about dirty clothes.

He opened the door, and looked back for a last reassurance. The sun streamed obliquely into the room. Still life, by Vermeer in rustic mood. He nodded, satisfied. He closed the door. Watchfully, he crossed the farmyard, and entered the olive grove.

This was sheltered ground. Even in the bad frost this year, these trees had had help from the winter sun. There were gray-green leaves on some of their branches, thriving on the warmth of the baking earth around their gnarled and twisted trunks. Then the grass of the field was under his feet, long and dry, but soft and yielding. Here the desultory breeze wandering aimlessly around the hills could stir the air gently with its warm breath, so that the rays of concentrated heat were broken and there was a feeling of almost coolness in comparison to the roasting oven around the olives. He reached the first green trees, the beginning of the wood. Bliss, bliss, this true coolness of dappled shade and softly stirring leaves. The wood was deep, a place for small game. He recalled now that of the dozen little shops he had passed that morning, scattered around the narrow streets, two had displayed good rifles, excellent shotguns. A lot of hunting took place among these little hill towns.

Under the cover of the trees, he could abandon his downward course. Abruptly, he turned to travel uphill toward the wall of the town. He began to worry that he might have gone beyond the gate in the wall that led to the gamekeeper's lodge. He reached the edge of the wood, and before him was the trail edging the vast encircling wall of Montesecco. Where now—to his left or to his right?

He turned to his right, his worry growing. Stupid, Joe had called him, and so, remembering that, he had been overcautious. Or had that been Joe's purpose? He increased his pace, angry with Joe, angry with himself. And then, as the trail curved round with the wall, he saw the gate just ahead of him. It was not a giant, like the other gates. It was simply a good-sized opening, handsome enough, probably constructed to let the owner of the house inside the wall enjoy his hunting without having to ride through the town.

Even as Lammiter took a deep breath of relief, a man stepped out from the trees and faced him, a man with a gun under his arm. A shotgun or a rifle? A rifle, Lammiter decided. Could this be Jacopone? Yet a gamekeeper usually carried a shotgun.

For a moment, Lammiter hesitated. Then he walked on. The man was dressed as the farmer had been, except that his trousers were tucked into high laced boots. His felt hat was pulled down over his forehead to shade his eyes. They never left Lammiter.

"*Buon giorno,*" Lammiter said, smiled, looked at the rifle. He got no reply. The man was old, his brown face wrinkled, many creases around his keen gray eyes. His face was thin, hawk-nosed; his hair was white. And Lammiter noted, too, that he himself was being studied, slowly and carefully, not a detail missed, whether it was his shoelaces or his haircut.

"*Americano,*" the old man said at last. He smiled. He had few teeth, and those were dark in color; but Lammiter thought it the finest smile he had seen in years.

"Jacopone? Giuseppe told me—"

"*Si, si.*" Jacopone turned to the gate, beckoning Lam-

miter to follow. Quietly, without another word, he opened
the gate and they entered. Carefully, the gate was locked
behind them. Lammiter's eyes left the coat of arms—
wolf's head, three beehives, this was the place all right—
and turned to look at the garden. He was standing at the
beginning of a short avenue of thick trees, their branches
meeting overhead to form a green tunnel. At the other
end of this short avenue, he could see a formal garden
of shrubs and graveled walls, and then a terrace, and
then a part of the house itself. But the tunnel of trees hid
any windows.

Jacopone touched his arm and began walking toward
a little cottage tucked well to one side of the gate. He
walked without talking, but without much concern either.
For there was a screen of shrubs and trees making sure
that the gamekeeper's cottage would give no offense to
any aesthetic eye looking out on the view from the Casa
Grande.

They passed the cottage. There was a wooden chair
at its door, and a large dog chained to a small tree beside it. The dog rose, faced Lammiter. But a word from
Jacopone silenced the beginning of a suspicious growl,
and the dog settled down again in its patch of cool
shade. It even thumped a heavy tail by way of apology.

They followed a path that kept close to the high wall
marking the boundary of the princess's land. But again
they could walk normally without fear of being seen, for
the path was hidden from the garden and the house by a
continuous hedge of tall rhododendrons. This, Lammiter decided, must be the servants' entrance. It was
probably as safe as old Jacopone seemed to think it was.

Quietly, Lammiter asked, "The American girl—is she
safe?"

The old man frowned at him. He had difficulty in understanding Lammiter's Italian accent. Then he raised
his shoulders for a brief moment: he didn't know, but he
hoped for the best.

"And the Signorina Rosana?"

Jacopone smiled. "She is brave, that one. The courage
of a man." Courage, he seemed to be saying, kept people
safe. He nodded. He made a quick signal for silence.

The distance to the house had been short. Here they
were, entering a neat square of hedged-in garden stand-

ing almost at the side of the house itself. It was the kitchen
garden, Lammiter noted, with vegetables and peach trees,
cutting flowers, vines, everything arranged in its own
neat space so that not one yard of earth was wasted. He
remembered how little room there was in this town: the
grounds of the house were small, even if they were constructed in the grand manner.

"Wait!" Jacopone whispered, backing Lammiter determinedly behind the shelter of a peach tree. He pointed
to himself, and then to the house. *"La signorina Rosana!"* he said, softly, hoarsely. "I tell her."

"I'll go with you." Lammiter took a step toward the
house.

The gamekeeper shook his head with unexpected
energy.

"But if there is any trouble—" Lammiter said.

The gamekeeper had understood that word, at least.
"Trouble?" He smiled, raised his rifle to his shoulder,
pointing its barrel into the sky. "I shoot."

"You'll give a warning shot if you need me?"

Jacopone frowned, and then gave up trying to understand. Again, he aimed a shot into the air, nodded, and
turned away. He stepped through an opening in the
hedge that lay nearest to this wing of the house, and vanished.

Patience, Lammiter told himself, patience: the old boy
has saved you at least half an hour of prowling around,
and you never could have climbed that wall in the first
place. He resigned himself to waiting, forced down his
rising anxiety, and studied the house.

From here, only the upper floors were visible, their
windows tightly shuttered against the afternoon sun, but
from the angles of the roofs he could make a guess at
the size and shape of the place. It was larger than it had
seemed from the street: that square of building could not
be solid, it must have a central courtyard. It was strong,
built in the days when the thickness of a wall was measured in feet, not in inches. No balconies, no loggias, only
smooth walls of stone decorated with softly painted gro-
tesques. The shuttered windows were large, spaced at wide
intervals not only between each other, but between the
floors themselves. Even a trained roof climber would
find no help in that façade. Better put your trust in

Jacopone, he thought, Jacopone and Rosana.

He glanced at his watch. Six minutes had passed since the old man had slipped through the hedge to find Rosana. Six minutes . . . seven . . .

He looked back at the house. Which was the room—what window? Or did the room, where Eleanor was left, face into the courtyard? Around him, the cicadas had become a permanent background of sound, no longer heard. The violence of brilliant light and black shadow, the contrast of scarlet flowers against blue sky, the heavy scent of sun-warmed fruit, the jagged rhythm of the yellow butterflies were no longer seen or felt. Nothing existed, nothing, except the silent house and the moving hand of his watch. Nine minutes now . . .

I'll give them one more, he thought, his anxiety shifting into foreboding. One more minute, an even ten altogether: no more. Then I'm going in.

Twenty-Three

ELEANOR STOOD at the window of the room where she had slept out her drugged sleep. Here, Luigi had talked to her. Here, Rosana had made constant excuses to visit her all that dreary morning. A square, high-ceilinged room, a museum piece quickly made ready for her: a prison, with cupids on its painted ceiling and a rosy Venus, one leg trailing from a golden couch of clouds, waiting. But, she thought, as she looked down into the central courtyard round which the house was built, she had felt every emotion in this room except the one for which it was designed. Bewilderment and fear and despair: these had been her companions. And now, the hope that Rosana had kindled was fading away. Down there in the courtyard, both cars had been made ready. And there, beyond them, was the gateway leading to the street, strong wooden doors, enormous, heavy, locked. Why did she keep watching them? As if she could will them to open and let Bill Lammiter come walking into the courtyard.

But he wouldn't come. Not today, Rosana had said: tomorrow he would come. It was all planned. But would tomorrow be time enough? Eleanor looked at the two cars: both seemed so ready for flight.

I wish, she thought, I wish Rosana would come back. Where has she gone? So quickly, without explanation. Something is going wrong. I know it. I know it. I've known it ever since the bell at the gateway rang, and the red-haired man walked into the courtyard.

I was eating the bread that Rosana had smuggled up to my room: bread and San Pellegrino water, both safe. I hadn't touched the food on the lunch tray: doubtful, Rosana had warned me. But the bread was good, and I was hungry at last. And then, talking together, we heard the bell ringing at the gate. How long ago was that? Ten minutes? Less? There is no clock in this room: Venus resents clocks. It doesn't matter; time has lost all sense today, except that the red-haired man is still with Luigi, and Rosana hasn't come back.

When the bell rang, I ran to the window. "It can't be Bill," Rosana said, as if she had read my thoughts. And she was explaining again that once the meeting in Perugia had taken place, Bill would be here. But not until then. Nothing must alarm Luigi, nothing must happen to make him send any warning to his friends. The meeting had to take place. Couldn't I understand that?

"It's a man, someone from the city," I said in disappointment, watching the stranger, neat in his movements, dapper in his dress, who was now talking to Alberto. The man took off his hat, wiped his brow, and raised his voice to make himself better understood. "A man with red hair."

"No!" Rosana was beside me then. "Oh, no!" she said, and for the first time I heard despair in her voice. Her face was filled with fear, fear and hate. It frightened me. Into silence. We stood together at the window. I began to feel sick again. For it was all so innocent down in the courtyard, with only Rosana's grip on my arm to warn me that there was danger, too. The man was a guide: he only wanted permission to show the Signorelli fresco in the chapel to his tourists on his next visit here. That was all.

"It's an excuse," Rosana whispered, "an excuse to talk to Luigi."

"But Luigi won't talk to a guide."

"He will!" she said. "He will!"

She was right, for Luigi came hurrying out. He looked as if he had slept well. He had shaved and changed his clothes. He was brisk and smiling. I don't think he actually knew the man, for he stood there, hesitating a little. And the man repeated his request. "I am sorry," Luigi said. "I'm afraid that is impossible." But he did not turn away. He still waited.

The guide said he was sorry, too. Dottore Vannucci, the great expert in Florence, had assured him the Signorelli fresco was superb.

"Would you care to see it yourself?" Luigi asked quickly. "Let me show you it. Of course, you understand that my aunt would not approve of tourists coming here." He was talking pleasantly as he led the way into the house.

Behind me, the room door opened. Before I could turn round, it had closed. And Rosana had gone.

Outside in the corridor, the man on guard spoke to her. I heard Rosana say cheerfully, "Are you still here? Why —you'll miss your bus if you aren't careful!" Then I heard the key turn in the lock again. And Rosana laughed at something the man said. Her footsteps were less and less, until they became nothing. The man got up from his chair—it scraped as it was pushed back against the wall —he tested the door, and for a moment my heart missed a beat: all morning the fear had been that the man would come in, and catch my wrist, and drug me again. But the man walked away, down the corridor. It must be nearly two o'clock then. That was the time, Rosana had told me, when the guards would leave Montesecco. By two o'clock they weren't needed any more to guard me; and, perhaps, if I had eaten the drugged food the men had brought upstairs for me, if Rosana hadn't told me the truth, instead of Luigi's story, I would not have needed even a child of three to watch me.

So the guards were gone. The key was left in the lock. Surely Rosana would come back now. She could open the door and let me out.

But she didn't come back.

It was odd, the stupid things I tried on that lock: a tooth broken out of my comb (it was too slight); a lipstick case (too bulky); a nail file (too broad); and then a small pencil. That fitted, but the key wouldn't move. It had been twisted in the lock so that it could not be pushed out. And it would have been so easy to pull it into the room through the wide crack at the bottom of the door that I stood with the useless pencil in my hand and cried with disappointment.

Odd, too, how one's mind trusts and then distrusts. I walked back to the table in the center of the room and stood looking down at the lunch tray. I began to wonder if Rosana had drugged me, too, in her own way. Not with food. She had warned me to touch nothing from the trays. Yes, give her credit for that. Give her credit, too, that she got the guard with that stupid smile on his face out of the room— I was still half dressed. "I'll see she takes her lunch," she told him. But as soon as he had gone, she whispered, "Touch nothing on that tray. He wouldn't allow me to carry it upstairs. He sent me ahead of him so I couldn't see what he added to Anna-Maria's cooking." Then she stood very still. "But why do they want to start drugging you again? So soon?"

So soon . . . Perhaps, then, as my heart sank, I did know that something was going wrong for us. Tomorrow Luigi would take me away. Tomorrow was time enough to start drugging me.

But Rosana found her own answer. "Perhaps Luigi doesn't trust my powers of persuasion. Or perhaps he doesn't think you are too easily persuaded. So they drug the food, just a little, just enough to keep you calm, unworried." She was cheerful again. She was so sure that everything would come out right. "All we have to do is wait. Tomorrow, once the meeting in Perugia starts, we can act. When Luigi is at the meeting, we'll leave. It will be easy."

I shook my head.

"Bill will come for you. Nothing will stop him. I know. I saw him." Then she was watching me, almost studying me. "You're beautiful, yes," she said, "but no more beautiful than others." She stood in front of the looking glass. "Luigi had twenty women and never married one of them. And you came along—" She laughed. "I begin to believe what his friends said. The little American has a very special secret weapon."

I stood staring at her.

"I'm sorry," she said, and stepped away from the looking glass. "That was foolish of me to repeat the gossip.
Of course, there is always gossip. . . . Jealousy makes
tongues bitter." Suddenly, she threw her arms round me
and kissed me. I never have liked people touching me, unless it was a man and I was in love with him. And there
were only two men I had loved, and the second one—

Can you fall into hate as quickly as you can fall into
love?

I shivered, and moved away from her, to pick up my
dress. It had been taken away from me last night to be
washed. "I'm cold," I said. I was wearing only a petti-
coat and brassière. "And thank Anna-Maria for laun-
dering my dress so nicely."

"Yes," she said, looking at me strangely, "you seem
cold. Yet you can't be." She laughed again, but this time
she was honestly amused and the moment of bitterness
had gone. "But don't put on your pretty dress yet. Keep
it fresh. When Bill comes—"

"*Will* he come?" I had got too tangled up in all my emotions. I began to cry. And Rosana changed again, into
someone gentle and kind. "I've done nothing but cry since
yesterday," I said angrily. "I've done nothing but—"

"Why shouldn't you?" Rosana said comfortingly. "But
don't let that barbarian outside the door hear you. You
are supposed to be placid, my dear, a little drugged,
and very much persuaded by clever Rosana. They are
expecting no trouble at all, from either you or me—or
from Bill."

Give Rosana all that credit: she comforted me with
the only name I wanted to hear.

Yet now, as I stood beside the little table with its
tray of cold congealed food, alone, Rosana gone, the key
in the locked door tantalizingly secure, the feeling of
being trapped came surging back. Has Rosana drugged
me with the promise of tomorrow? Only pretend to be
obedient, only play-act a little until tomorrow, and all
will be well. Would it? Was Bill really here in this little
town? Had she truly seen him?

Look, the other part of me told myself—and that's
how Bill always started an explanation—look, Rosana
did tell you the truth. She came to you this morning,

after Luigi had left you. She helped you, didn't she? You were almost believing what he had said, for you had nothing else to believe, and you were still a little sick, dazed, frightened, bewildered.

And I'm still bewildered. All I know that is bad about Luigi came from Rosana. His story was so different. If I had still been in love with him, I might have believed him. I wish I wouldn't have these waves of sickness.

The first one hit me as I got out of the car this morning, only half conscious, trying to fight my way to the surface of the hideous dream. Luigi's arms were around me, gentle as he always has been. I kept trying to push him away, to scream, "No, no!" But my voice was a whisper, and my hands were water. Two men were beside me. "Get away, get away!" Luigi said in anger.

Then quietly he said, "Take care of her," and two women came out of the shadows toward me.

His voice rose in a fury of bitter words. Not to me, not to the two women—one was young, the other old—who were trying to help me into the house. Luigi never spoke that way to women, not even when he was angry at Tivoli had he ever spoken like that. He was cursing the two men who had drugged me. I looked at the old woman who was helping me climb some stairs. I said, "But why did he let them do it?" My voice must have sounded like a child's, for the old wrinkled face pressed itself against my cheek and said something softly. In Italian. So she didn't understand what my question had been. But I kept repeating it to myself until the old woman and the girl brought me into a dark room. And then the second wave of sickness hit me.

I stood, twisted with nausea: long, long shuddering breaths of nausea. "Open the shutters," Luigi's voice said. "Get her undressed, into bed!"

I tried to tell them all, "Go away, go away, leave me alone!" But all I could do was to stand swaying like a drunken woman. I felt cold, ice-cold, as if winter had come, and the air from the unshuttered window were frost-edged.

"Rosana!" Luigi's voice said, "help Anna-Maria. Quick!" And the girl, who had kept away from me, began to help the old woman undress me. Someone pulled the sheets of the bed apart, someone lifted me in. So large, so tall was the bed, its posts soaring up into the ceiling, pink and white faces laughing down at me. And around me, the watching faces, the old and the young and Luigi's. I tried to pull the sheet over my shoulders. But all I could do was to close my eyes and blot out theirs.

"She'll be all right," Luigi was saying. Someone had brought a blanket and he folded it around me. "A little sleep . . ." He bent over me. I felt the roughness of his cheek on mine. "Darling, darling," he said softly in my ear, for me alone. His hand smoothed the hair back from my brow.

And that's how I fell asleep, Luigi's words soft in my ears, his hand gentle on my brow.

When I awoke, Luigi had come back. He was sitting on a chair, watching me, waiting for me to drift out of sleep. He sat quite still. He said nothing at all. And I lay still, not speaking. He hadn't changed his clothes, he couldn't have had any sleep as yet. He had just spent these first hours here, sitting beside me, watching. My anger left me; I felt only sad and miserable.

He rose and sat on the side of the bed and took my hand. He began talking to me. Gently. Everything he said and did was gentle, quieting my fears, calming my tense worry.

I think he believed what he said. His words were spoken so earnestly, so honestly. I think I would have believed him, too, except that I kept remembering last night. That shadow wouldn't go away, the shadow of all my unanswered questions, the shadow of a Luigi I had never known, of a world I had never imagined. And as I listened now to the Luigi I knew, my mind kept remembering the stranger. I lay quite silent, watching his face —a strong and noble face, proud, and yet, as at that moment, tender. I listened to his voice, filled with love and anxiety. And his words were right, too. Only remember all our weeks of happiness, he was saying: let them blot out the mistakes of the last three days, the stupid quarrels, the blunders. Forget, forget and forgive, and trust. Later, he could tell me the full story, but now it was enough to trust each other.

He would never question me again about Bill Lammiter. The man was an agent, in Rome on his own business, a man working with lies and hypocrisy, pulling me into suspicion and danger, thinking only of the information he could draw out of me. But forget all that now. Politics and love were two separate worlds. Luigi trusted me, as I must trust him. And now—today—I must rest and sleep and remember I was safe.

He bent down and kissed my cheek, as if I were a child who had wakened from a hideous dream and had to be comforted. I was safe, he told me again. He would place a guard outside my door and it would be locked. No one could harm me here. And he would send Rosana to keep me company. In a few days, we'd forget all this. Together, we'd forget. Meanwhile, I was safe. That was all that mattered.

But I felt only numbness in my heart, and my hand lay dead in his. "Sleep, darling," he said, "sleep some more." And then he left me.

I didn't sleep. I kept thinking of Luigi's words, last night, in Rome. I had listened then, and I had taken the first step into this trap. Or perhaps the first step had been my phone call to Bill. My two phone calls . . .

For they had brought Luigi to my apartment last night. His friends had been checking up at the hotel to make sure that Bill Lammiter was leaving Rome. And they had discovered I had been trying to get in touch with him. It was as simple as that.

I'll never forget the distraught look on Luigi's face as we stood together in the hall of my apartment. He gripped my arm and said, "Eleanor, *why* did you call him? *"Why?"*

I stared blankly at him. "But what's *wrong* with a telephone call?"

Luigi was watching my eyes. His grip slackened on my arm. "It linked you with Lammiter."

"Is that any of your business now?" I walked into the living room. I had a moment of guilt as I looked at the little table where Bill and I had had supper together. Luigi was jealous; that was all I could think. What would he do if he heard that Bill had been here? Or did he know that, as he knew about the telephone calls?

"Yes," Luigi said. "It *is* my business. Lammiter is an agent."

"An agent? What kind of agent?" I began to laugh.

"Stop that! Don't you see I'm trying to help you? Where are the photographs? I'm burning them. Immediately."

I found them for him. He examined them carefully, and then set them on fire, one by one, over the large ashtray. Thank God, I thought, I had emptied it of Bill's cigarette end. And then I felt my sense of guilt, mean guilt, deepen. But I was also afraid. Without knowing what all this meant, I was afraid.

"Are there any more?" he asked suddenly.

"Some didn't come out. The light—" I felt stifled. It was true. But the truth also covered a lie. The longer I didn't explain about Bill, the more difficult it was to give the full truth.

He had caught the sound of strain in my voice. "I didn't tell anyone you had taken these photographs, Eleanor," he said very quietly. "I had to keep you safe. That's why I broke our engagement. You didn't think I was serious about that, did you? All I wanted was to get you out of Rome, safely away."

"Safe from what?"

He looked up suddenly from the last twisting black ashes. "Safe from Lammiter. When he goes back to the hotel for his raincoat, he will find your message. He will come here. Won't he?"

So he didn't know that Bill had already been here. I was too relieved to answer.

He said, "There are some people who wouldn't like that. They would think he was questioning you, finding out what he could about the people you saw at Tivoli. They might even think you had been recruited—to spy on me."

I stared at him. "You—you *can't* believe that!" I must have looked both so astonished and so horrified that his last doubt vanished.

He came over to where I stood, and took my hands. "I don't believe it, but—" He hesitated.

"But some people do?"

"It's one of the oldest tricks. They've used it often enough themselves." He was smiling, as if it were a joke, now that he knew it was not being practiced against him.

I kept staring at him. "What kind of people are these? What have you got to do with them?"

"That's a story I'll tell you later. Now, you must leave."

"Leave?"

"Yes. I've come to get you away from here. Trust me, darling. I trust you. Remember?"

"Are these people your *friends?*" I was still groping for the truth. I knew too little, that was the trouble. Was Luigi an agent, working against them? He couldn't, surely he couldn't, be working with them. "It's all so mad, so completely crazy!" I said aloud.

"Not that. These people are realists. You've *got* to leave with me. Now. I'll take you to my aunt's villa. Then—" He laughed and didn't finish. He caught me in his arms and kissed me. "Don't worry about packing. I'll send someone to do that for you tomorrow. Leave a note for your maid. We don't want her running to the police and frightening everyone." His voice was soothing, unworried, confident. This is the only wise and reasonable thing to do, he seemed to believe. But I still hesitated. There was something wrong, something far wrong somewhere. I couldn't guess, I didn't know what to think. This secrecy, this haste, baffled me. I said, searching for a clue, "What if I don't go?"

"But you must! There's no other choice. Or else you'll prove that you *are* working with Lammiter."

"That's ridiculous!" I said impatiently. "You know that."

"Eleanor!" He pulled me round to face him. "I'm trying to keep you safe. Darling, believe me! These men have no time to waste. In a few days—nothing matters; but now —this is the moment of crisis. They cannot afford even a possible doubt. They will act—and act quickly."

His voice frightened me. Incredulously, I said, "Act? What do you mean?"

"They would have no remorse if you died."

"You mean, they'd kill me if necessary? Luigi, what *are* they?"

He didn't answer that directly. "They're fighting a war,"

he said. "Lammiter's friends are their enemies."

"If this is a kind of war," I said slowly, "then I'm on Bill's side."

"Because he's an American? You think that makes him right? But what makes you so sure that he is on the right side?"

I didn't quite follow. Was he saying that Bill was some kind of traitor? I couldn't believe that. "I know Bill—"

"Do you?" he asked bitterly. "Does one human being ever know another? Do you even know yourself?"

I looked at him. I shook my head. I knew Luigi least of all, I thought. And yet, watching him, I was sure of one thing: he did love me. And somehow I was also sure that, when he explained everything to me and I was no longer in ignorance, I would find honesty and courage in his story. It is difficult for a woman to admit that she could ever have fallen in love with a man who wasn't honest and courageous. These are the two qualities we value most, if any man wants to know.

Luigi was certainly honest then. "For God's sake, Eleanor, listen to me! You are in danger. So is Lammiter. Do you think these men will let either of you ruin months of careful planning?"

No, I had no doubt about that. "If I leave here, what will happen to Bill?"

"Nothing. He will be of no interest to anyone."

"Not even if he comes here?" For I knew he would come back.

"If he doesn't see you, how can he get the information he needs? He will be just another agent who failed in his mission." Then, sharply, "Why do you worry about him so much?"

"I don't want to be responsible for any man's death," I said, as easily as I could. "After all, I did make the telephone calls." Then I searched for a piece of paper and a pencil, and I wrote a message for the maid. There didn't seem to be much else I could do.

Later, I was thinking, we'll be able to talk at the villa. I'll learn the full truth then. (Yes, that's how stupid I was.)

At the villa, I learned nothing. I wasn't even allowed to talk to the princess alone. Poor old thing, she was as be-

wildered as I was. Her face enamel couldn't cover the
misgivings in her eyes. Her clever-cruel tongue was silenced for once. She was kind to me, she had never been
kinder, but she was just as helpless.

Then I knew I should never have come with Luigi to
the villa. I knew too late what I ought to have done in
the first place. Leave the apartment—yes, that had been
right—and after that, I ought to have gone to the Embassy: I ought to have had them telephone the police,
send out a warning to Bill, wherever he was. Only, would
Luigi have allowed me to go to the Embassy?

I didn't know the answer to that question until a car
came right up to the door of the villa. The two men, who
had been standing outside the little sitting room where I
was waiting for Luigi and the princess to come back,
urged me to leave. "Leave? But I'm supposed to stay *here*.
Leave for where?"

I went outside. I tried to run. I tried to scream to the
princess, to anyone who might be passing along that
quiet peaceful street. But the two men were beside me,
holding my mouth, my waist, my wrists.

And there they are now—the two men, crossing the
courtyard. Old Alberto is opening the gate. . . .

Eleanor stood at the window of her room, watching
the two men walk out of her life as abruptly as they had
entered it. Within a few minutes, the red-haired stranger
had followed them. Old Alberto locked the gate, with
Luigi standing beside him. The massive doors became a
solid wall once more.

Twenty-Four

LUIGI HAD NOT ENJOYED the guide's visit. Eleanor
could tell that by the way he stood down there in the
courtyard, feet apart, hands on hips, face still turned to
the locked gate as though his eyes could follow the red-
haired man's progress along the road.

Then he swung round on his heel, caught sight of Alberto, who had been hovering uncertainly nearby, and said angrily, "Bring down my suitcases and put them in the Lancia."

The old man—he was very fond of Luigi, Rosana had said—didn't move.

"At once!" Luigi's voice rose.

Still Alberto didn't move. Instead, he began talking. All day, he had been morose and silent; whenever Eleanor had caught a glimpse of him from her window, he had been going about his tasks, his head bent, answering no one, paying no attention to anything. But now the words poured out of him. She couldn't understand much of them—they came too quickly, in an accent new to her ear. He was saying something about the principessa: the principessa had given orders, the principessa had commanded. . . . His recital goaded Luigi. "My aunt is a fool." And Luigi turned angrily on his heel and left. Alberto followed him, talking, talking, his voice rising in anger, too. Perhaps no one, not even Luigi, could call the princess a fool.

Behind Eleanor, the room door opened. It was Rosana at last. She brought the key inside with her and turned it in the lock.

"Why didn't you come back and let me out?" Eleanor asked. "The gate was open for a few moments; we could have—"

"We could have done nothing," Rosana said, coming slowly away from the door. "Not with Sabatini here." She sat down on the edge of a chair as if her strength had suddenly been drained away. "We've lost," she said, dully. Her hands were trembling. She stared down at them and burst into tears. "Everything has gone wrong, everything. And everything will go more wrong." She brushed at her tears savagely with her knuckles. "And I couldn't wait to open your door. I *had* to get to the little gallery above the chapel before they entered. I *had* to find out why Sabatini came here. The man's a murderer. Don't you know that? And he is the man who is deciding about you—and me. He—" She caught hold of herself. The tears had gone but her hands still trembled.

Eleanor searched for a cigarette, lit it for her. She poured out the last of the water from the San Pellegrino bottle and handed the glass to Rosana. She said, not without respect, "You ran a terrible risk!"

"I got back, didn't I?" Rosana asked, almost fiercely. She took a deep shuddering breath. "Sabatini—he makes me feel sick, that man. Even to be in the same place as he is makes me feel—" Her whole body shuddered this time. "And Luigi—" she said contemptuously, "Luigi looking so noble, glistening, never objecting. I kept thinking, he can't, he won't ever agree to that. But he did, he did!"

She's near breaking point, Eleanor thought. More calmly than she felt, she said, "All right, all right . . . What's the bad news? Just how lost are we?" She even managed a smile.

"The meeting is today. I told Joe it was tomorrow. But it is *today*. This afternoon. At three o'clock. Three! And it's almost two now. An hour, that's all we have . . . an hour!"

We'd better keep the exclamation marks out of our voices, Eleanor thought. She said, "So we'll find Joe and tell him."

"But *where* is he? I don't know. He was coming here this evening, to check up. This *evening!*" Rosana made a gesture of despair. "And that's not all my bad news," she said quickly. "Luigi's orders have been changed. He isn't to attend the meeting. Oh, he is going to Perugia, all right. But he isn't to attend the meeting. Sabatini says there has been too much trouble—Luigi may be followed."

"Why send him to Perugia at all?"

"Because Sabatini is *clever*—didn't I tell you?"

"Yes, yes. I'm sorry. Go on. About Luigi."

"Luigi will drive to Perugia without any luggage, in his own car. He is to leave it at the Piazza Italia, but on no account must he go near the Corso Vanucci. That's the main street, where people walk and sit at the cafés."

"Yes, yes," Eleanor said again, her impatience growing.

"Don't you see—the Corso Vanucci is the last place you'd expect a group of conspirators to gather? It's so open, so innocent. But that's where the meeting is going to be held. Luigi is to avoid it, to lead anyone following him *away* from it. Don't you see? He's a—a—"

"Decoy?"

Rosana nodded. "He is to walk down by the market,

choose a little café there—any café, it doesn't matter—
go inside, sit at the back, look as though he were waiting.
After an hour, he can leave. Go back to his car, drive
over one of the hill roads to Gubbio. There are so many
small roads. He will lose anyone following him."

"What about the other car, the Lancia—and the suitcases?"

"These arrangements have not been changed," Rosana
said, avoiding Eleanor's eyes. "The mechanic will take you
in the Lancia, by the main route to Gubbio. And then
Luigi will drive you across the Apennines, to——" She
paused. "To Venice." She stared down at her hands.

Arrangements have not been changed. . . . Eleanor
stared in amazement.

"You mean, Luigi knew all along that——" Eleanor's lips
closed in anger, and she turned to the window. "And
what are the 'arrangements' for you?" she asked.

"The *carabinieri* will be notified that I am here. The
police in Rome want to question me." She added, almost
hopelessly, "About Tony Brewster's death."

"But the police must know you were his friend."

"Murder is murder."

Eleanor took a deep breath. "We *have* to find Joe."

Rosana said nothing.

"He is known in Montesecco, isn't he? He's the princess's chauffeur. Surely he has friends you could telephone, send them looking——"

"I can't get near the telephone. The mechanic is guarding it now." She rested her brow on her hands. "I'll *have*
to get out, that's all. Without being seen. If Luigi discovers
I'm missing——" She paused. She was thinking aloud now.
"Yes, I'll have to get out. But will Joe be at the farmhouse? And there is no telephone there. I may only
waste time searching for him." And then a new fear spread
over her face. "How do we even know he is still alive?
Sabatini could have seen him, Sabatini——"

"Stop that, Rosana! Stop it. You outwitted Sabatini in
the chapel. You'll do it again."

Rosana said slowly, "All day, you've been afraid.
Now——" She shook her head in wonder.

"We can't afford to be afraid both at the same time,"
Eleanor said sharply.

"If you knew what I knew——" Rosana flashed back at

her. Then she controlled her voice. "I'm sorry. I—I—" If only, she thought miserably, I didn't have to be responsible for both of us. The American is so helpless, so unaccustomed to danger.

"Rosana," said Eleanor, with a confidence that sounded real enough even to her own ears, "you *must* get to a telephone somewhere. Call Rome. Have your people there relay your message to Perugia. Isn't that possible?"

Rosana nodded. It was an idea to be considered. Only, she thought wearily, I wish I weren't alone. The American may give ideas, but no practical help. She means well, but— Rosana said, "I'll risk going out by the main gate. That will save fifteen minutes. I can telephone from the restaurant." She rose, frowning. "The post office is even nearer."

Eleanor looked down at the cars in the courtyard, and then back at the untouched luncheon tray on the little central table. "Telephone from here," she said, "That's quicker still." She walked over to the table. "I'll slash the tires. You give the mechanic the alarm. He'll leave that phone in a hurry." She picked up the knife and tested it. "Probably can't cut anything except spaghetti. Cooked spaghetti, at that. Still, woman with knife—always an alarming sight."

"You are mad," said Rosana, "quite mad." But there was interest in her eyes, and almost a smile on her lips.

Eleanor reached the door. She paused, her hand on the key. "Help me with my geography, in case I have to play hide-and-seek."

"Let me draw you a map."

"No time. The house is a square—four wings built around the courtyard. Where is the main staircase?"

"In the center of this wing."

"That's to my left as I go out of this door?"

"Yes. It leads down to the big hall, then into the courtyard. Then there are four other staircases, smaller ones—"

"Four?" I'll never remember them, Eleanor thought in alarm.

"It's quite simple—they lead out to the four corners of the courtyard."

"And where is the telephone?" Only one, of course. The princess no doubt thought telephones ruined her *décor,* all six centuries of it. But some might say that cupids playing around Venus were just as much of an anomaly to Signorelli's fresco.

"That's across the courtyard, in Alberto's office, beside the main gate. Alberto's quarters are over there, too."

"That's the east side," Eleanor said quickly, remembering the sun's rays that morning. "So we're in the west wing. What's in the north?"

Rosana looked at her. She has more brains than I guessed, Rosana thought: she has more courage, too. Her own confidence began to grow again. She said, "Kitchens, storerooms, stables, and garage."

"And Pirotta?"

She no longer called him Luigi, Rosana noticed again. "His rooms are in the south side of the house over the gun room and the chapel."

"Then, when the mechanic comes yelling into the courtyard, I run to the north," Eleanor said with a little smile. She unlocked the door and stepped into a shadowed corridor, with doors along one side, shuttered windows along the other. This was a good feeling, she thought, a good feeling to unlock a door and step out, of your own free will. Whatever happens now, I'm not going back into that room. Never, never . . .

"What's out there?" she whispered, pointing to the shuttered windows.

"The garden. The gamekeeper has his lodge down near the big wall. Jacopone. He's a friend."

Eleanor took a step to her left. "I'll go down the main staircase. And you?"

Rosana moved to her right. "North through the kitchen wing into the east one. Each wing is connected by corridors, upstairs and downstairs."

For a moment they stood looking at each other. Then they smiled.

"Remember," Eleanor said, "I escaped."

Rosana nodded. "You threatened me with that knife." Her smile deepened; she had to smother a laugh. Eleanor thought, at least she's out of the slump: she's all right. She's very much all right. Eleanor began walking toward the staircase.

The doors to the other rooms up here were all closed. Certainly it was comforting to know that Pirotta lived in another part of the house. But she was nervous, she might as well admit it. She could drop the pretense now that she wasn't afraid. Afraid? She was scared sick. She couldn't even laugh at the picture she must make, carrying this ridiculous knife in her hand. She could laugh later, if she was still free to laugh, at the comic relief. And then— Even thinking of comic relief made her feel a little better. She looked over her shoulder as she reached the staircase. The corridor behind her was empty. Rosana had been quick. There was no turning back now.

She started to descend the long flight of stairs. "Dear God," she was praying, "help us, help us." And then she added, praying fair, "If we are in the right. Dear God, just help those who are in the right."

The staircase running down the wall on her left had wide and shallow steps that stretched almost the full length of the hall. They were of stone, like the heavy balustrade, like the towering walls. This must be the oldest part of the house, perhaps the original building. No pink clouds and golden decorations here, no baroque twists and curves. The hall beneath seemed vast in its bareness. It was filled with shadows, dark and cold. At its large doorway, standing open, there was a stream of light slanting toward the foot of the staircase, at first strong, then weakening, then fading into the shadows. Outside, the heat blazed and shimmered.

She kept close to the wall of the staircase, sliding her left hand down its cool stone surface to steady her and keep her footsteps sure. A twisted ankle would be a foolish thing. I ought to take off my shoes, she thought, and paused for a moment to slip her feet out of them. She didn't stop to pick them up. She started to run lightly, noiselessly, down the broad steps. As she almost reached the pool of warm light, seeping up over the bottom steps, the oblique view through the doorway lengthened to show more of the courtyard. She could see part of the black shadow now cast by the south wing of the house, and the cars parked against the wall, carefully within the shade. And there, also, were two suitcases lying close to the Lancia's near wheel.

She stopped abruptly. From the opposite side of the hall came a little cry, quickly silenced. She looked over the balustrade. Anna-Maria and Alberto were down there, huddled together standing quite still, undecided, waiting. It had been Anna-Maria who had almost cried out: her hand was still over her lips. Now they both stared up at her in amazement and wonder.

"It is all right," she said, and smiled. But they didn't smile back. Alberto pointed to the courtyard warningly. She heard a movement out there, and then a man's confident stride, crisp, unhurried. It could only be Pirotta.

She retreated back against the wall. Were its shadows deep enough to hide her? She could see him now, as he dropped a third suitcase beside the others. Then he turned toward the hall.

Swiftly, Eleanor moved away from the wall back to the balustrade again, and sank down on the step behind its waist-high pillars. Was this safer? At least, it felt less vulnerable than standing up. Thank God she didn't feel sick any longer; but her legs were trembling, and so were her hands.

"Well," he said at the doorway, "is the rebellion over?"

For a moment of shock, she stared down at him from between the banisters. Then she saw he wasn't looking at her. His eyes, frowning as they accustomed themselves from the blaze of sunlight to the dark shadows, were searching the hall. "There you are," he told Alberto and Anna-Maria, "just as I thought."

Alberto took a few steps forward, trying to pull his arm free from his wife's sudden grip. She cried out, "Alberto! No! No! You've done enough. He will strike you again, he will kill you this time! No! No!—"

"You're a very foolish old woman," Pirotta said coldly. "I don't kill people. And I did not strike Alberto."

"I saw you—" she began hysterically.

"You did not. You saw him try to stop me from taking the suitcases to the cars—a job he should have been doing. I pushed him aside: that was all. What did you expect, Anna-Maria? In my place, what would you have done? You would have struck him, and hard, wouldn't you?" The voice of quiet reason subdued the old woman. Now it changed to sharp authority. "Go back to your kitchen before I do lose my temper. Do you want me to report him to the princess? You'd both be out on the street, soon enough!"

"He—he was only doing what the princess told him to do." Anna-Maria made her last protest. She looked at her husband and began to cry.

Alberto said, "That is the truth. The princess gave her orders—"

"You've told me all that!"

"But you have not listened. You must wait here, until she comes," Alberto insisted, his words gathering strength. "The princess must talk to you—she has much to say—I have never heard her so angry—"

Pirotta said impatiently, "I shall talk to her when I get back here. Alberto, can't you understand that the American is *ill?* We must drive her to the hospital in Assisi—"

The old man shook his head. "You must not take the princess's car! That will make her angrier. She did not give permission—"

Running footsteps came across the courtyard, slipping and clattering on the cobbled stones.

Pirotta spun round on his heel. "Giovanni! What the devil are you doing out here?"

Giovanni reached the Lancia and walked around it anxiously, looking at the wheels. "No, the tires are alright. Perhaps she damaged the engine." He opened the car's hood.

"Who?"

"The American girl. She's escaped."

"Who told you that?"

"Signorina Di Feo. The American girl escaped and—"

"You locked the office? You didn't leave it unlocked?"

Giovanni stared at him. "But there was no one there! And the car was being—"

"Signorina Di Feo? Where is she?"

"She went away—to try to find the American."

"You fool, you idiot, you blundering— Don't you see it's a lie? The cars are all right. No one has escaped. Get back to that telephone. No—I'll go myself."

"It isn't a lie," Eleanor said, and rose to her feet. He turned and looked up at her. It was the first time she ever remembered seeing him completely and absolutely amazed. Keep talking, she told herself: anything, anything to silence questions about Rosana. "I did escape. I did mean to damage the car." She held out the knife, gripped firmly in her right hand, and Anna-Maria let out a piercing scream.

"You see," Pirotta told Alberto, "The *signorina Americana* is ill." Swiftly he crossed over to the foot of the staircase.

In Italian, she said, "I am not ill—I am not ill. I want to stay here. I do not want to go. I—"

"Eleanor—" he said worriedly. He shook his head. "You *are* ill, you know." He turned to Alberto and Anna-Maria. "See—she has even forgotten her shoes. Her feet are bare. Help me, will you? She must leave at once. Anna-Maria: find the signorina's shoes, her coat—" He began to mount the stairs, slowly.

"I am *not* leaving," Eleanor told him. "*You* are the one who's crazy. Alberto—"

"What nonsense you talk! What nonsense you've let yourself believe!" Suddenly his arm reached out to catch her wrist, and then pulled back as she slashed at it with the knife. "God in heaven!" He stared at her unbelievingly. He gave an incredulous laugh. "You little idiot . . ." he said gently. "Do you still not realize that if it hadn't been for me you would be dead?" His voice hardened. "I risked everything for you. I gave my word that you'd go with me, leave Italy until everything was forgotten, all interest ended."

"Ended? Forgotten?"

"People forget," he reminded her. "They like to forget. And sometimes, they find new—new interpretations, which help them to forget. Eleanor—you've been told so much nonsense, so many lies! Come with me. My plan will work. You'll see. We aren't monsters. We are reasonable men."

She stared at him. This was the first time he had identified himself openly. "And if I don't go, what will you do? Kill me—like Tony Brewster?"

His face tightened. "I am not a murderer. You know that. You know I would not even hurt you. But there are others who will." He took a deep breath. "Don't force me to telephone them, and admit that my plan has failed." He stepped back into the hall, waiting. "Do I telephone? Or do you go with me?"

Rosana, she thought worriedly, Rosana must surely

have had the sense to lock herself securely inside the office, but she would need time. "Go—go where?" Anything to delay him, anything to let Rosana get that call through to Rome. How long did it take to get a call through, how long?

"Among friends. There is a freighter waiting now, ready to take us to them."

"Where?" she insisted.

He hesitated. Perhaps he was weighing the minimum truth he could tell her against a lie which would never be forgiven. Then, still evading a direct answer, "It will be a pleasant journey—through the Aegean, the Bosporus. . . ." He was watching her face. "It's only for a few months, darling. Then—we'll come back."

"You'll come back? To Italy?"

"I'll come back. Because I didn't leave in defeat." His confidence had returned. He had heard the worry, the uncertainty in her voice. He smiled, and held out his hand. Perhaps he never had any doubts about his power over a woman who had loved him, least of all when he loved her. Involuntarily, she flinched and took a step away from him. In that naked moment, he saw the contempt in her eyes. His smile faded as his hand dropped to his side. Grim-faced, he turned and moved to the door.

"Stop him, Alberto!" She ran down into the hall. She caught the old man's arm. "Rosana," she whispered, "Rosana," and she pointed across the courtyard. The old couple looked at each other: Anna-Maria, at least, began to understand something.

Pirotta had halted abruptly outside. He stood, puzzled, frowning, watching the solitary figure who had come out of the doorway near the gates in the east wing that led to the office and the servants' rooms.

"Jacopone!" Anna-Maria screamed. "Jacopone, we're here!"

The old man pulled his felt brim farther over his eyes to shield them from the glare, and he started across the courtyard, his heavy boots scraping on the cobbestones. He had a rifle under one arm.

Alberto shouted, pressing forward, "He's taking away the Americana—he's taking the car. He's—"

"Quiet!" Pirotta said angrily, pushing Alberto back into the hall. His eyes didn't leave Jacopone, or the rifle.

"Come here, you!" he told him. "What were you doing over there at the office?"

The old man halted. "There was no one in the kitchen," he said slowly, his eyes fixed on the doorway as if he were trying to see into the shadows of the hall. "So I came looking. . . ." His voice drifted away uneasily.

"For what?" Pirotta's voice was alert.

"Anna-Maria . . . Alberto. I went to their room." He jerked a thumb back over his shoulder.

"Where's Giovanni?"

The old man shifted his feet. "Back there," he said, and he gave a small smile.

"Stop scraping your damned feet! And give me that rifle. You don't carry a rifle around this house. Give me it!"

"No!" Eleanor cried out, and tried to run into the courtyard. Pirotta reached out, caught her wrist, twisted it, and the knife fell from her hand. He kicked it aside.

Jacopone looked at her. Then, calmly, he aimed into the sky and pulled the trigger. The sharp crack of the rifle cut through the heavy warm air, a flock of startled pigeons rose and swept in a bewildered cloud over the courtyard.

Pirotta stared at the old man, and then at Eleanor. He tightened his grip on her wrist. There was suspicion in his eyes, suspicion growing. . . . Then he dropped her wrist and ran toward Jacopone.

The old man was slowly reloading. Pirotta dealt him a savage blow, which sent him staggering, and wrenched the rifle from his hand. Eleanor raced across the short stretch of burning cobblestones. Behind her, she heard Alberto's hoarse shout, Anna-Maria's high scream; but in the blinding glare, she only saw Jacopone lying where he had fallen, and Pirotta standing menacingly over him. He caught her arm as she sank to her knees beside the old man, and pulled her up again to face him. "Where's Rosana?" he asked harshly. "Where is she?" He dropped her arm. "If you have betrayed me—" There was no need to finish his threat. She knew, then, that he would kill her. He began to run toward the office.

"Wrong direction, Pirotta," Bill Lammiter's voice called. "I'm over here."

Pirotta swung round to face the north end of the buildings. Lammiter left the shadow of the corner doorway, and stepped into the brilliant sunshine.

Twenty-Five

THERE WAS a long moment of silence, of complete surprise. No movement, no sound, except from Lammiter as he began to walk slowly across the courtyard. This long moment was in his favor. Nothing else. The sun was in his eyes. Joe's revolver was a .28, Belgian: he'd have to get at least twenty feet nearer. Against him, was a .22 one-shot rifle. He had heard that one shot fired as he stood in the deserted kitchen, but before he had been able to find a corridor that brought him out into the courtyard, there had been time for the rifle to be reloaded. Yes, it was loaded all right, judging by the way Pirotta faced him. One shot, then: he would drop flat on his face the moment Pirotta started raising that rifle above waist level, and fire from the ground. The books said it could be done. This was one time he hoped the books were right. At least, there was no one else within range.

Pirotta had recovered from his surprise. He watched the American walking slowly, steadily, toward him. "Isn't this unfair?" he asked with a smile. "You know so little about weapons, obviously. A man with a pistol never faces a man with a rifle." He raised the rifle a little. "Do you want me to complete your education?" He lowered the rifle. And then, quickly, he swung it to his shoulder and fired. Lammiter dropped flat on the ground. But there was no crack from a bullet.

It wasn't loaded, by God, it wasn't loaded, Lammiter thought, as the breath came painfully back into his body. And I was so damned busy hitting those cobblestones that I didn't even fire back. He rose. He began to laugh.

Pirotta looked with amazement at the rifle, and then at Jacopone. The old gamekeeper was rising to his feet, a broad grin on his wrinkled face. Pirotta flung the useless rifle at him, and turned to face Lammiter. The American began walking toward him again.

"You are close enough," Pirotta said contemptuously. "Or would you miss even at this distance?"

"I might at that," said Lammiter. Now he had time to glance at Eleanor. She was all right. She still had her hands clenched together at her lips in a kind of desperate prayer. Had that gesture been for him—or was it for Pirotta, even now? At that moment, she answered his thoughts: she dropped her hands, her eyes came to life again, and "Oh, Bill!" she said. That was all. But the way she said it was enough.

"Maybe," Lammiter told Pirotta, "I'd like to see you in a courtroom. Maybe I'd like to find out how many lies you can tell and still look noble." Odd, he was thinking: this morning he had said he would kill Pirotta. But now, he was finding it impossible to fire on someone just standing there, watching him. He ought to have shot at him the moment he dropped to the ground. Except, at that moment, every bone in his body had been jarred and he couldn't have hit an elephant.

Jacopone had picked up his rifle, examined it to make sure it had not been damaged. Now, with the bullet he had kept clenched in his right hand, he was reloading, expertly, definitely. He looked at Lammiter, his toothless grin widening, and nodded. Then with his deliberate pace he walked over to the cars and stood there, on guard, his eyes on Pirotta. Thank God for the Jacopones in this world, thought Lammiter.

Pirotta said derisively, "You can always shoot me in the back." He turned round. He looked at Jacopone. Then at Alberto. "Unlock the gates!" he told Alberto. But the old man made no move.

"You'll have to find a better solution than that for your problems," Lammiter said grimly. "But I'll tell you what I'll do for you— I'll shoot you in the leg if you start running for the gates. We'll just stay here until the *carabinieri* arrive. After all, I wasn't the only one who heard that rifle shot." He wasn't wholly bluffing: Joe must have heard the shot, and he would send someone.

"Rosana!" Eleanor called out, and everyone, even Pirotta, looked at the narrow doorway near the gate. Rosana was standing there, watching them all; and then, slowly, almost dejectedly, she stepped into the courtyard. "Rosana—" Eleanor began in alarm, "didn't you—"

"Yes," Rosana said quietly. "The warning went through. To Perugia." She looked away from Pirotta. She raised her voice. "I told them that the meeting was today at three o'clock. I told them to follow the two men who would arrive on the bus. I told them about Gubbio, about Venice. . . ." She looked at Pirotta, and her voice dropped. "I told them everything Sabatini told you, Luigi."

She began walking toward Lammiter.

Pirotta looked at his watch. His indecision ended. He ran swiftly toward the narrow door beside the gate.

"Rosana!" Lammiter yelled. "Get out of my way!" But she didn't. And before he could move to get a clear aim, Pirotta was safely inside. She caught Lammiter's arm as he started to follow.

"Are you crazy! He'll telephone his warning—" He pulled his arm free.

"No! No!" Rosana said. "His call won't go through." She caught his arm again. "Let him telephone. Let him give the number of the meeting place. That is all Joe needs to find its address." She turned to Eleanor, who had run over to join them. "Joe has had a man sitting beside the operator all day, waiting for every call from this house. I didn't have to telephone Rome after all." Suddenly she smiled and kissed Eleanor's cheek. "You and your funny old knife—you didn't do so badly, both of you, after all." Then the smile vanished, and she glanced across the courtyard at the door that led to the office. "Oh, I hate all this, I hate all this!" she burst out bitterly.

"Who started it all, anyway?" Lammiter said quietly. "Not you, not Joe, not Brewster."

She looked at him. "I keep forgetting that," she said. She drew away a little, her eyes once more on the door near the gate.

Lammiter asked, "What about that mechanic? Did he carry a gun?"

Rosana shook her head. "I told him if he didn't stop trying to force the door to the office, I'd name him to the police. And just as he was thinking about that, Jacopone came looking for Anna-Maria and Alberto. Their quarters are next door to the office. He locked the mechanic into Anna-Maria's bedroom."

"Joe heard the rifleshot, I hope."

"Yes. It was a signal he had prearranged."

"Damn it, I keep underestimating him."

"Who *is* he, Bill?"

"A Sicilian."

"Yes, yes, but . . ."

Eleanor looked at one and then at the other. There's so much I don't understand, she thought forlornly. There's so much I haven't been told. There's only one thing I do know: Bill never stopped loving me. Perhaps that's all I want to know, anyway. "The cobbles are hot," she said suddenly. "I'll find my shoes, I think." The excuse was real: now that the danger was over, she was aware, at last, of the pain in her burning feet. She tried to smile. Neither of them had heard her. They were listening for something else as they watched the door. I won't watch, she thought: I won't watch Pirotta come out. She turned toward the hall and ran. She heard Bill's voice, "Eleanor, wait—" And then, as she reached the dark silence of the hall, the stone floor, cold as the water of a mountain stream, under her burning feet, she heard the gate bell ring. That will be the police, she thought, the police or the *carabinieri*. . . . She didn't know why she should be crying.

She sank down on the bottom step of the staircase. She had suddenly no strength to climb toward her shoes. She sat, her head bowed, her hands covering her face. "If you have betrayed me—" he had said. Had she betrayed him? "You and your funny old knife," Rosana had said. Betrayed him? And then she remembered Bill's quiet voice back in the courtyard, "Who started it all, anyway?"

"Eleanor!" Lammiter tried to stop her, but she was already running toward the hall. That might be a safer place than the courtyard: he still had the worry that Pirotta would come out with a gun in his hand. Or with Giovanni. Or with both. He just didn't trust Pirotta. He started after Eleanor. "Wait for me!" He raised his voice. "Eleanor, wait for me in there!" And then he heard Pirotta's footsteps. He swung round again, cursing the moment.

Pirotta had come out from the doorway at the gate. He was alone and unarmed. For a brief moment, he had paused and looked at them all. Then it seemed as though

they no longer existed; as though he had blotted out the
whole picture of this courtyard from his mind. He began
to walk toward the south wing of the house. The gate bell
rang, but he paid no attention.

"What's over there?" Lammiter asked Rosana as he
watched Pirotta's determined pace. Pirotta passed the
cars. Jacopone made no attempt to stop him, and
Pirotta went on. He entered a doorway.

"His own rooms," Rosana said, and put a hand on
Lammiter's sleeve. "Don't follow him, Bill." She paused.
She hesitated. And then, slowly, she said, "The gun room
is over there, too."

"Locked?" he asked quickly. "Surely it's locked?"

"The princess told Alberto to unlock it. Those were the
orders."

"What?" He stared at her. He started toward the south
wing, but Rosana's hand tightened desperately on his arm.

"Do you want to stop him?" She shook her head. "What
other solution is there?"

"But—" He hesitated. He didn't know what to do.

"What else?" she said fiercely. There were tears in her
eyes. "What else? The princess is right. He has lived-
badly. Let him die well."

The gates were being opened. He pocketed Joe's revolver. "I just don't trust him," he said slowly.

Her tears changed to shocked anger. "Not even now?
He's defeated. He knows it. He knew it when his telephone call didn't go through!" She looked at him almost
accusingly. Then she pointed to the elderly captain and
two boys in dark green uniforms who were coming through
the gates. "They are in charge now, anyway."

"Suits me," he said. "I'll find Eleanor."

"And leave me to face the captain by myself?"

"Explain to him I'm a foreigner, can't speak the language." He turned toward the hall. This first meeting
with Eleanor—it would be difficult. Odd, how easy it could
have been five minutes ago, when she had called out "Oh,
Bill!" and looked as if she would run straight into his
arms. But Pirotta had been there, still undefeated, still dangerous. And now—how did you hold her and kiss her
when you were listening for a shot from the gun room?
Pirotta was still between them.

Rosana said, "Bill, what shall I tell him?" She was frightened. She made no move to go over to the captain and his two men.

Lammiter halted, and glanced at the little group moving away from the gate. Alberto and Anna-Maria had begun a long recital, no doubt making everything abundantly incomprehensible. Jacopone had added his stalwart silence to their story. "Tell him Jacopone was showing me how his rifle worked."

"And nothing else?"

"That's all he needs to know." And there I go, he thought savagely, starting to hush things up, just like the princess, just like Alberto.

"I suppose so." She wiped the tear marks from her cheeks. She added, pathetically, "It's so hard to remember what some know and others don't, and how much they can be told and can't be. Bill, I didn't say anything to Eleanor about Luigi's other—other organization. The narcotics one. I just told her about the politics. I thought that was—that was enough." She shivered and looked round the sunlit courtyard. "Strange that it should be here that everything was really decided. Not in Perugia. Here . . ."

Somehow, his worry grew as he watched the genial captain's stately progress slowed by that ancient mariner Alberto. Everyone was being so damned tactful and correct. Very serious were the two fresh-faced boys, and very impressed by the princess's Casa Grande. Yes, everyone was being so polite, so relieved that there was no ugly trouble to be found in this pleasant place after all. Decent, kindly people, trusting, ignorant. They had not one idea of the evil that had walked through this courtyard today. He looked at the south wing of the house. I still don't trust him, he thought.

Rosana, watching the captain approach her, said suddenly, "I—I don't think they've come to arrest me after all." She almost laughed in her relief. "That was the plan: Luigi was going to take Eleanor with him, but I was to be—"

"Rosana," Lammiter said urgently, "does this house all connect? Each wing leads into the other?"

She stared at him. "Bill!" she called out. But he was

already racing across the short stretch of cobblestones toward the main door. He was pulling out the revolver again. He was running, she thought in amazement, not to the south wing, not toward the gun room, but straight for the hall. Eleanor, she suddenly remembered, he's worried about Eleanor. . . . Quickly she signaled the astounded captain, and they began to run, too.

"Eleanor!" It was Luigi Pirotta's voice, far away, calling her, calling her urgently.

Or was he near, and the voice was low? It came again. "Eleanor!"

She raised her head from her hands. She half rose, turned slowly round. Outside, in the sunlit courtyard, there were footsteps and voices. Here, in the shadowed silence of the hall, was Pirotta. Somewhere in the hall, there was Pirotta.

She drew back, shrinking against the stone wall, and looked up the long flight of steps. He was standing there, at the head of the staircase, quite still. For a long moment, he stood looking at her. He raised the revolver he had held by his side.

From the door behind her, she heard a deafening explosion echoing around the high stone walls. She saw Pirotta's hand go to his right shoulder and hold it, his face twisted with pain. Then an arm swept round her waist and pulled her down into the hall behind the shelter of the balustrade. "It's all right, it's all right," Bill was saying, as she heard a second explosion, still louder, thunder through the hall.

There were people at the door.

"It's all right," Bill said again, his arms around her. And they stood there, together, her face pressed against his chest, his cheek against her hair, his arms around her, holding her, holding her, until their two bodies seemed to have been carved out of one piece of stone. She raised her head and their eyes met. Slowly, gently, he kissed her. "Never, never again—" he began; he couldn't go on. He kissed her hard, this time.

No one paid any attention to them. Everyone had started climbing the staircase. Someone began to speak. "Come away," Bill said, "come away from this place."

He led her toward the first room he could see. He wanted her away from the hall before Anna-Maria's cries became hysterics, before the captain would call out, "He's dead."

Twenty-Six

PERHAPS TWENTY MINUTES LATER, certainly no more than that, the door opened and the captain of the *carabinieri* came into the room where Eleanor lay. Lammiter had ripped a sheet from a velvet couch, and propped her up with cushions. He sat beside her, talking quietly, holding her hands between his in a firm grasp. Afterward, he had no idea what he talked about: it didn't matter. All that mattered was to get the shadows out of her eyes, the frightened look away from her lips. She had listened, and yet at the same time she had been following her own troubled thoughts. For suddenly she asked, just as the captain came into the room, "He would have killed himself, even if I hadn't been here?" There was a question in her voice, the last remnant of fear.

"Yes." He was sure of that.

"He said a strange thing." Her soft voice hesitated.

"That's all right, darling. Forget it," he said gently. He looked at the captain, who was watching them somberly.

But she had to tell him. "He said that he could and would come back to Italy because he didn't leave in defeat. And then—"

And then defeat had come, and it had been complete. How could Pirotta have faced his political masters with such an overwhelming disaster behind him? They would add up the total loss—Sabatini arrested; Evans extradited; the meeting not only a failure but a permanent danger to all those who had taken part—and even call it treachery. As Joe would say, it was in their pattern.

Eleanor said haltingly, watching him, "You don't blame me?" She closed her eyes and bit her lip. "He did."

"He made today's choice years ago. Long before he ever met you." He kissed her. Then he remembered the captain. He rose and faced the waiting man.

The captain had been remarkably patient. But he had found the little scene interesting. Each revelation, however small, was important. And he had got little help from Alberto or Anna-Maria: they were much too over-whelmed with grief. Jacopone, as usual, just stood around, saying and doing nothing. The Signorina Di Feo had told him a wild story of what she had seen as she entered the hall just ahead of him, and when he hadn't quite be-lieved it, she had rushed to the telephone over in the office. And a stranger, a mechanic, had been found locked in Anna-Maria's room next door to the office. (Anna-Maria had had hysterics at that point.) The man had not complained about his imprisonment: he kept saying he knew nothing about anything, which might be true. Only one thing was certain: the count had died on the staircase, by his own hand. Accidentally? Or had it been deliberate? A crime of passion? Perhaps . . . The poor count had lost this young woman to the American, and so he blew out his brains. What a tragedy, what a terrible unhappiness for everyone, what a disaster. . . .

The captain studied the young woman. Yes, she was very beautiful. They always were. He had entered this room prepared to dislike these foreigners for the trouble they had caused. And yet—watching them—he wasn't so sure now that this was a heartless creature, or that the American was a ruthless Hollywood ruffian. There was something very—yes, very touching in the way they looked at each other, in the way the man now stood pro-tectively over her. They were more like two people who had come through some frightful accident and could scarcely believe they were still alive. He had seen faces like these once, when a train had plunged over a bridge into a ravine and—but enough of disasters. Briskly, he held out a pair of high-heeled shoes. "These were found on the staircase," he said.

Thank God, he speaks English, Lammiter thought. "Thank you." He took the shoes and knelt to slip them on Eleanor's feet.

Now, the captain wondered, what is he thinking, what is he remembering? The American touched the girl's feet as if he had much to remember. (And indeed, Lammiter was remembering his first sight of Eleanor today, running across the burning cobblestones to reach Jacopone where the old man had fallen.) The girl was saying, "I was trying to escape. . . . I was afraid I'd twist my ankle—"

She glanced at Bill, wondering how foolish she must

now seem. But he didn't look as if he thought she had been foolish. She gave her first smile, a small one but real. "I'm much better now," she told him. "When can we leave?"

"Soon," he said. But that was the problem. He rose and led the captain away from the couch toward the window. "She didn't actually see what happened," he said quietly. "Please don't question her. Not now."

"Later, later," the captain agreed quickly. "She is very tired. I see that." And so are you, he thought, studying the American's exhausted face. "But now, one thing. You have a gun?"

Lammiter drew out Joe's revolver and handed it over. "One bullet—"

"The bullet in the shoulder." The captain examined the revolver with interest. "Why?"

"He was going to shoot—" Lammiter glanced back at Eleanor. "I fired from the door, and hit his shoulder. He changed his revolver to his left hand. And then—well, you arrived then. You saw what happened."

"Yes, yes."

Lammiter took a deep breath of relief.

From the courtyard came the ringing of the bell at its gate. The captain's worried face, no longer bland, was etched with down-drawn lines. "He would have killed her. You are sure?"

"Yes."

And that was what the Signorina Di Feo had insisted: she had arrived just a few seconds behind Signore Lammiter; she had seen the gun pointed at the *Americana*. "It is so difficult to believe," he said. "Suicide, yes. That is understandable." He glanced at the girl. "But murder, no."

"Most truths are difficult to believe."

The captain was staring out of the window. He sighed unhappily. "What shall we tell the princess?" His hands stretched out, as if asking help, and then fell to his sides, acknowledging no help was possible.

Lammiter glanced out of the window. A cream-colored sports car was coming through the gate now. The princess had arrived.

The captain frowned down at his highly polished boots, as if willing them to start moving toward the courtyard. He took a reluctant step. He sighed. "It would be kinder not to mention attempted murder, yes?" He spoke the word with distaste.

Lammiter nodded.

"Then," the captain said more cheerfully, "the bullet in the shoulder, it is probably of little importance now." But he did not hand over Joe's revolver. He slipped it into his pocket. Under the warm cloak of politeness, business was still business. The princess could have her myth meanwhile, but reports had to be made, forms filled out, evidence noted. He looked out of the window again, and squared his shoulders. Then, with an impressive salute, he marched quickly out of the room.

"The princess is here," Lammiter told Eleanor. He stood for a moment, watching the courtyard. "With that Englishman," he added in some surprise as he noted the driver of the car. "You know—Whitelaw, Bertrand Whitelaw." And he didn't know which astounded him the more: Whitelaw's excellent if raffish taste in cars, or the princess's willingness to travel in what she would call a "contraption." She was sitting very erect and motionless, her head and neck wrapped in layers of chiffon, her face a complete mask. At first, she didn't seem to notice Whitelaw offering her his hand to descend. She didn't even look at Alberto. And then she stepped slowly, carefully, out of the car, and stood, almost unwilling to face the door of her house. "She's afraid," Lammiter told Eleanor. "She's afraid to enter." He left the window.

"She knows? But how?"

Lammiter was thinking of Whitelaw now. He, too, had been uncertain, but for quite another reason: he had been glancing at his watch, a man torn between politeness and impatience. "What is Whitelaw doing in Umbria, anyway?" he suddenly asked aloud. He halted, looking back at the window.

"Bill—I don't want to see the princess. I don't want to stay here." Eleanor had risen and come over to him. He put an arm around her waist. "I can't bear this place, I can't bear it."

"We'll leave," he told her reassuringly. From outside, he now heard the captain asking politely about the princess's journey.

"But can you leave?" She was watching him anxiously.

"Why not? The captain is in charge. As soon as he gives the signal, I'm taking you right out of here."

"Bill," she said very quietly, "tell me one thing. Are you a secret agent?"

He looked down at her in amazement. "Good God, no!" He tightened his arm around her. "Everything I did was —strictly personal." He smiled, a little embarrassed. "All for you, funny face."

"That was what I hoped," she said gravely.

He stared at her. "Surely you never believed—"

"Everyone else does."

"*What?* But that's all nonsense. Ellie—it's absolute nonsense. You know that, don't you?"

She nodded. She gave her second smile. "Then your job is all over. You can leave with me?"

"Nothing is going to stop me." He pushed the hair back from the nape of her neck and kissed it.

"Now I really do feel better," she said. She glanced toward the window. "The poor captain . . . He is having a little trouble." They could hear his rich baritone still hedging around the distasteful task of being the sad bearer of tragic news.

Whitelaw said, with an undiplomatic abruptness that was quite apart from his usual character, "What bad news? What are you trying to say?"

And at last the truth was jolted out. "Luigi, Count Pirotta, has shot himself."

There was a long moment of silence. Then the princess's clear voice said, "When did it happen? This morning?"

"No, Principessa. Half an hour ago."

There was another silence. Lammiter could imagine the cold, sad face paling even under its careful mask of rouge and powder. She had, he thought grimly, been almost too early in arriving, after all.

Eleanor had walked back to the couch. She looked up at the high ceiling with its carved and painted beams, at the tall wall covered with the treasure of centuries, at the rows of high-backed chairs waiting under their dust covers for the parties that never would take place here any more, at the long windows elaborately curtained which once had opened on a courtyard filled with the

cheerful bustle of arriving guests, with the excitement
of people who had come to enjoy themselves, elegants
among elegance, an island of prerogative, of unreality, in
a sea of constant struggle. Now the Casa Grande would
become what it really was: a museum of beautiful things
and evil memories.

Bill Lammiter, beside her, was watching her anxiously.
"But perhaps," she said, letting him into her thoughts, "all
that happened today was as much a part of this house
as those pretty possessions." She pointed at random to a
Cellini candelabrum on a Florentine mosaic table, and
then to a Bronzino portrait of a handsome man, young,
richly dressed, melancholy, who looked gravely down at
her from his elaborately carved and gilded frame. Her
eyes widened suddenly as she stared up at the Renaissance man. "He looks like—" She didn't finish. Lammiter,
looking up at the portrait, saw the resemblance to Pirotta,
too.

Instinctively, he took her hand. But she was in control
of herself. She sat quite still, more curious than upset, as
though she were trying to solve the puzzle that anyone
who could bear a strong resemblance to such a noble face
should have been driven by the forces that had controlled
Pirotta. Was this, Lammiter wondered, the Pirotta she
had fallen in love with? And it was your own God-damned
fault, he cursed himself, remembering how he had let her
go last spring, hadn't followed her until he realized he
had lost her. She was watching him, holding his hand as if
he were the one who needed comforting. "I was a swollen-
headed fool," he said bitterly. "I was so busy giving away
pieces of myself to everyone and everything that I'd soon
have had nothing left to give to the only one who mattered." He paused. He gave a wry smile. "All a playwright has to do is to write good plays. All the rest is—
sawing sawdust." He paused again. He had never found
words so elusive and stupid. "I'm trying to say I am
sorry," he said almost desperately.

"No—not you. It's I who should be saying—" She
paused. The princess's voice came clearly from the hall.
"Oh, Bill—is she coming in here?"

Too late to close the door. He could hardly shut it in
the princess's face.

"It was an accident, of course," the princess told the

captain. "He was cleaning his rifle in the gun room."

"Perhaps it was an accident," the captain said unhappily. "But it happened on the staircase."

There was a long pause. "I think I shall rest here for a little," the princess said in a low voice. She stopped abruptly at the threshold of the room as she saw Eleanor, sitting so still. Then she looked at Lammiter. A strange expression, not unkind, not even surprised, softened her carefully painted lips for a fleeting moment. She nodded. She walked on.

Lammiter knelt beside Eleanor. He kissed her hands. She looked at him, and then she touched his brow gently, and she laid her cheek against his.

Rosana brought Eleanor's coat and purse. She spoke quickly, tonelessly, with all life dredged out of her voice. Perhaps this was the only way she could keep her emotions under control: to be businesslike and almost aloof—even if that was, or perhaps indeed because it was, contrary to her nature—that was how she could build a wall around her emotions. If she let one part of that wall be displaced, the whole barrier would come falling down. "Joe is waiting," she told Bill Lammiter.

"Where?"

"Outside the gate."

"What brought him here?"

"I telephoned. I thought the captain was going to be—difficult."

"Thank you." Lammiter looked at the pale face, now coldly beautiful, a marble statue going through human motions of politeness. "Again," he added gently, "thank you."

"You must hurry."

"Before the captain changes his mind?" he asked with a smile.

"He's been told your address for the next few days. He knows where to find you—if he needs you."

"My address? I haven't got any address." But Rosana didn't explain.

Eleanor said impulsively, "Rosana—you don't want to stay here either. Come with us."

Rosana's face softened for a moment. Her lips began to

tremble. "I must stay," she said, turning away. She walked back toward the door.

Lammiter took Eleanor's arm, and pressed her wrist gently. That warned her. She was still puzzled, but she said no more. She gave a last look round the white and green room, and then at the Bronzino portrait of the sad and proud young man. Rosana, waiting at the door for them, noticed that glance. She said, "Bronzino still enjoys his private joke. Every time someone stands in front of that portrait and exclaims 'What grace, what goodness! Ah—those were noble days!' then Bronzino's skeleton shakes with laughter. The Renaissance had its share of violence and evil. That young man was one of its monsters." She walked into the hall.

Quickly they followed her, quickly they passed over the stone-flagged floor. At the front door, Rosana halted. "Good-by," she said evenly. "I must go to the princess." She held out her hands to them both.

"Not good-by," he protested.

Rosana looked at him and then at Eleanor. She said, suddenly natural again, warm and vibrant, "You are my friends." She gave a smile that turned into a strangled sob as her guard went down. Then she turned abruptly, and retreated into the dark shadows of the vast hall. They began to walk, in silence, across the gold-lit courtyard.

It was a serene place, that courtyard. Under the five o'clock sun, warm and mellow, there was no movement except the flutter of a white pigeon over their heads, no sound except their footsteps on the stones. Near the gate, wide open now, showing the quiet little square outside, Lammiter suddenly said, "Where is Whitelaw?"

Eleanor looked at him in surprise. "I didn't hear him leave either." It was odd, she thought, that Whitelaw had left so immediately. He was a friend of the princess's, wasn't he? Strange that he should have left her at her doorstep. "Perhaps the princess sent him away."

"Perhaps."

"You're worried."

"I've reached the stage of worrying about everything," he told her. Then he thought, I never even noticed Whitelaw's car was gone until I had walked the breadth of this courtyard. What's gone wrong with your reactions, Lammiter? They are as slow as your feet at this moment.

He almost passed Jacopone. The gamekeeper was standing so motionless beside the gate that he might have been one of its carved decorations. He still carried his rifle under one arm. He looked at them both quite impassively. He nodded, and a smile entered those old watchful eyes. He seemed surprised and then pleased as Lammiter seized his free hand in a grasp that tightened as they stood in silence. *"Viva Garibaldi!"* Lammiter said suddenly.

A wide grin broke across the wrinkled face. *"Evviva!"* Jacopone said heartily. *"Viva Garibaldi!"* He pumped Lammiter's hand vigorously, clapped him on the shoulder with a hearty thump, smiled and nodded approvingly for Eleanor. *"Evviva!"* he said, and dropped Lammiter's hand. He turned and left them, clumping his way slowly toward the kitchen doorway.

"Now that you've stopped pinning medals on each other," Joe's voice said behind them, "shall we go and eat?"

Twenty-Seven

NORMAL, THAT WAS JOE. That was the cue he was giving me, Lammiter thought as he helped Eleanor into the back seat of the small Fiat. He followed her stiffly. Physically, he was more exhausted than he wanted to admit. Mentally— well, that was another matter. Now that they were out of the Casa Grande, out into the free air of Montesecco, the intense pressure had lifted and left him feeling almost lightheaded. He had the impulse to make several wild jokes, mad suggestions, all irresponsible, all delightful. But he'd have to brake heavily on his emotions, control them, and keep his inner excitement something secret. "This is service," he said, looking at his suitcase in the front seat beside Joe. And now he noticed, too, that Joe had found time enough to shave, brush his hair, put on his tie again, and don his jacket.

"We'll get your possessions back to you, one by one," Joe told him. He looked at Eleanor, and nodded approvingly as he started the car. She returned his smile, leaned her head against Lammiter's shoulder, settled into his comforting grasp, and closed her eyes. And Lammiter fell silent, watching the little streets of the town: here was the main piazza, now stirring into life with the approach of evening. This was where he had seen Sabatini, that was the street down which he had retreated, here was the gate of the town, the olive trees where he had talked with his two amiable maniacs, the farmhouse. . . . And, as he remembered the desperate misery of those waiting hours, the happiness that now enveloped him seemed completely incredible. Or let's put it this way, he told himself: this is real, this is normal; and that—he turned his head to look at the walled town—that was the hideous dream, the trial. But he must take his cue from Joe: no post-mortems. What was over was over, only to be remembered as a warning when life became too easy, too comfortable, for that was the funny thing about life: people always needed a warning every now and again, just to remind them of what might have been.

Down the hill, between the groves of olive trees, they traveled. Before them was the smiling placid valley, behind them the fortress walls.

"Not that way," Lammiter said sharply, as Joe swung the car to the right at the foot of Montesecco's hill. Joe slowed up. "You turn left for Rome."

"Rome's too far. Five minutes, and you'll be sitting down to a decent meal. Isn't that better?"

"And this decent meal is in Perugia?"

"It's the nearest place," Joe said cheerfully. "It's nice there. Good food, good hotels."

"We're staying there?" Lammiter was horrified.

"Why not? Rome's a long haul from here. Too much for Miss Halley."

That was true enough. "There's Assisi."

"Filled to the rafters with pilgrims. You'll be comfortable in Perugia."

"I'm not so sure," Lammiter said very quietly. "I don't want Eleanor to go near Perugia."

Joe halted the car and reached for a cigarette. He lit one for Lammiter. He said, watching a slow procession of farm carts coming back from work in the fields, "There is a small emergency."

"What?"

"About Evans," Joe said curtly. He was angry, but not at Lammiter. "Look, I didn't want this any more than you. My job's over: Sabatini was arrested, and none of his friends even know about it—yet. The meeting took place, and everyone attending it was observed and photographed: they will be watched when they get back to their own countries; all their contacts will be noted, and not one piece of advice or any reports from them will ever be accepted in good faith again. And, lastly, the big guy who organized a dope ring so efficiently that it could be taken over for political purposes by his Communist friends on the day they try to seize power—" he halted, looked at Lammiter, and was a little taken aback to find that the girl had opened her eyes and was watching him. He branched off. "You don't believe me? There's nothing Communism finds handier than a good tight organization with an efficient chain of command, all ready to be taken over. This one didn't even have to be infiltrated. It was created especially. It pulls in the money now. Later, it could supply the bully-boys, and whether they wear black, brown, or red shirts makes no difference." His mouth shut tightly. But he didn't finish his original sentence about the "big guy" who had organized a very efficient chain of command. Instead, he looked again at Eleanor. "My job's over. And so is yours. To hell with their emergencies. Let the English puzzle this one out. It's their headache. I'm only an underpaid Italian cop who hasn't had a night off in five weeks."

He must be pretty angry, Lammiter thought, to have broken his cover like that. He said, "What's this emergency?"

Joe gave a short laugh. "No one can identify Evans. A couple of fellows are being flown out from London right now. But there's no one here who knows him. Can you beat that?"

"But they saw him leave the meeting, didn't they? Don't tell me," Lammiter said in disgust, "that they let him slip between their fingers."

"No, no," Joe assured him. "They're keeping a close watch on the man. Tall, thin, fair hair—"

"Gray," Eleanor said.

He looked at her quickly. "Evans's description reads *fair hair*. And your photograph—"

"That was taken very late in the evening. The light was bad."

"So—" Joe said softly, "they have more reason for their doubts about Evans than they know."

Lammiter said, "What started the doubts?"

Joe shrugged his shoulders. "I wasn't there" was all he could say.

"And now," Lammiter said, his lips and voice tight, "they want Eleanor to make sure of the man they hope is Evans, but might not be. No, thanks. We are not taking Eleanor to Perugia."

"Then where? Back to Montesecco?"

"Stop being funny," Lammiter said sourly.

"But you don't find right places to eat and sleep in any little town. And your friend Camden has got a couple of good rooms for you in Perugia."

"Look, Joe—we don't need luxury. All we want is peace and quiet." He looked at Eleanor. "And safety."

There was a short silence.

Lammiter said testily, "I thought you said your job was over, you were glad it was over. Hell, what's this treatment, Joe? First you—"

Eleanor said, "Are there truly good restaurants in Perugia?" It's up to me, she thought wearily. Bill would go to Perugia if he were by himself and could identify the man Evans. And Joe, however much he doesn't feel like going, knows he must. The job is not over. It all began with Evans, and it must end with Evans.

Bill Lammiter said, "Eleanor—"

"I'm starving," she said. "Let's get all this business finished and then concentrate on us." She raised her voice, speaking to Joe now. "Let's go to Perugia."

Joe started the engine again. His furrowed face looked both pleased and unhappy. "Okay?" he asked Lammiter, his foot still on the brake.

Lammiter nodded. Two against one. He knew when he was in a minority. The car moved forward.

"How long were you in America, Joe?" Eleanor asked. A change of subject seemed advisable.

"Twelve years," said Joe. Then he gave her a startled look in the mirror. "Hey!" he said, "you know when to ask questions, don't you?" He grinned. Lammiter had to smile, too: he was willing to bet that Joe's true past was rarely jolted out of him.

"Only occasionally," Eleanor said. Too often, she thought, I've never asked any questions at all, just accepted everything on its surface value. But her inquiry had its effect: Joe was explaining those twelve years, Bill was interested, and blood pressure was falling back to normal all around her.

"Yes," Joe said. "Ten years as a kid; two years later on, as a college student in New York. I was brought up in Cleveland—I was only two when my father settled there. When he died, my mother brought the family back to Sicily. She had always kept talking about Sicily—the best place in the world, she said, the only place." Joe's smile broadened. "Funny thing, when she got to Sicily, she kept talking about America." He swerved round a pair of white oxen.

"Oh!" Eleanor sat up and looked at them.

"Want to take a photograph?" Joe asked, but he didn't slacken speed. "Or is the light not good enough? What color would their hair turn?"

She half smiled. She gave Bill's hand a little squeeze. See, she was telling him, I'm all right: I feel better every minute. And perhaps, she was thinking, I need this: I need to look out at the world, this heavenly scene of farmers and white oxen and rich fields and little hills and trees, all silhouetted so clearly against the western light. I need this sense of reality, as much as I need food or sleep. When Luigi and his two men brought me here, it was a nightmare journey through menacing shadows and grim black shapes. Now . . . She took a deep breath of the gentle air, with its first hint of coolness. Now, too, I begin to see the real reason behind everything Luigi did today. If this man Evans is so important, then now I see Luigi as clearly in perspective as these clear-cut hills. He lied, to the very end he lied to me. He wasn't taking me away to save me from danger. He was taking me away to make sure of saving Evans. And when he tried to kill me, it wasn't because he loved me so much, it wasn't any sweet romantic nonsense like that. He was simply protecting Evans. Luigi was the realist. It was not I who betrayed him. It was he who betrayed everyone who trusted him as a human being.

Bill was looking at her, worried again. She smiled for him. Some day, she thought, I'll talk to him about this. Not now. Some day . . . What makes a man into a machine? What kills conscience? Or did that die when self-criticism died? And did you stop criticizing yourself when you believed that anything you did was right? And if anyone else questioned you, there was always the Cause for an excuse? But how could you judge that a cause was good or bad unless you had enough feeling left in your veins for human beings? Not just "the people," a vague abstract mass, with as little real meaning as a linoleum pattern. But people like Rosana and Jacopone and Joe and old Alberto and Anna-Maria. People were not pawns, to be moved around and sacrificed, to be swept away if they did not fit into the grand design. People were this farmer here, riding slowly home with his daughter and son beside him; these two women walking with bundles of twigs on their backs; that boy on the bicycle; that man in the high-powered car; this bus load, Joe, Bill, me.

"Here we are," said Joe, swinging the car to his right.

They began to twist up the long arm of a hill between an avenue of trees. The town sprawled over the peak like a cap of snow on a Japanese mountain. Down here, the houses were new, neat modern shapes of plaster painted green or cream or pink, but above them the old buildings clustered together—perched, it seemed, on a precipice, an island of bleached stone and jutting shapes.

They had reached the end of the climb. They came into an open square with public buildings and a small park that overlooked the precipice. There, the main street began, the Corso Vanucci, running like a spine along the crest of the hill on which lay Perugia. There, too, the cars were parked, for the Corso itself was closed off to traffic. "It's usual," Joe told them as they got out. "At this hour, everyone strolls out to see the sunset."

"And one another," Lammiter added, looking at the groups of young girls walking arm in arm in their pretty dresses; of young men, tall and handsome, keeping together; of proud couples, with red-cheeked babies, all preened in starched frills. There was a strange hush over the street, broken only by the sound of light-soled shoes and the murmur of peaceful voices. The street was straight, wide, handsomely paved, and not very long. He could see the other end marked by a fountain, in front of a huge cathedral. Between the piazza, which they were leaving, and this stone giant, there was only a constant stream of gay clothes and well-brushed heads. Nothing could be more unlike Montesecco, he thought thankfully. He began to relax. And then, as they passed the last parked car and entered the wide stretch of street, he looked back swiftly.

"Yes?" asked Joe.

"That's Whitelaw's car. Bertrand Whitelaw. You know him?"

"I know about him."

"Where does he stand?"

"Does that matter?"

"He brought the princess from Rome. He knows Pirotta is dead."

Joe frowned. "Give me time. I'm slow. I have to think this out."

Lammiter looked at Eleanor. *Pirotta is dead,* he had said, as cold-bloodedly as though he had been talking about Mussolini or Stalin. But all she noticed now was his concern over her. "How far do we walk?" she asked, keeping her voice light.

"Another fifty yards," Joe said. "That's all. We start slanting over to our left." He steered them expertly across the street, between the strolling groups, toward the broad sidewalk which was filled with café tables.

"The foreigners," said Eleanor, looking at the tables, "are here in force."

"Keep watching," Joe told her quietly. They walked slowly along the edge of the sidewalk. Joe had taken her other arm. He pressed it suddenly. "Don't stare, just look," he told her. "Anyone you know?"

"No one," she said, when she thought it was safe to speak. "No one at all."

"Did you see that fair-haired man in the gray flannel suit?"

"Yes."

"You've never seen him before?"

"No."

"Into this restaurant," Joe directed them suddenly. He led the way across the sidewalk. He seemed neither disappointed nor hurried.

The restaurant was empty, of course, and unlighted. No one ate until the promenade outside, the *passeggiata,* was over. Now Joe let his pace increase. He led them through the cool dark room into a tiled kitchen where a solitary cook under a spreading tree of pots and pans suspended from an overhead beam was busy with a bubbling pot. The cook, a bulky man who looked as though he enjoyed his own cooking, scarcely glanced around. "You're late. I was beginning to think you weren't coming." He pointed with a ladle to a closed door.

Joe nodded. As he opened the door leading them into a back room, he called to the cook, "Serve it up!"

"Subito, subito!" The ladle went back to stirring.

Through the doorway was a tiled room, ill lit from the single window near its ceiling, but cool. Its wooden table was ready for supper. There was a scraping of chairs on its stone floor as four men rose to their feet.

"Hello there!" said Bunny Camden, coming forward to welcome them. He looked at Eleanor, then at Lammiter. "Good," he said. "It's good to see you." Then he turned to introduce two of the men. "A couple of friends," he said, "MacLaren from Canada. Oglethorpe from England."

The Englishman's eyes had a suspicion of a smile for the name Bunny had invented for him. A Canadian and an Englishman, Lammiter remembered suddenly: last night, in that open-air movie house behind the Esedra, they had been mentioned. They must indeed have been as interested in Evans as Bunny had guessed. But the fourth man, an Italian, middle-aged, dark-haired, with a thin intelligent face and mournful eyes, did not come forward. He nodded pleasantly, but he seemed to prefer the most shadowed wall of the room. Or, Lammiter thought, watching the clever worried face, he is only an observer from some branch of Italian intelligence, and is tactfully being subsidiary, leaving the main problems to the others. Joe, too, had retreated into the background: in fact, at this moment, he was leaving, quietly, unobtrusively.

Eleanor sat down. So did Lammiter. The others stood.

"Did you see Evans sitting outside?" the Englishman asked.

Eleanor shook her head.

"He was wearing a gray flannel suit," Oglethorpe told her as he watched her face.

"That was not the man I met at Tivoli."

"You're quite sure, Miss Halley?"

"Yes. Quite sure."

The men exchanged glances. "That's just what I thought," MacLaren said in disgust. In this moment of sharp disappointment, his voice held a pugnacious note surprisingly in contrast with his expressionless face. Like Oglethorpe, he could easily be misplaced in a crowd, an unremarkable man, with nondescript features, unobtrusive clothes, nothing dramatic or eccentric in his gestures or manner. The eyes were alert, though. These men were nobody's fools, Lammiter decided. How, then, had they been deceived? Or perhaps it was not their fault. He glanced at the silent Italian. Another sharp character. Then how had the failure developed? A split in authority, divided responsibility, conflicting methods, all the headaches of international co-operation? Lammiter passed the basket of half-sliced bread to Eleanor. "Eat slowly," he told her.

"I've eaten bread all day," she said dejectedly. "Bread and water. Everything else was drugged." And all this trouble for nothing, she thought: Evans is free. He has been the cause of everything that has happened to Bill and to me. We could have been killed, both of us, and he would have brushed us off his memory like a couple of dead flies from a window sill.

The Italian spoke suddenly. "You are thinking we have been stupid?" He shook his head. "Even in the best plans, there is the moment of luck, of accident."

Lammiter said, "I could wish the moment of bad luck would strike Mr. Evans, too."

"It may. There are few roads out of a hill town such as this. We have them watched. Every car is being stopped, every foreign passport is being examined."

"Evans is probably leaving disguised as a white ox," Lammiter said abruptly. Anticlimax was one frustration that he didn't accept very gracefully. "Can't you get some soup or something?" he asked sharply. Camden nodded and left. "How did this situation develop, anyway?" He looked at them, trying to keep his temper from breaking loose. We deserve some kind of explanation, he thought angrily. Damn it, are we among friends, or aren't we?

Oglethorpe and MacLaren, moving to the door, halted. "Have you any special interest in Evans?" Oglethorpe asked, seemingly only politely curious.

"A personal matter."

"But you didn't know him."

"I have a little bill I'd like him to settle for the trouble he has caused several of my friends." Brewster, chiefly.

"Haven't we all?" said MacLaren. He was anxious to leave.

"But," Lammiter kept on doggedly, "I do have a special interest in that meeting. Don't tell me you slipped up on that, too!"

Oglethorpe's mouth tightened. "We don't always fail, Lammiter."

"Look," Lammiter said (and here, thank God, was Bunny himself, carrying in a tureen of soup), "this girl was nearly murdered in front of my eyes. Don't expect sweetness and light from me." Quickly he served Eleanor a plate of *minestrone*. That would put some color back in her cheeks. "Slowly, now," he told her again.

"Would one success make you feel any better?" There was a smile, now, in the Englishman's eyes.

"Much better." Even knowing that there had been success was as good as the smell of the soup from the plate before him.

"Seven men attended that meeting. All were secretly photographed as they left." Oglethorpe paused, and then decided to add an extra bonus. "Three of them were government officials from NATO countries, two were from the Middle East: none under the least previous suspicion of being Communists. So that is one success we have had."

Lammiter said, "And a big one."

Oglethorpe nodded. "Have you seen the newspapers today?"

"Too busy." He nodded his thanks to Camden, who now brought in a bottle of Orvieto.

"There's trouble simmering in the Middle East," Oglethorpe said. "The Communists will certainly try to make that pot boil over. So, you see, these five photographed men are the best news I can give you. Even better than Sabatini's arrest."

"And what about the two other men?—There were seven at the meeting, you said." Lammiter's voice had lost its edge: the soup was good. We'll live, he thought, watching Eleanor carefully.

"Oh yes, these other two . . ." Oglethorpe seemed just to have remembered them. "One answered Evans's description. The other was totally unknown. No one could place him. At best, he seemed to be Evans's bodyguard. He wore a loose American jacket, a bright tie, a beret pulled down over his head, dark glasses. And there was a cigar clamped in his mouth. Distorts the jaw line, you know."

"Very neat," Lammiter agreed. "So all he had to do was to dodge into the nearest men's room after he left the meeting, take off all his accessories—"

"He did better than that. After all, we are prepared for tricks in a men's room. He went into the cathedral. You've noticed it?"

"It would be hard to miss." It was an enormous place, that unfinished cathedral, six centuries old, so vast in conception that people had long ago given up any idea of completing it.

"Inside, it's practically pitch black. Gigantic pillars all over the floor. Chapels. Alcoves. Confessionals. Railings. Groups of groping tourists. Everything made to order. Including," Oglethorpe added gloomily, "two main doorways. So all he had to do was to dodge from pillar to pillar, quickly peel off that jacket, stuff the beret and glasses and cigar into a pocket, bundle the whole thing up, drop it behind an empty confessional, choose a collection of tourists, and straggle out with them into the street."

"Smart fellow." There was a slight movement at the door. He glanced quickly. But it was only Joe returning to slip quietly into place.

"Too smart for a bodyguard," MacLaren said.

And that, Lammiter thought, was where the first doubts started. "Talking of bodyguards," he said, "do you know a man called Whitelaw?"

They obviously did. "Where does he come in?" MacLaren asked quietly.

"He's on stage right now. I saw his car near the piazza. A cream-colored Ferrari. Joe—you tell them about last night in the garden and today at the Casa Grande." He concentrated on his soup. It was better than good. A warm glow spread through his belly and up over his body. For the first time in thirty-six hours he began to relax properly, not altogether, but just enough to make him feel more normal, less strained. He gave Eleanor a broad smile, poured a second glass of wine for them both, and said, "We leave it all to the experts now." He thought, Our job is really done. We can do no more. That was a good feeling, too.

She nodded. "Funny," she said, "I was so hungry. And

now—I don't think I can eat anything more." She looked across the little room at Joe and at the men who listened to him so gravely.

"That's natural," he said. He studied her face, as if he were a doctor, carefully, unobtrusively. She looked all right, better than he could have hoped an hour ago. "To the prettiest girl in all Perugia," he said, lifting his glass. She smiled, as he always could make her smile, delighted and embarrassed in pleasing proportion. "You know what, Ellie? Apart from being in love with you, I like you. I like you very much. I like the way you smile, the way you tilt your head, that flutter of your eyelashes, the color coming and going in your cheeks, and your eyes—today they are blue, as blue as—" He paused. "Hell, what's the use of being a writer if I can't think of the right word?"

"You're falling asleep." She gave a little laugh. "And so am I. Oh, Bill! How do we get to the hotel?"

"We'll carry each other." He straightened his spine, stopped slouching comfortably. "The fresh air outside will wake us up enough. Too many people in here. Always too many people around." He looked across at the group of men. Even as he looked, they broke off their discussion. "It's one small chance," MacLaren, the Canadian, was saying as he began to move to the door, "but it isn't any more discouraging than searching a haystack for a needle."

"I've never understood," Lammiter told Eleanor, "why anyone should take her sewing out to a haystack in the first place, especially anyone who loses needles."

Oglethorpe, as he was leaving, called across to them, "Good-by. And thank you, Miss Halley, for coming here." His worried face relaxed for a moment. He had a singularly attractive smile. Or perhaps he liked to see two people holding hands so peaceably. MacLaren gave them a surprised look and a nod of farewell.

"A Scots Presbyterian, that one," said Lammiter. "Doesn't approve of mixing pleasure with business."

Bunny Camden looked down at them both. He grinned, shaking his head. "You're a couple of idiots," he said affectionately, and pulled up a chair. "Now eat! Both of you. Here's some chicken *cacciatore*." The jovial cook had brought in a tray laden with food. "And let's light the candles."

"Where's Joe? And that other Italian?" Lammiter asked, suddenly aware that Camden was the only one left.

"He had some friends to see."

"That's Joe. A friend in every hill town. Useful man to know." But he was disappointed a little, even if good-bys were probably unnecessary in Joe's business. "Come on, Ellie, keep me company." He helped her to some food. "Just pretend you're hungry, to please me. Besides, I'm going to have what New York calls a full-course dinner. While you talk, Bunny."

"Me?"

"About Bertrand Whitelaw."

"You're like a terrier with a rat."

Lammiter looked up. "Is he one? I hoped not."

"I was speaking metaphorically."

"The Marine Corps uses all the big words nowadays," Lammiter told Eleanor. "That comes from carrying a copy of Homer in their pockets, to while away the hours between battles."

Camden said with a grin, "All right, all right. What do you want to know? He's a sort of journalist, political reporting—"

"Yes, yes. Sober thoughts, upper-level stuff. But did he ever *know* Evans?"

"Yes. He went to college with him, Oglethorpe says. Defended Evans when he disappeared from England, would not believe the worst; and then, when Evans turned up blithely in Russia, he insisted that Evans must have been kidnaped and was acting under duress. I gather that the whole Evans business was a very nasty shock to Whitelaw."

"So Whitelaw is not a Communist?"

"No."

"Well, there's the man to help Oglethorpe. . . ."

"Oglethorpe isn't so sure about that."

"Why not?"

"Whitelaw is now a 'neutralist.' "

"Oh? What type?" There were those who just wanted to be left alone. And those who airily said they saw no difference between Russia and America. And those who were scared. And those who used neutralism as a cover, an alibi, to conceal their secret adherence to Communism.

"That's hard to judge. By his own account, he is second

to none in patriotism. And I think he is an honest British subject. But his judgment isn't always as good as he thinks it is. Evans was not the only hidden Communist who has used him as a transmission belt."

"He couldn't love England half so much, loved he not Whitelaw more?"

Camden smiled. "There's only one thing sure about Whitelaw. He will give no help to us. We are meddling in a matter that's strictly between two Englishmen: Whitelaw and Evans. Unjustifiable interference. Downright impertinence. Get it?"

"But Oglethorpe is as English as they come."

"To him, Oglethorpe is the contemptible instrument of a purely vindictive policy."

Suddenly, Eleanor spoke. "He just doesn't *know* enough. He just doesn't know what trouble Evans has caused . . . all of us. . . ." Her voice drifted away, unhappily.

"Or could cause," Camden added. "The sooner that man is extradited and taken out of circulation, the better for everyone. Today, his job here was obviously to receive last-minute reports, co-ordinate plans, give final instructions. A man like Evans is worth a whole armored division to the Russians."

"But what puzzles me—" Lammiter began.

"Yes?"

"How can he be extradited simply for having packed a bag and taken the first plane out of London?"

"He also packed a highly secret Cabinet report. Didn't have time to get it photographed, I expect." Camden frowned at the tablecloth and smoothed out the wrinkles that his hands had been busily folding into it.

"You're as troubled about Evans as Oglethorpe or MacLaren," Lammiter remarked. "Is he your business, too?"

"He is all our business. It isn't the first time an alliance has fallen apart because of a few carefully placed men whose secret instructions were sabotage. And if a small war starts, and the Western alliance crumbles, what will we have?—The big one."

"Tell that to Whitelaw."

Camden's eyes smiled. "You're recovering—started making your jokes again, have you?" Then, seriously, "In fact, Oglethorpe has gone searching for Whitelaw. Bevilacqua will help him, with phone calls to every hotel and lodginghouse."

"Oglethorpe really thinks that Whitelaw is in Perugia to meet Evans?"

"There are only two things possible: either Whitelaw is here for pleasure pure and simple or he is here on business."

"By business, you mean Evans?"

Camden nodded. "Oglethorpe thinks that Whitelaw may have heard Evans was in Italy. Or perhaps he saw Evans with Pirotta by accident, when they met in Rome. That could explain why he was so eager to see Pirotta: he was tracking Evans down."

"Why?" Lammiter asked bluntly.

"It's more than possible he still believes Evans is acting under duress. So if he could only talk to Evans, help him to escape from his bodyguards, help him to avoid us, then Evans would return of his own free will—always a most disarming gesture—and he would not be dragged back to England as a traitor. Evans could claim he had been kidnaped, and Whitelaw would feel happy that he had vindicated a friend. And, of course, his own judgment."

"I don't see why you're worrying about all that. Evans will never listen to Whitelaw."

"That's just the danger. Evans may pretend to listen. He may use Whitelaw as he has used him before. In that case, he will take any help offered, use it to leave Perugia, and a month later turn up in Moscow and give a press conference. What do you bet?"

Lammiter's lips tightened. "Nothing!" He pushed his plate away from him.

"So you can see why Oglethorpe is so eager to find Whitelaw," Camden said equably.

"And when he does find him—what then?"

"Whitelaw will be followed. He will lead Oglethorpe to Evans. Oglethorpe doesn't want to waste a precious hour in trying to convince Whitelaw that two and two make neither five nor three, nor even four and a half."

Lammiter reached over for Eleanor's hand. She had only pretended to eat. "Come on, you old unjustified interferer, you! To bed, to bed . . . Let's catch some sleep and forget Whitelaw." But, he thought, poor old Oglethorpe, poor old MacLaren, men fighting an unseen war to defeat any chance of a real one, getting little help from people like Whitelaw, who would be the first to scream out when the bombs started falling. Whitelaw, living in comfort, with money and prestige and applause; Oglethorpe and MacLaren, unthanked, ill paid, with hardship and danger as their reward. "Come on, darling," he repeated, very gently. Either she was already half asleep or she was lost in a world of her own. He turned to Camden. "How far is this hotel?"

"I'll take you there. But have some coffee first."

"We'd better leave," Lammiter said, his eyes on Eleanor. He didn't like that world into which she had retreated: there was a drawn look on her face, a look of tension and sadness.

"Black and bitter," Camden insisted, pouring coffee for them both. "You'll have to walk to the hotel—it isn't far —the *passeggiata* is still going on outside. Until darkness falls, in fact."

Eleanor spoke, avoiding their eyes, looking down at her slender hands. "Luigi Pirotta's orders were to drive from Perugia to Gubbio. I was to be brought to meet him. Then we were driving to Venice. There's a freighter there, ready to sail. For the Black Sea." She glanced up at Camden's astonished face. "Is that how Evans will leave Italy? By car to Venice, then by that ship?"

There was pity and tenderness in Lammiter's startled face as he watched her speak, and something of alarm, too. He wished she had been spared that knowledge. Today, Joe and he had made their guesses about Venice, but it was still a shock to find that the guesses had been actual truth. It will be a long job to make her forget all these things, he was thinking: but it would be the best job he could ever do.

Camden had recovered his usual unperturbed expression. "Could be," he said very quietly. He frowned, as he always did when he was making some decision. He picked a bread stick out of its glass on the table, and began breaking it absent-mindedly. "Finish your coffee," he said, "and then I'll get you to your hotel." And then, he thought, I'll have to search for Oglethorpe and tell him that piece of information. It could be vital.

"I hope someone is keeping an eye on Whitelaw's car," Lammiter said. "Evans may be a man in need of a good fast car."

"Whitelaw wouldn't be such a damned fool——" Camden

stopped abruptly. But Whitelaw might not have much choice in the matter. Once he made any contact with Evans, he would have no choice left. Camden's fingers snapped the bread stick into still smaller pieces. "Let's hope," he said, "that Oglethorpe finds Whitelaw in time. Are you ready to leave?"

"In time for what?"

Camden swept all the crumbs together and built them into a neat pyramid. "Let's get to the hotel," he suggested.

Lammiter rose, and went round to help Eleanor find her handbag. "You know," he said, keeping his voice as unperturbed as Bunny Camden's, "Whitelaw may have seen Evans with Pirotta in Rome, but how did he learn that Evans would be in Perugia today?"

Camden stared at him.

"It's been one of the best-arranged secrets of the year."

Camden nodded. True enough, Brewster had paid a heavy bill for uncovering it. Everyone who could have learned about Evans's visit had been living under a threat. But— He shook his head. "You think that Whitelaw was told, purposely? Do you mean that Evans telephoned him last night and—"

"No, this morning." Last night, Whitelaw had still been searching for information.

"All right—this morning, and laid on Whitelaw's visit here? Now, now, Bill—" He considered the idea from several angles. "I don't think Oglethorpe or MacLaren would buy that."

"Why not?"

"They'd say it would make a good plot for your next play," Camden replied with a smile as he rose. "All ready?" he asked Eleanor.

Lammiter, standing behind Eleanor's chair, her coat over his arm, faced Camden across the table. Doggedly, he said, "Look, Bunny—I *saw* Whitelaw in the courtyard at Montesecco. He could hardly wait, kept looking at his watch, didn't even stay long enough to help the princess face the first half hour in that house. He was a man with an urgent appointment. I tell you, Bunny, he was—"

"Then we're too late," Camden said. "If you are right, we're too late to prevent that appointment. Whitelaw and Evans could have met a couple of hours ago." He looked very directly at Lammiter. "If you are right," he repeated somberly.

"I know one thing for certain," Lammiter began, as he helped Eleanor to rise to her feet. He thought, I should never have let myself be persuaded to bring her here. "Damn it, I should never have let Eleanor come here," he exploded, his anger slipping to the surface in spite of his guard.

Eleanor's hand touched his arm gently. "It was my choice," she said. "Remember?" He mustn't blame himself so much. Bill looked down at her and knew her thoughts. He shook his head slowly. And I am to blame for all the danger she has known, he was thinking. If I had had more good sense back in New York, she would never have gone away without me.

Camden said, "If you would stop your interior conversations, we could start along the Corso. We'll keep arm in arm, and we'll talk about the weather, and look as though our only problem was where to find a dry Martini." He turned to Eleanor. "You can manage it?"

She nodded.

"Get him to smile," he told her with a grin, his eyes on Bill Lammiter.

"Will this do?" Lammiter asked sourly, and made a wide grimace.

"Diabolical," Camden pronounced. Eleanor began to laugh. Lammiter's face relaxed into a real smile.

"Hold it!" Camden said approvingly. They walked through the half-lit restaurant, still empty and still waiting for its customers, looking remarkably cheerful considering the giant worry that trod on their heels.

Twenty-Eight

OUTSIDE, DUSK WAS FALLING; the lights in the cafés and shops were being turned on. The tables were less crowded now, the strolling crowd had thinned out a little, too. But the three, Eleanor tightly gripped between Lammiter and Camden, looked a normal part of the scene as they walked westward along the smoothly paved Corso toward the piazza.

"Half-past seven," Camden said, glancing at his watch.

"By eight it will be dark, this street will be almost empty, and the traffic will start moving out of the town. There will be a steady stream of cars and Vespas going down that hill." And, he added gloomily to himself, not only will the light be bad, but the policemen at the roadblocks will be overworked and harried. That was always the moment of mistake.

"I thought this peace was too good to last," Lammiter said lightly for Eleanor's benefit, as he listened to the soft fall of light footsteps around them. Benignly, the eighteenth-century houses over the cafés and shops looked down on their progress. "How far now?" He could feel Eleanor's weight beginning to sag on his arm.

"The hotel is at the end of this street, not far, just beyond the piazz—"

"Hello!" called a clear young voice, surprised, delighted, friendly. A girl's tanned arm waved to them from a table littered with orange-juice bottles round which a crowd of American students were gathered. "See—we got here!" the girl called. "And isn't it *fun?*"

"Great fun," said Lammiter, recovering quickly, smiling, waving back, walking on.

"I like the green bow on her hair," Camden said. His eyes were as quick as ever. "Who is she?"

"A maniac, bless her. Without whose help we might not be walking down the Corso right now."

"Oh?"

But Lammiter did not respond to that cue. He was looking, now, along the final stretch of the Corso, toward the piazza. That was where the row of cars lay tightly boxed, like cigars. Beyond, the street continued into a little park with trees and benches, and ended in a balustrade cutting across the green-tinged sky. The park lay right at the edge of the cliff he had noticed when Joe's car climbed up from the plain. Dusk was coming rapidly, bringing a sudden breeze, the last gasp of a dying sun. The far edges of sky were washed with dark blue light.

"It's still there," Lammiter said with relief. "Whitelaw's car. That cream-colored job. Do we have to pass it?"

"Yes," said Camden. "The hotel is just beyond it, facing the park. But don't look interested in the car. Ignore it!"

"Am I just a little too worried, or do there seem to be more innocent bystanders than necessary on this stretch of sidewalk?"

"Keep walking," Camden said abruptly.

"There's someone following us."

"That's one of Bevilacqua's men." At least, Camden thought, I hope it is. Bevilacqua had promised a constant guard on Eleanor for the next twenty-four hours. By that time, the trouble would be over. Evans would either have escaped or have been arrested, and Perugia could go back to entertaining its summer-school guests.

"I'd like to meet Bevilacqua," Lammiter was saying.

"You did," Camden said absent-mindedly, as his eyes now studied the little park, with its benches and trees and small groups of people.

"Where? When?" And then Lammiter guessed. "You mean that dark-haired Italian, back in the restaurant? The one who talked about the moment of luck, of accident?"

"I see our Canadian friend. He seems to be as interested in that car as we are," Camden said very quietly. Mac-Laren was slumped on a stone bench, giving an excellent imitation of an exhausted tourist who hadn't strength enough left even to invent a good way to spend his evening. "And I see Joe, too." Joe was in the park, arm in close arm with a yielding brunette. "We've got our point men out," Camden said, with forced cheerfulness. "The situation is well in hand. I hope." Then he added, "I've been thinking over your suggestion—that guess you made—"

"My plot for a play?" Lammiter couldn't resist a touch of sarcasm in his voice.

"That's right," Camden said equably. "You know, you may have something there."

"But no one will buy it. So you said."

"I was halfway to buying it," Camden admitted. "Not quite, but almost. Now——" he shook his head "——I've seen the car, and it's too noticeable. Our Mr. E. wouldn't set one foot inside it, right there on the main piazza. He's waiting quietly around some corner. He's the type who likes to fool people." And, thank God, here was the hotel. He ushered them both quickly through the wide-open mahogany and plate-glass doors.

Lammiter had noticed, too, how obvious the car looked. He relinquished part of his theory, but with regret. Not altogether, though: he was still quite sure that Whitelaw had come to Perugia to keep an appointment. He said, "You don't have to come any farther, Bunny." Camden must have his own plans for this evening.

"I'll see you into your rooms," Camden said determinedly. Convoy duty didn't end within sight of land. "You stay with Eleanor." He went over to the reception desk at one side of the small lobby, more like the entrance to a men's club than to a hotel.

And that last order, thought Lammiter with a touch of annoyance, was totally unnecessary. Then he decided, as he led Eleanor toward a big room opening out of the lobby, and found a massive chair at its entrance, that Bunny was perhaps more worried than he had allowed himself to appear as they walked along the Corso together. The unnecessary order was often a sign of worry. If Bunny Camden had had his own free choice, he would not have brought Eleanor to Perugia any more than Lammiter would have. Or Joe. Here we are, Lammiter thought, as he settled Eleanor into her chair and sat on its arm and pretended to look around him nonchalantly, all of us, caught up in a business that is none of our choosing. What day is it now—Friday? The beginning of a weekend, the time for relaxing . . . He gave an outright scowl at a potted palm beside him.

The hotel had been built for the convenience of the rich Englishman of seventy years ago who demanded all the amenities of home when he traveled abroad. Now, judging from the people who were making their way toward the dining room, the visitors were mostly scholars, interested in Etruscan remains or early Renaissance act, or tourists making a comfortable overnight stay in their journey through the Italian hill towns. But the atmosphere of solid Victorian respectability still hung placidly over the hotel. An Italian family, the only native sons among so many French, German, English, and Americans, completely subdued into silence, stared in horrified fascination from their circle of heavy armchairs and lace antimacassars, less at the foreigners marching at funeral pace to a ridiculously early dinner than at the surroundings: Knightsbridge Victorian was far removed from Milan Modern.

Camden came over to them. "All we need are the documents. Eleanor—have you your Embassy identity card? Good. We'll need it. And your passport, Bill. You do have your passport, don't you?" This moment of anxiety passed as Lammiter nodded.

"A foreigner wouldn't get very far without one," Lammiter said, and then, his hand still in his pocket, he looked quickly at Camden.

"What's wrong?"

Lammiter's face was taut. He kept his voice low. "What if our Mr. E. didn't telephone Whitelaw just because of a car?"

"No?" Camden was smiling a little. Here we go again, he seemed to be saying: another of old Bill's twists and double twists.

"No. That's what we were supposed to think, perhaps, if we were clever little boys who were trying to reason out Whitelaw's arrival in Perugia."

"And what weren't we supposed to think?"

Lammeter pulled out his passport. "Our Mr. E. may be more in need of a good authentic British passport with a name that is known. Whitelaw wouldn't be questioned at any roadblock, would he?"

Quickly, Camden said to Eleanor, "Did you notice any resemblance between those two men?"

"Well—not exactly, but they are something of the same type: well brushed, well shaven, gaunt cheekbones, bony forehead. And, of course, gray hair." She exchanged a little smile with Lammiter, at some private joke.

"Height?"

"Tall. And thin. Both of them."

"That's enough," Camden said dispiritedly. A passport carried height and weight: its photograph often was only half a resemblance. "It's a crazy idea of yours," he told Lammiter, "but I'll telephone Bevilacqua while you get your registration forms all filled up and signed." He turned back into the lobby, toward the porter's desk, where pigeon-holed keys and letters, sedate post cards and newspapers and telephones were to be found. Lammiter and Eleanor crossed over to the other desk, where the assistant manager, a man of thirty-five, neatly tailored, politely mannered, was waiting for them with an enormous ledger spread wide on a polished desk, a pen already dipped in ink, and a welcoming smile for the young lady.

She was pale: perhaps tired with her journey. He rushed round his desk to offer her a chair, while the American filled out the registration forms. "So tedious,"

he commiserated with her. "But soon it will be over." He
made a sign over her shoulder to the policeman—a tourist policeman, but, *grazie a Dio,* in ordinary clothes, no
scandal, no publicity—to be more alert. The young lady
must be as important as she was beautiful to have been
given such an escort. Film stars and cabinet ministers
were always guarded like this. Who was she?

Bill Lammiter paused in filling out the registration details. "Eleanor, what date did you arrive in Italy?" He
looked up with a smile to cover the embarrassment of
his ignorance. And then he saw the strange look frozen
on her face (a mixture of puzzled memory and hesitating
doubt), and he turned to follow the direction of her eyes.
They were fixed on the back of a man, a short and thick-
set man, fair-haired, wearing a broad-shouldered suit of
extremely light gray, who was standing in front of the
porter's desk. The man turned to leave—his expansive
smile showed a mouthful of irregular teeth with lavish
metal trim—and Eleanor's head was bent, her face hidden, as she searched in her bag for a handkerchief.

"Who's that square-shaped character?" Lammiter
asked, as the man left the lobby.

"I—I've seen him—somewhere. Recently . . ."

The assitant manager said, "Signore Lammiter, if you
would just finish writing . . ."

"*Subito, subito,*" Lammiter said impatiently, and
turned back to Eleanor. "He must have been important,"
he suggested, "or you wouldn't have remembered you
ought to remember him."

"That's just the trouble. He wasn't someone important,
and yet—" She suddenly looked up at him. "I remember.
Tivoli."

"Well—" Camden had returned and was looking at
them worriedly. "What's the trouble?"

Quickly, quietly, Lammiter explained.

"You saw him out at Tivoli?" Camden insisted.

Eleanor nodded. "He served dinner. I'd never have
paid any attention to him except that I felt he was watching all the time, watching and listening. Remember," she
turned to Bill again, "I told you I was being inspected."

"By a servant?" Lammiter was a little incredulous. I
was too eager to have her identify that man, he thought:
I pushed her memory into being too helpful.

"Could be," Camden said. "That's the way they work.

It's often the Soviet Embassy servant who——"

"I know, I know. Never look at the Ambassador, look at his chauffeur."

"The registration——" It was the assistant manager again.

"Shortly. But first——who was the man who just went out? A hotel guest?"

"No." The assistant manager was nervous. Could this be trouble, just after he had been congratulating himself on the peace of the evening? "I think he was leaving a message."

Camden said, "Let's go and find out." They moved in a close group to the porter's desk.

"I'm afraid——" the assistant manager began.

Camden said to the porter, a capable-looking Etruscan watching them as unemotionally as one of his ancestors from his funeral couch deep down in the underground tombs, "The *signore* who was just talking to you——did he leave a message?"

The porter nodded, and his cold blue eyes measured them in turn. "A message and a package." His English was excellent.

"Could you tell us——"

"I am sorry," the assistant manager said most unhappily, "it is impossible to tell anyone what messages are left. You understand, such things are private matters."

"Wait here," Camden told Lammiter. "I'll go and fetch someone who can be told." He almost ran out of the hotel's entrance.

Lammiter said to the porter, "For whom were the message and the package delivered?"

"For Professor Stark."

"English?"

"He is," the assistant manager inserted, "the famous archaeologist from the University of London. He arrived yesterday for the summer school for foreigners. You have heard of him? He is an expert on Etruscan tombs. He is spending the week here."

"Oh . . ." Lammiter's voice drifted. The moment of excitement drained out of him. He smiled for Eleanor. It was possible that Tivoli and its ill-omened dinner party had become a little confused in her mind: too much had happened since, too many emotions had been stirred, too many tensions and fears. "Let's sit down and wait for

Bunny," he said, trying to lead her back to the chair, and failing.

"I didn't make a mistake," she told him, shaking her head. She was close to tears.

The porter—it was, of course, his normal routine, but Lammiter thought the man picked up the telephone very briskly—was now asking for room 67. "Professor Stark?" the porter asked. "Your taxi is waiting outside. And a package has been delivered for you. Shall we hold it here for you at the desk? Very good." And then to the assistant manager, "Professor Stark will collect the package on his way to the taxi." The porter's eyes, intelligent, sympathetic for all their coldness, swept over Eleanor's unhappy face as much to say, "There now, it wasn't very much to worry about, was it?" Then he scribbled a note on a pink slip and pushed it into pigeonhole 67 on the wall behind him.

Lammiter had automatically looked at pigeonhole No. 67. There was no package in it, only the pink slip, which possibly meant that a package too large for the pigeonhole was waiting to be collected. A passport, he thought, could surely have fitted into an envelope and be sitting in the pigeonhole right now. A passport?—He suddenly felt how ludicrous his suspicions had become. He had been trying to solve a puzzle simply by imagining himself the man Evans. It was the sure way to work the plot of a play, knowing his characters, being each of them in turn, letting the events form their decisions and their decisions shape events. But in real life, here in this hotel lobby, between his imagination and his belief in Eleanor, he had almost created an Evans whose NKVD guard had murdered Whitelaw to obtain a passport to safety. Not that Evan's friends wouldn't hesitate at eliminating anything that stood in the way of their purpose, but still . . . Our apologies to the learned Professor Stark, he said to himself as he took Eleanor's arm and insisted on steering her back to the large armchair at the entrance to the sitting room.

"The registration forms—" the assistant manager reminded him in a relieved voice.

"In a minute." He looked at the quiet man, an Italian, who had left his post beside a potted palm to come forward to Eleanor. "Who is this?"

The assistant manager was rattled enough to say, "He

is guarding the *signorina*. One of our tourist police. Very discreet, very capable."

"You can vouch for him? I mean, you know him?"

"But of course I know him. We went to school—"

"Then tell him to guard the *signorina* well." To Eleanor he said, "I'll be back in a moment. I just want to have one look at this taxi." He turned back to the lobby again.

The tourist policeman looked down at Eleanor, and then at the assistant manager. "There is some difficulty?" he asked.

"No," said the assistant manager and "Yes," said Eleanor, almost in unison. I'm so tired, she thought, I could scream. Instead, a few isolated tears forced their way to the surface.

"Ah," the policeman said, and looked protective. The assistant manager was visibly upset and apologetic. At least, Eleanor thought wearily, I could be in a country where men thought women were idiots and tears were ludicrous, but I am in Italy, where all women are beautiful and tears are a manifestation of charm. She gave them a little smile of thanks, and turned her eyes toward the door. Where was Bill? She waited, counting each second. There he was now, trying—as soon as he saw she was watching him—to look more cheerful. What was troubling him so much? Both he and Bunny Camden seemed to be sharing the same worry. And I never noticed anything, she thought; for the last half hour I've been in a kind of daze. I'm too tired, perhaps, just too tired. . . .

"The taxi was only a taxi," Bill told her. "No high-powered car." He sounded both relieved and disappointed. She looked at him, trying to follow his meaning, and failing. "Let's sign these registration forms, pick up the keys, and get upstairs." Gently, he helped her rise from the chair.

"This way—" The assistant manager was smiling now, and in his relief he became informative. "If you need a high-powered car, we could arrange to have that for you tomorrow. Usually, our guests only need the small Fiat to take them to the station."

"Station?" Then Lammiter added casually, "Professor Stark is leaving? Has he changed his mind about the summer school?" He smiled, turning his question into a little joke.

"No, no!" The assistant manager was very earnest. "He

is simply going to meet his old friend, Dr. Benvenuto
Corredi, who arrives tonight from Rome. Dr. Corredi is
our Etruscan expert. He is quite famous. You have heard
of him in America, no doubt?"

Lammiter thought, I wish that were the only kind of
doubt that kept buzzing round my head like a mosquito.
Then he had the unpleasant feeling that perhaps he had
let an idea become an obsession. That was the kind of
thing that happened when you were exhausted: your judgment warped.

"We have numbers of eminent scholars with us this
week end," the assistant manager went on. "A great
honor, a very great honor indeed." Scholars were peaceful men: no loud parties, no doubtful women. Virtue and
culture combined. That compensated, almost, for their
lack of spending power.

As Lammiter signed his name, he said, "I didn't realize
Perugia had a station. You hide it well."

"We have always congratulated ourselves that we kept
the railway where it belongs—down in the valley. A station is *not* a historical monument."

"Give it fifty more years," Lammiter predicted, and
crossed over to the porter's desk for the keys. Forget
everything, he told himself, except Eleanor: just get her
upstairs and into bed—she's on the point of collapse. Behind him, he heard her being forgiven for the little con-
tretemps she had initiated.

"Now," the assistant manager was saying to her with a
playful smile, "you are sure all the statements in your
registration card are true? It is a serious matter—" he
laughed to make it quite clear that he was joking, and he
looked at the policeman who was waiting beside her—
"most serious, if you sign your name to statements that
are not true. Eh, Giono?" But Giono, like Queen Vic-
toria, was not amused. It *was* a most serious matter. He
inclined his head as if he hadn't quite heard and upheld
the dignity of the law. The joke dropped at his feet and
crashed into silence.

Eleanor signed her name, and turned to look in Bill's
direction. What was the delay? A boy was waiting, keys
in hand, ready to conduct them both to their rooms.
"Luggage?" the porter asked firmly. And Bill was saying
that their luggage was outside, in a friend's car. Eleanor's
heart sank. Bill's suitcase—that was all the luggage.

More complications, more regulations; would she never reach that bedroom upstairs? She closed her eyes wearily; she would let Bill handle the problem of one suitcase between two people who had registered separately. Then she heard Bill say thankfully, "Bunny! Come and straighten this out, will you?" She opened her eyes. Camden had just entered, along with two neatly dressed, grave-faced Italians.

Behind Bill, one of the hotel guests was dropping his key on the porter's desk. He was a tall man, thin, with gray hair, dressed in a tweed jacket and unpressed flannel trousers. "Have you the package that was left for me?" he asked, annoyed with the porter's lack of attention.

"I'm sorry," the porter apologized. He had been watching the two grave-faced Italians with some apprehension: he knew a plain-clothes policeman when he saw one. And here were two. In *this* hotel? "I thought you would want me to keep it until you came back. It is only a magazine."

"I'll take it with me to read while I wait, thank you. One never knows how late the train may be, does one?" Professor Stark took the large, quarto-size envelope, and turned toward the door, unhurried and calm.

This, Eleanor thought, this is a dream. This, she almost cried out, cannot be real. But the man's voice took her back to Tivoli, to the garden beyond the shrubbery. . . . It was the same voice, cold, acid, superior. From here she could only see the back of his head—gray hair, yes, but now covered by the old felt hat he had pulled comfortably over his brow. This, she wanted to scream, is a nightmare—for there are Bill and Bunny Camden, talking together, turning back to the desk. And there is the man, passing behind them on his way to the door. No one knows, she thought, except me, and my feet won't move and my voice has gone. . . .

Then, suddenly, strength came back to her legs. She ran toward the door. You must be sure, she kept telling herself; you must see him as he faced you at Tivoli.

"Eleanor!" Bill cried, and started toward the doorway to intercept her.

At its threshold, she checked her mad flight and swung round to face the man who called himself Professor Stark. For a moment, their eyes met. For a moment, he halted. "Excuse me," he said coldly, trying to pass her. But Bill had reached her, had taken her arm. Together, they stood blocking the doorway.

Then strength returned to her voice, too. "Mr. Evans," she said. "How do you do, Mr. Evans. . . ."

Twenty-Nine

THE ASSISTANT MANAGER surveyed the quiet lobby as he was about to go off duty at ten o'clock. "There was a little trouble here tonight," he told the night reception-ist, who had just arrived, and then he fell silent: partly because the police (all kinds of policemen in plain clothes; *mamma mia*, had his hotel ever seen such a dis-aster as this?) had warned him against all discussion, partly because so many things had happened that he did not even know how to explain half of them, partly because it was superior wisdom to let the manager decide first.

"Oh?" said the night receptionist gloomily. Fortunate-ly, he was rarely interested in anything except the Tom-bola. He had lost again today.

"Ah well," the assistant manager said, "good night." At least, he had been saved from the impulse to talk too much. But he wondered, as he left the silent lobby, its lights already half subdued, whether any other assistant managers had ever been faced with the discovery that a guest was a liar (everything that man had entered in his registration form was false), a cheat (he was no more a professor than the name was Stark), a receiver of stolen property (the envelope had contained someone else's passport). And had a guest *ever* been arrested right in the middle of the lobby?

Giono had done that. Of course, he had been helped by the two detectives who accompanied Mr. Camden. Two detectives— Thoughts failed the assistant manager for a full minute. Anyway, Giono would get his promo-tion. Lucky Giono . . . But perhaps, thought the assistant manager, I may be promoted, too. After all, everything was handled so quietly, so simply that none of the other hotel guests, not even these impossible Milanese in the adjoining room, working up an enormous appetite for dinner, had noticed anything particularly wrong. Yes, he thought, all things considered, we were lucky.

The stranger who had left the stolen passport for Professor Stark had been found in a car waiting at the station, down in the valley. So Professor Stark—no, the real name was Evans—so Evans must have planned to get out of his taxi, step into this car, drive away. . . .

Then there was the man, poor soul, who owned the stolen passport, an Englishman, they said. He had been found at the foot of the precipice near the church of San Angelo. These foreigners were so stupid, so incredibly stupid: whatever made them walk near the precipices, by themselves, in fading light?

As he left the hotel, the assistant manager glanced up at the windows behind which most of his guests, thank God, were already safely in bed. Why, he asked himself angrily, why did that man Evans choose my hotel? Why couldn't he have found some miserable lodgings in one of the dark side streets? The American, Camden, had answered that question by saying that Evans chose the hotel for the simple reason that no one, *no one,* would ever suspect such effrontery, such temerity. And no one had, Signore Camden had said: Evans had not been discovered by suspicion; he had been discovered by the moment of accident, the moment of luck. Perhaps, the assistant manager thought as he walked through the soft night air of the little park to reach his motor bicycle, perhaps it is better if I do not try to understand too much about such things.

He halted and looked back at the hotel again. Now he could see the balconies of the Americans' rooms. (He had given them the best view he could provide, west and south, over the broad valley below, toward the further hills. It was a gesture of thanks on his part to the American girl, who had kept her voice so quiet. He could imagine his Maria facing such a man: all the guests would have been brought running from the dining room.) There was someone standing on the nearer balcony. That one belonged to the girl's room, but it was Signore Lammiter who was standing up there, facing this way, looking south. Ah well, the assistant manager thought, at least the trouble is over. And there will not even be any stories about it in the newspapers. The detectives had assured him of that.

He moved quickly away, to home and supper and Maria, who would count the minutes he was late. Out of sight of the hotel, he paused to light a cigarette, loosen his collar and tie, take off his carefully pressed jacket and fold it neatly over his arm. He unchained his Vespa, swung a leg over its seat, started the engine (it was splendidly unmuffled) and roared into the night. He was Colonel Eduardo Ricci, jet-propelled, breaking the sound barrier. . . .

Bill Lammiter, standing on the balcony, watched the stars come out. Far beneath him—for this hotel wall seemed to rise out of one of Perugia's encircling precipices—came the roar of a Vespa as it joined the noisy stream of cars and motor bicycles sweeping down the steep twisting hill to the plain. But tonight, strangely enough, his nerves were better, or perhaps they were exhausted into numbness: loud belches from watered-down gas, unmuffled roars no longer irritated him. Noise was those people's innocent pleasure: they were alive and enjoying it. He wished them well. He wished everyone well. He had never felt more kindly to his fellow men, to the innocent and naïve and uncomplicated who had simple ambitions and honest loyalties.

He lit a cigarette and looked southward again. The bright lights of the little houses flanking Perugia's hill gave way to the mystery of sleeping countryside. Against the night sky, the far hills were black shadows. That's the way I traveled last night, he thought; a long, long way. It is only two nights ago since I stood on another balcony, and wondered what lay north from Rome?

He heard a small movement from the room behind him. Quickly he stubbed out his cigarette, and left the balcony. Eleanor was still asleep. She had turned on her side, a light blanket over her legs had slithered to the floor. He picked it up, replacing it carefully, and stood watching her for a few minutes. Then he went back to the balcony again. Some people wanted to make speeches whenever they stood on a balcony. All he wanted to do was to give thanks. He gripped its iron railing. He felt strangely emotional, and then—as he overcame that unexpected and unusual onslaught—strangely at peace. A balcony was a very thanksgiving place.

"Bill," he heard her cry—a small, half-smothered cry of fear and bewilderment, "Bill—are you there?"

"Yes," he said, as he turned back into the room, "yes, I'm here."